the SAFELIGHT series

volume 1

chasing Reese.

Also by

IMY SANTIAGO

the SAFELIGHT series

volume 2

finding Reese.

chasing Reese.

a SAFELIGHT novel vol.1

IMY SANTIAGO

RISC BOOKS, NEW YORK

Published by RISC BOOKS.

chasing Reese. a SAFELIGHT novel vol.1

Editing by Kimberly Ito, Sakura Editing
Cover design by Marisa Shor, CoverMe, Darling, www.covermedarling.com
Cover image purchased at CanStockPhoto Royalty Free Stock Photography, #8185303
Formatting by Riane Holt & Imy Santiago

PUBLISHING HISTORY
RISC BOOKS eBook Edition / January 2015 - RISC BOOKS Paperback First Edition / January 2015

ISBN-13: 978-0-9863580-4-3

Adult Fiction–Contemporary Romance

MATURE CONTENT WARNING:
This novel contains graphic language and sexually explicit content intended for individuals over the age of eighteen, and includes subject matter such as *Alcoholism, Depression, Anxiety and Panic Disorder*, and *Post-traumatic Stress Disorder*. Your discretion is advised.

In Memory of Gil, the greatest brother I ever had.

For Izzy who motivates me to keep chasing after our dreams.

For Jc who said, "Go for it, baby!"

For Denise who read SAFELIGHT and said, "Pretty please!"

"When it comes down to it, it's pretty simple. Adventure is what you make it. And whether it's the travel, the discovery, or just the feeling of letting go, the only way we'll ever find out is to **get out there and do it.** *Enjoy the ride."*

-Travis Rice, The Art of Flight

PROLOGUE

Four years ago

Snow falls like soft whispers over the treetops. The weather is blustery cold and the skies are painted different shades of grey, like the backdrops of holiday greeting cards. The winding road is desolate and untraveled. The pavement is covered with ice and snow.

Catalina Pardo sits perched on the passenger seat while her fiancé, Blake Mackenzie, is behind the wheel. He is the love of her life and within Catalina's womb reposes the fruit of their undying love.

Blake takes a glimpse at the beautiful woman sitting across from him. His eyes appraise Catalina and glisten with fervent love. Blake removes one hand from the steering wheel and lays it on top of Catalina's, which is tenderly rubbing endless circles around her wee belly.

"I love you, Cat," Blake declares, as he lifts her hand to his mouth and showers Cat's knuckles with feathery kisses.

"I love you too, forever." Catalina tries to release her hand from Blake's with a giggle. "I know you love me, but you better keep your damn eyes on the road."

Blake scoffs and answers, "Your humor becomes you, honey," as he looks to her and threatens to tickle her.

She throws her head back in peals of laughter. But Catalina's merriment ends abruptly–the car hits a patch of black ice and swerves out of control. Blake tears his hand away from hers as he desperately tries to regain control of the car. Her eyes widen as she looks out the window. The trees move past them, unusually slow, the time continuum irrevocably broken. As a snow bank comes into view, her hands cover her mouth in horror.

Panicked, Blake slams on the brakes and yells, "Hold on, Cat!"

In a split second, the car slides a few feet and flips in the air three times until it lands upside down. Catalina's head hits the window, shattering it into countless pieces. She's in cutting pain, and blood rushes to her ears with the force of a freight train. All sounds diminish–she only hears a roaring hum. Her eyes blink rapidly–her body in shock–is going between patches of darkness and life.

Catalina tries to reach out for Blake but can't. He looks at her, pain etched on his features, his head dangling in front of the steering wheel. A large gash on his scalp forces a steady flow of blood to drip onto the ceiling of the upside-down car.

Blake coughs as he gasps for breath. "I'm sorry, Cat. I–"

He exhales one last time, and all the life disappears from his baby blue eyes. Catalina's voice breaks. "Blake? *Blake?*"

Catalina sobs inconsolably as she screams his name in vain. She tries to move but can't–crumpled metal restricts her, keeping her prisoner.

"God, please! No! Blake! Wake up, honey. Please don't leave me!"

A knife-edged pain grows inside her womb. Still suspended, Catalina tries to crane her head upwards. She looks to her lap. An ocean of red stains her maternity jeans. Losing all of her strength, she lets her head dangle back down.

"No, God. No! Please! Someone help us! Please!"

With hurried breaths, her eyes close. The snow falls like whispers in the wind.

CHAPTER ONE

Catalina

The intense sunlight through the window forces my eyes to open. Groaning, I roll over and reach out for Blake. His side of the bed still holds his warmth that lingers on the sheets. He hasn't left for work yet. I arch my body making inarticulate sounds as a few unladylike yawns escape my throat. I sit up on our bed and stretch my arms in front of me giving my vision a moment to adjust. The usual struggle with whether to get out of bed or curl back under the sheets is irrelevant today. The fact that Blake Mackenzie, my hot stud of a fiancé, is probably naked in the shower is incentive enough for me to get my shapely ass out of bed in double time.

As I tiptoe into the bathroom, the steam from the hot water smacks me in the face. *Hello, instant facial.* His throaty voice echoing in the shower singing about weary girls, and trying a little tenderness with them forces a small snicker to escape my throat. Blake's bath time concerts always make me smile. He can't sing for his life, but it's adorable when he does it with so much spirit. One time I caught him holding the bottle of body wash, pretending it was a microphone. The memory of that moment makes me grin.

My hand wipes off the fog covering the square mirror, and I settle into my morning routine. Finger-combing my long black hair, I twist the strands into a messy bun, thrilled that it's cooperating today. My slinky nightgown slides from my shoulders, making a whooshing sound as it pools around my feet. The creamy natural complexion of my skin works nicely with the dark brown hue of my almond shaped eyes.

When it boils down to fashion standards I'm an average woman–I'm 5'6" with considerable breasts, a medium waist and broad hips that sometimes have a hard time getting into jeans that aren't stretchy. I'm a size 14, not runway model thin like every other woman in this city. It's not a curse or a sin, God just graced me with extra curves and that's never discouraged the male population; I've had my share of admirers in the past. *If you got it, flaunt it.*

Quietly opening the glass of the shower enclosure I slip in. Blake's head is under the spray of water so I doubt he heard me sneak in. My arms reach out to embrace his lean, trim body. As my hands touch his skin, he turns around, startled. Hugging me with his muscular arms, Blake towers over me. His baby blues consider my naked body as a sexy grin lights up his face.

Gosh. That dopey smile of his drives me wild.

"Good morning, Catalina," he whispers sweetly against my lips.

His gaze pierces into the deepest parts of my soul. Smiling, I move the wet strands of blonde hair away from his eyes. My hands trace their way down to his cheeks, and I stroke them affectionately with my thumbs.

"Good morning," I reply lovingly. "How did you sleep?"

Using his thumb, he caresses my chin.

"Good. Very good, actually," Blake purrs, causing my body to heat with yearning.

"I missed you," I breathe.

Placing my hands over his heart, I feel it beating strong and lively; he's just as affected as me. My eyes travel down his abdomen, admiring his well-defined lines. I bite the insides of my cheek trying to bridle the desire burning within me.

My eyes reach the end of his happy trail and a wicked smile plays across my face. Blake's gorgeous cock is happy to see me. His manhood stands at attention, to my complete and utter delight. It doesn't matter that we've known each other for more than five years. Our mutual respect and love has kept the embers of our sex life very much alive. I must've been objectifying Blake, because the sound of him clearing his throat twice shifts my attention.

My eyes meet his, which are full of mischief and want, smoldering with desire.

"Cat, I'm pretty sure you were taught that it's not polite to stare," Blake taunts as his tongue seductively flicks the corner of his mouth.

In the blink of an eye, he swings me around so that the curve of my back faces his chest. Blake closes the gap between us and trails kisses down my spine, gently nibbling over my sweltering skin. I can feel his erection at the small of my back: hard, thick, and ready. I bite back a moan of pleasure as his hands trap mine over my head against the slippery shower walls.

Attempting to turn around is futile, as Blake's strength keeps me in place. His mouth reaches the bottom of my earlobe and nips at it. I feel his warm breath against my ear. "Wake up, Catalina," he murmurs.

Facing the wall, my nose wrinkles in confusion. It's enough to kill this moment. *Huh?* "Wake up, baby," Blake whispers again. Turning around, I look at him, puzzled.

"Blake? Honey, I'm awake." I mutter, slightly alarmed. When Blake doesn't respond, I huff and squeeze my eyes shut in irritation.

Beep. Beep. Beep. *What is that noise?*

Beep. Beep. Beep. The sound won't stop. Opening my eyes, I realize Blake no longer stands before me. I'm no longer in the shower but in my bed.

Beep. Beep. Beep.

"Fuck, I'm awake!" I shriek. I sit up in bed, breathing hard, unable to comprehend where I am. It takes me a minute to find my bearings. Closing my eyes, I clutch my comforter tightly. Slowly, the painful realization sinks in.

Beep. Beep. Beep.

My shaky hand reaches out for the alarm clock sitting on the night table, hitting it a couple of times for good measure until I turn it off. Taking a few deep breaths, I try to dispel the nerves brought on by my delusion. My hands cradle my head as the reality of this moment kicks me in the gut. Blake could not possibly be here. *He's dead.*

Irreconcilable tears fall from my eyes, staining my cheeks. It's been a long time since I've dreamt of him. Throwing myself back in bed, I close my eyes again, desperately trying to revive the dream. I beg God to bring him back, if only for a moment. Blake was as beautiful as I remember.

Completely shaken by the nightmare, I reach out for the sound system remote. Music is what I need. With one quick press of a button, "Reptilia" by The Strokes echoes loudly in my room.

I jump out of bed and walk straight to my bathroom. The cold tiled floor stings my feet. My reflection in the mirror disappoints me, tear stricken face, dark circles underneath my eyes, and my hair is longer and more unruly than ever. I'm older and to put things mildly, time has not been so kind.

With a deep sigh I brush my hair and pin it up, easing into my morning routine. Stepping into the shower, I set the water to the hottest setting I can tolerate. Soon, the stall is filling up with steam, the scent of lavender swirling in the air. I make a lather of the body wash and scrub myself clean, wishing it could wash away my sadness.

Yes, my body is feeling somewhat relaxed but my head is anything but. I abandon the stall, bundle myself in a terry cloth bathrobe, and stand in front of the vanity mirror. Music continues to play in the background as I prepare to put on make-up. My style has evolved since Blake passed away. I found comfort in alternative rock, and dark, rockabilly-meets-gothic outfits fill my closet.

I take my time applying the jet black eyeliner, making sure the wing tips are drawn to perfection. Accentuating the beauty mark on my left cheek, I complete the look with scarlet lipstick. I look nothing like the girl in my dream anymore, but I'm content with my image even though I'm slightly curvier than I was four years ago.

Losing Blake and our baby propelled me into a severe depression that took a toll on my psyche as well as my body. My change in style and image still turns heads everywhere I go, and I'm okay with that. I'm just a different person than I was back in the day.

I grab a pair of black leggings adorned with white skulls and pair them with a white long-sleeved tunic and my cherry red Doc Martens that lay strewn on the floor. One glance at the clock tells me if I leave the loft now, I'll have time to stop for coffee on the way to work.

I grab my messenger bag and winter gear, and run down the stairs to the main floor. New York City winters can be quite dreadful, especially if you walk everywhere.

I live in SoHo, a relatively small neighborhood in Lower Manhattan. After Blake passed away, I sold the apartment we shared Uptown and moved Downtown. I love the vibrancy of the art deco district. From the shops and art galleries, to the restaurants near my loft, I feel completely at home in SoHo.

Placing my cell phone headset into my ears, I listen to some of my favorite songs. I find that when I'm walking in the bitter cold, music makes the intolerable tolerable. Plus, it drowns out the incessant sounds of honking horns and screaming sirens that form part of the soundtrack of life in New York City. I just have to keep a close eye out for the cabbies. They'll run you over in a heartbeat, and you would never know what hit you.

I sigh contentedly as I reach the coffee shop. For once the place doesn't have a line out the door, probably because it's too cold. I grab my coffee, light and sweet, and opt to take a cab to work in Midtown Manhattan. I work as a journalist for *Xsports*–a magazine that publishes articles about daredevil athletes and, occasionally, celebrities.

I've worked there for almost six years, and for the most part, I'm satisfied with my career. I have been lucky enough to travel to different parts of the world. My editor, Marcia Reed, has been one of the coolest bosses I've ever worked with. She understands my antipathy for snow, so I'm typically assigned to cover sky divers, jousters, base jumpers and arena events.

I walk into the building and head straight for my cubicle. Placing my coffee on my desk, I sit and peruse the never ending flow of emails that drown my inbox. I usually scan the subject lines looking for important ones first. My eyes stumble upon one in particular: *PTO Policy Changes* flagged as high priority. Without a moment's hesitation, I click on it.

Catalina,

Our records indicate you have accumulated 450 hours of vacation time, the equivalent of three months. The company is gearing towards changes in paid vacation benefits. Starting the next fiscal year, all employees will be required to exhaust all accumulated time before June 1st. If not, all accumulated hours will be liquidated and dispersed in an off-cycle paycheck. Our records also indicate you have not taken a day off in almost four years. We encourage all employees to take periodic vacations. I advise you take a look at your calendar and make arrangements. Your loyal service to *Xsports* is unparalleled.

This email is being forwarded to your department head. Should you have any questions or concerns, please do not hesitate in reaching out to me or Marcia Reed.

All my best,

Emelina James, Human Resources Manager

I smile as I read through the departmental emails about assignments given to my peers. This job never gets old, and the twinge of excitement has not left my gut in almost a decade in the sports journalism world. I see that Aaron and Becky Jacobson, a husband and wife reporter/photographer team, were assigned to a press tour for the reigning Olympic snowboarding gold medalist Jackson Reese.

I snicker inwardly, recalling that infamous streaking fiasco during the Winter Olympics. As I'm multitasking between sips of coffee and reading and responding to emails, David Collins, one of my colleagues, stops by my cubicle. He knocks on my nameplate and I look up.

"Good morning, Pardo!" David greets me with a smile, his lips turning up to display his insanely bright and perfect teeth.

"Same to you, Collins," I reply with a grin. Collins is my closest colleague at *Xsports*. We have lunch at least once a week, assignments permitting.

"I stopped by to ask if you wanted a coffee, but I see you have one already." Collins shrugs his shoulders and pouts like a sad child.

Lifting the paper cup, I wiggle it. "It's almost gone. I could go for another one."

"I guess that was a given, huh?" Collins retorts. "You drink too much of that stuff. Come on, Pardo, we don't have all day."

"Calling the kettle black now, are we?" I counter, poking him on the chest. "I love you, Collins, but sometimes I wonder how your wife puts up with your shit. She *must* love you." I fire back.

Collins puts his hands on his hips and chuckles. "I know, right?" He pats me on the shoulder. "Always keeping it real huh, Pardo?"

"Just calling it like I see it. Now enough with the chit chat. Let's get some fuel. On our way there, we can talk about Andrea's birth plan. I want to know *all* about it."

Collins groans and rolls his eyes at me. He's going to be a dad any day now and like a true first time parent, he's freaking out. Does it make me evil that I tease him over it? No. It's just how our work dynamic is. Apart from being office buddies, Collins and I share a love for coffee and good books. It's great to have someone at work who understands you without having to ask too many questions.

"Okay, team. Before we wrap this meeting up, I want to introduce the athlete that will be gracing the cover of our magazine this upcoming April," Marcia announces, during our weekly staff meeting.

"*Xsports* has been lucky enough to be chosen to cover the reigning Olympic gold medalist of Men's Slope-Style Snowboarding. You're all familiar with Jackson Reese, courtesy of the unfortunate streaking incident a year ago," Immediately, groans and snickers fill the room.

I roll my eyes. I mean, who gets shitfaced, strips and snowboards in nothing but boots and a gold medal? I am not ashamed to admit I laughed my ass off at his bravado, but at the end of the day, it was foolish.

"His PR team has organized a six week-long press tour that will grant us, along with two other magazines, access to Reese's life on the slopes as well as off. Private jet, lush accommodations, you name it–all on his dime. I've selected team Jacobson to helm this project. I believe it's a perfect opportunity to have a relatable face on the cover. Despite his little incident, Jackson Reese has always been a phenomenal athlete. Having *Xsports* tell his story will help us sell more units. Let's face it. Sales have been slow."

Everyone in the boardroom nods. Some of my colleagues begin to chatter, forcing Marcia to clear her throat and continue.

"I know Team Jacobson will be a perfect fit for Reese given their experience at the Winter Olympics." She taps on a box sitting on the table. "This is the press kit Reese's team has sent over. I suggest you all take a moment to review it and offer support to the Jacobsons. The press tour begins in a month. All right guys, if there are no questions, meeting adjourned." Everyone vacates the boardroom, except Collins, the Jacobsons, and me. With purposeful steps I approach the box, curiosity getting the best of me. Perusing through the box like kids who've found treasure, Collins and I remove its contents. My eyes zone in on a DVD.

"May I?" I ask the Jacobsons and they nod.

Walking over to the media wall, I insert the DVD. It plays a sizzle reel of Jackson Reese on his snowboard shredding the slopes, as well as a replay of the unfortunate incident at the Winter Olympics. The trailer ends with Jackson facing the camera. He challenges with those crisp azure eyes, *"There's more to me than what you just saw. Do you want to know more? Join me."*

Wow. I'm not even covering him and *I'm* intrigued. Scanning the travel itinerary in the box, I groan. "Whistler, B.C.? Never been there but it's got to be cold as fuck," I mutter to no one in particular. My body shivers at the thought of being in the freezing tundra. Quickly, I shove the documents back into the box as if they could give me frostbite.

"Just imagine if *you* were the one picked to cover Jackson Reese in the Canadian snow… You'd be shitting a brick right about now," Collins smirks. I flip him the bird with a mouthed *fuck you* and Collins laughs, completely entertained.

"Good luck guys! Safe travels," I call out to the Jacobsons before walking out of the boardroom. Heading back to my desk, I decide to put in a request for time off. I think a vacation is long overdue.

Leaving work, I brave the cold and begin the trek home. My cell phone begins buzzing, and I smile when I realize Faith Mackenzie is calling. She has been my best friend for almost a decade now. We are the same age, thirty two, and among the many things we have in common, there's Blake. Faith is my late fiancé's youngest sibling. We usually hang out once a month but with the influx of out of town assignments this time of year, we haven't seen each other much.

"Hi, Cat!" Faith squeals. "Guess why I'm calling?"

I shrug, not really knowing what Faith could be suggesting. "I don't know..." I mumble, hoping she doesn't insist on making me guess.

Faith lets out a loud shriek, startling me. I inwardly curse her with all of my being because I'm pretty sure she has left me partially deaf.

"Matthew proposed last night! We're getting married!" she says in between giggles. Her excitement makes me smile. Matthew and Faith have been together a little over two years. Their love rivals those seen in romance novels.

"That's amazing! Congratulations, Faith!" In a heartbeat, she begins to tell me how Matthew proposed. I am beyond thrilled he surprised the ever living shit out of her. Good for him.

Faith's excited tone of voice changes into a serious one. She clears her throat and asks, "Catalina Pardo, will you be my maid of honor?"

My heart skips a beat; a mixture of bittersweet happiness taking over me. I cry over the phone–a little too energetically–"Well of-fucking-course!" I jump up and down in place, earning several awkward looks from passers-by.

"Hooray!" Faith cheers clearing her throat and speaking a mile a minute. "Mom and Dad will be hosting our engagement party at the house two weeks from now. You know Mom, she lives for organizing parties." She pauses to take a breath. "I really need to see you. I think we need to rejoice and be merry tonight. What do you say, Cat?"

I don't bat an eye. "Yes!" Blowing off steam with my best friend is definitely what the doctor ordered. "Velvet Box?"

"Yes," Faith responds. "I'll pick you up around nine. Sounds good?"

Happy with my decision, we end the call. Feeling rather celebratory, I decide it's time to buy a new dress, so I hail a cab.

"Where to?" the cabbie asks.

With a broad smile on my lips I reply, "34th and 7th."

"Tell me, have you met anyone new and interesting?" Faith asks me while sipping on her gin and tonic.

She's a little taller than me with porcelain skin and bright blue eyes. Her naturally blonde hair sweeps down past her shoulders in long cascading curls. Faith has a runway model-worthy body but absolutely refused to become one. Instead, she studied medicine and became a thoracic surgeon. I inwardly roll my eyes because as much as I love Faith, she can annoy the shit out of me. I know she means well and cares deeply for me, but no matter how often she asks me, I'm just not ready to move on. I find it ironic that my late fiancé's sister can't wait for me to meet someone new.

I also know that if I don't provide a satisfactory response, a barrage of questioning will ensue.

"No, not really," I answer. "I haven't set up that online dating account." I lift my bottle of beer. "Thanks for the gift certificate, by the way."

Faith smacks my arm playfully. "You know? I'm only watching out for you. It's been four years and here you sit, gorgeous as ever, single. Why?! I get it, you loved Blake, but he'd want you to meet someone new. I hope you know that,"

"I know, Faith. I just need time…" I finish my beer and signal the bartender for another, bracing myself for the inevitable lashing.

"Four years is enough time. Stop pussyfooting and put yourself out there. Just saying," Faith says emphatically. "Nobody wants to be lonely, Cat. Deep down you *know* I'm right." She pushes her empty glass across the bar. "I want to see you happy again. That's all." Faith takes a sip from her fresh drink and raises her eyebrow. "Stop mentally rolling your eyes at me. Don't think for one second I don't know you're doing it." She raises her hands in defeat and says, "I'm done nagging."

I giggle and roll my eyes at her. She breaks into laughter.

After talking about wedding planning for a bit and enjoying Faith's retelling of Matthew's romantic proposal, we sit back and enjoy the mellow jazz. I absolutely love music in all of its forms. It takes me back to the days I shared with my grandmother and how much she loved to sing and play the guitar. I guess you could say the apple didn't fall far from the tree.

Abuela taught me everything I know about life and music. Like her, I play the guitar and sing. I even dabbled in poetry and songwriting when I was a teenager. Abuela always told me that without music, the universe is an empty place filled with hollow souls. I smile wistfully remembering her, hearing her amazing voice still singing inside my head.

Abuela believed that music is a way of telling stories and expressing feelings. Blake loved when I sang for him. As I listen to the sultry jazz, I find my fingers in their usual spot, strumming against my left thigh while the other holds the neck of the beer bottle. I take slow, measured sips from it, enjoying the yeasty flavor. Closing my eyes, I allow myself this moment's indulgence. My body is relaxed, at peace. I haven't felt this at ease for a very long time.

After five rounds of drinks, Faith and I call it a night. Making our way towards the coat check area, we return our tickets to the clerk and wait for our coats.

"You know? I'm not going to miss being single," Faith muses as she gestures towards the people in the posh club. "This is fun in your twenties, but when you get to be our age, it gets old pretty quick."

I scoff at her words, and smile. My eyes take a quick survey of the patrons. It's always the same faces. Young women wearing sexy outfits hoping to meet Mr. Right and men standing around like hunters waiting to catch the perfect prey.

No one ever approaches me and that doesn't bother me one bit. I believe it will take a miracle for a man to keep up with the likes of me. But you sure as hell won't see me waiting for that stroke of luck to happen. Life moves on–I'm simply taking special care of myself in the romance department. No one will ever be able to fill the void Blake left inside me the day he died. *Ever.*

Our coats are handed to us and we help each other bundle up, giggling. I feel a little buzzed but not drunk. Faith on the other hand, is tipsy and won't stop laughing. Placing my hands on her shoulders, I push Faith out the door.

As we exit Velvet Box, the bitter cold of the night immediately hits us, both of our mouths chattering. Taking a few steps up the ramp, Faith smacks her forehead. "Shit! I left my clutch on top of the coat check counter. Give me a sec." She back tracks and heads back into the building. I walk up the ramp slowly, giving Faith time to recover her purse. A few steps from the top, I pause and wait for her. A few seconds later, Faith walks out holding her clutch high in victory.

I resume walking but my head is craned at Faith, making sure she makes it up the ramp without twisting her ankle. Suddenly, something crashes into me, and I land unceremoniously on my ass.

“Shit, that’s going to leave a mark,” I mutter, rubbing my sore backside with my hand. Slightly embarrassed by my unsuccessful attempts at getting back up, I begin to laugh hysterically.

Two masculine hands take hold of mine and help me up. Without looking up at my rescuer, I brush snow and salt from my coat and dress. My body shivers as a breeze of cold air seeps through the unclasped buttons of my coat. I immediately button them up and pat the elbow of the man who helped me up.

“Thanks,” I mumble, slightly mortified, avoiding any type of eye contact. I recite a mantra in my head, praying I don’t look like a sloppy drunk. Falling on my ass like that was freaking embarrassing.

CHAPTER TWO

Stryder

Walking through the long corridors of JFK Airport gives me a sense of relief that I'm finally home. I'm exhausted and in dire need of rest after my recent job in Sydney. Spending weeks, sometimes months at a time away on assignments takes its toll.

It's great being a freelance fast action sports photographer. I get to visit different countries, engage with diverse cultures and do what I love. But it's also a reminder of why I'm single. The demands of my job keep me away a lot, and women aren't too keen on long distance relationships. At least, that's what I learned from my experience with Olivia.

We were basically raised together, as our parents share a passion for dancing. As we grew older, our parents saw that we danced really well together and shortly afterwards, we became partners, winning competitions around the world.

In our early twenties, Oli and I fell in love. I thought I could trust my childhood friend and dance partner completely. After all the traveling we did when we were kids, you would think Oli would've been more understanding with the demands of my then–new career.

I guess she missed Wyoming, and the city became too big and lonely for her. Here I was sleeping in hotel beds in different cities for weeks at a time thinking how badly I missed her and wanted to come back home to her. We shared an apartment in Queens for over two years and after being together for over a decade, it was time for me to pop the question. To my delight, she said yes. I let her take care of the details and embarked on a three month long assignment overseas.

The first month, Oli was always in contact, but as time passed, I heard from her less and less. I figured she was busy with her job as a dance choreographer. She got to work with recording artists a lot, and music videos were her main source of income. But as the second month rolled in, her phone calls completely stopped, my emails remained unanswered, and my nights became restless.

One weekend, I flew back to surprise her but the one who ended up surprised was me. Opening the door to our apartment, the sounds of fucking make my head almost snap from my spine. Here I was in *my* apartment which *I* paid for listening to *my* fiancé fuck another dude. The rage I felt that day still simmers deep inside of me.

I wanted to destroy that man for killing the illusion of love inside of my head. You could say that was the day I became one jaded son of a bitch. Fuck being nice, and to hell with love. It's been two years and a couple of months since I called it quits with Olivia. It was the best decision I ever made.

After grabbing my bags, I catch a cab home. I now live in West Village. My career has earned me a pretty penny so I can afford certain luxuries I couldn't when I was with Oli. My life changed after our break-up, though I'm not entirely sure it was for the best. Walking through the doors of my apartment, I feel lonely. I'm going to take a nap, call up the escort service and treat a girl to a night on the town.

Arriving to Velvet Box, I exit the cab and extend my arm to help the pretty blonde the escort service set me up with. What's her name again? Tammy? Tracy? I don't know and I couldn't fucking care. Whatever possessed Blondie to wear a tiny dress with her legs exposed in single digit weather is beyond me. Nevertheless, she's hot and just what I asked for when I called the service.

One of the pitfalls of being single is going out on my own, but thankfully, tonight that's not the case. After giving the cabbie a generous tip, we walk carefully on the icy sidewalk and down the ramp towards the jazz club entrance. My phone chirps in my coat pocket, and wondering who it is, I unlink my arm from Blondie's tight grasp. Looking down at my cell's brightly lit screen, I move forward hearing my date's stilettos clicking behind me.

I probably shouldn't read emails while walking down a ramp. My lack of attention puts me in the path of a woman wearing an emerald dress and my moment of carelessness knocks her down. The sound of her ass hitting the icy pavement makes me wince. That *had* to hurt.

It all happened so quickly, and seeing her sprawled on the ground like that made me do a double take. Her overall look was pleasing, and for a guy who prefers a certain flavor in women, this one in particular gets my attention: skulls embroidered on the hem of her dress, long raven hair, ruby red lips, and tan skin with abundant curves. Fuck me when I say she takes my breath away. There she is, laughing her ass off trying to get up and here I stand, watching in awe.

Extending my arm, I help her up, and my heart skips a beat as soon as our hands meet. My spine stiffens when blood unexpectedly rushes south, stirring my cock. That's never happened before. Maybe it's because she's different from what I'm used to, but then again it could be the effect of the all the rye I had before I left West Village.

CHAPTER THREE

Catalina

"Are you okay?" His voice is kind and soft.

I simply nod, and desperately wish the earth would open up and swallow me whole. I stand immobilized and despite the wintry chill of the night, there is a bead of cold sweat running down the center of my back. There is something about his tone that immediately hooks me. Yet, I can't find the courage to look up into the eyes belonging to such a captivating voice.

"Are you sure?" the gentleman presses, his voice inquisitive, firm and steady.

I look down at his leather shoes, which contrast nicely with his graphite slacks. My eyes slowly work their way up, assessing, and stop at the base of his throat. His coat fits perfectly, as if it were custom tailored.

"Yes, thank you," I reply, my voice a little wobbly.

I glance to his side and survey the bombshell of a woman whose arm is linked with his. Her hair is up in a fashionable bun. Soft tendrils are placed strategically around her oval face, falling against her fair skin. Her make-up is soft yet elegant, just like her attractive face. Her lips are pursed, probably in irritation brought on by her boyfriend's mishap. It's obviously taking his focus and attention away from her and by the looks of it, she can't stand it.

"Ready?" she asks him in a smoky voice.

I am having a tough time understanding why he's still standing there. And while I am incapable of looking upwards to see his face, I know he is looking at me. I can feel his gaze upon me like a ray of light. My heart takes notice; I hear it beating inside my ears. I see his chest rising and falling with each intake and exhale of breath. Clearing his throat, he replies to his companion, "Yes," yet he does not move.

Three is a crowd. I turn around and walk towards the sidewalk to wait for Faith. She exclaims, "Holy crap! Are you okay?" as she maneuvers her way towards the top of the steep ramp.

"Yes, though my ass isn't. Damn. That hurt!" I complain, rubbing my sore backside. I'm going to have a bruise the size of Texas tomorrow morning.

Faith laughs and counters, "I wasn't referring to the fall, woman. I meant the hunk of a man that helped you up. Oh my God, Cat!" Her hand balls into a fist as she raises it to her mouth and softly bites it.

I shove her playfully. "I wouldn't know, because I never looked at him. Besides, you're drunk. How can I trust your judgment?" I retort in my most uninterested tone of voice. Without a warning, Faith wraps her hands around my shoulders as she precipitously and unceremoniously spins me around.

"Well, now is your chance, woman. Look!" she shrieks into my ear. I see the pair walking down the ramp, the bevy's arm still linked around his. Sadly, the only view I get of Mr. Mystery is his retreating form as he walks into Velvet Box with his companion.

"Cat, I would've melted into his arms if I was the one he helped up. Mind you, I'm taken," Faith says affectedly, fanning her face with her hand. "He was handsome. Black hair like yours and a chiseled jaw! Full lips I could kiss from here to eternity."

"I don't understand what the big deal is! He's *a man* like any other, Faith. Calm yourself will you?" I place my gloved hands inside the pockets of my coat and walk backwards. My best friend stares at me with her hands crossed over her chest obviously irritated. I smirk at Faith's annoyance and beckon her. "You coming? Let's go!"

"*That* is *exactly* what I'm talking about, Cat! Deflection," Faith spits at me vexed. "You're hell bent on not giving yourself a second chance, huh? But goddamn it woman, you're a fool! Your stubbornness confounds me."

Faith throws her head back and slaps her hands against her thighs obviously pissed. "He could've been *the man* for you! The one to break down your walls and give you a second chance! But you have this idiotic belief that no one will ever be as loving, kind or amazing as Blake. It's killing any possibilities fate could have in store for you!"

I shake my head. I cannot believe we are having this conversation again.

"No you don't, Mackenzie! You don't get to tell me what I can or can't feel." It's hard to keep my voice steady, but for now, I'm prevailing. "Our friendship is worth more than silver and gold, but I am exasperated with this motherfucking topic! I'm only going to say this one last time," I say, looking at Faith square in the eye.

"The only things I care about right now are my job and our friendship. I don't have the time, need, or care for anything beyond that. That includes men and relationships. I. Am. Not. Ready! No matter how often you try to tell me this or that about my life, you're not telling me something I don't *already* know!" I rant, swallowing hard and holding back the tears that threaten to fall.

Faith's hands rest on her hips, her leg tapping impatiently against the frosty sidewalk. "Fine," she sighs, "Have it your way, Cat. Let's get going."

We walk towards the street to hail a cab, both of us in stony silence. We have mulled over this topic for years now but never got into a fight over it. I know I overreacted, but at the same time, Faith should know by now I can be unpleasant when cornered.

As soon as we're inside the cab, Faith's arm tentatively reaches out for mine. "Listen, I'm sorry," she whispers. "I know I crossed the line back there. But I say and do these things because I love you. I just got carried away."

I look at Faith with a wry smile. I love her and understand where she's coming from. Deep inside my heart, I know she means well. I pull her to my side, sliding her butt against the vinyl seats.

"I know you do, because I love you too." I say. "Don't sweat it, okay?"

"What?" Faith deadpans, her eyes wide.

I laugh. "Well, for a second back there I thought you were going to take a swing at me." I close my eyes considering the possibility, and crack up even harder.

Smacking my arm, Faith bluntly informs me, "I would've except I know you'd have turned around and kicked my ass. So I pick my battles." She lifts a finger to my face. "But if it ever comes down to that, if it manages to knock some sense into you, well, that's a risk I'll take."

I clear my throat and say in a muted voice, "I'd be mad as hell at you, but I would totally understand why you did it. I would get over it because I love you and I know your heart is in the right place."

My throat tightens. "Give me time. I know it sounds like the same old song and dance to you. Trust me; there will come a time where you'll rejoice for me. Until that moment comes, be patient. I *will* get through this. Okay?"

Before I can even finish my sentence, Faith pulls me into a fierce hug. That's when the knot inside my throat unravels and unbidden tears spill down my cheeks.

As the driver travels down the icy streets of Manhattan en route to our homes, I notice him watching us in the rearview mirror. He makes eye contact with me and smiles, as if trying to say: *'Have hope. Don't give up.'*

With the whirlwind of activity at work, the past two weeks have been hellish. I just got back from Florida after covering a story of a man who accomplished his hundredth skydiving jump. I walked away from that assignment with one noteworthy lesson: *"Life is too short to waste it on bullshit. Don't live it based on past regrets. Live your life by simply being yourself."* Those simplest of words somehow moved me.

Upon my return, I submitted a draft of the article to Marcia's office for approval. She was very impressed with the turnaround time and artistry. We also sat down and discussed my upcoming time off. Marcia explained that my vacation time is approved and effective immediately. I couldn't hold back my excitement when she announced I would be off for an entire month. The timing couldn't be better. This weekend I'm going to Port Washington for Faith's engagement party.

When that's all said and done, I'll have all the time in the world to decide where I want to go. One thing is more than certain. I will not be spending my free time in New York City in the deep of winter. You can bet on that.

Glancing at my watch nervously, I board the Long Island Railroad from Penn Station. That is the train that will take me all the way to Port Washington. As I take my seat, I listen to music while looking up possible destinations on my phone.

After browsing countless travel websites, I come to the conclusion that my ultimate vacation spot is somewhere in the Caribbean and give myself an opportunity to fantasize. I'm at a secluded beach, perched on a hammock under a nice palm tree. I sigh and let my imagination run wild, daydreaming of a good book and a nice, and cold drink with an umbrella in it.

The screeching sound of the wheels braking brings me back to reality. When I open my eyes I look out the window. Snow blankets the ground. My mind wanders back to that horrific day when I lost the two lives that meant everything to me.

Whenever we had a chance, Blake and I would take a trip out here to take escape the craziness of the city. We were on our way to Blake's childhood home in Port Washington, when we got into a terrible car accident. I shiver at the memory, raising the volume of my music to keep myself from reliving that terrible day.

Visiting Port Washington has a tendency to hash up bad memories, but it makes me happy knowing I will see Faith's folks, who are like parents to me. I lost my own parents when I was seven. Their death was blamed on a natural gas leak that poisoned them. I was the lone survivor. Had I not woken up when I did and run for help, I would not be alive today.

After their death, Abuela, my father's mother–a humble Brooklyn bodega owner–raised me. She made sure I went to school, got good grades and stayed out of trouble. As a barrio kid, the odds of living an honest life were never in my favor, but Abuela made sure I had the right tools to make a future for myself. Imagine her pride when I got accepted into NYU on a full scholarship.

At the beginning of my sophomore year, Abuela was diagnosed with pancreatic cancer and her health deteriorated quickly. Six months after her diagnosis, she passed away. I had my arguments with God, asking why He kept taking the people I loved the most away from me. But then I would feel Abuela's presence over me like a soothing balm. So I stopped questioning things and accepted my new reality. Besides, if she were alive, she would be majorly pissed at me if she knew I was mad at God.

The years that followed were tough–being nineteen and an orphan, I had no choice but to grow up. I stayed in school, sold off her bodega and began living on my own. It wasn't until I interned at *ESPN the Magazine* that I met Blake. He was an editor and my internship supervisor. It wasn't until my internship was over that we gave into our feelings for one another.

The first time I met Blake's parents, they instantly claimed me as one of their own. The Mackenzies have a nurturing vibe about them so I felt like I was part of a family once again. When Blake passed away, a part of us died alongside him.

The train stops signaling its arrival so I gather my bags and wait for the doors to open. As I walk down the steps of the station, I smile widely when I see Carmichael, Mr. and Mrs. Mackenzie's driver, waiting for me with a grin.

"Catalina!" he booms in his wavering Italian accent, raising his hand. When Carmichael and I close in on each other, I open my arms and hug him. "Mi bella Catalina!" he bellows sweetly.

"Carmichael, so nice to see you dear friend," I exclaim. He takes my bags and opens the door of the silver SUV.

After loading my bags, Carmichael gets in and beams. "Everyone was thrilled when we found out you were visiting. It's been such a long time since you last came over. Are you excited for Miss Faith? I know we all are."

Fifteen minutes later, we arrive to the Mackenzies home. I have visited their residence many times, but it never ceases to take my breath away.

The Mackenzie Estate boasts large picture windows, elegant and detailed masonry, even a turret, the typical debonair of a Long Island Gold Coast mansion. There are several buildings on the estate, garages, a pool house and staff quarters. All the lights of the three story home facing the Long Island Sound are lit. The place looks absolutely majestic. Carmichael pulls the car up to the rotary in front of the main house and turns off the engine, then comes around and opens my door. I take a deep breath, realizing it has been two years since the last time I was here.

Carmichael opens the front door, and we both walk in. I stand awkwardly in the grand foyer, afraid to take a step further. The home has not changed at all.

The smell of exotic spices that remind me of an assignment in Egypt still remains. I take a few timid steps and look around. The main house has too many rooms to count, a kitchen the size of my loft, two swimming pools, and a library that I would lose myself in for hours at a time. I sigh at the memory of it all.

Blake's parents come from humble roots, despite the opulence of their home. Mr. Aedan Mackenzie was born and bred in the Bronx. He was a smart kid, so his parents worked extra hard to ensure he could go to college.

Aedan interned on Wall Street straight out of college. It was during that internship that he discovered he had a natural talent for commodities investments. Aedan amassed a wealth most people wouldn't dare to dream of. At thirty, his net worth was estimated at ninety million. Now in his late fifties, Aedan is a certified billionaire.

When Aedan turned twenty six, he visited Ireland for the first time with his parents. It was during that trip he met Deirdre O'Connor, the young Irish girl who would become his wife. Aedan met Deirdre at a bakery in Cork. She was a pastry chef, and legend has it Aedan fell in love with her at first sight. But if you ask Deirdre, she'll tell you it wasn't until Aedan tried her Apple Amber–an Irish version of an Apple Pie topped with meringue–that he truly fell in love.

I smile, remembering the playful bickering between Aedan and Deidre as they recounted the story of how they met during my first visit here. A delicious aroma of sinful sweetness wafts from the kitchen, distracting me completely. I walk towards it and upon my arrival, and Deirdre practically breaks into a run in my direction. Her blonde hair is cropped in a pixie, the longer layers flopping playfully as she jogs to greet me.

"Catalina, darling, it's been far too long!" Deirdre calls out to me with her thick Irish accent, wrapping me in her slim yet warm embrace. I simply nod and smile. Deirdre wears a cream colored cashmere sweater with black silk pants and nude ballet flats. Her make-up is modest but her whole appearance is elegant, and she's definitely rocking the look. I look down at my ripped jeans and scuffed boots and grimace. Deirdre laughs as if reading my thoughts.

"Cat, stop. You look wonderful. How have you been?"

I giggle, responding with my usual wit, "Deedee, Faith failed to mention you went blind. You seriously need to get your eyes checked. I look dreadful."

She arches one eyebrow and shakes her head. "Child, it's been far too long. I've missed you. These sensitive twits just don't get me," she mutters. It has been a while since Deedee and I bantered with each other. God, I've missed this.

"I'm sorry," I murmur, lowering my gaze. Deedee lifts my chin with her delicate hands and smiles. My heart stops. It reminds me of Blake. He looked so much like her, from his smile to his characteristic kindness and nurturing personality.

I ball my hand in a fist and rub my chest in circles, trying to sooth my aching heart. Being here just opens up a floodgate of feelings I have desperately tried to put behind me for all these years. Deedee rubs the sides of my arms, as if sharing my thoughts.

"What are you sorry for, Catalina? Never apologize for feeling, darling. Come," Deedee gestures me towards the kitchen island. She picks up a round tart and breathes, "Open up. It's a new creation. Tell me what you think," she says as she places a piece of the boysenberry pastry into my mouth.

"That tastes delectable, Deedee." I exclaim, my praise garbled by a mouth full of tart as Deedee smiles. She bends over to scribble in her recipe journal.

"Glad you liked it, dearie," she says enthusiastically. Before she can say another word, the kitchen phone rings, interrupting our moment.

As Deedee answers the call, I walk towards the cupboard and retrieve a mug. Desperately needing something warm inside my belly, I raid the pantry, grabbing a packet of instant hot chocolate. I smile to myself. Some things never change.

Sipping on my hot chocolate, I watch Aedan stop at the threshold of the kitchen, holding his jacket over his shoulder, one hand on his hip, bearing a dashing smile. When our eyes meet, he opens his arms. I place my mug on the counter and eagerly rush into them.

"Catalina!" Aedan exclaims. "The prodigal daughter returns," he declares with a hint of humor in his voice. I sigh in his arms feeling safe and secure, just like when Blake used to hold me.

"Dad," I reply. "I missed you, old man," I confess as Aedan lovingly tousles my hair.

"Welcome home, baby girl," he croons softly, so only I can hear, "I missed you. So much," Aedan says, finally releasing me. He walks over to the cupboard and retrieves a mug, fixing himself a hot chocolate. He places his jacket on the back of one of the barstools in the eat-in kitchen and takes a seat.

He hasn't aged a bit. Aedan is still dressed in his business suit, which means he just got back from the city. On the outside he looks like a billionaire, but when he takes off his shoes, hangs his jacket, and loosens his tie, he's just a Bronx kid like me. Aedan's reddish hair contrasts with his sharp blue eyes. He is a dashingly handsome man, when you pair him up with Deedee; it's no surprise their three children were born with their stunning looks.

"Cat," Aedan piped, "we're setting you up in Blake's old room. I hope you don't mind. Since Faith and Matt's guests are taking over the rest of the rooms, we figured you'd be more comfortable in there." His statement forces me to shiver deep inside my bones.

"That's fine," I croak, but the truth is I am anything *but* fine. This sudden news throws me for a loop. I wish I'd known this beforehand so I could've booked a hotel.

The last time I stayed in Blake's bedroom was when we found out we were pregnant. Blake and I used to come out to Port Washington at least once a month to visit the family and recharge our batteries. Our lives were a whirlwind and regular rest and relaxation was much needed.

During our stays, Blake would row and paddleboard on the sound. He would also take the boat out and we would go fishing from time to time. I became attached to this home because I felt part of it, like the bricks and mortar used to build it. This was our little piece of heaven away from the hustle and bustle of the city.

Walking towards the large picture window, I look at the stunning view of the Long Island Sound. The view is serene, and on clear days, you can see Connecticut on the other side. I glance down to the snow-covered steps that lead towards the private beach and dock. I try not to let my eyes wander towards the swing swaying lazily in the wintry breeze. My spine stiffens as my mind goes back in time.

The snow disappears and it's spring once again. Hibiscus vines wrap around the legs of the swing set, the flowers giving off a sweet tropical scent. I hold on tightly to the sailor ropes and move my legs forward, trying to gain momentum.

There is something special about this place. I always feel peaceful and utterly happy. The ocean breeze caresses my skin, flowing freely through my hair. As I fly absentmindedly on the swing, I hear Blake's voice call softly behind me.

I squeal with happiness when I feel his strong hands on my back, pushing me, making the swing soar higher. He chuckles with each nervous giggle I let out every time he propels me. After pushing me for several minutes, Blake stops and waits for the swing to stop. He stands in front of the swing set with both of his hands buried deep in his front pockets.

"Catalina, seeing you here so happy and peaceful makes my heart thud a little harder than usual," Blake confesses with a sheepish grin on his face.

My head snaps up and my eyes search his. They look down at me lovingly, those baby blues almost making me melt on the seat of the damn swing. I smile and let out a happy sigh, which makes Blake grin his signature smoldering smile right back at me.

I straighten myself on the seat and try to stand up. I don't know why but my heart races, I can feel it thump at the base of my throat. Blake raises his hands and shakes his head, telling me to stay in place. I look at him, alarmed, but his eyes softly tell me nothing is wrong. He glances towards the Sound and then back at me. Blake clears his throat and removes his hands from his pockets.

"My family adores you, and there's no question where I stand when it comes to us. I sometimes wonder how bleak my life would've been if I'd never met you," He kicks an imaginary pebble and takes a few steps towards me. "Sometimes I close my eyes and think what a lucky man I am to have such an incredible, beautiful girl by my side," Blake continues, placing his hands back into his pockets.

I close my eyes and smile in remembrance. Blake and I meeting the way we did was no chance encounter.

"One of the things I love most about you is that you are yourself. You don't let others dictate your life or your decisions. You're strong and assertive, and I pity the person who ever breaks your trust. You've been pulled apart more than once and you are like a bird that some way, somehow always flies through the storm," Blake says, his voice slightly cracking with each word.

Before I can panic, Blake smiles softly, reassuring me. "You're the woman I love the most and the one I want to be with for the rest of my life." Blake drops down on both knees before me.

I gasp, panicked, bringing my hands up to my mouth. Blake chuckles at my reaction as he pats the tops of my thighs sweetly, reassuringly.

"With my heart in my hands, I believe the time has come to make you mine. Manners and tradition dictate I ask you the most basic of questions so here goes," Blake says, exhaling a shaky breath. "Catalina Pardo, will you marry me? Will you be the woman I'll always come home to at the end of the day? Will you be mine?"

Elated tears fall freely down my cheeks, blurring my vision. One of his hands reaches up to my face and wipes the tears from my eyes. I smile and choke out, "Yes! Yes, Blake. *Yes!*"

He takes a deep breath and releases it, laughing wholeheartedly. He retrieves a velvet box from his pocket and opens it. My eyes focus on the ring and I gasp, completely shocked. It's made of white gold with too many diamonds to count. Its ornate and intricate design screams classic beauty, and instantly reminds of the 1940s. I absolutely love it.

Blake takes hold of my left hand, placing the ring on my finger. I giggle when he reverently kisses the ring, and then my fingers. Flinging myself at him, I wrap my arms around his neck, kissing him deeply.

We both land on the soft grass with his long, lean body hovering over mine. He regards me with tender eyes and kisses me softly. "You've made me the happiest man today, Cat. God, I love you so much!"

I take hold of his face with my hands and exclaim, "Blake, you've made me the happiest woman in the universe. I love you more than I could ever say."

My words become absorbed by a passionate kiss and when we are both breathless, he lifts me to my feet. Blake brushes grass from my dress and hugs me. We walk back towards the house, our hands intertwined. As we're walking, I look back at the swing and smile, knowing I will never forget this moment.

A soft hand touches the low of my back and I jump, my trip down memory lane interrupted. I close my eyes and a stray tear lands on my blouse. I wipe it away quickly, hating the fact that I'm back in the present.

"Come on, darling," Deedee says softly. "Let's get you settled in. The other guests are arriving, and dinner will be ready in an hour." She kisses my temple, as if knowing my thoughts.

Snow flurries fall over the swing set. Taking a deep breath I turn around, rubbing my fingers against the engagement ring that now hangs around my neck. I try my hardest not to allow this visit to consume me. This home is full of memories, and the more time I spend in it, the more my heart will ache.

CHAPTER FOUR

Catalina

I climb the staircase to Blake's childhood room, and with a shaky hand I turn the handle, opening the door. My heart races, blood rushing like a runaway train through my ears as I choke back tears, because the truth is, I'm terrified of walking inside. Closing my eyes, I walk over the threshold, softly closing the door behind me.

My eyes open, and I look around. Four long years have passed, yet it remains intact. The smell of polished wood and fresh linen is as I remember. My memories of this space are warm and cozy, but now it just feels cold and clinical. The emptiness of Blake's absence wraps around me, making me shiver to the depths of my soul.

The coldness of it makes me shudder, prompting me to walk out fast and close the door behind me. Flying down the stairs, I grab my coat from one of the hooks in the foyer and rush out the front door. I feel the scrunching of the snow beneath my boots with each hurried step that I take towards our old swing set.

Using my bare hand, I gently brush off the snow that has accumulated on the seat. When my hand makes contact with the cold wetness, my whole being trembles. I gingerly sit on the swing, praying the frigid conditions haven't weakened the ropes. After testing the seat a few times, making sure I won't fall, I lift my feet from the ground and swing softly. The cold air blowing in from the Sound makes my chest tighten.

I'm not a very religious woman, but I feel the urge to pray for Blake and for myself. Coming back here to this place threatens what little progress I've made over the past few years.

After crying for a while, I take a few deep breaths trying to steady my emotions and begin my trek back to the house. From a distance I see Sean on the deck by the kitchen door.

Sean is the youngest of the Mackenzie siblings, and the only one to have inherited their father's wavy red hair. He's not as tall as Blake was, and as a professional cyclist, Sean is in perfect shape. As we make eye contact, he lifts a red mug to me in salute. I make my way up the steep steps towards the deck, praying I don't slip on the icy path.

"Catty, how've you been, girl?" Sean asks as he places the red mug on the railing, and walking over to hug me. When he releases me, I see a frown on his face. "You've been crying. What's wrong?"

"It's been a while since I've had a bad day. Coming back here, well, it just brings a lot to the surface. You know what I mean?" I clear my throat, trying to prevent myself from falling apart again.

Sean nods, "You don't have to sugarcoat shit, doll. No matter how much time passes, we'll never fully recover. We just have to take each moment as they come and make the best of it. Come here," he says, pulling me close to his chest, his heart beating steady. "It's okay, Catty. It's going to be a-okay," Sean breathes into my hair. "I've missed you. We all have."

After enjoying dinner with over a dozen guests that have flown in from different parts of the country for Faith's engagement party, I reluctantly head back upstairs to Blake's bedroom. Taking a few steps towards his desk, I look up at the countless trophies lined up on one of the shelves. I smile, remembering the day Blake took me out on the Sound to kayak. He tried to teach me, but I was terrible at it. A small giggle escapes me.

Next to the trophies are pictures of Blake alongside the members of his collegiate rowing team. I pick one trophy up and hold it against my chest, desperately trying to connect with him through his personal effects. Feeling silly, I put the trophy back in its rightful spot and look at all the posters that still decorate the wall. Most of them are pictures of rock bands with a few movie posters in between. Blake and I shared a passion for alternative rock music.

I grab my toiletry bag from my duffel. After meticulously removing my make-up, I brush my teeth and finally braid my hair. Rummaging through the duffel bag I find my favorite pair of skulled flannel pajamas and slip into bed.

I sigh contentedly, realizing the mattress still has the dip in the middle that always forced Blake and I to sleep cocooned together. Every weekend we spent here, we would crack jokes about being forcefully spooned on this very bed. Deedee always complained the mattress needed replacing, but Blake would have none of it.

It makes me happy knowing she respects her son's wishes after all this time. I bunch the comforter underneath my chin. The night is rather cold and it was such a long day; to say I am exhausted is an understatement. It's not long before my eyelids feel heavy and I drift off to sleep.

Half asleep, I feel someone climbing into bed and nestling beside me. It takes me a split second to realize that it's Blake's body cocooning mine. I sigh, thrilled, and arching my spine I bring my back closer to his chest. His lips trail soft kisses along my hairline towards my mouth, stopping briefly to nibble my jaw and neck.

When his lips reach mine, his deep voice whispers, "I've missed you so much, Catalina."

As his words enter my heart it beats lively. For the first time in years, I feel whole again, and even though my subconscious is connected with Blake, my psyche knows I'm dreaming.

"Everything will be okay, my love. Everything is as it should be."

His statement robs a sob from my chest, making me heave with sorrow. "My life is so empty, Blake. Why did you have to go? My heart feels so hollow. Please come back to me. Please!" I cry bitterly as Blake kisses my temple.

"I don't know how else to say this, Cat, but you need to open up your heart in order to love again. I know it's hard for you, to trust completely in someone else after all you've been through, but I want you to. Please, don't be afraid," Blake whispers as he moves to stand before me. He glances over his shoulder, nodding, and slowly walks backwards with his hand clutching his chest.

"I know my absence has left you empty. One day, you'll meet someone, and he will make you smile and love you the way you deserve. Don't lose hope, and don't let fear get in the way. I'll always love you."

With each step Blake takes, my heart breaks. Sitting up in his bed, I beg between sobs, "Blake, please don't leave me here. Take me with you. I can't do this anymore."

Blake shakes his head. "Don't be afraid."

I squeeze my eyes shut stubbornly, but when I open them, Blake is gone. Once again, the room turns dark, a draft of cold air prickling my skin. With a racing heart I sit up, my thoughts completely scattered. I pick up his old pillow, praying his scent still lingers on it, but all I smell is fabric softener. Sobbing, I hold onto that pillow for dear life. My body feels beaten, my spirit corrupted and my heart irrevocably broken.

I wake up to the delicious scent of freshly brewed coffee. Ah, elixir of the gods. Opening my eyes, I see Sean's and Faith's giddy smiles, and both have trays full of breakfast.

"Good Morning, Sunshine!" they sing in unison. I can tell they are both amused.

Making inarticulate sounds that would certainly call my manners into question, I stretch. Tapping the bed, I invite them in.

"It's too early for this shit, man. I. Am. Not. Amused," I say in overly dramatic pauses. They both glance at each other and laugh, mocking me.

It doesn't matter that Faith is thirty two and Sean twenty nine, because right now they are acting like teenagers.

"You are such a moody bitch in the mornings, Cat," Faith says pretending to sneer. "Sean, give her the damn coffee. She'll be in a better mood once she has her caffeine drip."

Sean laughs hysterically, but hands over the mug of coffee–light and sweet, just how I like it. "Here you go, Catty. Drink up," he sings.

The three of us sit on Blake's bed sharing breakfast, picking food from each other's plates. After filling up on bacon and buttered croissants, Faith decides she needs some alone time with me. Tousling Sean's unruly hair she says, "You, out. Now. I need Cat for a moment."

I smack Faith on the arm. "Hey! That's not nice. Have some manners for fucks sake." They look at me wide-eyed and laugh hysterically. Sean gets up from the bed and waves goodbye, sporting a sad puppy face.

"So… How was your night?" Faith asks me dubiously. She's playing with her earring–something she does when she's nervous or uncomfortable.

I set my steaming mug of coffee on the tray beside me. "It was interesting. Why do you ask?"

Faith turns to face me. "I heard you crying last night. I was worried and came close to knocking on your door twice," she states, looking me square in the eye. I lower my head, a little embarrassed that my nocturnal sobbing was overheard by my best friend—and God knows who else.

Shrugging my shoulders, I reply as shortly and innocuously as I can. "I dreamed of Blake again, but I'm okay."

I can feel her sharp blue eyes regarding me, as if drilling into the confines of my mind. After a few moments, which feel like forever, Faith clears her throat.

"Well, get out of bed. Carmichael is taking us to town to get our hair and nails done. We have to be fabulous for the party tonight." I can tell Faith is forcing herself to not ask about my dream.

Carmichael drives us to downtown Port Washington to our favorite salon. As we are getting our pedicures, I gather the courage to share with Faith the dream I had about Blake last night. With each detail, she bites her lip nervously, her eyes full of unshed tears.

She lets out a shaky breath, "You know, Cat, even though it was a dream, he's right. It's time for you to move on. I know I promised not to give you a hard time over this, but he's definitely speaking the truth. Forgive yourself and let him go. No one's going to judge you for finding love again. We're all for it. Mom, Dad, Sean, me…"

I nod my head but stay mum. I can't disagree with her but I don't want to talk more about it. After a relaxing morning at the salon, we head back to the estate, where preparations for the grand party are in full swing. Snow has begun to fall heavily, heightening my levels of anxiety. Nothing good has ever come from snow after Blake's passing. Despite its beauty, the truth is, I fucking *hate* the goddamn snow.

I'm satisfied with the ensemble I picked for the engagement party. My make-up came out perfect, especially the wing tips over my eyelids. Ruby red lipstick makes my mouth look luscious and contrasts perfectly with the raven black hair curling down the sides of my face and curtaining down my back. I'm wearing a simple blood red dress with black platform heels.

Taking one last glance in the mirror, I hear soft knocks on the bedroom door. Exiting the bathroom in my killer heels, I try my best to not scratch the pristine hardwood floors. I open the door, and am greeted by the entire Mackenzie family.

"Wow, Catty, you look amazing." Sean exclaims sweetly. With red stained cheeks, I grin.

Aedan is holding a soft guitar case with a red bow on it. Looking at the family for answers, I come up empty handed. My hands reflectively grasp the engagement ring that hangs at the base of my neck.

"It's never been a good time to give this to you, sweetie," Aedan declares, shrugging. "Deedee and I always thought it would upset you, but I think the time has come. Before you think it's a present from us, well, it isn't–" Aedan smiles. "This was supposed to be your wedding gift from Blake, but things happened so fast. I kept this in my armoire waiting for the perfect moment."

"We all lost a piece of ourselves the day we lost Blake. Now that we have you here, it's important for me to pass on his last gift. He would have wanted that," Aedan whispers, his lips trembling with each word. A lone tear rolls down his cheek as I take the guitar.

Deedee offers a comforting smile. "You've always made incredible music with those talented fingers of yours. I don't know if you're up for it, but maybe you could sing a song for us tonight? For old times' sake?"

I nod as I look down at the guitar, not exactly knowing what to say.

Sean steps forward and places a card in my hands. "From Blake," he clarifies. "We'll give you a moment to yourself. See you downstairs, okay?" He says, squeezing my elbow.

I feel a knot forming in my throat, and try to hold in all of my feelings. "Yeah, no problem, see you in a bit. I'm going to tune the guitar and I'll be right down, okay?" Waving them goodbye, I close the door.

Placing the case on the bed, my unsteady hands tear through the envelope. It's a simple white card with Blake's messy handwriting. My hand tugs at the ring on my necklace, and clutching it tightly, I begin to read.

To the woman I will now call my wife,

You've made the music of my life so much brighter and happier since the day you walked into it. Figuring out the right kind of wedding present to give you was hard as hell. With a little help, I narrowed it down to a guitar. I once saw you looking at a similar one at the instrument shop in the city. I figured your old, battered guitar could benefit from a break. Here's to continuing writing that amazing soundtrack that we will forever play in our hearts. I love you so much Catalina Pardo-Mackenzie.

Your biggest fan and husband forever and ever,
Blake

The sadness I was holding in breaks free when fat, black tears run past my cheeks. I know it wasn't the Mackenzies intention to make me cry. Deep down I know they want me to address Blake's passing and acknowledge he's gone, no matter how hard I fight it. I know the Mackenzies will always be my family, even if I meet someone new. But one thing is certain—they want me to find happiness again.

I gather my wits and focus on the task at hand. Opening the zipper, I uncover a Ron Emory Fender acoustic guitar with an ash body and maple and butterscotch coloring. Getting the guitar stringed and tuned, I play the opening chords of the first song I ever learned. It's also the first song I ever sang to Blake, "Stand by Me" by Ben E. King.

After getting familiar with the guitar, I put it back in its case. Re-doing my make-up, I grab the guitar case along with my wristlet and make my way downstairs to the party. Arriving to the base of the staircase in the grand foyer, I hear music in the air. I faintly smile. The delicious aroma of grilled steak wafts in the air as a server comes by with a tray full of appetizers and champagne. Without giving it a second thought, I grab a flute and drink it in one swig, earning me a raised eyebrow from the server.

With the guitar in tow, I take my seat at the Mackenzie family table. My eyes marvel at the muted lighting brought on by pillar candles placed amongst the tables, which are adorned with centerpieces chock full of heavenly smelling lilies laced with pearls and gold feathers. The place settings boast elegant glassware, fine china and designer silverware. I can't help but feel enthralled with the magic and music swirling in the air.

After dinner and multiple toasts to the happy couple, Aedan thanks the throng of attendees before introducing me to the crowd. I take the stage and sit on a barstool with my new guitar. The band hired for the evening is seated behind me. Clearing my throat, I greet the guests, directing my attention to Faith and Matt.

"Matthew, you are such a lucky man. My best friend and sister will be your wife very soon. Please love each other madly and treasure one another. Live each minute together as if it were your last." I reminded him, my voice quivering slightly. "I want to dedicate this song to you guys because it has a special meaning to me. Marriage will have its good days and its fair share of bad ones. When those bad times come, remember to always stand by each other, no matter what. Stand by Me–this one's for you."

I begin strumming the introductory chords, and to my surprise, the band follows. My voice echoes across the great room; a large round of applause overwhelms me as soon as I finish the first verse. Guests and family members start to sing along. It's a magical moment, one I'll never forget.

As the song ends, everyone stands and claps as I make my way back to my seat. That was the first time I'd held a guitar, let alone sung, since Blake passed away.

I sit down and notice my wristlet vibrating against the table. Puzzled, I retrieve my cell phone from it and cringe when I see twelve missed calls, sixteen text messages and an influx of incoming emails.

It's my boss, who is, apparently, desperately trying to reach me. My brow furrows when I read one of her texts:

<MR: The Jacobsons are out. You're in. Call me ASAP. –m>

What the hell? My heart drops. Grabbing my phone I slip out of the party room and run for the library. Closing the door behind me with shaky hands, I call Marcia, who answers on the first ring. "Pardo? Thank goodness you answered!"

"I'm at an engagement party, Marcia. What's wrong?" In my heart of hearts I know where this conversation is going. Nevertheless, I hold my breath, praying I'm wrong.

I hear Marcia take a deep breath. "The Jacobsons can't make it to Whistler due to a family emergency. Everyone else is out on assignments and you're the only one who's free. I need you to go to Whistler for the Reese press tour. There's a private jet leaving JFK in two hours," she says, followed by a whispered *"Please."*

I groan in annoyance and kick off my platform heels, and then I let her have it. "You *know* I don't cover snow sports. You *know* why. Not to mention, I'm *on vacation*, Marcia. You said so yourself."

Marcia's apologetic tone tugs at my heartstrings. "I know, Pardo, I know. I wouldn't ask unless it was absolutely necessary. Please. I'll make it up to you. The magazine desperately needs this story. Please don't make me beg."

I raise my hand in frustration, balling and releasing my fist, trying to calm myself. "Fine," I relent. "But I can't make it to JFK tonight. I'm at an engagement party and will not bail on my best friend. Make other arrangements for the morning and I'll be there, okay?"

Marcia heaves a loud sigh of relief. "No problem, Pardo. Thanks so much. I'll make it up to you. I give you my word."

My mind races with anxiety over the news of this last minute assignment that has been forced on me. Off to the Canadian tundra I go. I swear God must really hate me.

CHAPTER FIVE

Stryder

"Hello?" I answer the phone on top of the bathroom counter. It's almost ten at night. Who would be calling now? I was about to go out for some drinks, but Jackson's name flashing on the screen makes me rush to answer. This kid has a tough time staying out of trouble.

"Well if it isn't Stryder Martynus. Thank God you answered." Jackson's voice booms over the receiver. Before I can even say hello, he goes on. "Listen, I have a huge motherfucking favor to ask you… Will you be free for the next six weeks or so?"

"Yeah, man. I just got back from overseas two days ago. I don't have anything slated for the next few months, and was thinking about taking some time off. Why?"

Jackson takes a deep breath. "I have this press tour, and one of the magazines' photographers can't make it. I really need *Xsports* there—you've heard of them, right?" Jackson asks.

"Yeah, I've heard of them."

"Okay, so their journalistic team had to bow out at the last minute. Family shit or something like that. Anyway, they're sending out a reporter but they're short a photographer… I figured, who better than my best friend and photographer to follow me for six weeks? What do you say?" I have nothing on my calendar and we haven't seen each other for awhile. I don't give it a second thought.

"Yes. I'll do it. Tell me where to go and I'll be there, Jax." I answer.

I hear Jackson chuckle, followed by a loud howl. His energy has always been infectious; it makes me chuckle in turn. Jax has always joked that I'm the sullen, overly serious one. I have him by four years which isn't much–but when you're around Jax, his adolescent behavior rubs off effortlessly.

"Okay, man. You're a lifesaver. I'll have K send you an email with your itinerary and stuff. All I know is that you have to be at JFK at the butt crack of dawn. Sorry if I'm ruining any plans of yours, dude," he says.

"It's nothing, man. Nothing I haven't done before," I reply, my brain formulating interrogatives. "So who am I working with? And where's the assignment?"

Jackson laughs and replies, without skipping a beat, "No fucking clue on the first one. Whistler, so you better bundle up!" He replies enthusiastically.

I love to snowboard, and some of the best times I've experienced have been with Jax. The more I think about it, the more excited I feel. This will be great; something in my gut tells me so.

"All right, Jax, see you tomorrow! I'll be waiting for the flight info. Can't wait, bro."

I don't know where tonight will lead me. It's always the usual humdrum when I'm back in town. Being away for weeks at a time leaves no space or time to have a stable relationship. The woman I thought I'd be with for the rest of my life turned out to be a complete flake. When the going got tough, Olivia just traded me in for someone else. I guess all those years we spent together meant nothing to her. *Absolutely nothing.*

I get it. I travel a lot, I'm rarely home but that doesn't mean your feelings just change overnight. Olivia meant the world to me. I just didn't see her cheating on me the way that she did. Am I bitter over it? *Yeah*, but does that rob me of sleep at night? *No*. I do what any guy would do in my situation. I put myself back on the market quickly but with a warning sign on my forehead that is clear as day–only fun and no attachments.

Tonight, after a few drinks and exchanged consent, I will find a pretty girl and let her take me home with her. It may sound cold, but that is just how I do things. Olivia made it very clear to me: I need to remain a bachelor forever because I love my job. I enjoy the travel that comes along with my assignments, and let's face it, I don't plan on quitting any time soon. I'm not able to offer the stability most women look for nowadays.

None of the women I meet and have sex with have a problem with casual encounters; it's not like I'm playing with their feelings or hearts. Consent leads to the understanding that I'm not available for anything beyond a night of fucking pleasure.

What I get out of it is a perfect opportunity to find release. It's been over two years since Olivia and I called it quits, and throughout that whole time, I thank God I haven't been trampled by a stage five clinger.

I'm not a liar and I don't make promises to women for the sake of rolling around in their beds. If they accept my terms, then baby, it's fair game. Do I like having meaningless sex? *Not really.* Maybe someday one of them will ensnare me, but until that moment comes, I will continue enjoying what's left of my prime years.

As I walk out of my West Village apartment building, Jerry, the overnight doorman greets me.

"Mr. Martynus, do you need me to hail you a cab, sir?" he asks with a smile.

I pat his shoulder. "No, Jerry. I got this. Thanks, though. How's the wife? Last I heard she got promoted or something like that?"

Jerry beams. "The missus got promoted to Senior Clerk and got a nice, fat raise. I think my days as a doorman are numbered, sir." He ends his remark with a wink.

I laugh because that's the usual exchange between us. Since we met, Jerry always declares his days are numbered, yet he's been a doorman in this building for almost twenty years. I shake my head, completely amused and fix my scarf as a gust of cold air almost blows it away.

"Okay, Jerry. We'll see about that, my man. Please congratulate the missus for me, okay? Well deserved," I say, nodding in respect.

Jerry grins and replies, "It will mean a lot to the missus, especially coming from you. She's a big fan of your pictures." He adjusts his hat. "I may have told her you were an award-winning photographer. She looked you up." He admits with a chuckle.

"Remind me to send her some prints then," I say with a wink. As a cab makes its way around the corner, I lift my hand to hail it.

When the cab stops, Jerry announces, "You're the best, Mr. Martynus, a world class act. She would love that. Thank you." I wave at him and grin.

The beauty of the Meat Packing District is the clubs and upscale restaurants, far away from the boisterous tourists that flow through the city. This is where real Manhattanites come out to blow off some steam. In this part of town, at any given club, there's a never ending flow of opportunity for a guy, such as myself, to have a good time.

I haven't been here for a good ten minutes and I can already tell someone has made me their target. So I let my body language do its thing. Before I have a chance to make it to the bar, a tall, thin blonde surrounded by other model-types makes eye contact with me. I smile at her and go about my business. Let them come to me, not the other way around.

The cute bartender, who's been trying to land me for quite some time, ignores the other patrons waiting for drinks with big bills in their hands. She saunters towards me and places a bottle of my favorite beer in my hands. I give her a mouthed 'Thanks" and slip her a twenty.

She mouths back sexily, 'You're welcome,' and struts back to the other side of the counter, to take care of other people.

I take a long pull from my beer and turn around, resting my elbows against the bar top and surveying the club. Sure enough, the leggy blonde who sized me up earlier walks towards me.

"Hey," she says, raising her voice over the music. She looks young—a little too young if you ask me—but attractive nevertheless.

"Hey," I reply. She bats her eyes, and I inwardly groan. *Trying too hard, sweetheart?* But I'm not a total asshole, so I play along.

Pointing at my chest, I try not to yell over the thumping dance music. "Stryder. Nice to meet you."

Her pretty green eyes light up, "Mandy… Nice to meet you too, Stryder." She giggles, tucking a long, artificially blonde curl behind her ear.

"How old are you, Mandy?" I challenge, and take another long pull from my beer. The cute bartender makes eye contact with me and shakes her head. I wink back at her. She shakes her head again and gets back to her job.

Mandy bites her lip. In a shaky voice, she answers, "Twenty five." She takes a sip of her drink and looks back at her friends, winking.

Her darting eyes and flushed expression give her away. I'm an old wolf; I've seen it all. Leaning down to her ear, I click my tongue, allowing my breath to caress her earlobe. That's the closest she will ever get to me.

"Darling, I suggest you try again. We both know you're not twenty five," I whisper, returning to my full height and take another pull from my beer.

She looks me dead in the eye. "You're an asshole, you know that?" Then she stomps away like a petulant child about to have a tantrum.

I smile, raise my bottle to her, and nod. *Good.* Now that I've weeded through that bullshit, it's time to enjoy my beer. I'm thirty four and my tolerance for bullshit is nil. Even an asshole like me has his standards. Plain and simple: I don't sleep with little girls, no matter how attractive they are.

I place my empty bottle on the bar top and before I know it, there's another one in its stead. I tip the bartender and make my way across the dance floor. The beat of the music soars through my body like an adrenaline rush. In a matter of seconds my brain processes the sounds and my legs and arms want to do their thing. But tonight, I didn't come here to dance.

I stop by a large window overlooking the Hudson River. My mind wanders as I watch the twinkling lights that flicker across the water. As I'm admiring the view, a hand caresses the length of my arm, the gesture makes my body shiver, and my mouth is unable to conceal a smile. When I look to my side, it's another tall, leggy blonde. I smile and nod my head at her. *She is definitely what I'm looking for.*

The sexy blonde comes over and purrs in my ear. "I know what you're looking for, and I can give you *exactly* what you need."

She has my attention. Turning my head, I whisper back, "And that would be..."

She leans over again and murmurs, "I'm looking to have some fun tonight." She moves to grab my cock and squeezes it commandingly, not caring where she is or who might be watching. I'll admit I'm turned on by her aggression. My dick is hard, pressing against the seam of my zipper.

If she's willing, then I am too. "Your place?" I suggest, counter-challenging her. She responds by grabbing my arm and dragging me out of the club quicker than the blink of an eye, as I smile salaciously. Like I said, let them come to me.

As she sleeps beside me, I stare at the ceiling of my bed mate's posh apartment on Park Avenue. Resting my hand over my forehead, I let my thoughts wander. Sure, the night was as to be expected, we fucked each other's brains out. Hell, she didn't ask what my name was and I didn't bother getting hers. I know this sounds all kinds of fucked up but that's how it usually goes.

I was surprised the dame didn't kick me out of her bed as soon as we were done. Instead, she wrapped her arms around my waist and fell asleep. I don't know why, but that felt nice. This woman filled my need for skin to skin contact. I'm not usually a spend-the-night kind of guy. It sends the wrong message, and blurry lines create major headaches. But given our exchange tonight, I'll let it slide.

My phone flashes in the dark room. Reaching for it, I see an email from Kaelan Porter, Jackson's personal assistant and a close friend of the family. Apparently, my flight is booked for 7:05 A.M. out of JFK. Looking at the time, I realize it's 3:47 in the morning. *Shit!*

Swinging my legs over the edge of the bed, I stand to gather my clothes. Once dressed, I tip toe back towards the bed where she is fast asleep. I press my lips softly against the curve of her shoulder. It's the least I can do.

During the cab ride back to West Village, the scent of sex and sweat hits me. That damn regret that usually accompanies my nightly adventures shows its nasty face. Placing my ear buds in, I let the music drown out my thoughts. On the way home, I make a mental list of the equipment I need for Whistler. Hurrying through my apartment doors, I jog to my office. I grab my equipment bag and sigh in relief. Everything is where it should be. Running into the walk-in closet, I grab my suitcase, still full of stuff from my recent trip, and drop it on the bed.

I get rid of the summer clothes and start packing as fast as I can. One glance at the clock confirms I have enough time to take a shower before heading to the airport. Placing my bags by the door, I race towards the bathroom and strip from my clothes.

The hot water feels so good, but I have no time to waste so I wash up fast. Too bad the washcloth can't get rid of my self-loathing, because I'm disgusted with myself right now. I enjoy casual sex, but this chasing game? It's getting old fast and I'm not getting younger either.

As I shower out of my self-hatred, I contemplate the possibility of taking some time off after Whistler to get my life in order. Ever since I ended things with Oli and moved into this apartment, I've never brought anyone home to spend the night. You could say this is my sanctuary, and I don't shit where I sleep–plain and simple.

My elbow accidentally knocks over the shampoo bottle and it falls on the floor with a bang. *Fuck!* I need to get out of here. After drying myself, I quickly dress, and leave my place in record time. Jerry hails me a cab and by 5 A.M. I am well on my way to JFK.

After checking in for my flight, I'm grateful the security checkpoint line wasn't unbearably long. As I sit in the First Class Lounge, my eyes begin to droop. I'm startled when someone taps me softly on the shoulder.

"Sir, your flight has begun the boarding process," a soft-spoken man tells me.

"Thanks," I mutter, as I stand up to stretch. I run my fingertips through my black hair, which is longer on the top and shorter in the back. My eyes feel tired and I'm pretty sure I look like shit.

I try to soften the wrinkles on my shirt. When I look forward, I see folks watching my every move, especially the ladies. I'm a decently tall guy–about 6'2"–and all those years of dancing have kept my body lean and trim. I button up my old grungy flannel shirt and bend over to re-lace my Chucks. Placing my equipment bag over my shoulder, I walk past the staring faces and bid them 'Good Morning.' I make it to the gate just in time for First Class boarding.

I see a mom with three kids, dad nowhere to be seen, struggling to get their bags, pushing a stroller, and corralling the older kids down the jet-way.

"Excuse me, how can I help?" I call softly.

She turns around with a giant look of relief on her face. "No... I think I got this," she replies, but deep down I know she doesn't.

I'm not going to take no for an answer. Noticing her tired eyes and obvious frustration, I smile in solidarity "Listen, I want to help however I can."

The woman stops in the middle of the jet-way and removes her toddler from the stroller. "Do you mind holding my daughter for a second while I close the stroller?" she asks kindly.

I nod. "Sure. She looks harmless enough."

The woman shakes her head. "You say that now because she's asleep. The Force is strong with this one, I'm afraid." Her *Star Wars* reference makes me smile.

The woman places the sleeping toddler in my arms. I gingerly hold her and ask the woman for a duffle bag so I can place it over my unoccupied shoulder. And just like that, we are making our way into the cabin. The courteous flight attendants take over, helping the woman stow her carry-on items and putting seatbelts on the squirmy, older children.

As I stand in the middle of the aisle with the sleeping toddler in my arms, the little girl opens her eyes and smiles. "Dada?" she coos.

I don't even know how to process what this beautiful child has said to me. Before I can correct her, she yawns and nestles deeper into the crook of my neck with a sleepy grin.

The woman smiles. "Wow. She really likes you if she's calling you Dada. We're on our way to see him," she informs, extending her arms to me so I can return the toddler.

"She is simply beautiful. You are so lucky," I tell the mother, and then ask her to take her seat so I can pass the child onto her. Once done, my shoulder suddenly misses the warmth of the sleeping child. Strange, alien feelings wash over me, making me miss something I've never had before.

The woman interrupts my thoughts by saying, "Children change a person, you know. I never knew such love until I held them in my arms for the first time."

Looking down at her I grin. "Yeah, I can see why. You have a beautiful family." I straighten my flannel shirt and pull down the t-shirt underneath it. "Enjoy your flight, ma'am."

"Thank you, kind sir, for everything," I hear the woman call to me. I turn around and wave, mirroring her smile.

Finding my seat placement, I put my ear buds in, and sit down. As the minutes pass, the cabin fills up. Looking at the empty seat beside me, I'm thrilled. No one will pester me. So far, this trip is going well.

I'm assigned to the aisle seat of the two passenger row. As I look out the small, oval window of the aircraft, the sun slowly rises in glorious splendor. Huge blasts of reds, oranges and yellows begin to color the sky, making the NYC skyline stunning. I am already strapped in my seat ready for takeoff, but a part of me wants to get my camera from the overhead bin and snap away.

In my line of work as a fast action sports photographer, I'm used to capturing images of people or objects in motion. But every now and then, whenever something or someone inspires me, I can't help but snap impromptu landscapes or portraits. This is one of those moments.

As the music continues to blare inside my ears, I look down and watch the ramp crew loading the luggage onto the plane. Further down, I see a flurry of people working like a well-oiled machine trying to get the plane off the ground on time.

Flight attendants work their way through the cabin, closing all the overhead bins in preparation for departure. I stop the track I'm listening to and browse my phone for a different song. After a couple clicks, the infectious opening piano solo of Coldplay's "Clocks" begins to play. That's when I see her barreling through the aircraft door.

I swear a tanned angel of devastating beauty just walked through the aisle of the First Class cabin. She's of medium height with curves that go on for days. Her hair is black like the feathers of a raven with bangs cut straight across. Half of her hair is up while the rest of it is curled down to her waist. She wears heavy make-up around her eyes with lips as red as an apple. I can't really tell her age underneath all of it, but she has to be at least in her mid to late twenties.

She looks like a modern day pin-up girl, except she's wearing a long blouse with a skull emblazoned on it with leggings under bright white knee-length boots. Raven Girl has my attention, all right.

Her cheeks are red and she appears to be out of breath, like she ran down the jet-way. She turns around, looking at the seat numbers when I notice the guitar case strapped to her back. Ah. That makes sense. The make-up, the get-up, it all makes sense. Raven Girl is a musician. She also looks familiar, like I've seen her before. She makes her way to my row and sighs in relief when she finds her seat.

"Thank fuck!" she mutters under her breath.

I remove my seatbelt and stand in the aisle so she can take her seat. A flight attendant comes over and collects Raven Girl's guitar. Once she hands it over, she sits down on her seat with a plop.

"Thank fucking God."

To say I'm amused with the amount of profanity coming out of this woman's mouth is an understatement. I try to hold back a snicker, but she looks like she would kick me in the balls if I did.

I take my seat beside her and clearing my throat, I ask, "Rough morning?"

Raven Girl scowls at me. That throws me for a loop. I guess I must've made a face because her eyes soften, and she grants me a smile that I feel deep inside my pants.

Damn. Luscious red lips curl up to give me a view of her perfect teeth, and when I realize there's a small dimple on her right cheek, that's it. I'm a goner.

"I guess you could say that," she replies, shrugging. "I almost didn't make it. Sorry if my manners suck testicles."

I cough, choking at her reply and try my damndest to contain my laughter. Oh, the mouth on her! I clear my throat again and tell her, "It's all right. No one's perfect."

After putting on my seatbelt, I notice she's taking a glance my way. I try to ignore it, but the tantalizing scent of her perfume is making it very hard to concentrate. It smells sweet, like candy.

As I take another peek at Raven Girl, I realize she looks a lot like the woman I accidentally knocked over at Velvet Box several weeks ago... No, it couldn't possibly be the same girl. I must be out of my mind.

I scroll through my music library, trying to find a way to avoid the stranger that sits beside me. We must be on the same wavelength, though, because she is doing the same. Placing headphones over her ears at a piercingly loud volume, I smile when I hear Audioslave's "Like a Stone" bleeding through. For a girl relatively young, it's an interesting song to choose, but with her headphones on, there's no way I can hold a conversation with her.

The plane takes off, and from the corner of my eye I see her playing air guitar. I try to focus on the music playing in my ear buds, but I stop the track and hunt for Audioslave, making sure to choose the same song. Raven Girl has taken my mood and concentration hostage.

A few minutes into the flight and my eyelids droop again. I fight the exhaustion of my sleepless night for as long as I can, but as the yawning progresses, I surrender to it and fall asleep in a matter of minutes.

The smell of coffee and the tell tale sounds of cans being opened in the galley disrupt my slumber. I feel overly warm, and the smell of sweet candy invades my nostrils. That's when I realize my row mate is sound asleep, on my shoulder, of all places.

Raven Girl looks so peaceful and beautiful against my shoulder. Through the fierce make-up and obviously strong personality, she looks delicate. Since she's fast asleep, I quickly assess her beauty before I get caught. Her long eyelashes fan against the tops of her cheeks and her skin looks slightly kissed by the sun. She must be Latina mixed with something else. Whatever her background, Raven Girl is ravishing.

The flight attendant taps my shoulder interrupting my staring session. Deciding to be bold, I order her a coffee–light and sweet, just like I take it–and a bottle of water. I try my best to stay still so I don't disrupt her nap. It takes all of my willpower to not brush away the strands of hair that cover one of her eyes. I struggle against the urge to caress her soft cheek and dimpled chin.

There's something about her energy that gets me. Having Raven Girl sound asleep, her skin pressed against my shirt, brings on feelings of comfort I usually get from my Mom. If she knew about this she would laugh. Italian boys have a strong bond with their mothers. I'm definitely not the exception to that unwritten rule.

As the flight progresses so does the urge to visit the lavatory, leaving me no choice but to wake her up. I hate having to do it because she is nestled perfectly on my shoulder, her breath warming the crook of my neck. I tap my fingers on her arm, praying she doesn't slap me when she realizes she's been sleeping on me all this time.

It takes me a few seconds to wake her. When her eyelids flutter open, I'm rewarded with a small smile from that heart-shaped mouth of hers, and that tiny dimple reappears. I return her smile, my eyes softening at this unexpected yet incredibly welcome moment. But the second I grin, Raven Girl frowns, her eyes widening apprehensively.

She abruptly lifts her head from my shoulder, the warmth of her cheeks and breath gone in an instant. I want to kick myself in the ass for waking her up.

Taken aback by her adverse reaction, I look at her closely–easily distracted by her mesmerizing eyes. They are like pools of melted dark chocolate. I must look like an idiot gawking at her. The longer we stare at each other, the deeper the clouds of pink forming on her cheeks grow. Her eyes soften, and I half smile like an awkward teenager. I don't know what to do or say. Raven Girl has ensnared me.

CHAPTER SIX

Catalina

The handsome guy sitting beside me has a kind semblance about him. He has vivid hazel eyes which pair well with his obsidian hair and the shape of his face. His lips are decently full and perfectly kissable. He's just sitting there staring at me with those expressive eyes, and the longer he stares, the more my body reacts. Blood rushes through my ears and a blanket of heat colors my skin.

No, this can't be happening. Lack of proper sleep must be bringing on this delusion.

Breaking the random stranger's gaze, I look down to my blouse and adjust it. I comb my fingers gently through my stylized curls, sweeping my bangs back across my forehead. My mind races a mile a minute wondering how on God's earth I fell asleep on his shoulder.

Did I snore, drool... or worse, did I shoot bunnies? Oh God.

Cringing in my seat, I cover my face with my palms. Earth, swallow me whole.

"How did you sleep?" he asks softly.

Once again I flush when he smiles at me. His hair falls lightly over his forehead; a few long strands skim over his defined cheekbones. He has the most beautiful jaw-line and dimpled chin I have ever seen. To put it simply, random stranger is absolutely dreamy. My eyes travel down to his chin and back up, and along the way our eyes meet.

His are full of amusement and mine avert embarrassed, like a child caught with her hand inside the cookie jar. His eyes bear pure mischief, even fascination towards me. He tries and fails to conceal a smile. I can't help but roll my eyes not at him, but at myself for being a complete nitwit. I mean, really. Who sleeps on a perfect stranger's shoulder? Who does that?! Only me.

Random stranger clears his throat. "Huh?" is all I can say.

This magnificent man smiles, and I honestly don't know what's happening inside me. I'm positive I just disintegrated onto the leather seat. My heart skips a beat, my nipples tingle and my stomach feels queasy. Desire wells deep inside my belly as the heat continues to move upwards, filling my cheeks, making the hairs on the back of my neck stand. I pray to God he doesn't notice I am completely and unequivocally aroused. Wait. *What?!*

"I just wanted to know how you slept?" he inquires with another panty combusting smile.

"Surprisingly well," I grin. "You know, from now on, I am going to hunt down random strangers' shoulders if I want to take a nap. Clearly, I sleep better on them than on my own. Who knew?"

The man throws his head back in unrestrained laughter, his throaty chuckles filling the cabin with the most beautiful sound. I can't help but giggle with him, softly at first, but as we both delve into our hysterics, our fellow first class passengers start throwing daggers with their eyes. Many are sleeping, but those who are awake clearly have no patience or sense of humor.

As our laughter dies down, my row-mate points to the tray table in front of me.

"While you slept, I took the liberty of ordering for you. I don't know what your poisons of choice are so I got you a bottle of water and a coffee." He looks at the mug with a smile. "Light and sweet, because that's how I take it."

My traitorous cheeks blush again when I thank him for his kindness. He simply nods and winks, making me a quivering mess. *Catalina, get your shit together!*

With shaky hands I lift the mug and take my first sip. As soon as the sweetness touches my lips, I close my eyes and moan appreciatively, thankful it's still hot. I feel his stare piercing me, sending chills throughout my body, and it's obvious my nipples are having a field day. I open my eyes and see him looking at me with a raised eyebrow and darkened eyes, biting the insides of his lower lip. I shake my head and decide to break the silence.

"This is absolutely delicious. Thank you." I give him thumbs up trying to conceal my nerves, but cringe when he gives me a smirk. Okay, that was awkward.

As I continue to sip on my coffee, he puts his ear buds in and closes his eyes. The ghost of a smile lingers on his lips. I look forward at the miniature TV screen in front of me, and while there's a movie playing, I can't focus on it. Instead, my brain goes haywire, thinking this is going to be the longest flight of my life.

Stryder

I thought *I* was affected by her mere presence, but when she moaned after taking that first sip of coffee, I couldn't help but fantasize it was me causing it. I imagined drawing moans from her mouth with my own, using my hands, my body, and most definitely my dick. I feel dirty thinking that way, especially after having ended a sexual rendezvous not even five hours ago. I know she feels it too. I can tell by the flush of her cheeks and her squirms on the leather seat.

This is becoming too much to handle, and I have to distract myself before I remove my seatbelt and assault those pretty red lips. My cock is hard and while the thought of taking care of it in the lavatory is tempting, it would be seedy of me to jerk off mid-flight. *Fuck.*

I scramble for my ear buds and shove them in. I pick "shuffle" and, Lynyrd Skynyrd's "Simple Man" plays. Closing my eyes, I focus on the song blaring inside my ears, but that distraction only lasts a few songs. Even with my eyes closed I can feel her examining me. My dick begins pulsing inside my pants, making me feel like a dirty old man. I shift in my seat uncomfortably, trying to imagine I'm wading naked in a frozen lake. That does it. God, this is going to be the longest flight ever.

I yank the ear buds out and reach for one of the in-flight beverage napkins. Taking the pen I always keep on hand, I begin sketching. I sneak a glance at the woman beside me—she's looking out of the window, immersed in her own little world.

By no means do I consider myself an artist, but my doodles are pretty damn good. In no time, I sketch her entrancing profile on the napkin. I draw a little further, enhancing the image to include myself, recreating the scene the flight attendant probably saw when we were sleeping against each other. Feeling an ounce of bravado, I write my phone number on the back.

I fold the finished doodle in half and place it in the front pocket of my flannel shirt. I smile inwardly, thankful she was oblivious to the fact that I sketched her. I take another glance at her; she is deep in thought. I would pay the highest price to know what she's thinking, to be inside her head right this very minute.

My musings are interrupted when the captain announces the initial descent into Vancouver International. My heart drops along with the plane, disappointed this flight is coming to an end. Never in my life have I connected with a perfect stranger, yet alone a woman, to the degree that I have today. Raven Girl begins to frown as she continues to look out the window. Before I can consider my words, they escape me.

"Don't frown," I tell her, clearing my throat. "A face as beautiful as yours should never frown."

She turns her head, as if in slow motion, and looks back at me with a forlorn expression, an obvious sadness reflected in those dark chocolate pools. Then she surprises me with a bright-eyed smile, forcing me to take a deep breath. It's amazing that beneath all that eyeliner, there is a genuine beauty that has left me breathless.

I return her grin and place my tray table in its upright position. She looks out the window again, but this time she's still smiling.

After landing, I stand in the aisle and help her retrieve her carry-on items. Shortly after, the flight attendant delivers her guitar. I let Raven Girl stand in the aisle and can't keep my eyes off of her as she straps the case to her back, the epitome of a sexy rock star.

"Hey, it's a shame I never heard you play..." I murmur. She turns around to face me and smiles.

My goodness, poems could be written about those grins. Every second I spend near her is agony. When I think this will be the last time my eyes will gaze upon her, my heart tightens inside my chest. The aircraft doors open and, reluctantly, I deplane like a lost puppy behind her.

As soon as our feet touch the jet-way, I call out, "What should I call you?"

I swear I die a little when she beams playfully and defiantly raises her chin. "Girl who sleeps better on a random stranger's shoulder."

I shake my head and sigh, pointing to myself. "Nice to meet you, girl who slept on *this* random stranger's shoulder. My name is 'Guy who let a beautiful raven-haired stranger sleep on his shoulder.'"

We both break out in laughter. After clearing Customs, we walk side by side giggling towards the baggage claim area. I feel like a teenage boy. I'm nervous, and once there, I can't stop shuffling my feet. I reach for my pocket and retrieve the napkin.

"Listen. I want to give you something. Please don't open it until you arrive at wherever you're headed. Don't ever stop smiling," I say and place the napkin in her open palm.

Again she shocks me by accepting the doodle. She offers me her hand, like a business person would, and shakes mine. "Very pleased to meet you. I don't recall a cross-country flight ever being so interesting and fun." Raven Girl abruptly turns on her heel and heads towards the baggage carousel with determined strides as I look after her with a goofy smile on my face.

I work my way through the throng of tired, grumpy passengers waiting for their baggage. I find an empty spot opposite her, the luggage carousel belt keeping us apart. As soon as her suitcase reaches her, a man offers to help and she waves him aside.

It is more than obvious that Raven Girl is an independent woman. It makes me smile when I realize she wasn't short with me. I guess I did something right in her eyes. This woman is like a puzzle that I need to figure out fast. I must find the corners and work my way in. If I move in too fast, she might scare away. Damn it. If only I had more time. My suitcase comes around and when it's in my possession, I get that unmistakable feeling she is gazing at me again.

My head snaps up and I see her smiling at me across the carousel. She holds the handle of her bag with both hands and shrugs.

"I guess this is goodbye," she says, with a sad smile.

Before I can say farewell, Raven Girl walks towards the elevators that lead to the ground level. I watch her press the button and when the doors open, she turns around, her eyes meeting mine. I lift my hand and wave, forcing a wide smile. She grins back as the elevator doors close, taking her away from me forever. I try my best to memorize each of her features, etching her into my memory. Then I feel my phone buzzing in my pocket and smile when I see a text from Jackson.

<JR: Go to ground level. Look for asshole with sign. It has your dumb name on it. –Jax>

I snicker, shaking my head, thankful for Jax's humor. Boarding the same elevator Raven Girl used, I reach the ground level and laugh when I see the driver holding up a sign with my name on it, replaying Jax's text in my head. There's another name beneath mine: *C. Pardo.*

I approach the man and introduce myself, showing him my passport. He escorts me out the glass doors towards an SUV parked on the curb. Before closing the door, he tells me we're waiting for another passenger.

As I wait, I take out my phone and text Jackson to let him know I've arrived. Outside it's snowing heavily. I wonder if it's safe to be driving through this. It's a two hour drive from Vancouver to Whistler and in this weather, it'll probably take forever, but then again, Canadians should have driving in blizzards down to a science.

Catalina

Turning on my cell phone I notice there are a few messages from my editor. I look out the window and see snowflakes the size of golf balls falling from the grey sky. This makes me very nervous and anxiety is getting the best of me. I shove the phone back into my coat pocket. *Fuck this weather, and fuck this shit.*

As I walk down the long corridor, I see a man holding up a sign with two names on it; one of them is mine. I introduce myself and he takes my bags walking me outside to the freezing air, and as soon as the driver opens the door for me, I see a familiar face. *Well I'll be damned.* My heart skids, and my breath catches. It's *him*.

The wind is whipping furiously, making my hair fly in all directions. Holding my hair with one hand and using the other to climb in, I slide onto the heated leather bench seat. His head turns and when his eyes meet mine, they widen in complete surprise. He starts laughing and I can't conceal my smile. I fumble with the seat belt, and when I look up, I see his right hand extended.

"Pleased to meet you officially, Miss Pardo," he says with a hint of humor in his voice.

As if I wasn't enthralled by him already, he flashes a mega-watt smile that makes my insides tingle. Oh dear. God has some sense of humor, putting me in this predicament.

I wrap my hand around his shaking it, and as soon as our skin makes contact, I feel a rush of energy flow from him to me and back, like an infinity circle.

"And you are...?" I ask casually, wishing I had taken the time to read the goddamn sign.

He looks deep into my eyes, keeping my hand hostage, and responds in a confident voice, "Stryder Martynus. A pleasure." For the umpteenth time today, I feel my jaw drop.

Cocking my head to the side, I wonder why his name sounds so familiar, and then, like a lightning bolt, it hits me. My eyes widen, and before the filter of my brain connects with my vocal chords I blurt, "*The award-winning fast action sports photographer Stryder Martynus?* You've got to be fucking with me, right?"

Stryder looks at me taken aback in confusion. He lets go of my hand and straightens in his seat. "I'm sorry, Miss Pardo, did I offend you somehow?"

I flush, completely embarrassed, and my mind scrambles into damage control mode trying to think of how to fix this major fuck up.

"I'm sorry. That was rude," I begin, looking down towards the hand that holds his. "I just... I hate the fucking snow. It makes me anxious, and the thought of driving through a goddamn blizzard freaks me out. My nerves are shot, sorry."

I aim for a smile as I look into his gorgeous eyes. "My name is Catalina, but everyone calls me Cat. Pleased to meet you, Stryder."

He smiles warmly, nodding. “It’s okay, I understand. Catalina... That’s a beautiful name,” He says, winking at me. “What brings you to Canada?”

“I’m a journalist sent on a last minute assignment,” I reply, aiming not to give too many details.

“So you’re a reporter. That’s awesome,” Stryder asserts with a glimmer in his eyes. I like talking to him. He makes me feel at ease and so flustered, all at the same time.

Trying to shake my impure thoughts, I ask, “Why are you here?”

He exhales and replies, “I’m meeting up with my best friend for some fun on the slopes. We haven’t seen each other for months. I can’t wait.”

As the driver continues along the slippery road away from Vancouver towards Whistler, I put my headphones on and blast Angels and Airwaves.

Stryder

I can’t help but notice Catalina is strumming her thigh again to the beat of the music bleeding through her headphones. Her body language screams discomfort, but at least I know it doesn’t have to do with me. I take out my tablet and review the press tour itinerary Kaelan sent me.

I glance over at Catalina, her eyes closed, lost in her world. I must be patient and proceed with caution. She’s obviously one tough cookie, yet I can’t help noticing there’s a vulnerable and soft side to her too. All my instincts scream to me I want her. I want Catalina Pardo.

Catalina

I have never heard anything negative about Stryder Martynus. He has always been the most talented photographer in the sports journalism field. Despite his fame and multiple awards in the industry, he’s never been involved in any scandals. A part of me wants to get to know him. Meeting him on the flight elicited feelings I haven't dealt with in a very long time. Plain and simple, I'm attracted to Stryder Martynus, but he's so out of my league. Besides, Stryder is a stranger, and I didn't come out all this way to mingle. I came out here to work, and that will be my top priority, as it's always been since Blake passed away.

I feel the SUV ascending a winding road. My instincts kick into high gear and I grab the oh-shit handle next to my door. My free hand takes hold of the seat and I'm pretty sure I am holding on for dear life.

Fuck! I feel my heart racing inside my chest, blood rushing through my ears with the speed of a bullet train. The air inside the SUV has turned thin and I'm finding it very hard to breathe.

I feel Stryder's hand softly tapping my shoulder. I open my eyes and see the worry etched on his face. He removes his seatbelt and sits as close to me as he can. He makes the bold choice of removing my headphones and squeezes my knee.

"Anything I can do to help?" Stryder asks looking me dead in the eye, and judging by his concern, I must be sporting a look of terror.

Somehow his voice soothes me, and having him so close makes me feel better. I let go of my death grip on the handle and place my hands over my face, breathing hard. He wraps his arm around my shoulders.

"Thank you," I whisper shakily. Just as I was beginning to relax, the SUV glides on a patch of ice and I scream. "Fuck! Let me out! Just let me the fuck out!"

Stryder's grip on my shoulder becomes tighter and his whispered words echo deep inside of me. "Whatever it is, I'm here and I won't let anything happen to you, okay? We can't stop in the middle of this blizzard. We run the risk of getting trapped in the snow. We're not too far away from Whistler. I presume that's where you're headed. What can I do, Catalina? Please tell me." Stryder whispers.

"I was in a bad car accident in the snow," I whisper. "I just need to get out of this car. I can't take it. I'm so sorry!"

He moves to grab his tablet, placing it on my lap. He taps on his photo gallery, showing me pictures he took of the last Winter Olympics. As he glides his finger over the pictures, he talks about the photographs, giving details about each one.

My anxiety eases; I'm instantly mesmerized by the stunning images. Stryder must've spread himself thin covering so many sports: hockey, skiing, snowboarding and figure skating among many, many others. My eyes land on a particular male figure skater doing a triple axel. You can see the skater's concentration, starting from his face all the way down to the crossed arms tightly pressed against his chest.

Another image that I loved was one of Jackson Reese, the very man I was sent here to interview. In it he's coming down the slope and going up a steep ramp made from snow. As he reaches the top of the ramp, he flips in the air, one of his hands gripping the board tightly while the other is extended over his head. The image captures the body-contorting move flawlessly. There are close to twenty five pictures showing the move as it happened in real time. Each one is better than the next.

I go from basket case to reporter mode, asking questions, and getting insight. Stryder must like my line of questioning because he opens another file and shows me his professional portfolio; the same images I've seen in magazines, which have garnished him many awards. I'm amazed and honored that someone like him would take the time to discuss his work with me. Any reporter in my shoes would do back flips over an opportunity like this.

"A lot of these were flukes, Catalina. I notice my best shots are the ones I don't plan. I just press the trigger and hope for the best. I guess I'm just lucky," Stryder tells me with a broad smile.

Just as he ends his sentence, the lodge comes into view, and while my conversation with him has alleviated my anxiety, knowing I'll be sheltered from the treacherous snow fills me with peace. I'm grateful the journey in the SUV has come to an end. Stryder looks at me and says in a resigned voice, "I guess this is goodbye. Have fun with your assignment. It was a real pleasure to have met you."

He clears his throat and says quietly, "Listen, I gave you a napkin at the airport. On it is my cell number. Since we're both based in the city, I would love to show you my gallery next time we're both in town. Give me a call, okay?" He bends down to collect his bags and I look at him, confused. The driver opens the door and Stryder slips out, stretching his beautiful body and collecting his bag. I get out of the SUV and grab my luggage, strapping the guitar to my back. Stryder eyes me with his head cocked, and beams.

I scoff and say, "You've got to be shitting me. You're staying here too?"

Tipping the driver, Stryder approaches me, and peers down into my eyes. "All evidence would show that's the case. Does it bother you we're staying in the same hotel?"

His bluntness makes me blush. "No… It's just weird that I keep bumping into you. It's like the gods are playing a practical joke on us."

"Maybe we can meet up for a coffee at some point? I'm serious. Just give me a call if you ever feel the need to nap," he says, with a devilish wink, "on this stranger's shoulder."

I shake my head. "Sure thing, Stryder, but seriously, thanks for putting up with my emotional shit on the way here. I can't thank you enough. See you around," I say, winking back.

CHAPTER SEVEN

Stryder

My hands fumble in my pocket for my cell phone, and I remove my leather gloves and tap the camera icon. Sure, it's not my wide lens, but it'll have to do. Standing behind Catalina, I try to get the best picture.

I love her stance, as if she's defying the terrain with a fierce look on her face, her chin pointed upwards as her hair whips around and that guitar strapped to her back. Satisfied with my shots, I put the phone in my pocket just in time to see her walk towards the lodge. She stops at the foyer and waves at me with a smile, and my heart races like a prized steed.

I really can't believe my good fortune, and this is my chance to get to know Catalina. Giving her some space so she can check in sans me, I stop on the walkway and retrieve my camera. Finding the right lens is easy; getting into the right frame of mind isn't.

The lodge sits in the middle of the snow covered mountains, with a frozen lake on the horizon. The lodge buildings look like multi-level log cabins. While I have been to Whistler before, I've never stayed at this particular lodge.

I'm guessing the harsh weather conditions kept all the guests indoors during the morning. Since the bad weather broke, the staff is working to clear the walkways that lead to the ski lift.

My camera's shutter clicks loudly as I document the alpine tundra. There's a serene beauty about this place and my heart skips a beat knowing Catalina is here. My mind replays the last few hours, and I can't help but smile like a smitten asshole.

The bounce in my step fades when I think about her little episode on the way here. My best guess is that she suffers from some kind of trauma that has to do with that accident she mentioned. I know it's none of my business but I want to know more about it. At least I have the comfort of knowing I was there for her when she needed me.

Maybe I'm thinking too much into it, but I want to know all of her: the good and bad. I hate how she put herself down after the panic attack. There's nothing wrong with bearing your emotions, especially when you can't control them. Even the toughest person breaks down every now and then.

Putting my thoughts of Catalina on hold, I approach the front desk and check in. Once there, I get a text from Jackson.

<JR: Meet me at the Lobby Bar. Be there in 5. –Jax>

I shake my head, partly concerned he might want to share a few drinks, partly thrilled because it's been far too long since we've seen each other. Walking into the bar, I sit on one of the stools and order a beer.

After a few swigs, my body feels tingly. I don't know if it's because of the sleepless night or the elevation, but whatever it is, by the time I finish this beer, I'll be drunk off my ass. I nurse the bottle, almost choking on the small sip as a solid whack on my back forces the beer down the wrong pipe.

"Motherfucker! You couldn't wait for me?" Jackson's voice booms into my ears.

I try to clear my throat, coughing up the yeasty taste. Standing up from the stool, I rub my burning throat. I tousle Jackson's reddish-blonde hair, which hangs over the collar of his thermal shirt. It's a big brother/baby brother thing we do every time we see each other. His big blue eyes are smiling. Yeah. The little shit is happy I'm here.

"Jax, whack me one more time while I'm drinking and I will beat your ass," I chide, patting his shoulder.

Jackson laughs loudly, smacking me in the back once more. I glare at him and he says, "Jupiter, it was long overdue." He shakes my hand and pulls me in for a brotherly embrace.

"I know, kid. I know. How are you these days?" I don't want to bring up the streaking incident. If he wants to talk about it, he will.

Jackson motions the bartender over, who brings us two bottles of Labatt Blue. "Well, everyday's a struggle. New place, new adventures, no slam piece, the usual," he says, taking a long pull from his beer.

Jackson Reese drinks a little too much and in recent years, he's gotten worse. He shouldn't be having that beer, but something about his slow pace with it tells me he's in control.

I clear my throat and take a sip. "No slam piece? Girls love you... It's always been that way since you were a kid. I mean, now you're a gold medalist. That bumps up the popularity with women, right?" I ask him.

Jackson shrugs his shoulders, but says nothing so I carry on. "If I recall, you were the one caught in the dressing rooms making out with the competition!" I say, laughing at the memory. Jackson's lips turn up smiling.

Our parents are professional ballroom dancers, so whenever they traveled for competitions, we went together. Jackson's parents always kept a close eye on him. He was a stick of dynamite growing up. Still is.

Jackson takes another long, brooding pull. This is so unlike him, and I wonder what's going on in that head of his.

"Tell me about this press tour," I ask, and he takes the bait.

He tells me it was a plan devised by his public relations firm to repair his image. The press tour is slated for six weeks and three magazines have been granted interviews. It's an interesting concept, because Jackson is so much more than what people read in newspapers or see on TV. All the media has seen is the public persona who acted foolishly.

We both sit, nursing our beers and talk until my eyes begin to droop. I've been up for twenty four hours straight. I pay the tab and ditch Jackson, telling him I need some shut eye before the press mixer tonight.

Battling severe exhaustion, I stumble towards my room. I'm thankful it isn't far away from the main building. Once there, I place my bags the first place I see and throw myself on the bed. I don't know if it's because I'm exhausted, but I hear the faint notes of a guitar. After taking off my coat and shoes, I fall asleep as soon as my head touches the pillow.

Catalina

As I'm approaching the conference center, Marcia calls. I roll my eyes thrice when she won't stop apologizing. I reassure her that I'm fine and this time, I mean it. Before ending the call, Marcia goes over several key points she would like for me to address during the one-on-one session with Jackson Reese. It's slated for tomorrow after his first practice run.

I'm a little nervous about that solo meeting because while the Jacobsons know Jackson on a first-name basis, I haven't even met him. I wonder if he'll make an appearance tonight. I hope so.

My stomach rumbles unceremoniously. I look around, hoping no one heard. Please God, let there be appetizers because I'm freaking hungry. I look at my watch, but I don't have time to eat dinner. Using the lodge map on the back of my press pass, I try to navigate my way to the nearest vending machine. I sigh in frustration when I keep walking further away from the ballroom and the machines are nowhere in sight.

My eyes focus on the tiny map as my legs trek forward, and before I know what hit me, I stumble to the floor, landing on my ass and wincing. *What is up with these falls lately?* Clearly I must be having foot coordination problems because this is the second time in a month my clumsy ass has landed on the floor.

"Fuck! Not again..." I mutter. "Could you *watch* where you're going?"

My sullen mood completely vanishes as my eyes land on some sexy as hell black Doc Martens belonging to a man who smells of incense and citrus, and towers over me.

He offers his hand and helps me up. Before I manage to make eye contact, a familiar chuckle forces my head up in attention.

"I'm starting to believe you're keeping tabs on me, Catalina," Stryder says, in a smoky voice. "Are you okay?"

As I look into his playful, sensual eyes, my insides begin to quiver. I try to steady myself, absentmindedly placing one hand over his shoulder.

"Well there, Mr. Martynus, I *am* a reporter. Keeping tabs on people is part of the job description."

"So you're basically stalking me?" Stryder challenges, looking at me square in the eye.

I raise my chin defiantly, mocking his seriousness and reply, "Perhaps I am, Mr. Martynus."

But my body betrays me as his gaze falls over me, warming me from the inside out. I feel the heat radiating in my cheeks. *Catalina Pardo, stop flirting with this man.* God, I can't find in my mental dictionary the right adjectives to describe him.

A rush of electricity runs up my spine when his hand covers mine on top of his shoulder. His lips quirk up and I hastily break eye contact, removing my hand. I look down to my heels and smooth out the wrinkles from my dress, wondering how to oust the chaos inside me.

"How's your butt? Will it live?" Stryder asks in between chuckles.

I look at him with wide eyes and playfully smack him on the arm. In the end, I'm laughing with him. He's so freaking adorable.

"Bruised, but not in need of first aid, thank you very much," I reply with burning cheeks.

We both crack up laughing, and God, it feels so good. Stryder smiles down at me and I lose myself in his eyes.

"Are you hungry? Would you like to grab something to eat?" he asks.

"I have this work thing I have to go to. Can I take a rain check?" I reply, hoping Stryder doesn't take my rebuff the wrong way. "I'm headed to one of the ballrooms. I have to go. See you around." I turn on my heel and start walking.

"Catalina! Wait! I'll walk with you. I'm meeting my buddy in one of the meeting rooms." Stryder calls out, jogging to catch up with me.

We slow our hurried steps and walk together in silence. Up ahead, I see a restroom, and couldn't be more thankful. I stop in front of the bathroom entrance, clutching my coat in one hand, and shift my heels.

"It was nice bumping into you, Stryder. See you around." I tell him, feeling overwhelmingly shy.

Stryder places his hands into the back pockets of his jeans and asks, "Would you like to have a drink with me after your meeting? I'll be at the lobby bar after 9:30. I would like it very much if you could join me."

Stryder's invitation is tempting, but it has been a long day; I really need to rest.

"I would love to, except I haven't slept in over twenty four hours. I have a big day tomorrow and really need to get some shut-eye. I'm sorry. See you around?"

I feel terrible looking at the disappointment etched on his face. I wave goodbye as I walk into the restroom.

My hands clutch the edge of the porcelain sink. I look into the mirror and the woman that looks back at me is someone entirely different. Her pupils are dilated, with cheeks flushed a deep shade of red, and her pulse is visible against the tanned skin of her neck.

I can't believe for one second that woman is me. I close my eyes, enjoying the faint scent of his cologne as it embraces me. I live in denial about many things, but this feeling inside me, I certainly can't ignore.

Per usual, the alarms of my defense mechanisms ring loud and clear. Stryder Martynus is making me feel again. While I enjoy the sudden breath of life his presence has given me, he is trouble and must be avoided. End of story.

I take a deep breath, repeating those words like a mantra. Then I take one last glance at the woman in the mirror and walk out. Work awaits me.

Stryder

As soon as I walk in, I forego the welcome table and make a beeline towards the bar. I can't believe I just did that. Sometimes I forget I'm a thirty four year old man and act like a hormonal teenage boy. Damn it.

I want to kick myself in the ass for being so impatient. Why couldn't I just let her come to me? But no, I jumped the gun and scared her away. Maybe it's the sting of rejection that has me so wound up. I have to kick this fast. As soon as I walk up to the bar, the pretty, young thing behind it receives me with a flirtatious smile. Quite frankly, I'm not in the mood. I ask for a beer. The girl tries to make polite conversation but quickly gets the hint. I take a long draw from the bottle and the bartender leaves me alone with my thoughts.

Why the hell is Catalina so guarded? I could swear she was flirting with me, but then again, maybe that was me seeing something that wasn't there. She doesn't wear a wedding ring, but maybe she's in a relationship? If she is, then her rejection would be warranted.

My back is facing the small group of people gathered for the press mixer. As minutes pass, the background noise gets louder. I groan when Jackson manhandles me playfully, tousling my hair. I'm not in the mood for his shit right now.

"Keep your hands to yourself, Jax," I say in a clipped voice.

He stares at me, bewildered. "What crawled up your ass and croaked?" He crosses his arms over his chest.

"Sorry, Jax, but we're not kids anymore. Your guests will think we play for the same team. You know that won't help your current image crisis," I say sardonically.

And I should've known Jackson would play on my words. He wraps me in his arms, caressing me playfully and even kisses my cheek. I try to break free from his overstated display of affection.

"Baby, let's not hide it anymore. Let our love be free!" Jackson almost shouts, making the press look at us and laugh.

I look on, relieved, and laugh my ass off. "You are something else, jackass."

"Seriously though, what's bugging you? You're standing at this bar brooding like an angry old man. Want to talk about it?"

I really don't want to talk about it, so I pat him on the shoulder and let him know everything is okay, that I had a long day. I'm thankful when he changes the subject, saying how thrilled he is I'm here.

Resting his elbows on the edge of the bar and facing the members of the press, he says, "Being a photographer sure beats being an Olympic champion with a questionable reputation. I mean, look at these fuckers. They're all dying for a piece of me." He pauses as he takes a swig from my beer. "It's the price you pay for celebrity. I miss the days when I could hit the slopes or go on dates without the paparazzi following. This sucks, man." Jackson continues, gesturing towards the people behind us, "My publicist ensured me this would fix the mess I made at the Olympics. I made an ass of myself. I thought I was being funny, clearly that backfired, and now I have to deal with this shit."

I smile, understanding Jackson's predicament. I give him a one-armed hug in solidarity. "Don't go crazy drinking during this thing and you'll be fine. Now give me my beer back," I demand.

Trying to get my head into the job I came all this way for, I ask about the person I'll be working with.

"Hey, Jax, when am I going to meet the journalist from *Xsports*? Is he going to be here tonight? I need to go over some stuff with him about his plans for you. I want to make sure you look good," I state, nodding my head assertively. "I got your back, buddy."

But Jackson doesn't reply. He just stands there with a scrunched forehead and crinkled nose as if confused. His eyes are following someone across the ballroom, but since my back is facing the bar, I can't tell who it is.

"She's obviously lost," Jackson mutters.

I shrug, not wanting to pay more attention to his nonsense. Lifting my empty bottle, I gesture the bartender for another.

"Who is that?" Jackson mutters again, and this time he points to someone across the ballroom where the members of the press are mingling. I turn around, following his finger and recognize the tall fellow he's referring to.

"That's the photographer for *Sports Visual*. We run into each other from time to time. He's a decent guy. What about him?" I ask Jackson curiously.

I guess I must have a different vantage point because he retorts, "No, not him. *Her.*"

Then the tall guy moves aside, revealing a face I already know. What is she doing in this ballroom?

I blink twice just to make sure I'm not imagining Catalina is here of all places, mingling with members of the press. God, she looks beautiful and in her element, her fierce persona up front, and center. I'm beyond stupefied.

Jackson looks at me long and hard, and a knowing smile lights up his face.

"Do you know her?" Jackson asks amused. "And don't try to bullshit me on this. I know you. Damn well I might add."

I shrug my shoulders unable to conceal my zeal. "Know her? Not really, but I've seen her before. On the flight on my way here and in the SUV that drove us from the airport."

"Right... Shit! I totally forgot. Kaelan mentioned this to me last night... *Xsports*... She's the last minute replacement!" Jackson says, scratching his beard.

He shakes his head and slaps me on the shoulder, and pulling me away from the bar, Jackson walks towards Catalina. With a determined voice I know all too well, he says, "Come on, let us mingle. Introduce me."

So I'm competing with Jackson Reese? Well, isn't that fucking grand.

Catalina

I make my way across the ballroom to where my colleagues stand. I'm so glad to see so many familiar faces here. Luckily, our paths have crossed more than once, so witnessing them here is actually nice. My fellow journalists are talking about the press tour, but I can't ignore how hungry I am. A server comes by with a tray of appetizers; I thank my lucky stars. Without shame, I take three risotto balls and shove them into my mouth.

"Pardo? Come back from Lala Land, girl," says Jimmy from *Graphic Sports*.

"Huh?" I mutter through a mouth full of rice. I chew as quickly as I can, wishing I had a drink in my hand to wash down the clump of food.

Jimmy snickers. "I just asked if you knew what happened to the Jacobsons. Last I heard, they were coming, yet here you are. Everyone knows you don't do these types of stories."

I nod, but before I can respond, someone clears their throat behind me, a little too loudly. Some people are unaware of personal space, seriously.

A second clearing of a throat prompts me to turn around and see who the hell is being so annoying.

But the joke is on me when I see Stryder, flanked by none other than Jackson Reese. I blink twice, trying to dismiss this daydream that has meshed into my line of sight. Stryder is wearing the same press pass lanyard as me. When our gazes meet, his eyes regard mine with unmasked surprise.

This really isn't happening. I don't need my personal life trickling into my work life.

I gather what little courage I have and put up a serious front. I offer Stryder my hand, and say through tight lips, "Mr. Martynus, it would appear we seem to find ourselves in the same place at the same time once again. How are you doing this evening?"

I can tell Stryder is taken aback by my cold approach, yet he wraps his hand around mine, shaking it. A rogue thumb caresses the top of my palms as our hands greet each other. That mere gesture shoots a torrent of heat all over my body, beginning deep inside and working its way out. My body is a complete traitor.

Our eyes meet and time stops. The sounds of people talking, laughing, the clanging of glassware, ceases. I swear I can hear the thumping of my heart inside my ears.

Both our breaths hitch as electricity ebbs from his body, and works itself into mine. Stryder looks at my hand with his lips parted; the movement in his chest, unmistakable as it rises and falls with each breath.

Someone clears their throat and brings both of us back to Earth. Hesitating, Stryder lets go of my hand and rakes his hair. It takes him a split second to get his bearings before he speaks.

"There's someone I would like for you to meet," Stryder says.

Jackson Reese is much taller in person than he is on television or in print. In fact, he's a very handsome guy with a dazzling smile that could easily land him an ad with a toothpaste manufacturer. Stryder's obsidian hair and olive oil skin contrast heavily with Jackson's strawberry-blonde locks and pale skin. Watching these two men standing side by side is quite the sight to behold.

Flashing me a slow, sexy smile, Jackson Reese extends his hand. When our hands meet, he takes one look at my press pass and purrs, "Pleased to meet you, Catalina."

"Catalina Pardo with *Xsports* Magazine. The pleasure is mine, Mr. Reese. Thank you for having me on such short notice."

With a raised eyebrow and curious blue eyes, he replies. "Please, call me Jackson. Snowboarders aren't big on formalities. Jackson, Jax, dude, bro, and amigo are the names I prefer." The humor behind his words wins me over, if only a little, but I'm not stupid. Jackson is trying to flirt with me, or at the very least being a tease.

I smile politely. "Mr. Reese, everything happened so quickly. I'm afraid I haven't met my photographer. I would like to coordinate with your publicity team to obtain whatever footage of the press tour you have."

Jackson beams at me and replies, "There's no need, Ms. Pardo. You're being paired with my personal photographer. It's all settled."

Marcia made no mention of this during our call. I look at Stryder with questioning eyes. His eyes glimmer as the cogs inside his gorgeous head turn.

"I'm sorry, but you have me at a disadvantage. I'm thrilled it's settled, but when will I meet your photographer? There are things I would like to work out with them."

Jackson looks at me as if I'm stupid. His bewilderment quickly morphs into a hearty laugh and says, "You are looking at him, Ms. Pardo. It's clear to me you two aren't in need of an introduction. But as you are so fond of formalities, please meet my best friend *and* personal photographer, Stryder Martynus."

Stryder and I look at each other, both unquestionably stunned. We gaze at each other in complete and utter shock as we both try to process the bomb of epic proportions Jackson Reese has just dropped. My mind is strapped to a rollercoaster seat set to cruise on terminal velocity. Stryder and me were booked on the same flight, and shared the same car service; bumping into each other on the way here was inevitable. *It all makes sense!*

My eyes land on Jackson and then move back to Stryder. "Are you fucking kidding me?" I mutter. Stryder groans, his hands raking his hair, and before I know it, he storms off to the bar without a word to Jackson or me. I look at Jackson Reese out of the corner of my eye. His hands are wedged deep inside the front pockets of his jeans.

"Okay?" Jackson exhales. He's obviously wondering what the hell just happened.

CHAPTER EIGHT

Stryder

I ask the bartender for another beer, trying my damnedest not to be rude. As soon as she places it in front of me, I chug it. The bartender looks at me with an arched eyebrow as I slam the empty bottle on the counter, and without asking if I want more, she places another one in front of me.

"It's on the house. Just take it easy, eh?" she sympathizes before turning to grab a beer for someone else.

Before I hear Catalina, my body stiffens, well aware of her presence. "Can I have the same thing he's having?" I hear her ask.

It amuses me how rancorous women are towards each other. The bartender looks long and hard at Catalina and answers, rather curtly, "Sure." She gets the beer and slams it against the mahogany counter. This time, *I'm* the one with the raised eyebrow. The bartender winks at me as she walks away.

Catalina scoffs then takes a long pull from her beer. Taking a deep breath, she takes a seat on the stool next to me. "Did you know anything about this?" Okay. I see how this is going to go. I throw her insolence right back at her.

"No," I reply flatly. "But that explains everything. Why we were seated next to each other on the same flight, why we shared the ride here, and why we're currently sitting next to each other drinking beer and loathing our very existence."

I immediately regret my contemptuous response when Catalina throws back the remains of her beer in one swig. Standing up, she throws a ten dollar bill on the counter and storms away from the bar and out of the ballroom like a fucking tornado.

You stupid asshole! I chastise myself for behaving like a complete jackass. That could've gone a lot smoother, but I had to act like a teenager. Throwing another set of bills on the bar top, I exit the ballroom to chase after Catalina.

As I reach the bank of elevators that lead to the lobby, I see her standing in the hall with her hands over her face. Hearing my footsteps, she uncovers her face and looks at me with wearisome eyes. The elevator chime echoes loudly, breaking the silence between us. As soon as the door opens, I plant myself in front of her, trying to catch my breath. There is no way in hell she's getting into the elevator without answering my questions.

"Catalina, why are you so mad?" I ask, frustrated as fuck, looking into her eyes. "Who are you so mad at? Me? Because if it is, I deserve to know why..." Again, she just stares at me as if I have two heads. For all that is holy, this woman is impossible.

My psyche screams, desperate to crack the code to Catalina's mind. Reaching for her elbow, I try my best not to make the situation worse by pressuring her. "Cat, will you please talk to me?" I whisper, gently squeezing the elbow I'm holding hostage.

She takes a few steps backwards, leaning her head on the wall. I walk with her, holding onto that elbow for dear life. I'll be damned if I allow her to break this moment. I can't ignore the worry etched on her face or the sadness emanating from those beautiful eyes.

"Stryder, I don't like being here. I shouldn't be here. I was supposed to be on vacation. The first one since Bl–well, I haven't had a break in years." Catalina replies softly. I crouch to hear her barely audible whisper. "I want to go home."

I'm having a tough time riding the emotional rollercoaster she has subjected me to since the moment we first saw each other. I'm not going to lie, if it was another person, I'd say fuck this shit and move on with my life. Although I can't explain why, I want to be with her. I just need to dress myself with patience. I welcome a challenge. Hell, I've cracked worse puzzles than this. Catalina will *not* be the exception.

She's revealed some information about herself, but all I can gather is that she's overworked and wants to go home. Not happening. The elevator has come and gone as we stand in the vestibule in silence. Pressing the call button, I squeeze Catalina's elbow once more.

"Catalina, have dinner with me. I think we need to properly introduce ourselves. If we're going to be working together, we need to get to know each other." I say, commanding the moment. I let go of her elbow and look deep into her bewitching eyes.

I extend my hand to her like a lamb about to enter a lion's den. "Please." I beckon.

Her eyes immediately transform from sad to warm. My heart dances in my chest when I see the corners her of eyes crinkle, and a smile appears on her lips. Damn. Catalina is stunning, her beauty completely alluring. I return her smile with a sincere, elated grin.

"Come on, Cat. We both know those appetizers didn't make a dent and we've had a trying day. What do you say?"

Catalina straightens, all the confidence she lost in the ballroom returning with the force of a hurricane. The energy between us charges and this time, we acknowledge it. The elevator car arrives–its unmistakable ding interrupting our little moment. I die a little when she wraps her hand around mine.

We step into the elevator, holding hands for the very first time. I've held the hands of many women on the dance floor, but I've never felt the way I do right now.

As the elevator rises, I rub my thumb over the soft skin above Catalina's knuckles, and she gently squeezes my hand in response. I am thankful the elevator has no mirrors because I'm certain I have the cheekiest grin spread across my face.

Glancing to my side, I see Catalina's head lowered, looking down to her feet. Some of her long raven locks block my view of her mesmerizing face. Her hand is my prisoner, so I squeeze it, silently beckoning her to look at me. Catalina lifts her bashful gaze to meet mine, combing her hair with her free hand.

"Stryder?" she whispers. "I swear I don't know what's gotten into me lately. I want to apologize for the multiple meltdowns you've had to put up with in such a short time. You must think I'm some misadjusted freak and–"

"Catalina," I halt her in her tracks. "Stop, please. Don't spoil this moment with unwarranted assumptions. You have no idea what's going on inside my head, and I can assure you, it's far from that."

Shifting my feet, I contemplate this beautiful woman standing before me. With trembling fingers, I raise her dimpled chin so all that she can see is me, and fight the urge to kiss her heart-shaped lips. I'm a thirsty man who has found an oasis in the middle of a scorching hot desert. But mind over matter trumps all my physiological needs. My body gives into the commands of my brain, ignoring the Neanderthal inside me. Yet my hand goes rogue moving to caress the curve of Catalina's jaw. When she closes her eyes, cradling her face against it, my body sings.

Catalina's pulse makes the skin of her neck flutter, her tanned skin turning pink as desire courses through her. I can barely breathe inside the confines of this elevator. My breathing accelerates, aware that her body is reacting to my touch. My manhood awakens, painfully pressing against the taut fabric of my jeans.

"Catalina," I whisper, wanting to kiss her lips, and wishing my tongue could explore the curves that dress her body.

Before she can answer, the elevator arrives to the main level. As the doors open, we exit still hand in hand. Catalina giggles as I maneuver us through the crowd of people who are gathered by the entrance of the restaurant. Her presence is a soothing balm, filling all the crevices of my hollow heart. This woman is working her way into my soul, and I'm not going to fight destiny. I will bide my time, but eventually, Catalina will be mine.

Catalina

I don't know what possessed him to hold my hand, but I don't fight it. I love the warmth and softness of his skin. Each time he squeezes my hand, I try to contain the fireworks going off inside my body. As we walk, my mind trails off to the past, taking a stroll down memory lane. It has been a little over four years since I felt the tenderness of a man. No one has even come close to breaking through my barriers like Stryder Martynus has. *No one.*

Blake.

The simmering of my body dissipates at the mere thought of Blake. Guilt washes over me. For the first time since Stryder caught up to me in front of the elevators, I feel ashamed of myself. I loved Blake with all my heart and still do, yet another part of me looks back at those pretty hazel eyes and I'm drawn to them mercilessly–like a moth to flame. Deep down I feel wrecked, torn by my past and curious about the future. *Curiosity always kills the cat.*

Picking up the menu, trying hard not to look like the hot mess that I am, I feel Stryder's eyes studying me. His scrutiny makes me squirm in my seat, forcing me to my clench my thighs tightly together. It's difficult to assuage the ache of lust his presence evokes in me.

He orders two bottles of water for us. My gaze meets his; in order for me to relax, I'm going to require liquid courage, so I arch my eyebrow at his beverage choice. As if reading my mind, Stryder breaks the silence.

"We have business to talk about. Level heads must prevail." Stryder speaks softly yet determinedly. "First off, I want to tell you I had no idea about this arrangement. Had I known who you were, I would've acted more professionally and for that I want to apologize. I know it's been one hell of a long day for both of us," Stryder says with a hint of pink on his cheeks.

I feel like he threw a snowball right into my face. We had *moments*, yes, but none that required apologizing. *I* was the one that was off the handle. *I'm* the one who owes Stryder an apology, not the other way around.

The server arrives with our waters. Stryder clears his throat after taking a sip from the bottle. "Tomorrow will be the official first day of the press tour. I would like to know what your plans are for Jackson, objectives, ideas. Have you covered winter sports before?" he asks rather bluntly.

I sit there stoically, as an appropriate response eludes me. I take a deep breath and say whatever comes to mind.

"Mr. Martynus. There is no need to apologize. Life has a sick, twisted sense of humor. Honestly, the one who has acted unprofessionally from the start is me..." I reply, exhaling a shaky breath. "Now, to answer your question, I have not covered winter sports because I hate the snow. I'm well versed in summer sports and arena events."

Stryder looks at me, his elbows on the table while his gorgeous chin rests on top of his crossed fingers. I sit back in my chair, taking a sip from my bottled water. Uneasy with his silence, I start to play with the soggy cocktail napkin.

His soothing voice forces me to look up at him again. "Maybe this assignment could change your perspective about snow. Maybe it could right a wrong."

After eating our meal in silence, exchanging furtive glances at one another, this time it's my turn to break the ice. "How long have you and Reese known each other?"

Stryder runs his fingers through his hair, something I notice he does quite frequently.

"Jax and I go way back, since he was a baby. Our families are close, so we grew up together. As the years passed, he went off to travel the world snowboarding, and I went to college in the city. We didn't see each other as much, but I owe my career to Jax. My rookie portfolio was full of pictures of him shredding the lines.

"Those early pictures of him got me into the spotlight. Next thing I know I'm getting calls to cover other pros and as they say, the rest is history. Here I am, back to the start," Stryder concludes with a smile on his face.

I know there is more meat to this pie, and the urge to ask questions about Jackson Reese's personal life is too tempting. Maybe it's not such a bad idea I was paired with Stryder. He is, after all, Jackson's best friend.

As I'm about to ask him more about Jackson's past, the server arrives with our check. With a full belly and a tired body, my internal clock catches up with me. I grab my credit card from my wristlet and attempt to pay for the meal, but Stryder pushes my hand away, shaking his head while mouthing, "No."

"The next time we have dinner, it will be on me," I declare, unwilling to take no for an answer. When a lazy smile spreads across his face, I swear I melt like butter on a freshly-baked loaf of bread. Stryder pulls back my chair. With a nod, he offers his arm and I wrap mine around it, walking out of the restaurant with a smile on my face.

Stryder

I was right about the up and downs with Catalina. Maybe I'm just tired and in dire need of rest, but damn, we go from cold to hot in seconds just to go from hot to cold in nanoseconds. I'm so fucking frustrated with this entire situation. Here I am one minute, meeting this intriguingly beautiful woman, and the next I have to work with her.

There is no doubt in my mind I want to spend more time with Catalina. But under these circumstances, where I need to be strictly professional, it's going to be a crucible. She was right though, life has a sick sense of humor. As we walk out of the restaurant arm in arm, I feel something humming inside me. It must be happiness, because I've never felt this way with anyone else, and as tired as I am, I don't want this night to end. I want to stay close to Catalina even if it tears me apart.

One thing I know for sure, Catalina is the look-but-don't-touch-me type. Not physically, but emotionally. The more I think about it, I realize there's nothing but a dead end waiting for me, yet, my heart and gut tell me not to give up. I can't expect to win if I don't cross the starting line. It's just that right now, the timing and the circumstances aren't right.

Catalina

The elevator arrives, and we both get in. We reach to press the same button; I can't conceal my smug smile. "West Wing too?" I ask. It's a stupid question because I already know the answer.

Stryder looks at me with a half smirk. Pursing his lips, he answers, "Yes..."

I throw my head back in laughter. "Want to bet your room is next to mine? Twenty dollars, do you want in?" I challenge, grabbing a twenty dollar bill from my wristlet, and waving it in front of him.

"Oh, it's on, Pardo. There's no way in hell you'd win that bet!" Stryder answers me playfully, like when we said our first goodbye at the airport.

He flashes me a smoldering smile; that sexy grin of his making my insides go buck wild.

"I bet to win, Martynus. Not to lose. It's best that you know that beforehand," I wink.

As the elevator works its way up, he looks into my eyes. I feel myself lost inside those eyes of his, wanting to know his past, enjoy the present and discover the future. But Stryder Martynus is fire and I am ice, and I must remain that way if I want to get through this assignment in one piece. Or, at the very least, try.

As the elevator ascends, we stand beside each other in silence. The cool air crackles as the magnetic pull that draws me to Stryder overpowers me. Even in such a small, enclosed space, the tension in the air feels like a cobra coiling upon itself before striking.

The throbbing between my thighs has returned in full force. I let out a ragged sigh, my feet shifting in place, a desperate attempt to ignore my traitorous body. I can't deny the fact that I'm craving Stryder's touch, and just looking at him makes my insides quiver.

It's only three floors up, yet this ride is taking forever. I pick fibers from my coat, doing anything to avoid looking into Stryder's eyes. All it takes is one slip. I can't break my resolve. I *must* keep this relationship professional.

The elevator picks up passengers and as the car loads up, I stand on the side of the elevator opposite Stryder. His eyes lock on mine and I swear the Earth stops turning once again. His eyes darken, and with one finger he traces his lips absentmindedly. The elevator stops on our floor. I take a deep breath and brace for the frigid air that awaits us.

"Ready?" Stryder asks tenderly. I look into his eyes and nod.

I have to breathe really hard as the cold air smacks me in the face.

"Sweet Lord," I squeal, covering my face with gloved hands.

I can hear Stryder chuckling beside me. My room is on the top floor of the three story lodge, facing the mountains. Naturally, the walkways are exposed to the elements. I trek forward, making a left where the sign points towards the west wing. Stryder laughs again, walking behind me.

There is a thin sheet of ice covering the walkways, so I tread with caution. I don't need to add another bruise to my collection. Stryder's route has not deviated from mine. I stop in the middle of the walkway and call to him.

"Are you ready, Martynus? The time has come to pay the piper." Stryder stops in his tracks, leaning against the wall. He closes his eyes dramatically, as if saying a silent prayer.

"Tsk tsk. Come on now. Let's see. Who will be twenty dollars richer, you or me?" I taunt him with a smug smile on my face.

Stryder straightens out from against the wall, and strides beside me grinning.

CHAPTER NINE

Stryder

Catalina Pardo, if only I could tell you I don't care about this silly bet. The fact that I know you quiver under my gaze is incentive enough for me to not lose hope. I am a gentleman but a man nonetheless.

My affections for Catalina, while precipitated, are more than just a quick game of seduction. I refuse to allow this thing between us to turn into a lustful fuck and later act like nothing happened. This woman, with her curves and sass, insecurities and bravado intrigues me. The more I know her, the more I want her.

As we walk together, I feel her penetrating gaze on me. It's like déjà vu from the flight on our way here. I walk faster, taunting her to chase after me. I hear her hurried steps behind me.

"Catch me if you can, Pardo!" I yell. Turning my head, I see Catalina running with her arms stretched out, balancing herself.

"Come on girl, hustle!" I boom once more, clapping.

I don't understand why this childish game excites me so much. I feel liberated around this woman. I mean, seriously, I don't have to saunter towards Catalina to get her attention. She has obliterated all of my thoughts and desires of being chased. Technically she is walking behind me, but figuratively speaking, I am the one chasing her. I notice the patch of ice a little too late. My boot slips and, quicker than I can think, I land on my ass with a thud.

Catalina stops dead in her tracks, doing her best to walk briskly towards me without suffering the same demise. She extends her hand, offering to help me up. There is no doubt she's trying hard not to laugh, so I smile at her, enjoying this moment.

"Go ahead, Cat. You can laugh. There's no use holding it in." I try to sound bruised, but instead it comes out in chokes of laughter.

Catalina lets out a snort that quickly morphs into giggles. She laughs so hard, she has to lean against the wall, holding her abdomen with eyes full of tears. Her feet slowly slide forward and in no time, she's sitting beside me. Just when I thought Catalina couldn't be any cuter, she says something that makes me blush. Yeah, I said it. *Blush.*

"How's your ass, Martynus, other than well-made?"

All our laughter dies in a fraction of a second, and my neck almost snaps with the comment.

I'm in complete awe of her flushed skin–the way it colors her cheeks and neck under her thin scarf. I don't want to assume, but her red face tells me she didn't think her words through.

Catalina Pardo has been checking me out.

Placing one hand over her mouth, she looks down to the floor. Her head hangs low between her knees, and her hands stroke her shins. As we sit on the ice cold floor, I wonder. Why does Catalina cower whenever a part of her personality shines through? It's like her brain is on lockdown. Every now and then she lets some of herself come through, but the majority of the time, I can tell she is holding back. *I need to know.* What is she so afraid of? Placing my hand on her shoulder and shaking her softly, I speak.

"Look at me, Pardo,"

When she doesn't comply, I take off my leather gloves and bring my hand to her chin. I tilt it, forcing her gaze to meet mine.

"Cat, open your eyes. Please."

When she opens those dark eyes, I can't control my smile. I couldn't give three shits if I look like a smitten asshole right now. I'm not going to prohibit myself from enjoying this burst of happiness.

Her eyes reflect many things–confusion, fear, kindness–but the most evident is relief.

Without sugarcoating anything, I tell her my thoughts of this very moment. "There are many things I find beautiful in life. Maybe it's because I have spent most of my life admiring my fellow man's actions and words through a lens, and without one. The most important thing I've learned is not to feel shame or embarrassment when you speak with your heart. Life is too short to dwell on the little stuff, Pardo."

I stand up and brush the snow from my jeans and hands. I extend my hand to Catalina and lift her from the cold floor. I don't care if this move earns me a slap; I help her dust the snow from her coat, gently tapping the material that covers her round ass.

Satisfied I have removed all the snow from my beautiful Raven Girl, I take hold of her face with my bare hands, looking deep into those dark eyes. "Never feel embarrassed when you're around me. Never apologize for being yourself, and never be anyone *but* yourself when you're with me, okay?"

Before she can nod her assent, she cradles her face in my hands. My heart skips a beat. Man, I need to distance myself for a second because right now, all I want is to pin her up against the wall and kiss her senseless. I say a silent prayer for strength. When my resolve remains unbroken, I look into her eyes and tease her.

"My 'well-made' and quite flattered ass is fine at the moment. Thanks for asking," I reply to her earlier remark, winking as I step away.

She smiles, and I'm glad there's at least a foot between us. That grin of hers does wild, dirty things to me.

"It was unprofessional of me to say things like that. It's just that, well… you make me feel comfortable and I *never* feel comfortable around anyone. Not since… Anyway, it won't happen again."

Catalina clutches the lapels of her coat, forcing herself not to look at me. Is she nervous? *What is it?* "You… Ugh," she pauses, taking a deep breath. "I just–well, you…"

"Just fucking spit it out, Catalina," I interrupt, more forcefully than necessary. She's obviously trying to tell me something, but her insecurities are flooding in. She needs coaxing and if I have learned anything from her thus far, Catalina responds to strength.

Her eyes meet mine, her chin raised in defiance with a fierce fire in them. "When I'm around you, I feel different. You make me feel comfortable and I seldom feel that, especially with a perfect stranger.

It throws me for a loop. I'm sorry." I struggle with the urge to bring Catalina to my chest and hug her fiercely.

My entire being wants nothing more than to caress her from head to toe, and protect her from everyone and everything that could cause her pain. I know there is hurt in her eyes, and I want to dispel that sadness. From the outside, it would appear I'm calm and collected, but on the inside, I'm not. There's evidence of that riot, stretching painfully against the zipper of my jeans. You would think my cock would be in hiding given the subzero breeze drafting down the hallway. *No.* Catalina unmans me without even trying. She's topping me from the bottom without a single touch, and *I love it.*

I smile at her with all that I have, and then shake my head–a meager effort to sway my cock's wayward reactions. Pulling the gloves from my jacket pocket, I hurriedly put them on, because it's fucking freezing.

"Ready to claim your twenty dollar bill, Pardo?" I ask Catalina, trying to shift her focus. I'm rewarded with a smile and a snarky remark.

"Like that was even a question, Martynus. Just don't fall on your ass again, got it?"

We begin to walk slowly, ribbing each other. As soon we reach my door, she walks to the door next to me. I insert my keycard and Catalina hers. When both doors click open, we just lose our shit laughing.

"Dammit!" I curse between chuckles.

Catalina struts towards me with a smug grin. Extending her hand, she says, "I believe you owe me twenty dollars, Martynus." She flexes it, asking for the bill.

This woman is adorable. She has a playful nature that taunts my sensibilities. I can't wait to see her personality completely unrestrained. I give her one of my signature smiles, and the hitch in her breath tells me she felt that grin in between her thighs.

"Okay, you got me, Pardo. I'll pay up," I tell her, removing a twenty dollar bill from my wallet, and placing it in the palm of her hand. I use my hand to close hers so the money doesn't fly away. I need to tell her something. Words, please don't fail me now. "You were right, Pardo. The universe has a sense of humor that I am now starting to understand," I concede, inserting my key card into my door once again.

"Good night, Catalina. Sleep well. The slopes are unforgiving, and you will begin to treasure your rest tomorrow night."

Catalina smiles at me and walks the five steps to her door. "Sweet dreams, Stryder," she says with the sweetest smile. Then she opens her door and waves goodbye.

I wave back. Catalina hasn't closed her door and I'm already missing her. "Sweet dreams, Catalina."

I can't take my teenage boy behavior anymore. I slip into my room, closing the door softly behind me. Taking off my coat, scarf and gloves, I lean against the door, and take a few deep breaths. I hang my head low and look down at the massive tent in my pants. *Fuck.*

I push myself away from the door and walk towards the bathroom, leaving a trail of clothes in my wake. Frustration can unsettle you, rattle you to the core. Desire? Don't even get me started. It can make the sanest of men complete fools. The awareness that this is going to be the most challenging assignment of my career overwhelms me. I have never dealt with this kind of situation before.

Work is work, pleasure is pleasure. I've never allowed those two worlds to collide. Yet here I stand, in the solace of my room, considering the playing field. Since I met Catalina Pardo my world has been shaken, rattled, tossed, and put back together again. It hasn't even been twenty four hours, and not once have I dealt with the emotional rollercoaster I'm on right now. Let's be real. When it comes to women, I've never had to think with my head, only with my cock.

The scalding hot water of the shower soothes my tired body but not my battered mind. I feel the trails of water trickle down my lean and defined body. Feeling exhausted, I sit on the tiled floor of the shower enclosure. As the water falls, I sit there thinking, wondering.

I'm conflicted with the emotions rioting inside me, my judgment completely clouded. All this time I've never cared about companionship. The closest feeling would be another woman's skin sliding against mine in a rushed race towards an orgasm, ending with her screaming my name.

Just when I thought I had my priorities straight, I meet this woman and I'm drawn to her like a magnet. Catalina Pardo is branding my soul with all kinds of feelings that are foreign, but incredibly welcome.

Yet, I don't know where I stand with her. It's been a series of knee jerking moments. Catalina and me have no choice but to work together. She stressed the importance of being professional when she apologized to me earlier. How the hell am I going to work with a woman who makes me hard every time I see her?

I have to do my best to keep a safe distance from Catalina. Whatever interactions I have with her must be strictly professional–more for my sake than hers. As I close my eyes, I envision her smile, the laugh that makes the corners of her eyes crinkle, and her sudden shyness towards me when we're alone, and that tough, grueling persona when she's in her element.

Sitting there on that tiled floor dwelling on Catalina Pardo isn't doing me any favors. She has ensnared me, there's no doubt about that. Where do I go from here? I know what I want and I usually get what I want, but when it boils down to Catalina Pardo, she isn't easily attainable. She isn't some woman... She is *the* woman.

Sighing, I get up from the floor, and turn off the water. I see my body in the mirror, but to me, it's just the skin that wraps my soul. Resigned to the sudden melancholy that has come over me, I head straight for bed. As I lay there, my eyes focus on the wooden beams above the king size bed. I wonder if my beautiful Raven Girl is in her bed and if her thoughts are of me.

Catalina

Taking a deep breath, I close the door of my mini suite, and lean my tired head against it. I close my eyes, the events of today unfolding like a movie before me. It's been four long years since I invited a stranger into my life, and Stryder Martynus waltzed into mine like he owned the damn place.

Ever since we met less than twenty four hours ago, I haven't been able to think about anything else. Stryder makes me feel so alive. His physical appearance is alluring, yeah, even I can't deny that. *He is fucking gorgeous.* But men cannot live on bread alone. Stryder's personality is the main attraction here. Compassion, kindness–those qualities most men nowadays lack, he has in excess. In my eyes, he is a ten, hands down. I can't deny the chemistry between us. I may have my dumb moments, but I'm not stupid. There *is* something there.

I can't ignore the pulsing of my hollow core clenching–radiating heat–causing my thoughts and desires to go haywire. I made a commitment to myself to never allow anyone into my heart–or bed–until I was absolutely ready. Until I felt it was respectful to Blake's memory to move on.

My body is starved. It has been four long years without sex, four years without the caress of a man–not even a kiss. In my thirties, everything is changing. My hormones feel crazier than in my teens or twenties, but like the disciplined woman that I am, I've managed to squeak by untouched and untarnished.

The question at the forefront of my mind is: What does *he* feel? But the answer really doesn't matter. The shitty predicament Stryder and I are in leaves no room for a quest to find answers. This is some fucked up cosmic joke that isn't funny at all.

The point is, I traveled all this way to perform a job and that is exactly what I intend to do. I can't let a shiny new toy like Stryder Martynus lead me onto a path I cannot follow. I know where it will lead me, and happiness is not guaranteed.

I am physically and emotionally drained, and it takes a lot of effort to remove my shoes. I sit on the bed, still wrapped in my coat and gloves. I look up to the beautifully adorned wooden slats on the ceiling with my palms resting on top of my vacant womb.

My eyelids become heavy as sleep deprivation sets in. I think about Stryder, wondering if he's asleep and dreaming happy dreams. I sigh like a schoolgirl when I fantasize it's me he's dreaming about. A girl can wish, right?

Beep, beep. Beep, beep.

I wish I had a bat so I could smash the damn alarm clock. I roll to my side and silence the sound from hell. My body is still running on Eastern Standard Time and if I'm honest, I don't feel rested at all.

I look around me in amusement. There's a messy pile of winter gear next to me. I recall wearing my coat and gloves when I drifted off to sleep. This was not due to the cold, but to exhaustion. Somehow in my fatigued state, I managed to take them off. This time difference is going to take some getting used to.

I wiggle out of my leggings, and throw on my black oversized t-shirt. Crawling back into bed, my hands caress the Sherpa comforter. Grinning, I snuggle back underneath it. It feels so soft against my bare legs and arms. Let's just say it feels like complete heaven. In matter of seconds, I drift off to sleep.

Knock, knock. Knock, knock.

I must be dreaming. Who could possibly be knocking at this hour? Curling into myself, I try to fall asleep again.

Knock, knock. Knock, knock.

In a fight or flight panic, I get out of bed with a jolt. I try to stop in front of the mirror to look at myself, but the persistent knocking makes that impossible. I'm confident I look completely disheveled; looking like a plow ran over me. In my rush to get to the door, I trip over a suitcase. My pinkie toe, which has done nothing terrible in its life, gets stubbed in the process. As I dance in place, I curse the inventor of suitcases and toes. *Fuck, that hurt!* Limping towards the door, I swing it open without even looking through the peep hole.

The arctic air slaps me in the face and if that wasn't bad enough, the sunshine is bouncing off the fresh snow at the foot of the mountain, creates a blinding glare. I have to shield my eyes and cross my legs simultaneously, something reminiscent of a 1980s dance move.

"Fuck!" I curse loudly as a draft of cold air breezes through the open door.

"Well, good morning to you too," says a familiar voice.

I quickly forget the cold and the glare, and let my hands fall from my eyes. Stryder Martynus stands in my doorway, fully dressed in super sexy snow gear holding two Styrofoam cups, with his equipment bag lying at his feet.

His eyes travel from my face down to my bare legs, and a slow smile appears on his lips. I gasp, realizing I answered the door half naked. I close the door enough to cover myself, but with ample room to peek my head out. My teeth begin to chatter.

"What the hell?" I blurt.

Stryder just stands there and smiles, with a twinkle of excitement in his eyes. "Good morning, Pardo," he purrs.

The unmistakable warmth of desire begins to blossom within me. I clench my thighs tightly together, trying to make the deliciousness of his words and gaze to go away. I feel my cheeks heat up. *Get a grip, girl.*

"Good morning, Martynus. To what do I owe this visit so damn early in the morning?" I quip, annoyed yet pleased at the same time. "It's fucking cold!"

Stryder chuckles, revealing a dimple high on his left cheek bone I hadn't noticed before.

"Have you taken a look at the time?" he replies amused. He begins to nod when he sees my face, registering the fact that I overslept.

I turn my head into the room looking for the time. 9:48 in the morning. *Shit!* I let go of the door, and run to my cursed suitcase to get something to wear. A blast of cold air rushes into the room, forcing the door to open wide.

Stryder's voice calls out. "Pardo, I'm coming in!"

Stryder

I walk into Catalina's room rather uncomfortably, but it's cold outside. Besides, I brought her a coffee and I'll be damned if she doesn't accept it. Walking in, I remind myself to avert my eyes in respect to her privacy.

The air swooshes as Catalina rushes past me to grab something from her suitcase. Her shapely legs are fully exposed and utterly gorgeous as she bends over. I swallow hard against the desires of my inner devil, and I look the other way. I wish the same could be said for my dick. *Think other thoughts, Stryder.*

"Excuse me," Catalina says, snapping me right out of my wayward thoughts.

I look at her trying to appear calm, hoping she doesn't see the massive hard-on in my snow pants. I clear my throat and smile.

"Is that coffee? If it is, I will kiss your feet right now," Catalina tells me with thirsty eyes.

"Yes, indeed it is. No kiss required." I try my best to sound unaffected. Who am I kidding? I'd kill for the opportunity to kiss her lips and discover the taste of her body. She takes the cup from my hand and winks. “Sorry I woke you up. You must have been in a deep sleep. We have to be at the lifts by 10:15 for a briefing. After that we’ll meet Jackson at the foot of Village Peak where we’ll watch his practice runs,” I ramble, trying to sound professional when my thoughts are anything but.

Catalina looks up to me, listening intently to my every word in her t-shirt and bed head. I swear she’s so fucking beautiful. I need to remind myself that she’s also a no-fly zone. But my eyes betray me as I look at her–hungry–wanting to feel her lips against mine, and her hands pulling my hair. I must be mentally ill because I can’t control my thoughts around Catalina.

“I’ll head out and wait for you by the ski lifts,” I blurt, trying to sound casual.

“Let me just get a few sips in. Can you hold tight for a few minutes?” Catalina asks, throwing the remote on my lap. I flinch as it grazes my dick.

“Watch something. I’ll be ready in fifteen minutes,” she says, putting the coffee down, grabbing her clothes, and racing into the bathroom. I try to avoid looking at her beautiful shape as she runs past me. Before closing the door, she takes a peek out and gifts me a smile. “Thank you,” she says softly.

Opting to keep my mind occupied while Catalina gets ready, I check my equipment bag, and as soon as I place it on my lap, I notice it is other equipment that needs checking. I do last minute checks to my camera, lenses and back-up batteries.

As soon as I hear the water running, my mind starts to wander, but before my thoughts go to that wayward place again, my phone rings.

It’s Olivia–someone I have no desire to talk to, especially now. I ignore the call, and stand up. Then the bathroom door opens, and a fresh-faced and beaming Catalina walks over to me. She looks stunning.

CHAPTER TEN

Catalina

I grab my coffee from Stryder's powerful hands, thankful it's still hot. After a few sips, I put the cup down to pull on my coat, gloves, and skull-covered beret. Stryder puts his bag over his shoulder and walks toward the door in complete silence.

Our eyes meet and I can see him watching me, as if trying to take in my new look. He must approve, because he won't stop staring. Removing a pair of polarized sunglasses from my messenger bag, I place them over the bridge of my nose.

"Come on, Martynus. We don't have all day."

I take a quick glance at Stryder as I walk out of the room and chuckle when I see him standing there, just shaking his head with an amused smirk.

As we walk together towards the bank of elevators sipping our coffee, I tell Stryder how much I'm looking forward to the one-on-one time block we have scheduled with Jackson Reese.

"I think it's a smart strategy that Reese's team has designated members of the press exclusive time with him. I want to get to know the side of Jackson Reese the world doesn't know about. I really want to ask him what prompted him to go streaking after he won gold," I say, my words coming out like a snide remark. Stryder continues sipping his coffee, completely quiet. He glances at me, eyeing me with suspicion. Then I remember–he is, after all, Jackson's best friend.

Guilt washes like a wave over me. I didn't intend my words to be snide; they just came out that way. Reporters are curious beings by nature, and the truth is, I want to know what Reese's thought process was that night.

As we reach the bank of elevators, I see Jackson Reese waiting with a bag strapped to his back. He hears our steps and turns around. He immediately smiles, his eyes shining brightly. I roll my eyes when he completely disregards Stryder in favor of me. Jackson removes his skull beanie, and with his free hand he tousles his unruly locks.

"Good morning, Catalina!" his voice booms maybe a little too warmly.

Wait. Is he flirting with me?

Stryder

I don't know what takes over first, possessiveness or anger. I stand on shaky ground as I watch Jackson and Catalina interact with each other. I know Jackson all too well. He is quite the charmer and is being overly sweet to Cat. I mean, how could he not?

Catalina takes a step back in caution. She is astute and shrewd; there is no doubt about that. That simple move backwards helps me relax a little. I may not know Catalina too well, but I know she will have no problem putting Jax in his place if he ever crosses the line.

"Good morning, Jackson," she answers professionally, nodding her head.

Before he can reply, the elevator arrives. On our way down, I try to break the awkward silence.

"The weather report looks great this morning. Are you ready, Jax?" I ask, genuinely thrilled about the possibilities that are in store for us today. I love snowboarding, especially with my best friend and little brother.

Jackson claps his gloves and responds with a mischievous smile I know all too well. "I have a surprise for the press today. Heli…" he hints, wiggling his eyebrows, and raising his index finger to rotate it in an endless circle.

I can see the curiosity etched on Catalina's face. Those gorgeous furrowed eyebrows of hers give her away. She must be dying to know what Jax meant but she keeps quiet trying to appear uninterested.

"You'll have to wait and see. I just hope you're warm enough," he says smugly.

I know exactly how Jax operates. An announcement like this means whatever he has planned will be entirely risqué mind blowing fun for his benefit and no one else's.

As the elevator arrives at the main level, Jackson turns to face Catalina.

"We have a one-on-one planned for today. It'll be fun, I can promise you that. I bet this will be the craziest story of your career. The question is, are you ready for it?"

Before Catalina has a chance to answer, Jax tells me, "Strapped to the side like last time. The press will love it." He turns back to Catalina, and with a wide grin on his face, he says, "See you up there, Cat."

Catalina looks at me for answers, but I just shoot her a reassuring smile and carry on down the walkway to the ski lift. As soon as we walk out the doors, the splendor of Village Peak comes into view. Catalina's eyes widen, and despite repeatedly saying how much she hates the snow, the look on her face screams the contrary.

Catalina

"Come on, Pardo. The view is even better from the top," Stryder calls out to me, as if reading my thoughts. He grabs my elbow, and gently prompts me forward.

We have to meet up with the other members of the press, and we're definitely behind schedule. As we stand waiting for our turn on the ski lift, I ask Stryder about Jackson.

"Is Jackson always so sure of himself? It's kind of a turnoff. It's a shame really. He's kind of cute…"

I can see Stryder struggling with his response. He shuffles in place, fixing the collar of his coat with one hand and taking a rather large gulp of coffee with the other, avoiding my gaze. *What is he thinking?*

"Jackson is used to winning and getting his way. It's part of who he is. Smug? Yeah. A self-confident, arrogant asshole? *Totally.*" Stryder answers nonchalantly as he tosses the remnants of his coffee into a nearby trash bin.

As the line for the lift progresses, Stryder takes out his digital SLR camera and clicks on a wide lens. He begins taking pictures of the landscape, testing and adjusting the focus and zoom.

As he does his camera checks, I ask, "Stryder? It feels kind of awkward asking this, but I have some input for you during this assignment. For the spread I need some candid shots of Jackson. Realness always shines through candid images. Jackson Reese is a puzzle I want to figure out. Is that okay?"

He nods in understanding, then to my complete and utter shock, Stryder starts taking random pictures of me. I place my hand in front of my face, trying to hide from the lens, but he continues snapping pictures relentlessly.

With a resigned tone, he says, "Let's get to it, Pardo. The sooner we get the job done, the quicker we can resume our lives."

I don't know what prompted Stryder to go all gloom and doom on me all of a sudden. A flicker of emotion crosses his eyes and not knowing what it is frustrates me. My thoughts are halted when the lift car arrives and the attendant signals our turn. Stryder moves to the side, and motions me to board. There is *no way in hell* I will sit down and go up this mountain on my own. I look into his eyes pleading, and reach for his hand refusing to accept 'no' for an answer. "Please don't let me ride this on my own. We're a team now, and the truth is, I'm scared and I will feel loads better if you are next to me. Please?" I practically beg; my voice raised an octave. I don't care if this makes me look weak. I need him.

Stryder takes a firm grasp of my hand with a sure smile on his face. "Don't worry, Pardo. I'm not letting you out of my sight." As soon as we're strapped in, the lift starts ascending. I feel Stryder's hand gently squeeze mine. "Don't look down, Pardo. Keep your eyes focused forward. Take in the view. It's simply majestic up here; and if that doesn't do it, then just look at me," he whispers, looking intently into my eyes. *My God. He is so beautiful.* Taking in a deep breath, he says, "I won't let anything happen to you on my watch, Pardo." I simply smile, and let out a shaky breath.

As the lift car makes its way up to Village Peak, he makes it a point to take candid shots of me. At first I'm a little annoyed, but as time passes, I can't help laughing. Stryder chuckles as he tries to wrestle my hand away from the lens.

"Either you sit there and let me take these pictures or you will be forced to ride back down all by yourself," he says with a serious face, yet the gleam in his eyes screams mischief.

The sudden desire to kiss the lips of this kind and hotter than hell man sitting beside me is overwhelming. "Is that a threat, Martynus?" I retort with a raised eyebrow.

And just when I think I've gotten away with my insolence, he removes my polarized sunglasses in one swift move. As if that wasn't enough to make my heart race, his thumb delicately traces my jaw, making my breath hitch, and urging my eyes to close for a split second. All of my barriers begin to crumble helplessly under his touch.

"Fucking yes, so deal with it, Pardo," he challenges, those damn beautiful hazel eyes of his peering into my soul.

My eyes open wide as heat fills my cheeks once again. I'm completely enjoying his commanding attitude. You got my attention handsome. *You so do.*

"Shoot away, Martynus. I don't know what I enjoy more. It's either your loss of patience, or your sudden use of profanity. Clearly I'm a negative influence on your oh-so-gentlemanly ways. I approve," I quip, loving this moment.

"Are you going to stop running your mouth and let me do my job?"

I can't restrain my laughter; I throw my head back allowing happiness to flow through my body. Nothing matters more right now than this interaction between Stryder and me. I hear the shutter of the camera click endlessly. I playfully try to cover my face. When I open my eyes he is glaring at me, quirking his neck from side to side, trying to be patient.

All laughter stops when his eyes meet mine. Time stops, like when we saw each other at the press mixer last night. Every cell of my body stands at attention in the commanding presence of this man. I try to swallow the golf ball that has suddenly lodged itself in my throat. The energy between us shifts and the truth is I *need* to know the taste of his lips. But–at least for now–he's my coworker, and coworkers don't kiss each other.

Stryder lifts the camera once more to his eyes and murmurs, "Beautiful. That a girl. Breathe, little lady."

After a few more snapshots, the car arrives to the top of Village Peak, interrupting the photo shoot. Vacating the lift, I see other members of the press congregated by a tent set up at the foot of the mountain. We walk up just in time for a run through of today's itinerary.

My gaze wanders over to the small helicopter parked off to the side of the tent. Jackson Reese is having an animated conversation with the pilot. Stryder politely excuses himself and walks towards Jackson. They begin to talk, every so often taking a glance my way. Oh, to be a fly on the wall right now.

I approach my colleagues, leaving my curiosity about Stryder and Jackson's conversation behind me. Everyone present is thrilled with the "big surprise" Jackson has in store for us. The word is Jackson Reese loves to ride down the highest of mountains, pushing vertical limits.

I look upwards to the mountains and see the snow blowing off the mountaintops like powder in the wind. The sun is shining in its bright splendor and even with my polarized sunglasses on; I have to use both my gloved hands to shield my eyes. The tallest peak looks treacherous as the wind blows the snow across the icy terrain.

I glance towards the helicopter, and notice Stryder's uncomfortable expression. Our eyes meet for the briefest of seconds, but I break the connection to speak to a colleague. Everyone congregates in one of the tents over protein bars and hot drinks. Given that I only had a coffee, I make a beeline for the basket with the frozen protein bars and scarf one down as quickly as I can.

I want to kick myself in the ass for not waking up early. The itinerary for today leaves little time to venture back and forth from the mountain to the lodge. Everything is set to take place outdoors and without proper sustenance, I'm afraid today will suck big time. Without hesitation, I grab another protein bar and make myself another coffee.

As I start on my second protein bar, Jackson enters the tent, flanked by Stryder. Jackson gets the attention of the press by announcing he will be making two runs today: one from the highest point of Village Peak, and another from halfway down. Everyone else seems completely enthralled with the news. I snicker to myself, thinking how happy I am to be keeping both feet on the snowy ground.

Jackson walks out of the tent with Stryder. His team makes last minute adjustments to his equipment. The rotors of the helicopter begin to spin, blowing powdered snow in all directions. It was already cold, but with each turn of the rotors, it becomes unbearably freezing. We all huddle by the entrance of the tent watching Jackson, Stryder, and a videographer preparing to board the helicopter.

Inside the tent, a makeshift projector screen shows a live telecast of Jackson's practice runs. Again, I am thankful I get to stay on solid ground. Just as I'm making myself comfortable next to a portable heating unit, I feel two strong hands grab me by the shoulders.

"Come with me," Jackson whispers into my ear.

I turn around, completely surprised at his request. Is he out of his freaking mind? There is no way in hell I'm going in a helicopter up a dangerous mountain. I'm afraid of heights. *Hell no*.

I look over his shoulders, refusing to make eye contact. Stryder is nowhere to be seen. My heart is beating furiously inside my chest, and I'm sure a panic attack is looming. My colleagues are looking at me with puzzled expressions. If the invitation were extended to them, they wouldn't hesitate. Exclusivity in our business is a big deal.

I shrug my shoulders and follow Jackson outside. When we reach the helicopter, he turns to face me. He looks down at me and it's like I'm seeing a different person. His eyes are intense, full of seriousness and truth–a huge contrast from our prior encounters.

"I figured you'd like an up close and personal account of a sport you know nothing of. I want you up there with me," Jackson states with a tinge of authority.

I stand there like he threw a brick at me. "With all due respect, Jackson, while I appreciate the offer, I find it unwise to sit in a deathtrap. Thanks, but no thanks," I tell him, shaking my head with my arms crossed against my chest defiantly.

Jackson's playfulness returns when he grabs my hand and pulls me towards the helicopter. As we get closer, we have to bend down, and he yells at me because the roar of the rotors is deafening.

"I promise you will be safe. I have never allowed anyone who isn't part of my team to see me this close. I insist. You're being offered a once in a lifetime opportunity. Take it, Pardo."

Stryder slides the door open, and helps me up into the helicopter. Jackson takes his seat and motions me to sit on a bench opposite him. Stryder sits beside me with a furrowed brow.

"You okay, Pardo?" he asks. He looks worried, and I can tell he isn't exactly thrilled I'm here.

"Um, if sitting inside a metal coffin with a rotor going up a tall peak covered in snow qualifies as being okay, then I am fine, damn, motherfucking skippy!" I snap. Stryder can't be blamed for my current discomfort, but my nerves egg me on.

I cringe, waiting for him to snap back. Instead, Stryder smiles. I feel immediately comforted, his eyes telling me everything is going to be okay. Kneeling before me, he secures my five point buckle harness, giving the seatbelt a tug for good measure.

Looking deep into my eyes he whispers, "You won't move an inch. You're good to go, Cat."

His kindness makes me feel like an utter jerk. I give him a mouthed "Thank you." He gets the message, nodding, and winks at me. Stryder sits on the bench once again. Our eyes meet, and I decide to return the favor. Grabbing his seatbelt, I give it a good tug. Stryder's eyes widen, amused.

"Safe and secure, handsome," I inform him, winking. I can tell something about our little exchange affected him. His tongue darts out of his mouth to wet his lips and in his eyes there's a fleeting look.

Jackson looks at both of us, as if trying to figure out exactly what is going on. He leans forward and gives me a headset. As soon as I put it on, Jackson's voice booms loud in my ears. It's a welcome sound as it dulls the deafening roar of the helicopter.

"All right guys, it's a fucking beautiful day at Village Peak. The powder is perfect for a ride down Tiny Twist. Stryder, the pilot will angle the bird so you can do your thing," Jackson instructs like the seasoned athlete he is.

He clears his throat. "Please, give Pardo a very warm welcome. First time on a helicopter, first time up a mountain, first time on the slopes... Too many fucking firsts if you ask me. Up we go!" Jackson rambles happily, throwing a wink my way. Before I can even consider the reality of his words, the helicopter rises, forcing my stomach to drop to my knees and boomerang up into my chest.

"Holy shit!" I yell, louder than I intended.

Through the receiver, Jackson laughs. "Holy shit is right! Ready for the thrill of your life, Pardo?"

I swear this man-child is out of his mind. Does he find my discomfort hysterical? I look into his eyes, my spine completely straight, and ball my fists.

"Abso-fucking-lutely not!"

Stryder chimes in. "Cat, look at me."

I turn my head and see him gesturing me to press the button that will mute my microphone. I nod and mute the cursed thing. Stryder's lips move slowly so that I can read them. I wouldn't be able to hear him anyway, over the roar of the helicopter.

"Don't be afraid. I'm right here." When I nod, he extends his hand to me reassuringly. "Take a deep breath and hold my hand."

Without thinking, I grasp his hand and squeeze it. The corners of his eyes crinkle as a wide smile curls his lips. There is so much promise in his eyes that I feel it's just him and me inside this metal coffin rising into the sky.

Stryder returns my squeeze, and with his free hand, he points toward the window, "Look how beautiful," he mouths.

I turn my head and look at the snow-covered mountains in all their glory. The sun shines brightly, making it impossible to look towards the horizon without squinting. We must be up quite a bit because the lodge looks like a small speck in the white powdery snow. To my left I see the ski trails with skiers that resemble ants going down the mountain.

The helicopter soars to the side, gaining altitude with each second. It's only a matter of minutes before it stops rising, and simply hovers over the top of Village Peak. There's a flurry of activity inside the helicopter. Jackson is stepping onto his board, and his videographer is making last minute adjustments to the head cam on his helmet. Stryder takes out his camera and begins snapping pictures of Jackson.

Once satisfied with the prep photos, Stryder places a hook into a safety harness strapped across his body. Everything is happening so quickly, and my fears have reduced me to a heap of motionless nothing. Jackson's voice booms over the headset, startling me.

"Ready, fuckers? Stryder, circle loop on the north side," Jackson instructs. I have no idea what that even means. Stryder nods and Jackson gets closer and says something to him. I can't hear their exchange because both have muted their microphones. It must've been short and sweet though, because once again, Jackson yells confidently over the headset, "Let's do this!"

The door of the helicopter slides open, and the arctic air crowds the vessel so quickly I feel my bones rattle deep inside me. My heart drops to my feet when I see Jackson hover over the exit, sticking his head out, and looking down. He calls through the headset to the pilot: "Drop it a few meters."

The helicopter circles around and lowers. Satisfied, Jackson nods. Stryder walks to the edge of the exit and gives his harness a good tug. Before I know it, Jackson's videographer jumps. I close my eyes and cringe, praying these two nut jobs don't die in the process.

A few seconds later, Jackson yells to me, "Pardo, see you down below!" He jumps out of the exit; everything is happening in slow motion. The only sound I hear is my heartbeat roaring in my ears.

The once deafening sound of the rotors dwindles to a low hum. I exhale in relief when I see Jackson's board touch the snow, causing small cascades of powder to trickle down behind him. That's the moment when I throw all my presumptions about Jackson Reese out the window. He's not a man-child. Jackson Reese is a brave, talented man with balls of steel.

Sound and relativity return as the helicopter dips down, following Jackson's path down Tiny Twist. Jackson looks like a small rock tumbling down the mountain.

For the first time in a very long time I can appreciate the beauty of the snow-covered mountain, not once dwelling on what it took from me. My *Chionophobia* was because I associated snow with tragedy, not because I fear the snow itself. This experience, while brief, will definitely help me move past my fears. I also get to learn more about this sport, and a weird part of me finds snowboarding invigorating and exhilarating. What once I deemed as fear now turns into adrenaline-infused adventure.

The helicopter follows Jackson all the way down Village Peak. It seems to take forever for Jackson and his videographer to traverse

Tiny Twist, and I watch enthralled. Now I understand why Jackson insisted I accompany him during this jump. Personally, I don't think I have it in me to strap my feet onto a board and go down a mountain like Jackson Reese can. Seeing the path left by Jackson's board against the pristine white snow as he treks down Tiny Twist from this vantage point will be an experience I will never forget for the rest of my life.

Stryder walks back into the cabin, removing the clip of his nylon harness. He beams at me when he sees my wide-eyed grin. We both stumble into our seats as the helicopter lands on a soft patch of snow. The rotors stop, prompting Stryder to release me from the bonds of the harness. As I'm getting up, Jackson pops his head in the doorway.

"Hey Pardo, how's that for a one-on-one experience? I wish you could've been there with me during the run. It was fucking amazing. The powder was absolutely perfect. I'm three seconds away from believing you're my lucky charm!" He rambles, clearly on an adrenaline rush. "So tell me, did you like it?

I am at a loss for words. I step out of the helicopter, and take a few steps forward, resting my hands on my waist. I look upwards to the mountain and then at Jackson Reese.

Jackson walks towards me with his hands crossed against his chest, obviously expecting an answer. I look towards the helicopter; Stryder's leaning against the door, watching Jackson and me closely. I fumble in my coat pocket, looking for my digital voice recorder.

Jackson stands in front of me, his eyes searching mine for answers. I whip out the recorder and ask, "So tell me, Jackson Reese, how does it feel to be back on the slopes after the Olympics?"

CHAPTER ELEVEN

Catalina

I can tell Jackson isn't thrilled with my lack of response to his question. He stands in front of me, breathing heavily, steam emanating from his mouth as he breathes. His crisp blue eyes are hard like stones, yet there's a smirk that creeps its way out from the corners of his chapped lips.

Jackson steps forward, extending his hand. I look at him, puzzled and irritated that he's refusing to answer my question. I hold my voice recorder in the space between us, waiting for his response.

"May I?" Jackson asks in a hushed tone. He shocks me further when his hand gently removes the recorder from mine and shuts it off. To add insult to injury, he opens a cargo zipper in his pants and slips *my* voice recorder into his pocket. *What the...?*

"Pardo, I don't want to talk to a recorder. I want to talk to you. You stand here asking me a question, obviously irked I haven't answered it, yet you failed to answer me first." He takes a step forward and places a hand on my shoulder, his eyes asking for permission. "Did you like it?"

I lower my eyes, embarrassed at having been put on the spot. In a low voice, I answer as best I can.

"Jackson, I'm here to cover facts, not my emotions." I step away. "But to be fair, and not come across as rude, I'll answer." Raising my gloved hands to my head, I give him the response he is so eager for. "I felt a mixture of exhilaration and fear. I still feel adrenaline coursing through my body. It was fucking unreal. I can't possibly imagine how you feel when it's you going down the mountain."

I see Jackson go from serious to elation in the blink of an eye. He walks towards me, and this time he grabs my shoulders giving them a reassuring squeeze. He looks into my eyes and decrees.

"That's precisely why I brought you up here with me, Pardo! Reporters seldom understand me, what I do. All they do is dissect my fuck-ups and run with them on the evening news. At the end of the day, they don't know me, they don't know my story. They don't have a fucking clue of what it takes to tackle a mountain and curtail exhilaration and fear in the same breath."

I stand here, in front of this remarkable athlete, completely stupefied. It was never my mission to follow Jackson Reese's career, but I see in him something that is rare these days: truth. I shake my head in disbelief, lowering my gaze to the icy ground as I try to find the right words. I place my hands on my hips and tell Jackson exactly what's on my mind.

"Jackson, in all my years as a journalist, it's a rare thing to be left speechless. And you, my friend, have rendered me speechless."I extend my arm and pat his. "Thank you for choosing me to see this side of you. Thank you for letting me in."

Jackson looks down at me, smiling. "I knew I wasn't wrong about you after all." Jackson nods and walks towards the helicopter where Stryder stands. His words confuse me, but I can't over-analyze them. They were probably excited utterances brought on by the moment.

Stryder stands with his arms crossed, one leg propped against the body of the helicopter. When our eyes meet, he cuts the connection with a shake of his head, and turns to look up at the mountain.

Stryder

I should've known better. This was bound to happen. It doesn't come as a surprise that Catalina would fall for Jackson's charm and appeal. After all, he is a superstar athlete with a gold medal and the sole reason why we're here. I hate this feeling inside of me. It's taking over my emotions. I feel the sudden urge to punch someone, that someone being Jackson Reese.

I push myself off the helicopter and walk towards them, reminding myself to stand tall, but feeling defeated inside. I stand next to Jackson and hand him my camera so he can view the preliminary pictures I took during his run. I focus on Catalina as Jackson reviews the shots. I need to know where I stand. I need her to know that this job—and Jackson—won't get in between whatever is brewing between us.

Jackson

What is up with this motherfucker? Ever since he got here he hasn't been himself. If I didn't know better, I'd think he's acting like a jealous boyfriend. I've known Jupiter for a very long time. He's interested in Catalina. He's got to be! I mean, he would be dumb not to.

She's cute, strong, and banging hot. I sure as hell have never seen a woman quite like her. Catalina feels familiar and she has this sadness about her that I can relate to. She may fool everyone else, but she can't fool me. I intend on figuring her out. My gut tells me she can be trusted, and after all the shit I've been through, I could use a good friend. Someone who can see me for me, and not the constant fuck-up I've been.

I click through the pictures Jupiter took today and I can't act surprised over the beauty my best friend and brother has captured. Picture after picture, they're fucking awesome. I wouldn't expect anything less from him. The crazy thing about Jupiter is that he's got natural talent, and even though he's made it big, he's still humble.

Honestly, anything he sets out to do he does so fucking well. It's been hard living under his shadow after all these years. I wish I could keep my shit together the way he does.

Just when I thought I was done, I stumble across pictures of Catalina on the helicopter and on the ski lift. Yep, Stryder is hot for her, and rightfully so. Smirking, I return the camera to him. He has no idea I caught him red handed, and I'll sit on this hot little piece of information until the time is right.

"Great shots, man," I tell Stryder, patting his back with a smirk on my face. I glance at my watch. "It's lunch time at the landing with the rest of the crew. Let's go."

Catalina stands beside Stryder, looking at the helicopter with a worried face. She's probably shitting herself again thinking we'll take the heli back to camp. It took a lot not to make fun of her in the helicopter ride earlier, and I'm glad Stryder told me about Catalina's fears before I jumped. I felt like an asshole after that, so I won't subject her to the same experience twice in one day.

I look at the snowmobiles parked nearby and make a mental note to thank Kaelan for arranging them at such short notice–she's fucking awesome.

Smiling, I call to Stryder, "You take Cat on the snowmobile, and I'll follow."

Stryder

"Snowmobile? Wait. No helicopter back?" Catalina asks me nervously. I look towards Jackson, wondering why he assigned me to drive her rather than doing it himself. Surely Jax would want to capitalize on the opportunity to have Catalina's arms wrapped tightly around his waist. I shudder at the thought. I'm more than happy to oblige with the task at hand.

"Have you ever been on a snowmobile before?" I ask Catalina, but I already know her response based on the dirty, snarky look she's giving me. *Oh, Raven Girl, I love it when you get angsty.*

"What do you think, Captain Obvious?" she retorts with her arms crossed over her chest.

I laugh because she is so damn cute right now. Her lips are practically pouting.

I nod towards the helicopter. "Well, you can always take the helicopter back..."

Catalina shakes her head and groans, throwing her head back in obvious irritation. "Uh, no thanks," she says, walking towards the snowmobiles.

She does one full lap around them and looks into my eyes, worried. "Do you know how to operate this thing? Like, on a scale of one to ten, how confident do you feel we'll arrive to our destination alive?"

I cover my mouth trying my damndest not to laugh. I would look like a total douche if I did. "Ten." I put on my helmet and offer the second one to Catalina. I scoff when she looks at it as if it had teeth. "Just sit, Pardo. I'll take care of it."

I take hold of the long braided strands of raven hair and place the helmet gently over her head. Our gloved hands touch when she adjusts it over her face. I knock on the helmet playfully, and ask her, "Ready, little lady?" Catalina shakes her head, and I respond with a chuckle, "Okay, I'll take that as a yes."

I take my place in front of her on the snowmobile and turn the motor on. Making sure Catalina is safe and secure; I grab her calves, and pull her towards my back, closing the gap between us. When our legs meet, they grip each other instinctively. A familiar jolt of electricity arcs between us as our bodies touch.

I reach for her arms and wrap them tightly around my waist. As our bodies mold onto each others, I can't help but smile. There's no other place I'd rather be right now. I instruct her to hold on tight, and if she feels like she might fall off, to simply squeeze my chest several times. Catalina nods.

I pat her leg, signaling that we'll begin moving. Jackson starts maneuvering on the snow like the wild reckless boy that he is. I slowly move forward, making sure Catalina is okay and that she doesn't break hold.

I feel her squeeze my waist as we inch forward. I start to get a feel for the terrain and begin to move a little faster, just to make sure we don't fall behind Jackson and lose our way. I can't see Catalina, but I know she's nervous–she's pressing her head against my back.

I yell over the lapping sound of the wind and the loud motor. "You okay there, Pardo?"

"Yep. Just dandy, Martynus!" Catalina yells sarcastically. I allow myself to laugh, because she's so adorable when she's nervous.

I'm so thrilled to be in such close proximity to Catalina, yet I can't completely rejoice when she's so uncomfortable. I make a bold move. I let go of one of the steers and gently stroke Catalina's arms, wrapped tightly around me, her hands clutching my abs. Without speaking, I reassure her that everything is going to be just fine. I can't hear her, but I feel her body sag in relief. Before placing my hand back onto the steer, I squeeze one of her gloved hands, and when she squeezes back, my heart skips a beat.

As we trek through the snow, coming close to the landing, I decide to slow down, and park the snowmobile. Catalina lets go and lifts her head from my back when I tap her thigh. I get off the snowmobile and remove my helmet, looking over the edge to take in the scenery. I hear Catalina's steps against the crunchy snow. Standing beside me, she removes her helmet, and turns to face me.

"Why did we stop?" she asks in a soft, muted voice. I swear the sound of it is enough to get my engine going.

I look at her, trying to contain the vortex of emotions inside me. "Just look down and tell me if this view isn't simply remarkable."

Catalina moves closer to the edge and looks down. I can tell by the look on her face she agrees. The snowed-in landscape looks so serene. As we both take in the scenery, Catalina surprises me by pulling me close, and snaking her arm around my waist. I don't know what possessed her to do that, but I'm not one to complain. I feel the reverberations of her audacious giggle mix with mine.

She leans her head against my chest and looks up to me with quite possibly her prettiest smile to date. Sighing, I smile back at her, communicating without words how much she affects me. I pray Catalina can't see how hard I am right now.

Shaking my head, trying to regain control of my biological urges, I cradle my head with hers. We stand silent next to each other, but the energy between us is anything but quiet.

"I'm glad I get to see this," Catalina whispers. "I typically don't like the winter, but this, *my friend*, is something else."

I sigh, accepting once again that Catalina is a coworker. I shouldn't let my feelings for her get in the way of the job we are being paid to do. "Well, I'm glad you're enjoying it. I've been on different mountains with Jackson for as long as he's been a snowboarder. Views like this shouldn't surprise me anymore, but being here with you, I guess I get to see it through your eyes. It feels like the very first time. It's nice."

I hear the low hum of a motor and see Jackson approaching the landing on the snowmobile he is sharing with his videographer. We should get moving.

"What's going on between us, Stryder?" Catalina blurts. I break our hold and look at her. She appears shocked by her own words, as if she spoke her mind by mistake.

Oh boy. How do I answer this one? It has to be a safe response, one that won't admit what I'm feeling deep inside. Catalina doesn't need to know about my growing feelings for her. What if she doesn't reciprocate? Now is not the time. It breaks my heart to say half-truths.

"I'll admit we have great chemistry which is going to work great for us during the tour. We're a team and nothing can happen between us," I reply, wincing at my lie. Clearing my throat, I decide to end this conversation in fear that I might lose my resolve. "We have to get going, Pardo. We're going to be late for lunch."

I think my words have stunned her, but with Catalina you can never be sure. I'm just biding my time here, to protect my heart from disappointment until I know for certain she feels the same way about me.

Putting on my helmet, I walk back to the snowmobile. I sit down and pat the seat so that Catalina can sit. I offer to help with her helmet, but she snaps at me, "I got it."

Something about our conversation threw her off, and while she holds onto my chest on the way down, I can tell she's anywhere but here.

"Dude, what took you guys so long?" Jackson asks me with a smirk. He repeatedly throws Catalina's helmet in the air, catching it every time. *Nothing escapes him, does it?*

"It's not what you're thinking. I stopped to show her the view of the lodge halfway down," I answer without missing a beat. "You know, Jax? That poor girl lives her life freaking out about stuff I don't know or care to understand." Jax shakes his head with a knowing smile.

"Do you like her, Jupiter? Like '*like her*' like her? Or do you feel comfortable working with her?" he asks.

Damn it. Jackson's intuition has always been spot on, and I don't know how long it will take him to figure out the clusterfuck of emotions Catalina Pardo evokes in me. It's going to be awkward as hell when the time comes to admit the truth. I can't confide to him that the more time I spend with Cat, the more I'm drawn to her. So once again, I stick with half-truths that hopefully will appease his curiosity.

"I think she's an amazing woman. Shrewd, smart, and goal oriented, but other than that? I can't tell you because I don't know her."

Jackson crosses his arms across his chest and raises an eyebrow. His look says he thinks I'm full of shit.

"So you don't think she's hot? I mean, she's a little all over the place for my liking, but fucking gorgeous nevertheless," he says, wiggling his eyebrows, and placing Catalina's helmet on the snowmobile seat.

I would give anything in this world to punch the grin plastered on Jackson's face right now. Standing tall, I raise my index finger to his face. "No, she's not hot. Catalina Pardo is not a piece of meat, Jackson Reese. And she's not emotional, she's just scared. There's a difference!" I growl, my body shaking with irrational anger at his poor choice of words.

Jackson takes a step back, raising his hands in surrender. "Whoa there, buddy! Simmer down! It was just a question… No need to get feisty with me," he says, chuckling at my reaction. "Dude, you seem a little wound up. When was the last time you got laid?"

This kid needs to shut his mouth before I knock his teeth out. "Two nights ago, okay? Happy?" I answer, slamming my helmet onto his chest, and walking away from him before I act on my thoughts. As I'm walking away, I see Jackson standing there, holding onto my helmet with a knowing smile. He's not stupid, and that shit-grin on his face tells me he's going to fuck with me until I admit the truth. What can I say? Jax knows me too well.

Catalina

After lunch, Jackson's team sets up for a Q&A session. I'm impressed that Jackson answers all of our questions, even when the line of questioning transitions back to the Winter Olympics. A fellow journalist asks if Jackson Reese had any regrets over his actions at the recent Winter Games, and Jackson replies, "I appreciate the question. I really do. Whatever I've done in the past is in no way a reflection of who I am today. I don't make it a habit to snowboard naked. It does terrible things to my, uh, image, but we're here to cover my journey towards the World Championships, so let's focus on that. Next question, please."

Stryder stands beside me in stony silence, his mind elsewhere. Since we arrived at the landing he's been quiet and distant. Something must've happened between him and Jackson. After Jackson answers the last question, he informs us his afternoon run is cancelled due to personal reasons. The news disappoints me. After the thrill of this morning, I was looking forward to a repeat performance. I reluctantly gather my things and decide to go back to my room. As I'm walking out of the tent, Jackson stops Stryder and me.

"Guys, do you mind staying behind for a bit?" he asks, rather seriously.

I glance at Stryder wondering what could be so pressing. He only shrugs.

"What's up, bud?" Stryder asks cautiously.

"Here's the thing. I had a great morning with you two and I feel like playing hooky," Jackson replies with a devilish grin on his face.

"If your definition of playing hooky entails getting on another deathtrap, I'm afraid I must decline. I've had my share of excitement for one day," I inform him, amused. "This morning was fun, but it's getting colder and I'm overly tired." Shifting in place, I bring my gloved hands to my mouth and blow into them. "It's cold!"

Jackson laughs. "It's not every day you get a snowboarding lesson from a legend, Pardo. I wanted to take you to a beginners slope and teach you what you need to know. I promise an afternoon of unadulterated fun... Plus, Stryder is one hell of a snowboarder too, so you'll be in great hands. What do you say? You in?"

Stryder gives Jackson a long, hard look, but a second later, he claps his gloved hands and hoots. "Well, if Pardo isn't in, I sure am."

Jackson smacks Stryder loudly on his shoulder and shoves him playfully. I look at both of them flabbergasted.

"You two are out of your damn minds." Lifting my fingers as if counting I blurt, "One, I would love to live to see another day. Two, I don't have any equipment, or energy for that matter."

Jackson and Stryder stand next to each other, and when I'm done with my little rant, they look at each other and laugh. Jackson winks at Stryder, taking a few steps towards me. Looking keenly into my eyes, speaking ever so seriously, he whispers, "Pardo, rest assured I have *all* the equipment to satisfy your requirements." He ends his statement, and when I quirk my head in disbelief, he chuckles loudly.

It's impossible for me to hold back laughter. "Shut up! You're gross. Eww!" I respond in between laughs. "Okay. I'll agree on one condition."

"And that would be?" Jackson asks.

"If you tell me the details about how your friendship came to be, over drinks and dinner at some point of the press tour, I'll agree to your ridiculous request."

Jackson looks at Stryder with a grin. "She's a curious one isn't she Ju-*ahem*-Stryder. What says you?" he inquires, feigning seriousness. Jackson exchanges a knowing glance with Stryder, and then he lifts his arms in the air and-dare I say-dances in front of me.

Even though Jackson Reese is clad in thick winter gear, his movement is positively fluid and has me enthralled. His hips sway effortlessly across the snow. I don't know what possessed him to dance in front of me like that, but one thing is certain. He got my attention.

Jackson offers me a hand as if asking me to dance, but I cross my arms against my chest, and raise an eyebrow at him. Stryder walks over, laughing like the saving grace that he is. "Okay, Cat. I'll agree to your terms, but only if you allow me to foot the bill."

Stryder looks into my eyes, but it's different from when Jackson does it. Where Jackson's eyes are playful and full of mischief, Stryder's are serious, dark, and full of unspoken words. Every time he looks at me like that, it sets off a chain reaction inside my body. A delicious heat begins to flow through it, causing me to shiver. It's not because we're in the great outdoors or in the freezing weather; it's because Stryder makes me feel. I'm no longer numb when I'm around him, and while it overwhelms me a little, I welcome the feeling.

As I lose myself in Stryder's gaze, not caring if I look like a sick puppy, Jackson settles between us, and throws his arms around both of us. "All right, bitches, let's do this then!" he cheers, and the three of us laugh into the arctic air.

We board our snowmobiles and trek up to a small ridge that, according to Jackson, is the most popular spot to snowboard 'freestyle'. As I get off of the snowmobile and walk to the top, I look down and shudder. It's not steep, but for someone who has zero experience, it looks like a chasm that will swallow me whole. What if I fall and injure myself? Then what?

Sensing my hesitation, Jackson stands next to me and whispers, "You'll be just fine. I wouldn't put you in danger." Patting my back reassuringly, he calls to Stryder, who is unloading a large bag bungeed on the back of Jackson's snowmobile. "Come on, kids! I paid the resort a hefty sum to have this little slope all to ourselves today," he says with a chuckle. "Let's just say there's a horde of unhappy folk slumming on the other slopes."

Stryder lays out three snowboards, three helmets with *GoPro* cameras attached to them and snowboarding gloves. Who would have thought a little over twenty four hours ago I was dreading being in the snow? Look at me now, about to go down a ridge, on a snowboard no less. God help me.

CHAPTER TWELVE

Stryder

Uncertainty is getting the best of me. Why would Jackson go through all this trouble and cancel a practice run to go snowboarding with just us? I'm not stupid. He has an ulterior motive, and it makes my stomach turn thinking it's because he wants to impress Catalina. As I'm sorting out the equipment, I can't bite my tongue any further. Catalina is standing just out of earshot. Jackson is humming ridiculously, and I swear it takes everything in me not to punch him in the throat to make him stop. I don't know why I'm feeling so temperamental around him. Maybe it's because of his interaction with Catalina after the helicopter jump.

"What's your plan here?" I ask. "If you want to woo her, you don't need to jump through all these hoops. She's already impressed..."

Jackson looks at me with a wicked gleam in his eye. I can tell he sees the cracks in my armor. "Ha ha ha! You are such a fool, Stryder! I'm not making a move on her," he says matter-of-factly, testing his boots on his board.

I contain the urge to yell at him. I don't take it too kindly when people lie to me, and I certainly don't like being mocked.

"Come on, man. Who do you think you're kidding? Not me!" I spit through gritted teeth.

Jackson gets off of his board and takes a step closer, leaving just a foot or so between us. He adjusts the Velcro on his glove, and looks into my eyes. "Why are you acting so jealous and possessive of Catalina, huh? This is your second blow-out over her today. It's getting old, asshole."

I swallow hard, not wanting to admit he's right. He places his hands on his waist and challenges me. "Come on now. I'm waiting for an answer."

I really don't know how to answer Jax right now. It's not like Catalina is my girlfriend or anything. Yet, I feel the urge to shelter her—and yes, I'm being possessive. I don't need the added pressure of competition, especially when it's my best friend.

Jackson Reese has been in my life since he was born, and even though we don't share the same DNA, that doesn't matter because blood doesn't define family. I've seen blood relatives treat each other like shit, bad seed and greed getting the best of them, and let me tell you, miserable people like that don't deserve to be called family. Family is anyone who respects you, and cherishes you. Family is those who love you unconditionally and support you no matter what. That is precisely what Jackson Reese is to me.

So imagine how hard it is to find myself in this predicament with him. The lines between us have never been blurred and now, for the first time in our adult lives, I resent him. Shaking my head, I crouch down over the equipment, trying to dismiss his question.

"Silence, huh? Okay. Well guess what, fucker. I'm not making a move on the reporter so stop with the jealous boyfriend act, and get your head out of your ass!" he says, pacing in front of me. "And while we're on the subject, she's not yours to have anyways. But maybe, if you admitted to yourself how you feel about her, perhaps *you* could be smart enough to make a move on her you *stupid asshole!*" Jackson spits.

"I don't give three fucks about this press tour. I was ready to cancel the whole thing before it even started, but that all changed when I met Catalina. Before you start getting the wrong idea, know this. I have fucked up too many times to keep count. I don't have any friends other than you and my crew, but some way, somehow, I felt a connection with Catalina–like we could be friends, and your reaction towards her reinforces that thought," he continues, placing his hands over his beanie-covered head. "I must be out of my mind to think I could be friends with a reporter."

"What the hell are you talking about?"

Jackson raises his hands in frustration. "What the hell am I talking about? Are you really that dense, man? Open your eyes! What are you so afraid of? Why can't you admit this woman is throwing your world off balance?" He clamps his jaw, taking a glance in Catalina's direction. "And if I didn't know any better, I'd say you're rocking her world too!"

"Shut the fuck up, Jackson! She's right there, for God's sake. I didn't anticipate any of this! Since I first laid eyes on her, she's taken control of me. Goddamn it. There you have it! Yes, I *like* her. It's damn ironic to come so close and lose the race before it even starts. It can't happen, and you know why. So drop it, and let's do what we came here to do."

As my chest rises and falls with residual anger, Jackson looks at me like I'm a moron.

"Okay, but this conversation is far from over. Do you understand me?" Jackson hushes me reproachfully.

Catalina walks over to us with a hesitant look on her face. "Is everything okay?"

"Yeah, why do you ask?" I reply, trying hard to conceal my discomfort.

"You both seem, I don't know, tense. What's going on?" Catalina asks, peering into my eyes.

"Nothing is wrong, girl. This knucklehead here thinks you're not ready to snowboard. I say, throw caution to the wind! Oh! Pardo?" Jackson speaks, easing Catalina's curious mind.

"Yes?"

"Could you do me a huge favor? Put the reporter away for a bit. I know there's an adventurous girl trapped in there somewhere."

Catalina smiles and watches us prep the equipment. Once done, Jax and I help her put on the gear. Jax gives her a quick rundown of safety instructions and basic moves.

"It's as simple as riding a skateboard, Pardo," Jackson says, snickering, and when Catalina gives him a snide look, we both laugh. "Okay, if you've ever been on one. Come on, we don't have much time."

As Catalina scoots over the snow, I smile because she looks so damn adorable. I can tell Jackson cares about her by the way he scoops her from the ground and places her at the top of the hill. He places her hands over his forearms, securing her, as he gives instructions

"Okay, girl, we're going down. Hold my hand!" Jackson demands, and coaxes Catalina down the first dip of the hill.

I quickly follow, knowing that soon we won't be able to keep the same speed.

Sensing Catalina's fear, I speak so only she can hear me. "Just let go. Your legs and arms will do the work. Don't think, just do."

Slowly but surely she descends the hill holding onto Jackson's hand. At first, she lets out a string of expletives that would make a pirate blush, but as she keeps going, her words, while still profane, become elated. I follow her every move, documenting this awesome moment.

"Oh my goodness, I'm snowboarding! Yes! Woo hoo!"

"That a girl, Pardo. Let go of my hand," Jax instructs her.

Catalina unclasps her hand and gains speed, shredding the slope well for a first-timer. Her hips move side to side, her hands mimicking their movement. My jaw drops to the floor, and judging by Jax's remarks, I'd say he's equally impressed.

"Oh, man. Look at her go! She's a natural!" he yells with the widest of grins. Giving her thumbs up, he chases after her like a proud papa duck following his duckling.

I fall behind on purpose. I can't hide the pride and joy I feel. Two days ago, Catalina Pardo was unable to be in the snow without getting anxious, and look at her now, almost at the foot of a hill with a snowboard strapped to her boots.

Catalina arrives to the baseline, landing abruptly on her ass. I get there a split second later and all I hear is Jackson laughing, holding onto his stomach. She darts her eyes at him saying, "Okay, asshole. Whenever you're done pissing your pants, can you help me up?"

When we process her snarky remark, we laugh even harder, but this time she joins in, delving into our hysterics until we can't breathe. When our laughter subsides, I walk over to Catalina and help her remove the board. I hoist her up, but my boot slips on a small patch of ice, sending both of us toppling down with a thud. Catalina lands on my chest, her gloved hands clasped on the lapels of my coat.

Our eyes meet. I can tell she's nervous by the rapid movement of her eyes as she struggles to catch her breath. I couldn't care less about anything right now, except for the woman returning my gaze. I remove one of my gloves with my teeth to caress her cheek.

"Hey, you okay?" I ask Catalina, holding onto her for as long as she will allow.

My hand continues to stroke her cheek while the other holds onto the small of her back. My heart drums inside my chest when she smiles, her eyes turning into liquid heat. My hand leaves her cheek to move a strand of hair that made its way out of her helmet, tucking it behind her ear.

Catalina closes her eyes, humming while cradling her face into my hand. *Holy fuck*. I find it very hard to breathe right now, and my pants feel overly tight. *Again*. It's taking all my effort to not kiss those lips of hers. I feel her hands pressing down on my abdominal muscles, and a wicked grin turns her lips up. *Goddamit*. The hardening in my pants has me all kinds of frustrated. I throw my head back onto the snow, closing my eyes, and exhaling loudly.

I lay there on the snow with Catalina cradled on my chest, my mind going batty with all the possible scenarios that could gain me entry into her heart. Despite telling Jackson that I wasn't ready, this *thing* going on between us is damn frustrating. I want to explore the possibilities. I want to taste her lips, lose myself in her embrace. There is no doubt in my mind I want Catalina Pardo.

The sound of crunching snow forces me to open my eyes. Jackson is crouched beside me with a smug look on his face. I know that look all too well. He's giving me the 'Oh, you're in so deep, it's not even funny' look.

"I don't mean to be an asshole and break up such a... uh, how do I put this? Fucking tender moment, but it's getting late. I'm fucking famished," Jax jokes, standing up. "One last run?"

Jackson

Look at these two... Well I'll be fucking damned. I know it's none of my business, and let's be honest; I don't give a shit about this press tour. I don't find it fun having my life scrutinized by these hypocrites for a damn story. That's all I am to them, *a fucking story*. But watching these two around each other is like watching a goddamn movie.

Yes, Catalina is a reporter, but she's no hypocrite. She's awesome and I know she has come into both our lives for a good reason. Stryder's an asshole if he doesn't realize she's falling fucking hard for him. She is tough in reporter mode; even with me, but when she looks at Stryder, she turns into putty.

As I stand there looking at the two lovebirds lying on top each other, I want to know more about Catalina. I know what's holding Jupiter back, but what about her? It's clear to me she's struggling with some demons herself. I can tell by the lifeless look in her eyes when she thinks no one is looking. *I can tell.*

You see, my demons usually get the best of me, but having these two here is the best distraction I could've ever asked for. I look forward to spending time with them and I'll be damned if anyone cuts our time short.

"One last run?" I ask, and Catalina scrambles off Jupiter's chest, trying to dust the snow from her coat while refusing to make eye contact with either of us.

"Sure," Catalina mumbles.

Jupiter stands and removes his helmet in frustration, finger-combing his hair with a pensive look, but says nothing. These two are so stubborn and ridiculous, and I laugh because it's fucking hysterical.

My chuckles are brought on by happiness because I haven't felt this peaceful in like, fucking forever. My career is demanding. It's easy to forget who you are to be '*the someone*' the public expects, and damn, being this carefree around them feels so fucking good. That's what Jupiter and Catalina evoke within me: Laughter, happiness and friendship.

She may not know it yet, but she means a lot to me. Ever felt like you've known someone forever? Yeah, that's how I feel about her, and I could give three shits what my sister has to say about the matter. She'll get the memo–eventually.

Stryder

"So tell me, on a scale of one to ten, how sexually frustrated are you?" I shake my head at Jax's idiotic question. Instead of answering, I take a long pull from my beer and look away. I know what he means, but it's none of his business. His mother taught him better manners than that.

"What? Did I say something wrong? I felt out of place watching the exchange between you two back there. It was like, intimate and shit. You know? Like when you do a little five on one in the bathroom… I felt like a goddamn voyeur. It was damn cold out, but watching you guys made my dude stand up and wave hello."

I try hard to ignore his words. I know he's trying to be funny, but I'm just not in the mood. I keep my eyes trained on the bottles lined up on the wall.

"Come on, Jupiter. Talk to me! I want to know what's making you all gloomy and shit. Is it Cat? Is it O? What is it, man?"

Irritated by Jax's persistence, I slam the beer bottle down against the bar top.

"I don't want to fucking talk about it, okay? Just back off! I can't give you answers I don't have. The only thing I do know is that I crossed the professional line back there. I don't know what it is about her. I keep telling myself this is a job, that she's a colleague and nothing else, but the harder I try to stay away from her, the more I want to be closer."

Jackson Reese rarely acts serious, so imagine my surprise when his reply includes *her*.

"If you're worried I'm opposed to the idea of you starting a life with someone else, then don't. Regardless of the fact that Olivia is my sister, she did you wrong. Blood or not, you're my brother," he says, patting my shoulder.

"You've done well with your career, and the days of letting life slide by are done and over. I don't know how this Catalina thing is going to pan out for you, but I'll say this. Stop being a pussy. The sexual tension between you two is more than noticeable. Just watching gave me a chubby." Jackson pauses. "It's... it's intense. I don't know if it's love or lust, but whatever it is, stop wondering and start doing." I glare at him and struggle with the idea of hugging or punching him.

Jackson Reese is giving me his blessing. I really don't need it, but it means so much. I just hate the fact that he talks about Catalina like she's just another girl.

"If you even as much refer to Catalina like a fucking piece of meat again, I will rip off the ball sack from your body. Never *ever* speak of her like that in front of me."

As soon as Jackson smiles back at me, I am defenseless trying to hide my feelings. I take another sip of my beer and focus on the liquor bottles again.

"The fact that you're so defensive when it comes to Catalina tells me you want her. Stop pussy footing around and give yourself a chance," Jax says as he pats my back. "And I'm sorry about my poor choice of words. I seem to forget what a sensitive asshole you can be. Sorry, man."

Jackson stands and offers me his hand like a gentleman, drawing me into a fierce hug. I chuckle, and mumble my apology. Then he whispers something about having tampons and Midol in his room. I can't be mad at him. He's right. I've been touchy about Catalina since the moment we met. It's time to admit exactly how I feel.

"Are you ready for this?" I pause, shifting awkwardly in my seat. When Jax nods, I continue. "I more than like Catalina Pardo. Between us, I'm struggling with feelings I can't really describe. Before we met, I was jaded but as soon as she walked in, she changed it all. She makes me want to pull her close and do things. This isn't about sex. It's about intimacy, and the frustration I feel is driving me nuts. Can I tell you something, man?" I clear my throat, embarrassed.

"She makes me... Fuck. I'm frustrated all the time when she's near. It's not because she's done anything to me. That smile of hers is enough to get me going. I've never felt that way before. Yep, I'm fucked. Maybe it's cruising syndrome." I sigh and place my head on the bar top.

"What the *fuck* is cruising syndrome?" Jackson asks.

"Do you remember how my sister met her husband? She went on a cruise with a bunch of friends. She met the guy and fell madly in love after they'd only known each other for a week. Do you recall Mom losing her shit when Maddie eloped after dating the guy for a week?"

"Yeah, how could I forget? So you think you're falling for Pardo because you guys have no choice but to be around each other? We are in a big-ass lodge yet you always gravitate towards each other. It's not cruising whatever the hell you call it. Plain and simple, this that you feel is called love, so stop fighting it. What was your first impression of her?" Jackson asks, genuinely interested.

"Wow. Where to begin? I was on the plane, listening to music when I saw her running into the galley. When she stepped foot in the cabin, I couldn't believe my eyes. There she stood, raven hair, dark garb with a guitar strapped to her back. I mean, Catalina isn't what I would normally be attracted to, you know? When she plopped herself next to me, I just couldn't tear my eyes away, and her scent, fuck, I don't even know how to describe it other than candy, but I was instantly addicted. Call me crazy, Jackson, but I swear I've seen her before… in the city? I don't know. And if I wasn't balls deep already, she falls asleep on my shoulder. It was the best feeling. I'm not one to cuddle or get attached since Oli, you know? I mean, I literally hooked up hours before the flight so it wasn't like I was deprived or anything.

"We said our goodbyes at the airport. Next thing you know we're sharing a car. Then we find out we're working together and to make matters worse, there's literally one wall that separates her room from mine.

"From the second Catalina Pardo made her way into my life, I've been starving for her, but this is a job and once it's done, we have to continue with our lives. I can't get attached because I don't think she feels the same way about me. My heart has taken a beating. I can't let anyone crush it again. This blows."

Jackson stares at me in silence. He signals the bartender for another round. "Listen, man… It's probably the pot calling the kettle black, but you need to stop assuming Pardo isn't into you. She likes you. I'm telling you, I've seen it in her eyes. There is something there and if you don't act on it, you're going to regret it for the rest of your life. Catalina could very well be the woman of your dreams. Think about it, but first, drink up. I'll help you."

CHAPTER THIRTEEN

Catalina

Unable to ignore the rumbling of my stomach, I get out of bed to shower and get ready for dinner. Deciding to go retro with my outfit, I style my hair nicely, and after making sure my trademark eyeliner and red lipstick are on point, I leave the suite for the lodge restaurant. Waiting for the elevator, my heart skips a beat when thoughts of Stryder Martynus invade my mind. I shift my cherry red Doc Martens in anticipation. I hope I don't look like I'm trying too hard.

A part of me wants to give into my feelings while another struggles with self-doubt. I know Stryder made it clear we are colleagues and while that is most certainly true, a woman knows when a man is into her. I know Stryder is intrigued, and it would be silly to not admit the feeling is mutual.

The elevator car arrives and I step in. There's an extra bounce in my step, perhaps brought on by the possibility of bumping into Stryder again. The walls barricading my heart are slowly coming down. During the ride down, I smile to myself. I look good, and this time, it's because I feel freaking awesome.

The lobby bar is packed with other hotel guests. The music is loud, but my eye catches Jackson and Stryder sitting at the bar. I quirk my head and frown; they're still in their winter wear and look like they've been there for hours, but they're laughing so I walk over to say hi.

They are obviously the life of the party. Jackson says something that makes Stryder laugh so hard he falls off the barstool. I stop in my tracks and watch them closer. It's nice to see them in their element, having a good time as friends. It is obvious they are much closer to each other than I ever imagined. I wonder what their connection is.

Seeing Stryder on the floor makes me want to help him up. His eyes light up obviously happy to see me.

"Hey, Pardo, what a pleasant surprise!" he slurs. *Oh dear.* One whiff of him and I'm drunk already. I crouch beside Stryder and help him up. "You look so pretty and damn, you smell so good."

"Hey, you," I reply sweetly, trying to get him off the floor.

I try hard not to snicker at his in vino veritas state. Jackson seems tipsy, but not entirely drunk like Stryder is.

"You're so busted, man!" Jackson quips as he stumbles to help me pick Stryder up.

Stryder's arm snakes around my waist, and Jackson and me work together to help him stand upright. Once on his feet, Stryder looks into my eyes, hunger registering in his gaze. I feel his admiration all over my body, his arm refusing to leave my waist. Jackson whistles faintly, but I ignore it because right now, I've lost all sense of place and time. I've never felt this level of attraction before. I'm thirty two, yet the way my hormones act around him, I feel more like eighteen.

I shake my head, trying to connect my thoughts to my mouth. "Hey, guys. How's your evening? Wait. I already know the answer–overly fun?"

Jackson chuckles, nodding his head, but Stryder keeps his eyes transfixed on me, with his relentless grip around my waist. I try to dismiss the hum of excitement that is brought on by his touch.

"I was on my way to have dinner. I just wanted to stop by and say hi. Now that I have, see you guys tomorrow," I say, slowly walking away, and breaking the hold between Stryder and me. I stop in my tracks and tell them, "Oh and word to the wise. You guys should quit while you're ahead. You're both trashed."

Jackson groans, "Why? Party's barely starting. Come. Join us and have a few drinks. Let it loose, girl!" He gestures the bartender to bring me a drink.

"No thanks, Reese. I haven't had dinner, and that would be a really bad idea. I'll see you in the morning." Pointing at them I announce, "Which, by the way, will definitely suck if you don't stop now, and eat, then go to bed." Turning on my heel I walk out and wave at them.

"Cat. Wait!"

Stryder's voice halts my steps. I turn around and see him patting Jackson on the shoulder, followed by unsteady steps as he walks towards me. As soon as he reaches me, he places his hands on his knees, breathing hard. He looks really pale. Standing upright, he looks around frantically looking for something.

"Cat, I'll be right back," he says, and bolts towards the restrooms.

I sit on a bench across from the restrooms and wait for Stryder to come out. After about fifteen minutes, I begin to worry. I walk towards the restroom and call for him.

"Stryder? Are you okay?"

His response is muffled. "Yeah, I'll be out in a minute."

I wait another five minutes and when I hear two guys talking about someone sick inside the bathroom; I rush to the door.

"Stryder? I'm coming in."

I barge in. There are two stalls and thankfully, no one else is in there. Stryder is kneeling in front of the toilet. His face is white as paper, his brow sweating profusely, and the stench of vomit swirls in the air.

"Oh, Stryder… Anything I can do to help?"

His eyes grow wide in alarm, his cheeks turning red with embarrassment. "Why are you in here? Please tell me I didn't go in the ladies' room."

I smile and crouch down to his level. "No… I got worried. I waited a while and you didn't come out. Since I knew you had a little too much to drink, I was concerned you passed out or something." I brush the hair from his forehead and grab some toilet paper to wipe his brow and mouth.

"Come on, babe. Let's get you better. Up you go."

I cradle Stryder's waist and we walk slowly towards the elevators in silence. On the way up he moves to the opposite side of the lift, away from me. He looks at me and mouths, "Vomit breath." I smile at his thoughtfulness. He clears his throat. "I'm sorry about what happened downstairs. One thing though, you look amazing tonight."

"Why thank you, Stryder. I wish I could say the same about you."

His face turns red like a tomato, and he looks at me with a raised eyebrow. I giggle letting him know my words were in jest, and he chuckles in understanding. The car arrives at our floor and once again we tread carefully on the walkways, making sure not to fall.

"Come on, drunkie. Off to bed we go." I extend my hand and clasp his, guiding and steadying him. "Hey, where do you think you're going?" I ask, as Stryder unlocks the door to his room.

He stands there in front of his door like a deer caught in headlights.

"Um, I really need to shower," Stryder responds, pointing at his chest. "There's a whole lot of unpleasantness going on right now."

"You're not going into your room until I'm sure you've eaten. Just grab some clothes and you can shower in my room. I'm worried you'll slip and crack your head." He looks at me like I have two heads. "I would appreciate you getting a move on. I'm freezing," I joke, tapping my foot.

Stryder beams at me and walks into his room. I stand in the hallway, waiting, and my teeth begin to chatter. Reaching for my room key, I shuffle in place, a fruitless attempt to stay warm. He returns, and I couldn't be more grateful. We slip into my room, Stryder closing the door softly behind us.

I walk into the toasty warmth, taking off all my winter gear except my boots. I wasn't expecting to have company, so I quickly scan the surfaces, tidying up as I go. Satisfied the room is decent I sit on the king size bed and begin unlacing my boots.

"Wait. Allow me. You've been patient with me," Stryder says, placing his clothes on the corner of the bed. Kneeling in front of me, he unlaces my Doc Martens.

"You don't need to do this for me, Stryder. I'm very capable of taking off my own shoes, you know." My words come out like a whisper. I look at the man kneeling before me. Despite having glazed over eyes and smelling like a bottle of isopropyl alcohol, he still looks incredible.

His hair is spiked in all sorts of directions. I watch intently as his hands loosen my laces one by one. Extending my leg, he tugs twice, and the first boot comes off. His bare fingers touch the silken fabric of my leggings, forcing a gasp from both of us. He lets go of my leg as if it burned him.

Stryder's eyes look up to meet my gaze. I don't know him too well, but I know he's turned on. I feel like a hormone-raged teenager; my heart is racing, my stomach feels queasy, and my breath comes out a little ragged. He breaks our eye contact and looks down at the remaining boot. After loosening the laces, he removes it, and places my foot back on the rug.

My body almost cries at the loss of contact. I squirm in place, trying to appear unaffected, and silly me, the movement causes my core to clench, boiling my blood red hot and making me horny as hell.

Stryder looks up to me and smiles. "Better?"

"Yeah, I'm demolished. Today was a long day. How are you feeling?"

Looking into my eyes, he replies, "I'm alright. A little dizzy, but couldn't be in a better place if I tried, you know?"

I gaze into his mesmerizing hazel eyes. They're so full of heat that I have to look away. His fingers touch my foot again, forcing another gasp to escape my mouth.

Stryder extends my left leg, allowing his fingers to lazily trail over my ankle and shin. He applies gentle pressure to the back of my calf. His touch feels so good, so right. I close my eyes and let them roll to the back of my head in delight, and a small moan leaves my throat.

Stryder's chuckle snaps my eyes open, and he looks at me with a sly smile.

"Better?" he asks again.

I'm hot and out of breath. "Yes. Thank you."

Stryder sits back on his heels and places his hands on top of my knees.

"Listen, I need to go to my room real quick. I'll shower there, and I'll be right back. I need to show you the footage from today."

I frown. I don't want him to leave the room, and I don't want to be deprived of his touch, no matter how innocent it may be.

"I promise I won't fall and crack my ass bone, okay? Ten minutes is all I'm asking for," Stryder quips with a broad smile.

"If you're not back here in ten minutes, I will go and get you myself. There's only so many Labatt Blues a man can handle at this altitude. I simply... I worry, that's all." His adorable face makes my insides puddle. He stands up and kisses my cheek.

"Yes, mother," he winks, as he grabs his clothes, and closes the door behind him.

I throw my head back against the mattress and hold my chest. *Man that was intense.* My mind races a mile a minute, replaying what just happened. His fingers touching my legs, his hands massaging my calves... The ache between my legs is undeniable. Working with Stryder is going to be more challenging than I originally thought.

I change into my pajamas and order room service for us. While I wait, I get some work done. I begin composing an entry into my work journal. It makes it easier to remember the little details when I begin to write the story. It's a method I learned in college, and it has stuck with me ever since.

Soft taps on the door startle me. Looking at the clock, I realize I've lost track of time. Room Service has arrived, yet Stryder is nowhere to be seen. I let the folks set up the trays of food on the table, and sit waiting for Stryder to return.

Stryder

The cold water hits my back with such force I can barely breathe. That stunt I pulled in Catalina's room has given me an unforgiving hard-on, and the frigid water hasn't been able to put my dick into submission.

It's been over ten minutes. Shit.

I have no choice but to take care of my not-so-little situation if I want to be able to hang out with her tonight. No one has ever elicited this kind of response from me before. I mean, I am a man, and yes, I get wood all the time. But the way my dick reacts around Catalina, like a thirteen year old, where the wind hits you right, and you have tented pants... yeah, that's never happened in my thirties. As the water continues to pummel down, I wrap my hand around my twitching cock and stroke, starting at the root and working up to the crest.

With each tug, my body shudders, my muted groans echoing against the tiles of the glass enclosure. I cup my balls with my free hand, and increase the tempo, the sound of skin and moisture heightening my turn-on. I close my eyes and Catalina's sweet scent takes over my wild imagination.

I see her eyes and smile; my mind has done one hell of a job memorizing her features. I squeeze my hardened cock, tipping closer to the edge of that sweet, satisfying relief. The hand that once cupped my sac extends against the tiled wall for balance. My hips thrust in synchrony with my hand, and when my mind replays the moan of pleasure Catalina let out when I massaged her calves, I come. My jaw clenches, and the sounds that erupt from me are uncontrollable as my essence shoots out.

Coming down from my high, I let go of my dick. I brush off that momentary feeling of shame that follows jerking off and wash up. I dress as fast as I can, grabbing my bag before leaving the room. I knock on Catalina's door and her worried face answers.

"Hey! Come in. I got you something." She pulls my hand and takes me to the table, where dinner awaits. The smell of bacon cheeseburgers is freaking amazing. She smirks with red cheeks, and I squeeze her hand, giving her an appreciative grin.

"Wow. Burgers, one of my favorite foods! You didn't have to, Cat."

Catalina raises her hand, silencing me. "Well, if tomorrow is anything like today, I need you to be in tip-top shape. Let's soak up whatever Labatt is left in your system and prevent the ugly monster from showing up in the morning. Plus, I kind of wanted to have dinner with you, and I'm fucking hungry. Park your ass in that chair and eat," she commands. *She can boss me around whenever she wants.* It's hot.

I pull the chair out for her. "Allow me. It's the least I can do."

"You don't have to be chivalrous, Stryder. It's only burgers," Catalina mocks with a laugh.

I walk by her and watch her inhale deeply. Her eyes soften and I could've sworn she said "Mmm." Her eyes close, and I realize she's taking in my scent. I scurry to my seat to take a front row seat to her musings. The beauty mark on her left cheek is alluring. She's changed into pajamas, but her hair and make-up are intact. I can tell she suffers my same affliction. Her cheeks are red and her heartbeat is visible at the base of her throat. I smile, knowing exactly how she feels.

"Chivalry or not, my mother taught me manners. Maybe you should shut your trap and let me do something nice for you for a change." Catalina squirms in her seat in response to my words. At first her glance is hard, but when she understands it is friendly banter, she winks at me. *God, she's so breathtaking.*

We sit in silence, eating dinner. I ask her to pass me the ketchup. She's looking at my body, and under that gaze I feel my dick harden again, pressing against the seam of my pants.

"Cat?" I ask, smirking.

Catalina blinks returning from wherever she was. "Yes?"

"I was asking if you could pass the ketchup. Are you okay?"

"Yeah, I zoned out. I'm tired and this food isn't helping me stay awake."

We resume eating and the silence is deafening. Retrieving my cell, I choose a song before putting the phone on the table. The soulful tunes fill the room. I watch for her reaction.

"I never pegged you for a country music fan. What's the name of the song? It's beautiful."

"It's *Violin* by Amos Lee. After long days like these, it's the first song I play when I need to unwind.

The song comes to an end. "Can you play it again? Please?" Catalina asks sweetly. I am more than happy to comply. "I love your playlist, Stryder. I must steal it," Catalina praises, as she takes a sip from her bottled water.

I watch in rapt attention as her lips wrap the mouth of the bottle. If only I were that bottle. *Take a deep breath, man.*

Catalina pushes her plate forward. "That was amazing. I'm stuffed. How was your dinner?"

"It was good. Thank you so much, it was very thoughtful of you." I pick up a plate of yellow cake covered in chocolate frosting. "There's still dessert."

"Oh, no you don't, Martynus. That is *my* cake, and if you even dare look at it, I will cut you. All my knowledge of etiquette will be out the window," she declares with a mischievous glint in her eye.

"Oh come on, Pardo. It's just cake." I slice a piece of the dessert with the fork. Leaning forward, I offer it to Catalina. She opens her mouth and accepts it. Her eyes close and I stiffen when she moans in appreciation.

"Mmm. That tastes so good," she says with her eyes still shut.

I'm pretty sure I look like a love-sick fool. My hand is in the air, holding the fork a few inches from her gorgeous face. My lips suddenly feel dry, my tongue flicking them, savoring this unexpected yet arousing moment. The ache in my balls returns as my dick twitches against the seam of my pajama pants in agreement.

My mind wanders to that wayward place where I take hold of Catalina's face and smear that delicious frosting over her lips, devouring her mouth with ravenous hunger. She has no idea how much I desire her. I want to cover her body with kisses, and lap her up until she's consumed with want and lost inside me.

I shake my thoughts away and clear my throat. "I wish I could taste it, but I'm afraid the cake police wouldn't approve," I quip mockingly.

She opens her eyes. "Give me the fork, mister." So I hand it to her.

Catalina slices a generous piece of the yellow cake and walks to my side of the table.

"Open."

I oblige and take the piece of heaven she's given me. I try not to focus on the fact that her lips hugged the fork before mine did, that her taste is mingling with mine. With Catalina standing so close to me, it's hard not to dream of stealing a chocolate flavored kiss from her, professionalism be damned.

"Mmm. You're right. That *is* good."

"I know, right?" she says with a smile.

As if her smile wasn't enough to bring me to my knees, she bends forward, her face inches from mine. Our eyes meet, and my breath catches in her proximity. She lifts her index finger and caresses the corner of my mouth.

In a sultry voice she tells me, "You have chocolate right here." She swabs it off with her fingertip and lifts it to her mouth. "This can't go to waste."

Without preamble, she inserts the assaulting finger into her mouth and sucks it clean.

I blink hard, not believing what my eyes just witnessed. My thoughts, pre-conceived notions, and basically everything I know about Catalina has been cast aside. The primal desire to claim her takes over. Oh, I want this woman. What makes her even more alluring is that she's unaware of her appeal. She has no clue she is causing a goddamn riot inside my goddamn pants right now.

"Can I use your bathroom real quick?" I ask, as I rush past her.

"Stryder?" I hear Catalina call out softly as I close the bathroom door.

"Just give me a minute, Cat. I'm fine."

Standing in front of the sink I let the water run on the coldest setting. I splash my face with it, shocked that ice cubes aren't coming out of the faucet. I look in the mirror, trying to reason with my conscious. *Just calm down Stryder. Calm. The. Fuck. Down. Breathe, asshole, breathe.*

I repeat the words like a prayer. I look down at my pants feeling the swell going down. *Thank God.* I wash my hands and dry them, and taking a deep breath, I open the door and put on my game face–trying to shield myself from embarrassment.

She's clearing the table and I jump in to help. In minutes, the dining area is neat and the room service trays are outside awaiting pick up. Back inside, I grab my bag and settle on the sofa beside her. I can't conceal my pride when Catalina praises me for the pictures I took today.

"Stryder, these are breathtaking. How do you do it?"

I look at Catalina, my eyes holding her gaze. "I don't know. When I see something I like, I zoom in, capture it, and pray for the best."

I know she didn't grasp the double entendre, but I love how she holds on to my every word. Minutes pass, our conversation evolving into shop talk. A good hour passes and we both begin to yawn. I place my camera back into the equipment bag and stand.

"It's getting late, and I'm feeling way better. Thank you for taking good care of me tonight. I was an asshat earlier."

Catalina stands, looking adorable as ever with her sleepy eyes and mussed up hair. "No problem, Martynus. You weren't an asshat. You had a little too much to drink. There's a difference. You're welcome."

I lean close and place a chaste kiss on her cheek. "Goodnight, little lady," I whisper.

"Don't go," she whispers back. My back stiffens. I wonder if I imagined her words. "Don't go," she whispers again.

"You don't mean that. You're tired. Let's get you into bed," I say, fighting the urge to comply with her request right then and there.

"I have to remove my make-up and get the pins out of my hair. Give me a sec," Catalina declares, as she walks briskly towards the bathroom. I follow her, not knowing what to do. My thoughts are conflicted–physiology clashing with morality in a never ending battle.

My body wants Catalina, but I know it's not right to take advantage of this moment. I'm not a child who acts on impulse. I'm a guy, but I'm also a man. I want to be *the man* for Catalina Pardo, and she deserves no less. I stand with my arms crossed, watching her rub a cotton ball all over her face, removing all traces of make-up. She washes her face and brushes her teeth. She seems unfazed that I'm right beside her and I'm shocked with how comfortable I am. It seems so domestic.

As her hands reach up to remove her hairpins, I gently grab them and bring them down to her sides. "Allow me," I whisper, and remove the black pins from her hair one at a time. I comb her locks with my fingers, making sure I've removed all of them. Her raven hair is so long and soft. I look at her reflection in the mirror. Make-up enhances a woman's natural beauty, but to me, natural beauty trumps any artificially enhanced look. Her skin is slightly olive and the shape of her eyes is exquisite. I fight a primal urge to tilt her chin up and kiss those lips that taunt me effortlessly. My arms want to embrace her and never let go, but reality sinks in, and as much as it hurts me to end this moment, I have to.

"All done... You can open your eyes now," I murmur, placing a chaste kiss on her temple.

She just stands there bracing herself with her eyes squeezed shut. She leans into my chest and breathes, "Stay." Her eyes, meet mine in the mirror. "Just stay."

How can I say no to her? How can I turn down this opportunity?

I take a deep breath and tell her, as kindly as I can, "It's been a long day for us and we're tired. I've had a lot to drink, and you haven't had much sleep since you got here. Let me tuck you into bed and I'll leave."

Catalina looks away; her disappointment is more than visible. She walks out of the bathroom towards the bed, peeling the comforter back. She quietly curls in place, placing her arm over her forehead, shielding her face from me. I sit on the edge of the bed, trying to find the words so she doesn't feel dejected.

"Just don't, Stryder. Good night."

I take her hand and squeeze it. "Cat, I..." I sigh, because words are failing me. I lift her soft hand to my lips and kiss it.

"I really want–I..." *Goddamn it.* I rake my hair in frustration.

"Just fucking spit it out, Stryder!" she snaps.

"I want to stay. I just don't know how."

Catalina sits up in bed forcefully, taking a pillow and plopping her hands on it. "I'm not asking you to stay for a quick fuck and tomorrow act like nothing happened. I'm not that kind of girl. I don't know what you're thinking about, but I can assure you, I'm not asking for sex. So if that's what's troubling you, stop." Catalina takes a deep breath and sighs.

"It's been a while since I've slept with anyone–years, actually. I'd be a liar if I said I don't miss sex. I definitely do, but what I miss most is cuddling. I asked you to stay to cuddle. I know it sounds juvenile of me... I didn't want to sound like a prissy little girl saying it like that. I'm sorry if I led you on."

I stand up and turn off all the lights in the room, then lift the covers and crawl in beside her. I place my arm over her waist and pull her against me. Kissing her hair, I speak from my heart.

"You haven't led me on, Catalina. Don't apologize for how you are with me. I have something to confess."

"And that would be?"

"It's kind of a dirty secret of mine. I'm an awesome cuddle partner. I just haven't found the right person yet. Let's see how you fare."

Giggling, she cradles into my hold and fights for control over the comforter. I overpower her, pinning her arms on both sides of her face, my body hovering over hers. Our breathing is hard, and our chests heave from wrestling.

I let go of one of her hands and brush the hair away from her face. The room is dark, but not so dark that we can't see each other. "I'm so happy to have met you," I confess looking into her eyes. I can sense her arousal, and pray she can't feel mine against her hip. She shifts underneath me, the slight movement making us gasp at the same time.

"Me too," Catalina whispers.

I lean in and kiss her forehead. As soon as my lips make contact, a fire ignites within me. Judging by her shuddering breaths, she must feel the same. I don't want to overwhelm her, so I move to her side, nuzzling my head into her neck. “Am I crushing you?” I murmur.

“No,” Catalina whispers.

I nod into her neck and stroke her hair. When she hums in appreciation, my blood sings.

“Sleep my lady and sweet dreams.”

I lay beside her, an emotional energy connecting us. This is the first time in my adult life I’ve spent the night beside a beautiful woman that I haven’t had sex with.

I’m a lucky asshole if you ask me. Tonight I’m sleeping with the most amazing woman. She rocks my world in every sense of the word. My heart swells, overjoyed that she trusts me enough to share her bed.

I shift our bodies so that her plush curves mold against my body. My hand holds onto her waist and when I’m certain she’s asleep, I whisper into the night.

“I’m yours Cat. All of me, completely yours.”

CHAPTER FOURTEEN

Stryder

"Stryder."

"Open the door, asshole!"

"Jupiter!"

A constant knocking wakes me up. I feel slightly disorientated and my heart is racing like a prized horse. I'd forgotten I was in Catalina's bed. Sitting up, I perk my ear and recognize the voice.

Jackson.

"Stryder! You lousy fuck. Open the door!" he screams as he continues to pound the door.

Fuck. Fuck. *Fuck*. Catalina begins to stir, and I know it'll only be a matter of seconds before he wakes her up. I sneak out of bed, put on my coat, and open the door, making sure to put the stopper so I don't get locked out. Jackson stands in front of my door, leaning against it. I know this stance. *Dammit.*

"What the hell do you think you're doing? It's four in the goddamn morning," I hiss.

"Hold up. I must be extremely drunk because I was knocking on this door," Jackson slurs, pointing to my hotel room door, "yet you come out of that one. Someone at the front desk fucked up. They said 1104…" he mumbles with a look of extreme confusion written all over his face.

"What do you want, Jackson? It's cold out and you're drunk as fuck. Did you eat anything?"

"No, man. I just drank until I got kicked out. You know me," Jackson slurs, laughing as if it were the funniest joke in the world. He staggers towards me, barely able to walk in a straight line.

"I sure as hell do, Jackson," I retort, walking towards him, and helping him stand straight. "Let me remind you why we're here. You drank too much at the Olympics. You made an ass of yourself in public. The world thinks you're a joke. Your media team got all of us together to prove you aren't what they claim you are and that you've changed your ways. That you're no longer the same belligerent alcoholic asshole the press makes you out to be!" I snarl.

"What's going on guys? Why are you arguing?" Catalina asks, coming up behind me, and startling us both.

I look at her nervously, wondering how the hell I'm going to cover for Jackson when he's practically falling on his ass in front of her. She's dear to me, but she's also a reporter commissioned to write his story. *Fuck.*

Jackson looks at me and then at Catalina. His eyes light up. Raising his fists in the air, he lets out a loud whoop, and he begins to laugh hysterically.

The look on Catalina's face screams trouble for Jackson. This is the last thing he needs.

"Why, you motherfucker," Jackson quips with a huge grin on his face.

Before he can make things worse for himself, I place my hand over his mouth.

"He's obviously had too much to drink. Drunk-knocking trumps drunk-dialing when we're staying at the same hotel, right, Jackson?" I explain, praying Catalina sees the humor behind my words and nothing more. Jackson nods with my hand still wrapped over his mouth.

"Well don't stand there! It's fucking freezing," Catalina says, gesturing Jackson into her room.

Jackson rips my hand away and replies, minding his manners for once. “Actually, I was just leaving. Sorry to have interrupted your sleep.”

“What he really meant was, he was asking for my room key. Weren’t you, Jackson?” I prompt, shooting daggers his way.

“Uh, yes. Yes. I’m pretty lit up like a Christmas tree. I think it’s better if I crash with Stryder,” Jackson explains as he extends his palm, demanding my key.

“Good night, Jackson. Sweet dreams,” Catalina says, and then walks inside. I follow. My mission is to get my room key, get Jackson into bed and return to Catalina’s.

“I’ll be back in a minute. I’m going to get him settled and come back to bed. That is, if you’ll have me again.”

Catalina smiles. “Don’t take too long. I was sleeping like a baby.”

I nod eagerly, and walk out.

Opening the door of my room, I make sure Jackson makes it in. When he throws himself face forward onto my bed, I give him a piece of my mind.

“This conversation is far from over, asswipe. Catalina is really cool, but don’t forget she’s also a reporter. You can’t afford to be seen like this again. You got me?”

Jackson moves his head to the side and mumbles, “Yeah, man. I’m going to sleep it off. I’m sorry, Jup. I really am. I had an awesome day and got carried away. It made my day spending time with you both, and by the looks of it, it made yours too.” He wiggles his eyebrows at me and gives me a knowing smile. “Are you going to address the motherfucking elephant in the room or what?”

I kick the mattress. “Get your ass in gear. This isn’t a game. Sleep it off and we’ll talk tomorrow.”

“I may be drunk, but I’m not stupid. You’re blushing, Stryder Martynus.” Jackson mocks, this time laughing really hard.

I shake my head, concealing my amusement, and head for the door. “See you tomorrow, Jax.” I say, and close the door behind me.

As I stand in front of Catalina’s door, I let Jackson’s words sink in. He has no clue how deep I am with Catalina. Taking a deep breath, I open her door, and climb into bed, praying Jackson stays put and sleeps it off.

"Is he okay?" Catalina asks, yawning.

"Yeah, he just had a little too much to drink tonight. That's all."

"It sounded like you were arguing. Is everything okay between you guys?"

"No, it's just Jax being Jax, living it loud, but he's good now," I reply with chattering teeth.

"Come here. You're freezing," she beckons, patting the side of the bed I was sleeping on. I crawl under the covers and lay on my back with my forearm over my head. Catalina lies on her stomach, resting her head on her folded arms. "You don't suppose Reese thinks, we, well... you know?" she asks rather cutely.

I roll onto my side, resting my head on my bent arm. "No. He won't remember anything in the morning. Besides, if he did, would it bother you?"

Catalina clears her throat. "No, it wouldn't, but it wouldn't feel right for him to assume we're, you know... I'd hate for the members of the press to think I'm getting exclusives by sleeping around with his staff... Sorry, I'm delusional, assuming something like that could ever happen."

She rolls onto her back, embarrassed, putting a pillow over her face. "Sorry. That came out way uglier than it should have. I really need to learn to filter my thoughts before I speak," Catalina mutters. Her reaction makes me chuckle.

"You're not delusional, Cat. I want you to know everything about me before we get to know each other more intimately. Besides, I don't kiss and tell. I'm a grown man, in case you haven't noticed. Come here, Cat." I pull her into my embrace. "I'm freezing, and you're hot like a furnace."

"Has that line worked for you in the past? That was cheesy as hell, Martynus," she mocks, nudging me with her elbow.

"You got close, didn't you?" I whisper into her hair. My fingers find their way back to her scalp, and once again she hums gratefully. "Sleep, little lady. Sorry about Jackson."

I continue my affections until I feel her drifting away. Before she falls asleep, I confess, "I can't remember the last time I felt this comfortable."

In a sleepy voice she whispers, "Me neither."

Catalina

I'm warm, and the ache in between my legs has disrupted my sleep. Stryder lies beside me, and for a split second, I forgot he spent the night. He has a vice hold on my waist, and his head is nuzzled deep into the crook of my neck. I lift his hand so that I can roll onto my side.

Stryder Martynus is a sight to behold. He looks so peaceful asleep. His obsidian hair is going in all directions, some of it covering his eyes. My fingers want to brush it away. His lips are slightly parted, a small hiss exiting them with each exhale of breath. I find myself daydreaming of his kiss. His sex appeal makes me wonder if he's a great kisser. I wonder how old Stryder is. He looks like he could be my age, though I'm not sure.

The more I look, the more aroused I get. It's gotten to the point where the throbbing of my core has become unbearable. I try to dismiss the urge, but right now my bodily needs have surpassed all reason, and demand release.

Slipping out of bed, I tip toe into the bathroom, and turn on the shower. The spray of the blasting hot water sends my hypersensitive skin into overdrive, and my nipples harden. Every square inch of my skin is prickled. Water seeps through my hair until it's soaked, and then runs down my back. I close my eyes, indulging in the luxurious feel of the water on my body.

I imagine Stryder's strong hands encircling my waist, his lazy fingers trailing circles on my skin. Soft moans escape my throat as I'm pleasured by his affections. He presses me close to his strong chest; one of his hands is splayed against the small of my back while the other tilts my chin up.

Our lips are close; our breaths share the same air, and his thumb caresses my jaw. Winding my arms around his neck, I hug him close–our bodies pressed flush against each other's. The contours of his muscles mold deliciously against my soft curves and the evidence of his arousal is ever present, twitching against my belly.

Stryder smiles softly, knowing we've gone past the point of no return. Our mouths meet, his tongue gently tracing the outlines of my mouth. He nibbles my tender flesh, drawing low moans from me, and like a match against an ignition strip, our desire grows, our shy kisses morphing into unrestrained passion. Sliding his hand down my neck and onto my chest, his fingertips caress the swell of my breasts, gently flicking my nipples that harden under his touch. Reaching my waist, the same finger traces circles lazily around my navel.

His arms move to the top of my shoulders, and his fingernails trace the length of my back, all the way down to the swell of my bottom. Firm hands take hold of my backside as he squeezes softly. Using my cheeks as leverage, he pushes our bodies closer, his hard length squeezed in between us. With flattened palms, he rubs my hips, sending shivers throughout my body. He drops to his knees inside the glass enclosure. Lifting my foot, he kisses me gently, starting at my ankle and working his way up to the apex of my thighs. Hooded, lust-filled eyes look up at me reverently, asking for consent.

I'm startled by a soft knock.

"Cat?" Stryder calls from the other side of the bathroom door.

My eyes snap open at the sound of his voice, my body convulsing as it finds its release. Placing my free hand over my mouth, I conceal the sounds of my pleasure.

"Yes?" I gasp, cringing at the possibility that he heard my little moment.

"Are you okay?" Stryder asks, his voice sounding muffled. *Oh darkened soil of the earth, swallow me whole.* He heard me.

"Yes," I answer assertively, but on the inside, I'm mortified.

"Listen, I'm running next door to wake Jax up. I'll be back soon, okay?"

"Okay," I reply, shutting off the water, and wrapping myself in a fluffy white bathrobe. I wait until I hear the door close before I leave the bathroom.

I sit on the edge of the bed and think. I can't believe what just happened. I've never done something like that while thinking of someone other than Blake. It felt amazingly real, and I can't stop replaying the images of Stryder in my head. I feel like a traitor. It's like I'm taking a huge shit on Blake's memory. *Goddamn it.* But I can't control how I feel or how my body reacts when Stryder is near...

Stryder

I can't even begin to describe the mess I walk into when I open the door to my room. The stench of urine and vomit is overwhelming. My eyes search for Jackson, but he's nowhere to be seen. Alarmed, I run into the bathroom and what I find crushes my heart. Jackson is passed out on the cold tiled floor. His chest is rising and falling, so at least he isn't dead.

This has always been one of my biggest fears when it comes to Jackson Reese. I've known him his entire life, and I really don't understand what motivated him to drink in the first place. He was always a happy-go-lucky child, but as he grew up, he started drinking. Jax's first trip to rehab was when he was nineteen; and he's been in and out ever since.

Kneeling beside him, I shake his shoulders. "Jax, come on, buddy. It's time to wake up." It takes him a minute to rouse, but he eventually does. Jackson groans, curling into himself. "Jax."

"Turn the goddamn volume down. My fucking head feels like it's about to explode," he groans.

"Come on, buddy. Let's get you back to your room, okay?" I say, reaching for his hand.

I lead a staggering Jackson back to his suite, praying no one–especially Catalina–sees him in this state. Jackson needs to get his act together, and this is the last place he can pull this stunt.

Kaelan Porter, Jackson's personal assistant, and good friend of our families, greets us at his suite. Tall and lean with short, blonde hair that is combed back, Kaelan is the eminency of all things Jackson Reese. Her stern green eyes meet us, and she isn't happy. Not one bit.

"Oh, Jackson, what trouble did we get ourselves into?" Kaelan asks, her forehead looking scrunched with worry. Extending her hands, she helps me walk Jackson towards the bedroom.

Kaelan removes Jackson's boots, and peels away every article of clothing except his boxers. I smile at her motherly ways. Despite Kaelan's modern look and youthful face, she's our mothers' age.

"Luckily, he ended up in my room, which reminds me, you need to get a cleaning crew up there as soon as possible."

"Was it that bad?" Kaelan asks, visibly disappointed.

Something tells me she isn't surprised, which makes me wonder how often Jackson gets like this. My career demands intense traveling so naturally, I'm never around. On the other hand, Kaelan is, and I don't know if his drinking has increased recently, but she would.

"I thought he'd gotten better, Kaelan. After dodging vomit and piss, I found Jax passed out face first on the bathroom floor. It scared me. Did he get bad news or something? I mean, we had a couple drinks last night, but not enough to get him sick like this. I was feeling buzzed and Cat... I called it a night."

"No bad news that I know of, Jupiter." Kaelan replies, shaking her head.

"Stop talking to each other like I'm not in the motherfucking room! In case you've forgotten, I'm right here." Jackson yells belligerently. "Kaelan, clear the calendar; I'm staying in. Find these cocksucker asshole members of the fucking press something to do.

"These assholes... I don't even know why I agreed to do this shit in the first place! I want them gone by the end of the week. Find a way, Kaelan. Do whatever is necessary. Operation '*Let's Pretend I'm Well*' is fucking over. I don't want to do this anymore."

Kaelan and I face each other, and watch Jackson slam the door, the sound it makes is deafening. I feel terrible for not cutting Jackson off. I was so preoccupied with Catalina I totally forgot.

Sighing deeply I tell Kaelan, "I agree. He doesn't need the public to know he's struggling. He made a fool of himself once. I'm not going to allow it again."

Kaelan takes a few steps towards me and smiles. She rests her hands on my shoulders, like only a mother would. "So you're staying, sweetheart?" she asks with hopeful eyes. When I nod, she gives me a fierce hug. "He was doing so well and lately, he's been a good boy. I don't know what triggered this episode, but I'll look into it. In the meantime, talk to him. We need to get him back on track."

"KAELAN!" Jackson screams angrily.

Sighing deeply, Kaelan lowers my chin so she can observe me. "It makes me happy to see you smiling again. The ruckus Jackson is causing doesn't give me time to talk properly about it, so we'll be in touch. Now go, before I whip this child on the behind with his own hand." Placing a loving kiss on Kaelan's cheek, I make a confession.

"I'm feeling very much alive today."

As she walks towards the bathroom, Kaelan turns around and winks. *She knows.* I've never been able to get anything past Kaelan, even when Jackson and I were kids. She has always treated me like a son, and she always knows what to say. It didn't surprise me when Jax brought her on board with his snowboarding. She's the only person in this world besides his mother who knows how to deal with him.

"Call me if you need help with the angry bear. My schedule cleared up," I call to Kaelan before leaving.

Turning the doorknob to Jackson's door, she says rather slyly, "You're an idiot if you don't take advantage of this opportunity to get well acquainted with your *colleague*. You were the smartest of the bunch, at least I thought you were," Kaelan looks on, her green eyes sparkling with mischief.

Chuckling, I shake my head, and stick my tongue out at her. As I'm walking out of the bedroom, Kaelan calls, "Jupiter, next time you let my boy get drunk, make sure to give me a call. It's easier for me to contain if I know what's going on. Now go!"

Leaving Jackson's suite, I hang my head low at Kaelan's final comment. She's right. I let her and Jackson down. My heart is heavy, knowing Jackson's intention to cancel the press tour means Catalina will be returning to NYC. I storm into my room, ignoring the cleaning crew's long faces. *Great. They think I did this.* It isn't until I look for my clothes that I realize my belongings are gathered by the door. Before I can ask what the hell is going on, a hotel representative informs me that I will be switched to another room.

I walk out and knock on Catalina's door. "Good morning, Martynus!" She greets me with a grin.

Praying this move doesn't get me in deep shit, I place a kiss on her cheek, loving the flush that warms her skin despite the arctic breeze. "Good morning, Catalina. How was your night?"

She replies in a low whisper, looking at her boots, "Better than I'll ever care to admit." Tucking a wayward strand of hair behind her ear, Catalina meets my gaze. *God, the things she does to me when she looks at me that way.* "How was your night, Stryder?"

I love how my name flows through her lips. Smiling, I answer. "It was all right. Your snoring kept waking me up, but other than that it was nice."

Catalina scoffs, and shoves her hands deep into her pockets. "I do not snore. Liar."

Stringing her along is a lot of fun, so I keep teasing. "Um, yes you do. It's okay. It's not loud... just a whistle, and a few snorts here and there. It's cute, really." She shoves me playfully, and I pout. "Ouch. That hurt!"

"Oh, stop," she says, smirking.

"Kiss it. Make it better. Now," I demand wickedly.

Her eyes widen at my poker face. She looks at my arm as if considering my request. As she starts to bend closer to kiss it, I chuckle devilishly, and wrap her in a fierce hug.

"Just kidding, Cat. I can't believe you were actually going to kiss it."

"Asshole," she gripes, giggling in my arms.

Her hands clutch at my waist as if afraid to let go. I feel her heart beating against my own racing drum. My breath catches in awareness of her, and I sigh contentedly.

Breaking her hold, she looks up to me with questioning eyes. "What?"

Busted. Clearing my throat, and shuffling my feet I say, "Nothing. It just feels nice to be hugged."

I'm slightly embarrassed with the fact that I can't keep my feelings for Catalina concealed, no matter how hard I try. It's like the armor of my soul keeps cracking, my rooted feelings trickling out. As I stand there in contemplation, I feel a hand lowering my chin, her thumb rubbing against the stubble of my imminent winter beard.

"Hey," she whispers. "Come here."

Her delicate hands draw me closer into her hold. This time, Catalina's arms snake around my neck. I can feel her breath warming my skin. I instinctively nuzzle Raven Girl, my arms reciprocating her affections.

"Thank you," I whisper into her hair. "I needed that."

"Me too," she sighs in return.

We stand at the doorway of her room, hugging. The sound of a clearing throat interrupts our moment. A housekeeping manager and a bellhop help Catalina place her bags into the same cart mine are on.

With a raised eyebrow, I ask Catalina, "Switching rooms too? Where?" Before she can answer, the manager replies.

"Your new accommodations are near Mr. Reese's suite. I will escort you there. Are you ready to go, or do you need a moment?"

"We're ready," Catalina and I reply in unison, laughter erupting from both of us.

As we follow the housekeeping manager to our newly assigned rooms, I survey the beautiful wintry horizon. My heart pounds a furious beat inside my chest as hope begins to swell deep within me. Just thinking Catalina may like me more than just her colleague puts an extra bounce in my step. I'm pretty sure the smitten asshole smile is on my face again. Beside me, Catalina looks down at her phone, and her brow is furrowed in concentration.

"Did you get this email? Reese canceled all practice runs today. All interview slots are being rescheduled due to a last minute engagement. You don't suppose it was because of last night?" Catalina asks, placing the cell phone back into her coat pocket. "I hope he's okay."

I nod, and let my body language do the talking. There are some things related to Jackson that Catalina needs to be left out of. I'm not saying I don't trust her… I don't think she's the type of woman to use personal knowledge for professional gain. I just want to make sure I keep Jackson's private stuff far away from the press, and right now, Kaelan is in damage control mode and I support that.

"I doubt we'll be in adjacent rooms again," I say wistfully. "For what it's worth, I'll miss my sassy neighbor."

CHAPTER FIFTEEN

Catalina

The bellhop inserts the key to the door next to Jackson's suite and walks us through the mahogany archway. I gasp when my eyes take in the luxurious suite his team has given us.

"Holy hell," I say, and Stryder snickers.

The suite has two floors with cedar beams adorning the ceiling, and large windowpanes showcase the majestic beauty of the mountains, allowing plenty of natural light that brighten up the space. A large fireplace in the sunken living room sizzles and crackles, warming me instantly. I admire the full size industrial kitchen, all while brushing my fingertips against the basket of fresh fruit placed on the counter. My footsteps click against the hardwood flooring as I explore the vast space.

Man, I could totally get used to this.

"This suite has two bedrooms, one on the loft level, and the other on the main floor. There's also a fully equipped office. Welcome," the housekeeping manager announces. "Who will occupy the loft master suite?" Stryder looks at me with a miffed expression. I control the urge to snicker. I guess he didn't read his email after all.

"I'm staying here? With you?" he asks incredulously.

"Indeed you are, Martynus. You really need to catch up on your emails." I direct my attention to the manager, and reply, "Sir, I'll take the main level room. I like having the office close by. Is that okay, Stryder?"

Both men nod their heads. The bellhop takes my bags in, and I follow him, dying to see what awaits me.

Stryder

The bellhop tips his hat in appreciation to my generous tip. Closing the door behind him, I run upstairs to my room, and dial Kaelan.

"Yes, darling?" she sings.

"Is Jackson up? If so, put the asshole on the phone."

"He's sleeping. I gather you're settling into your new rooming situation?" Kaelan asks. "I hope it's not too much. You said you'd stay..."

"Wait a minute," I halt her mid-sentence. "This wasn't him. It was you!"

Kaelan laughs at my overreaction. "Well, darling boy, now you know what to do with your unexpected day off. Oh, I forgot to tell you. Brunch is on its way. I love you, sweetheart." And then she hangs up on me.

I throw myself on the bed, my fingers tapping against each other on my chest as I lose myself in thought. *Well, I'll be damned.*

I prepare Catalina a coffee just the way she likes it, light and sweet, and head over to her room. As I get closer, I hear her voice echoing down the hallway.

"... Yeah... He stayed the night... No! It's not like that... He couldn't possibly... Well, how the fuck should I know?! Yes... Really... No... Not going to happen. Because! Just drop it, Faith... How many times are we going to beat a dead horse, Faith? We had an agreement... Yeah... I know... Okay... Love you... Bye."

Just as I'm about to knock on her door, I hear Catalina say, "*I don't know what to do. I love you, Faith, but not all of us can have a happy ending.*"

My heart drops. Hearing those defeated words coming out of Catalina's mouth shocks me. She's so strong, sassy, beautiful, and amazing. There aren't enough pages in a notebook to write all the words I could describe her with.

Then it hits me. Sadness... I have seen it carved in her eyes. It's fleeting, but it's there. I have to figure out the cause of it. Straightening my spine and pretending I didn't overhear her conversation with this Faith person, I knock on her door.

"Cat? Can I come in?"

"Hey, you," Catalina replies as she walks towards me. "Nice digs, huh?"

I shake my head, trying to understand how she can be frustrated one minute and happy the next. Something's up. I just don't know what that something is. I offer her the mug of coffee. "I made you coffee–light and sweet–just how you like it."

A wide grin spreads across her mesmerizing lips. "Why, thank you, Stryder," she says sweetly.

"Listen, there's brunch on the dining table if you're interested." I point towards the main room. "After all, I did offer breakfast."

If I've learned anything about Catalina Pardo, is that she's always full of surprises. Her soft hand laces with mine, and when our skin makes contact, a rush of energy goes through my body. Her lips part as a gasp leaves her mouth. *Good, she feels it too.*

We walk hand in hand towards the dining table, and I pull out her chair so she can sit, and push it in like a gentleman should. When I sit on my chair, I notice Catalina is watching me closely.

"What?" I ask, amused.

Catalina simply giggles, failing to respond. *Okay.* I decide to play her game. *Staring contest? Bring it.* Our eyes lock onto each other's. The longer I hold her gaze, the more flustered she gets, until the color in her eyes deepens, darkening with desire. The redness of her cheeks increases as her boot taps the hardwood floor impatiently. Catalina tilts her head, placing an elbow on the table and resting her cheek on the palm of her hand. Her beautiful black eyelashes tease me as her confidence gives her the upper hand in this game.

Now it's me who's squirming on the chair. Okay. *Screw this.* My dick is bulging in my pants again. I break eye contact to 'adjust' the napkin on my lap. Clearing my throat, I break the silence. "How's your coffee, Pardo?"

Catalina coquettishly mouths, "Good." Her seductive response isn't making the riot inside my pants any better. This continues for the duration of our meal. I don't know how long I can handle this. I'm tempted to get out of my chair and kiss her senseless for teasing me.

"Let's cut to the chase, shall we?" Catalina's amused voice cuts through my wayward thoughts. "Did you have anything to do with this, Stryder? I don't believe in coincidences."

"I have everything to do with this breakfast. Hell, I even made you coffee. Why do you ask?"

"Don't be coy, Martynus. I'm not talking about breakfast," Catalina says, and gestures towards the expanse of the room. "I'm talking about our rooming situation."

Great. She thinks I'm behind this, and since she doesn't believe in coincidences, she'll never believe me.

"I can assure you I had nothing to do with this, Catalina. I'm just as surprised as you, but if it makes you feel more comfortable, I can grab my bags and room with Jackson." Irked, I throw my napkin on the table, and head to my room, closing the door behind me.

Catalina

The sound of Stryder's door closing makes me slump in my seat. If I had kept my mouth shut and trusted his word, this awkward exchange would've never happened. The more I think about it, the more I feel like shit. Upstairs, Stryder's phone rings, so I begin to clear the dishes.

I know room service will come by to collect them, but I need to keep my mind occupied. Four days ago, I was in New York getting ready to go on vacation, and now I'm far from home, in the company of some awesome folks. Stryder Martynus and Jackson Reese have burst into my life, bringing along with them feelings I had long forgotten.

For years I've been quite masterful at controlling my emotions. Now, they're beyond my grasp. There's a raging war inside of me and it has been going on for far too long. I'm not sure I want to fight myself or the demons that haunt me for much longer. When Blake passed away, I put myself in a metaphorical prison—a place where I'm safe, and where no one can hurt me ever again. You see, everyone I love dies. It started with Mom and Dad, then Abuela, and ended with Blake and our precious baby. I had accepted the fact that I will never love anyone, not because I'm incapable of loving, but because I don't want to feel abandonment again.

I never expected Stryder to come along with his dashing looks and beautiful spirit, breaking all conventions, and stealing my heart away. He was supposed to be some random stranger on a flight. Our paths were never meant to cross again once we arrived to Whistler. Yet they did. Little did I know I'd end up feeling the way I do. I know things happen for a reason, and all my dreams foretold that this day would come. I would meet someone and become whole again, but what I feel right now is more like broken apart.

What would Blake think of me? I feel so guilty. Even though it's been four years, I feel like I'm cheating on the love of my life. Yet when I think about Stryder, my heart races, and my stomach turns into knots. I can't deny how much I enjoy being near him. For years Faith has insisted I give myself a shot at meeting someone new, but now I'm scared, and I don't know where I stand when it comes to Stryder.

My entire being hums in his presence, and my heart skips a beat deep inside my chest. The physical reaction Stryder sparks within me is undeniable. My body hasn't reacted like this since Blake, but I don't know what Stryder's intentions are. My growing feelings for him might not be reciprocated, and that scares the shit out of me.

I didn't give it much thought when I asked him to stay last night—beyond the thought that I wanted him. I fantasized about his lips meeting mine—our tongues dancing a sensual tango with our bodies aligned, his hardness against my softness, our bodies melding into one. My entire body fights the urge to run up the stairs and tell him the truth about why I wanted him to stay. And then there's the little spat we just had. I dislike that my words upset him, and hate that I doubted him without tangible proof. Stryder wasn't lying; because he looked equally shocked. I should've known better.

Damn it. Using the backs of my hands I wipe the unbidden tears from my cheeks. I'm so used to being in control of everything, but I can't control this. Placing the last plate on the counter, I allow myself to sink to the kitchen floor. *Blake... our baby... the future we planned...*

Memories of our past together swirl inside my head, and sobs wrack my chest as my hands instinctively circle the vast emptiness of my womb when I think about them. I'm tired of not grieving. I'm tired of pretending they'll find a way to come back to me. They are gone. For such a long time I convinced myself I was strong, and nothing could break me after all I've been through. But the truth is, I'm past the point of broken, and I need to let them go, no matter how much that thought scares me.

I need to move on, and not because the Mackenzies want me to. I need to grieve for my losses, and give myself a fresh start. If not, I'll continue to miss out on happiness like I have for so many years. I need to stop bargaining with myself and move towards acceptance. I deserve to live, to love again.

Stryder

Catalina's sobs travel softly through the closed door of my room. Alarmed, I jump out of bed, and lean my ear against the door, trying to listen through the rich mahogany. It takes me a few seconds to zone in on the sounds, but when I confirm what I heard the first time, I turn the handle and race down the steps in search of Catalina.

The first place I check is her room, swinging the door open without care or regard for her privacy. I tip toe towards the bathroom; it's empty. I hear the gentle sobs once again and realize they aren't coming from that side of the suite. I walk towards the kitchen, but I don't see her, yet the sounds are coming from within.

Walking around the kitchen island, I see her. Catalina's knees are pressed up against her chest, her head resting on top of her folded arms. With each sob, her whole body shakes, and I debate if I should go back to my room and let her cry, or embrace her. I care for this woman too much, and I can't possibly walk away from her. Not now, and not like this.

Sitting in front of her, I rest my palms tentatively on top of her knees, and my touch startles her. Catalina raises her head slowly, trying to wipe away the tears that continue to fall. One look at her and I want to cry too. I reach for the travel size packet of tissues I always keep in my back pocket, and offer one to her. She accepts my tissue and slowly wipes her face. Her raw vulnerability destroys me. How could someone so beautiful cry like this? I cringe when I think her tears could be my fault, and I feel like a jerk for overreacting earlier. As Catalina's crying continues, my nervous hands reflexively stroke her knees in soft circles.

As the minutes pass, her sobs fade away. I grab more tissues and take matters into my own hands. I lift her chin, gaining better access to her face. Pressing the tissue against her tan silken skin, I gently wipe the tears away, wishing the soft paper also had the ability to remove her sadness. Satisfied that her cheeks are dry, my eyes search hers, praying I can make contact with the inner reaches of her soul.

I kneel in front of Catalina, and take hold of the sides of her face, drawing her close to me. My lips tenderly kiss her scrunched forehead, and whispering, I express what my heart needs to say. "I'm sorry, Cat. I didn't mean to be a jerk." I allow my hands to rub the lengths of her shins. She hasn't responded to words, but I try once more.

"Cat?" I beseech, looking into her dark eyes. "I didn't mean things to go down as they did. I hope you understand that." I exhale, louder than I expected, and I continue speaking, "I think all these sudden events in my life are overwhelming me, and I'm finding it hard to process it all. It breaks my heart to hurt anyone's feelings, especially yours."

Catalina nods and swallows loudly. Her eyes begin to water again, and I can't let that happen. Scooting over, I bridge the gap between us.

"Once upon a time I met this raven-haired girl who fell asleep on this complete and random stranger's shoulder. She told me she needs to fall asleep on random strangers' shoulders more often. She needs to know right this second this shoulder isn't just meant for sleeping. It's also designed to catch and hold her tears." Placing my arm around her shoulders, I pull her close. "Cry if you need to, okay? It's okay to not be strong. Sometimes you just have to fall apart so you can be pieced back together again."

Catalina nods as tears stream down her cheeks. I rub her shoulder repeatedly, and shower her hair with countless kisses. After her tears subside, we sit in silence for God knows how long.

I jump, startled when she speaks. "Thank you for dealing with my damn emotions. I know I've been a mess since we met… Up and down like a goddamn roller coaster. Like you, I'm coping with a clusterfuck of shit that I don't how to deal with." Sighing she continues, "You need to know that this isn't your fault. I'm the one who needs to apologize for being a bitch. This trip… it came at the wrong time."

"No, Pardo, I beg to differ. I think this assignment happened at the right time. We barely know each other, but I know we were meant to meet. I'm a firm believer in destiny and fate. We're here for a reason. Look at me."

Catalina turns her face away. In a barely audible squeak she says, "Why? So you can look at my ugly, swollen, snot-filled face? No thanks, mister."

Even at her lowest, Catalina is so damn alluring. Her humor is infectious, more so when she isn't even trying. Her words force a chuckle out, followed by a wide grin.

"There she is. Hey, you have to be thankful you don't cry ugly, right?" I say with a tinge of humor. "Look at me, Pardo." This time, my words come out softer, gentler. Catalina turns her head, her eyes meeting mine. "I'm happy you're here. That has to count for something." Breaking our hold, I stand and offer my hand to help her up. "Come."

Even though her eyes are swollen, I see mischief in them and couldn't be more grateful. She places her hand in mine and blurts, "Okay, but if you slip a disk helping me up, please don't sue me."

I flex my biceps dramatically, showing off my sculpted arms and look deeply into her eyes. "I may look a little on the lean side, but I'm strong."

Catalina giggles and pats my biceps as soon as she's on her feet. "Okay, Rambo. Put the guns away," she teases, rolling her eyes, and mocking me. One look at each other and we burst out in unrestrained laughter.

As our laughter subsides, the energy between us shifts, energy buzzes in the air. Something changes within her, shyness taking over. Lowering her gaze, she says, "Thank you, Stryder, for everything.

Thanks for listening, and for being here, and dealing with my bullshit. If it ever becomes too much, please let me know."

I smile down at her, "And if I ever behave like an ass, please let me know." Without thinking, I press Catalina against my chest and hug her. Whispering, I confess a half-truth. "I'll always be here for you. You've gained a friend for life."

I'm not a love guru but I can tell when a woman melts into my arms. Her nose tickles my neck, and when she draws in my scent in long, repeated pulls, I smile like the lucky bastard that I am. "Ditto," she replies sweetly.

Catalina's body trembles against my own. "Cold?" I ask, wishing we could stay like this a little longer. Feeling her nod, I regretfully break our embrace. Wrapping my arm around her shoulders, we walk towards the sunken living room and sit on the large sectional in front of the fireplace. There is a plush blanket draped across the arm of the sofa. Pulling it over, I tuck Catalina in, and sit beside her.

"Better?" I ask.

"Yes, much better. Thank you."

"Good. So this is the part where we get to know each other. I want to know everything about you: from the good, the bad and the ugly. Being that you flooded the place with tears, I'll take the lead. Ask me any question, but first, I need to know you're okay with this."

Catalina stiffens. Clearing her throat, she says, "That's fine. But understand there are things about me I'm not ready to share with you. Not yet."

"That's fine. Take all the time you need. We have all day," I tell her with a wicked wink. *Here goes nothing.* "My name is Stryder Martynus. I'm thirty four, Capricorn, making a living as an award-winning fast action sports photographer. I've never been married, and don't have any children. I was engaged once and it ended badly. I've focused on my career over the past few years, leaving no room for sentimental entanglements. You already know my best friend. I love the outdoors, spending time with family, and I love to meet new people.

"My favorite colors are black and red. I am, among these cool things, an arrogant, jaded selfish prick who gave up on love. Blame my ex for that. So when I'm not spending time behind a lens, in a darkroom or in the great outdoors, I like to spend my time with women.

"I seldom care for their names or get to know them. They are aware of who I am and what I have to offer. I'm not a liar. Since the break-up, you could say I've become emotionally detached. That was until very recently. You might be curious to know why I just spilled the contents of my closet. I'm an open book. What you see is what you get, Pardo, the good, the bad and the ugly.

"I want you to know me. I want us to be friends. I want us to be able to talk over the phone once this assignment wraps. I want to be able to call you up, and meet with you for a coffee whenever we're in the same city. I hope you're open to this idea, and since you asked how Jax and I know each other, I'll let you in on the secret. Truth is, we both love to dance."

Catalina's jaw visibly drops.

"Before you're tempted to ask the sordid details of my past, please understand I'll need time to answer them, but I want to emphasize on two things. I was emotionally detached before I met you and yes, I love to dance."

Catalina's curious gaze morphs into amazement. An incredulous grin spreads across her beautiful lips. Her hand suddenly covers her mouth, but her eyes are still scandalized by my confessions.

"No fucking way. Prove it, Martynus," she challenges.

"Which part, my emotions or the dancing?" I quip. Kneeling before her, and resting my hands on her knees, I gaze deeply into her eyes. "Emotions, well, I'm pretty much immune to all women–except for one, and the bit about dancing? Well, you'll just have to wait and see."

Catalina smiles sweetly. "You're more interesting than me. Go on," she urges, waving her hand. I feel elated knowing she didn't use my shortcomings as ammunition against me.

We sit there in front of the fireplace chatting for hours, just talking about me. I share with her my countless journeys, my highs and my lows. I've told her everything about me except for the name of my ex and how she links me to Jackson. The level of comfort I feel with Catalina is indescribable.

It's like we've known each other our entire lives. While I desperately want to know more about her, some things are worth waiting for.

Gentle knocks interrupt our conversation. Walking to the door, I look through the peephole. It's Kaelan. Opening the door, I greet her with a genuine smile. "May I come in?" Kaelan asks, obviously amused.

"Come on K, you know you don't need to ask," I scold. Grabbing her hand, I walk her towards the sectional.

Catalina stands to greet Kaelan. It's interesting to watch her go from personal to professional in the blink of an eye. One hand smoothes her hair while the other extends to shake Kaelan's.

"Catalina Pardo, this is Ms. Kaelan Porter. She is Jackson Reese's personal secretary, and a close family friend."

"It's nice to meet you, Ms. Porter. It's a real pleasure."

Kaelan steps back and smiles. "Oh, dear girl, I'm not one for handshakes. I'm a hugger." She pulls Catalina in for a warm hug. "The pleasure is mine, darling." Looking at both of us, she goes on. "I hope I wasn't too invasive with your room change. I figured since you're working together, you might benefit from the amenities this suite has to offer. I apologize for any inconvenience."

I smile wickedly.

"No need to apologize, Ms. Porter. Thank you for your thoughtfulness," Catalina beams, totally missing the double entendre.

Kaelan smiles at Catalina. "I also came by to deliver these. Jackson feels terrible he is unable to comply with the itinerary for today. He is offering all members of the press a night on the town on his dime." Placing the tickets in Catalina's hand, she walks towards the door. "I've made arrangements for dinner to be served here before your departure. All the details about tonight's festivities are in the envelope. Please enjoy yourselves."

I see Kaelan out. Standing at the doorway, she waves to Catalina. "It was nice meeting you, Ms. Pardo. See you around." Then she pats my back and tells me, "Be a good boy, Jupiter," as she walks out of the suite, and closing the door behind her.

CHAPTER SIXTEEN

Catalina

"Jupiter?" I ask.

Stryder turns around, his handsome face bearing a shy smile. His cheeks flood with red, his ears and neck following suit.

"You heard that, didn't you?" he replies, sheepishly.

"How could I not? Ms. Porter's warning kind of stood out," I mock. "We spent hours talking about you, and not once did you make mention of 'Jupiter'. You know what I think? You're holding out on me. Spill the beans, Martynus," I challenge, tapping my foot determinedly.

Stryder's wide grin and twinkling eyes are a dead giveaway that he is, in fact withholding information from me. Chuckling, he stalks towards me. "It's a childhood nickname. Only friends and family call me by it."

My eyes press him, unspoken words challenging Stryder for a real answer. He raises his hands in defeat, knowing he owes me the truth.

"It was–it was..." Stryder stutters, shuffling in place.

I smirk at him. Of all the things he could be flustered about, he's freaking out over a name? This has *juicy* written all over it.

"It was my dancing name when I was a kid," he mumbles hurriedly. He rakes his hair and looks across the room, obviously embarrassed. When he returns my gaze, I greet him with a smile.

"So *Jupiter*, what type of dancing are we talking about here?" I ask, still tapping my foot childishly. "I'm waiting."

Stryder walks towards the sofa and picks up his coat. Buttoning it up, he answers confidently, in a smoky voice. "I'd love to tell you, but I'd have to kill you." He comes closer, and places a tender kiss on my cheek.

Walking towards the door, he announces, "I'm going over to Jackson's. I'll be back in a bit. See you before dinner? Text me if you need anything. Oh! I meant to tell you. The footage is already saved on my laptop. It's upstairs if you need it. The password is 'Jupiter.'"

"No problem, Stryder. You're off the hook, for now. Please tell Jackson I said hi." Stryder nods, with a broad smile on his face as he closes the door.

The vast space is so quiet, Stryder's absence echoing inside me. I decide to catch up on work in the suite's office. As soon as I check my inbox, an email in caps draws my attention: JACKSON REESE CALLING OFF PRESS TOUR. My heart sinks. In a fit of panic, I read the body of the email sent by my editor.

> C. Just got word from Reese's team. They're calling off the press tour, and they aren't giving a reason other than a shift in Reese's competition schedule. It's postponed indefinitely. You're there... Something is up. Have you heard anything? Do you know anything? I got word from Sports Telegraph that their team overheard from hotel staff Reese was seen drunk, and acting disorderly at the lodge. Juicy gossip... You might be able to get inside information. Martynus is his personal photographer... Can you ask him? I'd hate to lose this opportunity. We NEED this story. How's your assignment so far? Do you have any dirt? Let me know as soon as possible, okay? Oh. I know you haven't been content with this assignment from the get go. I appreciate you stepping in at the last minute. –Marcia

I read the email twice for good measure. I can't believe this shit. Until I have concrete information, I refuse to give credibility to rumors made by the competing magazines. Yes, I did see Jackson Reese drunk, but at the same time, we all get drunk every once in a while. We're all human. I decide to reply to Marcia's email before she decides to pester me over the phone.

> Hey, M. His team hasn't approached me about any of this... They just relocated me to a different room due to a booking error. His personal secretary, Ms. Porter, left the room not so long ago and made no mention of the press tour being cancelled... I honestly don't know anything about the behavior you described. His team has been very accommodating and I actually got exclusive access to his first practice run from a helicopter. Not to mention he gave me private snowboarding lessons. The guy is really cool... I'm just as befuddled as you. Rest assured, I'll let you know if I get any information on it. Plus, IF it's cancelled, I have enough footage and material to secure that cover. He's been really kind to *Xsports*. Trust me on this one. Catch you later. And hey, no problem. ;) –c

My computer pings as Marcia's response arrives.

> Okay, Pardo. Just keep me posted. When you can, send me an outline of what you have so far with any footage I can work with. I want something I can show to the big guys, okay? And C, I can't see your face but I know your style of writing. If anything, I can say this assignment seems to agree with you... :) –Marcia

Marcia's response makes me smile. She's never been the kind of boss I can sit down with, and offload my sad life story. It's always been strictly business between us because of her low tolerance for bullshit. If anything, I've learned to be the same way. While I feel slightly guilty for not telling her I saw Jackson Reese drunk, I know in my heart I did the right thing.

Opening a blank page on my computer, I begin writing an outline of my story. Jackson Reese isn't the person I thought he was. Like many, I rely on the press for information. Sadly, there are multiple sides to any story, and I'm glad to have been proven wrong on more than one account when it comes to Jackson. He is kind, adventurous, and someone I feel I can relate to. Readers will love that.

Taking a break from writing, I venture upstairs to retrieve Stryder's laptop. Bringing it into the office, I enter the password. While searching for the footage, I notice another file titled 'Raven Girl'. With a racing heart, and looking to my sides making sure Stryder hasn't entered the suite, I open it.

I'm not sure what I feel when I see there are countless pictures of me. My heart beats furiously inside my chest, adrenaline rushing up my spine. My jaw drops at the beauty of these photographs. Some are candid shots taken on the ski lift, in the helicopter, and snowboarding. I never knew I could look so calm, happy, and pretty.

The sound of a door opening, and closing disrupts my unapologetic invasion of Stryder's privacy. With shaky hands I close the file and power down the laptop. Walking swiftly from the office en route to the living room, I meet Stryder. I awkwardly wave at him, and he looks down at me with curious eyes.

"What?" I ask, praying he never finds out I looked at those pictures.

"I don't know. Were you running or something? You're shaking like a leaf." He points to my trembling hands, "Are you okay?"

"I was working in the office and lost track of time. When I heard you come in I realized it was getting late. Listen, I got an email about the press tour being cancelled. Did you know about that?"

Removing his coat, and placing it on the coat rack he answers. "I just found out. The press tour is cancelled effective Friday; however, Jackson has other plans for *Xsports*. He's working out the details with the heads of your magazine and his team. Tomorrow there's a meeting to talk it out between all parties. If you haven't spoken with your editor, hold off until they iron out the details." Stryder takes off his shoes and sits on the sofa with a contented grin. "Jackson wanted me to tell you 'Hi, what's up girl.'"

"Aww," I reply, removing my hair from the bun on the top of my head, and letting it cascade down my back. "Okay, off to get ready. There's a copper bathtub with my name written all over it. See you later!" I call, as I begin walking backwards, and waving goodbye. Stryder looks down at his lap, and I follow suit. I turn around thrilled, and mortified at the same time. I don't know what I said or did to get him hard, but damn me if I say I'm not proud of it.

The smells of lavender and vanilla swirl in the air, begging me to close my eyes. My naked body lies in the sunken copper bathtub surrounded by bubbles. The only light in the room comes from several pillar candles aligned next to the window as Mumford & Sons' "Below My Feet" plays in the background. The hot water is so welcome after being exposed to the wintry elements for two days.

As I lay there, my thoughts reside purely on Stryder Martynus. My mind wanders back to all the conversations we've shared. Stryder has made it a point to be open and honest with me, and has on multiple occasions mentioned friendship, yet his actions contradict that. Maybe I just want to be noticed by him because it's been so damn long since someone made me feel alive again.

My eyes flutter open and I look down at my body. I have more meat on my bones than the average girl, the scar on my abdomen, reminds me every day of all that I've lost. There's no way a man as handsome and fit as Stryder Martynus could possibly be interested in little old me. During the Blake days I was curvy, but fit. His death brought on baggage, both mentally and physically. Surely Stryder is the kind of man who prefers the company of leggy blondes and not some average woman like me.

Taking a deep breath, I slip under the warm water trying to dismiss further thoughts of him, but as I lay there with my eyes closed, his beautiful face pops up. Surfacing, I search for the remote belonging to the bathroom sound system. One of my favorite songs starts playing in the background–Audioslave's "Like a Stone." Letting Chris Cornell's sultry voice soothe me, I finish my bath, and start dressing for our night on the town.

Going through the closet, I find one of my favorite outfits: a black and red pencil dress that hugs my curves in all the right places, and match it with harlot-red peep toe pumps. I style my hair with victory rolls, and decorate my eyes with black eyeliner, and my lips are fire engine red. I look like a 1950s pin-up girl. Dabbing a few drops of perfume on my neck and pulse points, I exit my room with an extra bounce in my step.

The room service team arrives with our dinner. When it's all laid out on the table, I carefully head upstairs praying I don't roll my ankles up the steep steps. Stryder's door is wide open, and there's music playing softly in the background.

Knocking on the door, I call for him. "Stryder? May I come in?"

I don't know what possesses me to march into the room uninvited. As I'm walking in, I see Stryder walking towards the bed–completely and deliciously naked. I stop mid-stride and gasp. My eyes scan his features, starting from his damp, tousled hair, down his beautifully defined chest, across his Apollo's belt, looking at his manhood which stands at attention, and all the way down to his toes. I turn around, scandalized–my insides fill with heat and lustful desire, and my heart is fluttering intensely in my chest. I'm sure I need to change my panties after this show and tell. Placing my palms against my fire hot cheeks, I whisper my apologies.

"I… I'm so sorry!" I stammer. "I knocked and called for you. I'm so sorry! Shit. Fuck." Raising my hands I walk towards the door. "Okay, leaving now."

"It's okay," Stryder laughs. "Don't apologize. Give me a second." I hear his footsteps behind me, and the music playing in the room ceases. The tell-tale sounds of rustled clothing echo loudly in my ears. I want to turn around and watch, and let curiosity to get the best of me. *Keep it together, Cat.*

"Okay, I'm decent," Stryder jokes. "You can turn around now." I reluctantly turn around, making sure to keep my eyes focused on the floor.

"Wow!" he exclaims, "You look gorgeous. Absolutely stunning, Pardo!"

Shyly, I look up to meet his eyes. Stryder stands before me wearing jeans and nothing more, his perfectly chiseled chest on full display. I remind myself not to gawk, but damn, it's so hard not to. My hand begs to feel the contours of his skin, and my eyes lower to the waistband of his jeans that hang low on his hips, giving me a stunning view of his Adonis arrow.

The room feels hotter by the second, and I find myself having to clench my thighs to abate the ache of desire pooling there. My eyes work their way back to his face, and a slow smile escapes my lips when I see his taut jaw and clean-shaven face. My heart skips a beat when our gazes meet, his hazel eyes twinkling devilishly, and a wide smile is etched on his amazing lips.

"I can't help noticing you like what you see," Stryder breathes, raising an eyebrow as his hands gesture down the length of his torso.

I flush, knowing he saw me gawking at him a mere second ago. My nipples harden underneath my dress, my breath accelerating with each passing second. A myriad of sensations occur simultaneously, taunting and teasing my poor, deprived body. My throat feels dry so I clear it.

"I beg your pardon?" I ask, rolling my eyes, and trying to appear unaffected by his fucking gorgeous self. Stryder chuckles again and counters me.

"Don't be coy, Pardo. You were totally checking me out."

Crossing my arms defensively across my bosom, I look away. "Walking in on a buff, naked man and being caught by surprise does not qualify as checking you out."

Stryder clicks his tongue, and walking forward, he closes the space between us. Like me, he crosses his sculpted arms over his chest. Leaning forward, he whispers into my ear, "Bullshit."

Oh my word. Nope. Not going to admit to anything. No way! With my eyes focused on the floor, I dismiss his statement. "Dinner is served downstairs. Whenever you're ready, come down."

Turning on my heel, I walk downstairs, clutching the banister a little too tightly to keep my legs from buckling beneath me. Reaching the landing I exhale loudly, feeling my heartbeat drumming wildly inside of my chest. *Holy hell.*

With determined steps I return to my room. I throw myself on the bed, and fight the urge to lull the ache in between my legs. I don't think my poor heart can take another moment like that. What I feel for Stryder goes beyond physical. Yes, the visual stimulation is there, but it's his personality and soul that makes his outward appearance more enticing.

Damn this man, and damn me for walking into his room like that. Goddamn my body for betraying me like an awkward adolescent who has never seen a naked man before! Shit.

Taking a deep breath, I get off the bed and walk back to the living room. The clicking of my heels alerts Stryder, who is standing fully dressed in front of the fireplace with a glass of amber liquid in his hands, to my presence. He looks even more amazing dressed up; dinner jacket tailored perfectly to his trim body, dark slacks, and some expensive looking shoes.

God help me.

CHAPTER SEVENTEEN

Stryder

The warmth of the fireplace combined with the heat of the whiskey going down my throat pale in comparison with the intensity I feel right now. Catalina walking in on me like that was the last thing I imagined happening. I probably should've closed the door, but then again, I have no regrets. There is no doubt in my mind Catalina loved what she saw.

I could tell by the way her eyes glazed over when she stared at me naked. Catalina's lustful gaze touched every part of my body. There's no denying how she kept squirming in my presence with red-hot cheeks and accelerated breaths. Catalina was aroused, and I'd be a liar if I said I didn't reciprocate.

Having her standing before me started a clusterfuck of emotions swirling inside my head. Naturally, biological responses always happen first. I know she saw my hard-on, and it took a lot from me not to grab her by the shoulders and press her flush against me, and claim her once and for all. Yet my feelings and respect for Catalina go beyond a quick fuck we'll both regret, and I'm determined to win her heart and be the man she deserves.

The echo of her heels against the hardwood floor prompts me to take another swig of whiskey, and after placing the empty tumbler on the mantelpiece, I turn around. Given our little rendezvous upstairs I wasn't able to focus one hundred percent on her appearance. God, she looks absolutely stunning, bringing to mind the pin up posters my grandfather used to have plastered all over the walls of his garage. From the hair to the outfit, there isn't a single inch of Catalina that is unattractive, and those curves–God, they go for days.

"Hey," I croak as Catalina steps closer.

"Hey," she replies softly, averting her eyes.

We walk towards the dining table in awkward silence. I play some music, hoping it will lighten the mood, and pour wine for both of us.

"Thank you," Catalina whispers, a smirk decorating those cherry-red lips of hers.

"You're welcome, Pardo," I respond with a smile. "Not too fond of the salmon?"

Catalina pours herself another glass of wine. "It's delicious. I just don't have an appetite at the moment. The wine, however, is another story."

Smirking at her response, I pour myself another glass, and take notice of the time. The shuttle should be arriving shortly to take us to downtown Whistler. Standing, I begin clearing the table, and Catalina follows suit.

She walks in silence towards the coat rack by the door. Standing beside her, I hold her jacket so she can get into it.

"Catalina, don't make this more difficult than it already is," I plead in frustration. This is *not* how I saw this evening panning out.

"I'm sorry to have barged in on you like that. I'm just... well, I'm embarrassed," she replies sighing. "Let's just go out and have some fun, and pretend none of this ever happened."

Shaking my head at her sudden recoil, I turn her around and tilt her head up. She tries to avoid my gaze, but I won't have it. "Shh. Don't feel embarrassed because I'm not," I confess smiling. "I told you, I'm an open book, remember? What you see is what you get, figuratively and quite literally," I joke, trying to diffuse her more than obvious discomfort.

She begins to laugh, relief etched in those alluring eyes of hers. The dulcet tones of her laughter encourage my own.

Catching her breath, Catalina mocks me with a raised eyebrow, "You should've made some type of disclosure regarding the imminent potential of nakedness in our friendship, you asswipe!"

I grab Catalina by her shoulders and push her against the door of our suite, my arms pinning her in place. My heart races with my sudden display of aggression. Catalina gasps loudly when I bring my mouth to the soft, silken skin of her neck. I kiss her gently, feeling her pulse fluttering against my lips.

"Don't make fun of me, Pardo. It's not nice," I whisper, my nose trailing up this delectable territory of hers. I inhale her delicious scent without shame or regard. "God, you smell like candy."

Gently removing my lips from her delicate skin I raise my head, my eyes beseeching hers. Removing one hand from the door, I allow it to caress the skin of her jaw, my thumb tracing circles on the low of her cheek.

Catalina's shuddered breaths fuel me further. I move in closer and feel the rising and falling of her chest with each breath she takes. Desire rolls through me, my dick twitching in my pants. She looks at me drunk with lust, and that gives me all the reassurance I need. I would never pull this stunt on just any woman because it's the quickest way to get kicked in the balls, but my need for Catalina goes beyond all reason.

Inching closer, my nose collides with hers. Her whole body tenses, and a low moan escapes from her throat. When Catalina closes her eyes, I let out a long-drawn breath.

"You're unraveling me, Catalina."

Catalina nods and lets out a sigh, her breath caressing my lips. She replies softly, "And you're breaking me."

I tear myself away, her words burning me like hot coals. Looking at her breaks my heart. So close, yet so far. Catalina scrunches her brow. Backing away, I place my hands in my pockets, ashamed of my impulses.

"Oh, no you don't, Stryder," Catalina says, sauntering towards me.

She grabs the collar of my shirt, pulling me into her embrace. *God.* I think I might go into cardiac arrest. Her soft hands cradle my face, and this time, I'm the one surrendering under her touch. Catalina's fingertips caress my jaw and eyebrows, and my eyes close in response. She grabs my shoulders, and I feel her body rise, trying to reach my face. It's then when I feel her fleshy lips kiss my forehead with a tenderness I've never known before. I open my eyes, and her darkened eyes greet mine. I see incorruptible beauty and honesty. Catalina Pardo is different from any other woman I've ever met.

She beguiles me, unraveling me to the core of my very existence. I knew I wasn't jumping the gun when I told her I was hers. She may not know it yet, but Catalina has taken full ownership of my heart.

I reach for her face, stroking her cheek. The silence between us is no longer awkward–it's full of promise and hope. After taking a moment to recover, I speak.

"Ready, Pardo?"

"As ever," Catalina grins.

Smiling, I open the door of our suite. With our arms linked, we walk down the long corridor that leads to the hotel lobby. I must look like a love-sick fool, because the happiness I feel is indescribable.

Catalina

The cold, brisk air brings me back to the present, and knowing we are approaching the lobby makes me tense. Releasing Stryder's arm, I walk beside him, making sure to keep a reasonable distance between us. While Stryder is my photojournalist for this assignment, he's also Jackson Reese's personal photographer, and the last thing I need is for my colleagues to assume I'm getting preferential treatment because of Stryder's ties to Jackson.

The other members of the press are already in the lobby. Some keep to themselves, others are huddled talking with each other. As I'm walking to join them, I halt mid-stride when I hear the murmurings.

"I left my family for three days, only to come back home with nothing but chapped lips and a serious dislike for this guy."

The derogatory statements go on and on, and quite frankly, it's pissing me off.

"Gents, let's act professional here. We don't work for the tabloids," I chastise, my voice laced with disdain.

"That's easy to say coming from the woman with the exclusive... Come on, Pardo, you'd be agreeing with us had you not secured one-on-one time with the drunk asshole and you know it," the guy tells me, prompting a snicker from another journalist standing nearby.

"What the fuck are you implying, asshole? We both know our job holds no time or space to be subjective, but only to report the facts. Indulge me with your fact checking. Tell me exactly what you mean."

"Come on, Pardo. Everyone here knows you went snowboarding with Reese. The following day you're reassigned to a new room which happens to be next door to Jackson Reese's suite. Now tell me if that doesn't scream preferential treatment. To what lengths are you willing to go for an exclusive, Pardo? Why don't you give us something to report? Say, how good Jackson Reese is in bed?"

Before I am able to process the terrible things this jerk is saying, my hand rises and slaps him across the cheek, the sound echoing against the walls of the atrium. The foyer, which was buzzing with chatter upon our arrival, suddenly becomes so silent you could hear a pin drop. All I hear is the constant opening and closing of the automatic doors that lead to the drop-off area. I see everyone is staring at me.

In the corner of my eye I see Stryder standing close by, his hands balled into fists, his chest rising and falling in fury. He moves to stand beside me, his taut jaw ticking. He takes a deep breath as if trying to pacify his indignation.

"Those are some serious accusations, buddy. What proof do you have?" Stryder growls, his voice laced with anger.

"Says the drunk's best friend," the horrible colleague challenges.

Taking a step forward, Stryder Martynus towers over the jerk journalist. He stands there like a valiant avenger, his whole body vibrating with anger.

"I was taught to behave like a gentleman, especially when there are ladies present. However, I'm willing to forego my manners and beat that smug look off your face, you piece of shit."

Stryder pokes the man against the chest, causing him to lose his balance. "Come on, you lousy fuck," Stryder challenges, his voice flat. "It'll be the last thing you say before I knock out all of your teeth."

Another journalist pulls the jerk away from Stryder. "You crossed the line. Apologize to Pardo; this guy is right," he demands, pointing at Stryder.

"I'm not apologizing for shit," the man shouts, commanding the crowd. "Come on, everyone here was talking about it yesterday. Don't criticize me for voicing everyone's thoughts. If anyone is being unprofessional here, it's Pardo!"

I stand between Stryder and the douche bag, stretching my arms to separate them. As soon as my hand touches Stryder's chest, I feel his body vibrating, his breaths rapid. My eyes rise to meet his as I plead for him to calm down. Our silent conversation seems to work because Stryder lowers his fists, and takes a step back. After making sure he's okay, I face my accuser. Metaphorically speaking, my gloves are off and I'm ready to fight. This time, it's my body that shakes with unrestrained fury. I direct my attention to the members of the press who are eating up this pathetic display like hungry vultures.

"You don't get to disrespect me like this. You don't get to behave like pompous children. I believed you were better than that." I pause to catch my breath and gather my wits. Resting my hands against my hips, I continue. "I'm not fucking anyone here for a story. Oh, if Blake were here now! If the thought that Jackson Reese is parading inside my panties makes your dull lives exciting, well eat it up, you sick fucks," I exclaim amid tears.

Everyone looks at me stunned. When I dropped Blake's name, everyone was taken aback. Watching me cry unsettles them, their discomfort etched on their faces. I'm not known to be emotional, yet here I am, upset, and crying over the stupid words of a jealous colleague.

Stryder pulls me closer to him, but I won't have it. Shoving him aside, I try to run away, but my damn heels won't let me. I kick them off and run down the long corridor, desperately holding the sobs that threaten my chest. Having my colleagues think I'm less than professional agitates me. I have forged this career with blood, sweat and tears. I never cut corners or slept my way to the top. The more I think about it, the harder I cry.

Arriving at the bank of elevators I press the call button repeatedly. When the elevator arrives, the doors open to reveal a very angry Jackson Reese. As soon as our eyes meet, he opens his arms wide, and I run into them. He presses a button, and the elevator ascends. My cries turn into full blown sobs. I don't care if he sees me like this. I stand there crying as he hugs me fiercely.

"There, there. Shh," Jackson whispers gently. "Everything's going to be all right, you hear?

I nod against his chest and allow grief to consume me. I really can't recall exactly how Jackson and I arrived at my suite, but as soon as the door closes, I run towards my room and throw myself on the bed, crying bitter tears. A dip on the bed startles me. I look up and see Jackson sitting beside me with a worried expression.

"You should go," I beg between sobs.

"The fuck I will! What happened downstairs?" Jackson asks, trying to mask his anger. When I fail to respond, he inches closer, placing my head on his lap, his fingertips tracing circles on my forehead. We sit like that for a long time. "Do you want to talk about it?" Jackson whispers and when I shake my head, he asks, "Where's Ju–Stryder?"

After taking a few calming gulps of air, I'm finally able to speak. "He probably beat the shit out of the asshole downstairs. I just ran off. I couldn't stand there and allow them to insult me."

I look up into Jackson's eyes. "Well, let's hope he did," Jackson says smirking. "Do you feel better?"

I shake my head. "No. They think you and I are sleeping together, and that's why I'm getting exclusive time and preferential treatment from your team."

A smile curls Jackson's lips. "Well I'll be damned," he quips. "That's a new one. Usually their reports are spot on."

Watching him bite his lip holding back laughter makes me smile. It's interesting to see how unfazed he is by the rumors.

"Go on, laugh," I chide, as Jackson's bellied laughs jerk my head against his lap. I join in, thinking how ridiculous the accusations brought forth by my colleagues truly are.

"I wouldn't crumble like that over a rumor, but when my motives are questioned, even when they know about my past with Blake, that shit just makes my head spin." My eyes well up with tears at the mere mention of his name.

Jackson looks at me, his forehead wrinkled in confusion. "Who's Blake?"

Sighing, I appease his curiosity. "Blake was my fiancé. He was a journalist as well," I reply, closing my eyes in remembrance.

Jackson helps me up. Using his fingertips, he brushes away a few strands of hair and tucks them behind my ears.

"I don't get why a dude's name makes you sad. Want to talk about it?" Jackson asks earnestly.

I don't know why, but I feel like I'm sitting in front of someone else, not the cocky snowboarder I thought I'd figured out. Can he be trusted? They say the eyes are the windows to the soul, and from where's I'm sitting, I know Jackson Reese has a beautiful spirit.

"Why do you want to know, Jackson?" I inquire, looking into his eyes and trying to decipher his intentions. A part of me knows he's harmless, but one can never be sure.

Jackson looks away as if unsure of what to say. "Cat, I'm not one to open up to strangers because there's so much that can be used against me. I know we don't know each other well, and I'd hate for those invisible lines between us to be crossed, but one thing I do know is that you're special. You're different from all those assholes downstairs." Jackson sighs deeply, shifting his gaze back towards me. "I don't know why, but I get this feeling deep inside that you and I are very similar. I have this draw towards you, and before you think I'm coming onto you, I'm not. I chose you to deliver my story because I feel like you're the only one who can.

"There's something about you that allows me to be 'me'. I feel like I don't have to sugarcoat anything or pretend anymore. I want us to be friends even after this press tour is said and done." Jackson raises his pinky finger with a sheepish grin. "Deal?"

I'm at the very least shocked by Jackson's request and genuinely flattered by his proposition. His kindness rubs off on me. Without dwelling on it any further, I raise my pinky with a smirk. Our pinkies meet, and the next thing I know, Jackson is pulling me in for a hug.

"Thank you. I needed that," I confess, whispering my words into his chest.

Jackson pulls back from me, assessing my features and cupping my face with his hands. "It's all good, girl," he croons sweetly. "Tell me Pardo. I want to know about Blake."

Sighing loudly, I throw my head back onto the pillows, and Jackson follows suit. Lying there I open up about the death of my parents, Abuela and Blake and pretty much everything that has anything to do with my troubled past. When I tell him I lost the baby the same day Blake died, Jackson curls beside me, crying openly without shame as he holds me. Hearing his sobs bring back my own.

"Fuck! I'm so sorry, Cat. I'm so *so* sorry!" Jackson whispers in between his tears.

When our tears subside, we both stand up from the bed, Jackson getting us tissues from the night table. Drying our tears, we break into peals of laughter when we both blow our noses at the same time. If that isn't bonding, then I don't know what bonding is.

The door of the suite slams shut, startling me.

"Cat?" Stryder's voice booms throughout the suite.

Jackson and I look at each other, both curious to see if Stryder has returned intact. His heavy footsteps echo against the hardwood flooring, and the sound increases as he walks down the hallway that leads to my room. Stryder's eyes look weary and his brow is scrunched. As soon as our eyes meet, I crash into his arms, not caring that Jackson is there. After all, the three of us have crossed the fine line between professional and personal in one way or another. All this time, I haven't been thinking, I've only acted on instinct.

Stryder hugs me fiercely, and the mixture of his cologne with his natural scent beckons me to take it all in. With just one whiff, my nose works upwards to the crook of his neck. Halting there, I relish the delicious smell emanating from him. Stryder's flesh pimples as soon my lips make contact with his skin. A low, pleased hum comes from his throat. My insides quiver, forgetting, if only for a minute, the bullshit that led up to this moment.

Lifting my head from his neck, I look deeply into Stryder's eyes. I don't care that my eyes are swollen, or that make-up has run down my face. Judging by his sweet gaze, I know he doesn't care about it either.

"Thank you for having my back down there," I whisper, completely immersed in his hold.

Stryder smiles and holds my cheeks with his palms, stroking his thumbs against my humid skin. "Hey, it's okay. I'd do that and more to assholes like him. Are you okay?"

I cover his hands with my own, and smiling softly, I whisper, "Yes, I'm okay."

We stand there, speaking with our hearts and our eyes, enjoying this perfect moment. It's only when I feel two strong arms embrace Stryder and me that I remember Jackson is still in the room.

"*Trifecta*," Jackson cheers. His unexpected quip makes the three of us burst into a fit of giggles. Clearing his throat, Jackson says, "Guys, tonight was a shite night, but tomorrow will be a glorious day. Wait and see." Jackson's eyes twinkle mischievously as he watches Stryder and me. It's as if he's pleased. I wonder what he has planned.

"Stryder, do you mind coming over real quick? There's something I need to run by you." Stryder frowns but nods his head. "Nothing personal, Catalina, but surely you don't want to be bored with weather watches, right?" Jackson asks, trying to conceal a smile.

Rolling my eyes dramatically, I raise my hands in surrender. "No, thank you. Knock yourselves out."

Stryder looks deeply into my eyes, as if apologizing for having to leave. "I'll be back as soon as I can. We need to talk."

Nodding, I wave at both men as they leave my room. As I begin unzipping my dress, Stryder walks back in, and without saying a word, he plants a chaste kiss on my cheek and quickly walks away. I raise my hand to my cheek, and across my lips a happy smile unfolds.

CHAPTER EIGHTEEN

Stryder

As we walk towards the door, Jackson looks over his shoulder making sure Catalina is nowhere in sight.

He whispers through gritted teeth, "I need to know exactly what happened in the lobby."

Exhaling a little too loudly, I give him a play-by-play version, trying to keep my voice low just in case Catalina comes out of her room. Jackson balls his fists, his anger visible.

"I'm going to make sure that prick pays for the world of hurt he caused Cat tonight. Consider that a promise, Jupiter!"

It becomes clear to me that Catalina and Jackson spoke about what happened. When I walked into Catalina's room, Jackson was the last person I expected to be there. While he's made it very clear to me he isn't interested in Catalina, a part of me questions his motives. You see, even though I've known Jackson my whole life, there's a part of him he has always kept private. Catalina must've been overly upset for Jackson to react with tears. I need to and deserve to know why.

"Why were you upset, Jax? Don't bullshit me. Does it have to do with Blake? Did she talk about Blake?" I prod, my eyes narrowing as

Jackson stiffens under my questions. "I'm confused, man. I don't understand why a name would make her cry like that. Did she tell you?" This time, my eyes plead because I know he knows.

Jackson nods. "Yes, she spoke to me about Blake. It's so fucking sad I had no choice but to cry, man."

I turn my palms up expecting an answer that never comes. Frustrated with his silence, I ask again. This time, my words are laced with sarcasm. "Well, are you going to tell me?"

Jackson shakes his head. "No. It's not my story to tell, but that makes me want to ask, how serious are you about Cat?"

His question, while warranted, pisses me off beyond belief. "You question my motivations or feelings for her one more time and I will make sure you understand them with my fists. Got it?"

Jackson has zero intention of backing down. His protectiveness over Catalina alarms me. He looks back at me defiantly.

"Good," Jackson points towards Catalina's room, "because that girl deserves the world and then some. I'm not going to allow any asshole, including you, to fuck around with her heart. She's been through enough already. Do you understand me?"

His seriousness grips me. What does he know that I don't?

"What the hell happened to her? You have to tell me!"

Once again, Jackson dismisses my interrogatives by shaking his head. "No, but mess with her and I will tear you to pieces, Jupiter. You got that?" Jackson crosses his arms defensively, and his impassive eyes meet mine. I nod, and Jackson exhales. "She's family now, and I take care of my family, understood?"

I don't know what possessed Jackson to go into papa bear mode, but this much I understand: Catalina is worth protecting–even I know that.

Nodding, I rein in my frustration for both their sakes. I hate that he holds the cards here, but Jackson Reese is stubborn so for now, I'll relent.

Jackson surprises me when he wraps me into a hug. Murmuring into my ear, his words throw all of my doubts and insecurities out the window.

"Go get her. You have my blessing." Patting my back loudly, Jackson opens the door and walks out with a satisfied smirk.

With my hands on my hips and my eyes focused on the wooden beams in the ceiling, I say a silent prayer. Earlier, I walked back to Catalina's room with the sole intention of kissing her lips, communicating all my feelings into that single kiss, but at the last second, reason took over, and I'm glad it did. My body hungers for Catalina's. My thoughts want hers. My heart yearns for Catalina, but I need to know the truth.

I know that once I go back into her room, I'll have to put my feelings aside and let her do the talking–that's if she even wants to talk. Sighing, I bend down to pick up Catalina's high heels I brought back from the lobby. Walking towards her room, my heart whacks furiously against my ribcage. I don't want to be too forward with Catalina, especially after her evening was completely ruined.

Discovering her door open wide turns my lips up devilishly as my mind recalls the little walk-in incident earlier today. Thinking about her flushed skin and her shallow breathing when she laid eyes on *all* of me rouses my cock. The swelling hardness presses against the zipper of my pants. I look down at myself, and I place both hands on my temples in frustration. *Back to being thirteen, I suppose.* I adjust my stance so as to not scare Catalina with my raging hard-on when she greets me at the door.

"Hey," Catalina chimes, her smile revealing that single dimple on her right cheek. Simply clothed in a t-shirt and flannel pajama pants, she makes my heart leap with her presence.

Lifting her high heels, I explain the reason for my visit. "I stopped by to return your torture devices you so recklessly abandoned." Admiring the stilettos one last time, I place them in her hands.

"Thank you," Catalina replies. Playing along, she puts the shoes on one foot at a time with such grace I swear it's unfair. With a raised eyebrow, and a wicked gleam she says, "You're right, they're torture."

The way those words slip from her tongue and roll against her lips take all of my willpower away. The energy between us becomes palpable, electric. Catalina regards me with lust-filled eyes, and flushed cheeks. She's turned on, all right.

"Oh, but what a sweet torture," I admit seductively, hoping she caught the double entendre.

My hands grab her luscious waist and pull her flush against me. The sound she makes when I take hold of her body makes me even harder. Catalina quivers in my arms, an obvious confirmation that my actions are welcomed. Her head nestles sweetly against my chest, and I'm sure she can hear my riotous heartbeats, just as much as I can feel hers fluttering against my chest.

Allowing one of my hands to roam the expanse of her back, I tuck my fingers underneath the hem of her t-shirt, causing another whimper to escape her lips. Raising my palm, I tilt her chin upwards, beckoning Catalina to look at me. My voice, hoarse and fueled by desire, commands her attention.

"I'm going to do something I have wanted to do since the moment I first laid eyes on you."

Without hesitation, my mouth crashes into the moist flesh of Catalina's beautiful lips, confessing all of my secrets, and sealing them into that one precious kiss. Both of my hands tenderly rub her jaw, willing it to relax. In seconds, her body gives into me, and her arms wrap around my neck, locking me in.

My hunger for Catalina increases as I deepen the kiss. Opening my mouth I explore hers, our tongues shy at first but wasting no time greeting each other, and what began as a slow spark quickly ignites into a raging blaze. My tongue probes Catalina's, enjoying the sheer ecstasy of this divine moment. Catalina's teeth gently graze my lower lip, and her mewls of satisfaction resonate within me, making their way down to my twitching shaft.

Her fingers find their way into my hair, tugging possessively, claiming me. I don't know what paradise is other than a place we go when we die. Well, if this is paradise, then this is the way to go, and I would die a happy man. Her kiss feels so right–I don't know what regrets she'll have when my lips unlock from hers, but this is the moment I realize Catalina genuinely wants me.

Catalina

Hearing Stryder groan as he deepens the kiss taunts my core as arousal dampens my panties. I feel the softest of caresses trailing down the sides of my ribcage, making my already heightened senses go into overdrive. Goose-pimpled flesh spreads throughout my body–an endless torrent of heat and lust devouring me whole.

I make no attempt to hide my pleasure; as I moan into Stryder's mouth with every flick of his tongue and movement of his hands. He pulls me closer, and it would be impossible to be more connected. Feeling his length brush against my pelvis instinctually brings me to roll my hips. Stryder hisses into my mouth, his hands moving towards the round of my backside and squeezing it possessively.

Our kisses move into that dangerous territory where self-control could be easily lost. My body is thirsty, famished for Stryder. It's been far too long since a man has held me, let alone kissed me, taking all of my will and making it his. I want this just as much as he does, but the consequences of our actions could be detrimental.

Stryder abruptly ends the kiss, and holds my face with his strong hands. We breathe into each other's faces with small smiles curling our lips.

"Whoa," I breathe, completely flustered, and trying hard to control my labored breathing.

Stryder smirks, and raises his lips to my forehead kissing it, while his palms gently cradle the back of my neck. Unhooking my arms from his neck, I take hold of his taut jaw, and pull him down. This time it's me who kisses him with all the force of my being, reciprocating his declaration. Licking his lips, and taking no prisoners, I end our kiss with a soft bite on his lower lip.

"Holy fucking, whoa," Stryder mumbles.

The suite is silent except for the sounds of us panting heavily into the air. My lips feel bruised and my heightened desire bars me from talking, so I let my eyes do it for me. Damn, the kiss was amazing, but the connection we share never ceases to amaze me.

Approaching the bed, Stryder takes off my stilettos, and massages my sore feet. I don't know how long we kissed and it awes me that he didn't press to take this a step further. The desire is there, but level heads prevailed in the end. Stryder's eyes scream at me, telling me he really wants me, but there's a fleeting look in them that disconnects us. I understand because my mind has wandered back and forth too. The last lips I kissed before Stryder's were Blake's.

As I sit here watching him shower me with affection, I fight against my guilty feelings over what just happened between the two of us. Stryder breaks the sudden silence between us.

"I am a man, and it has taken every single ounce of my will to not take you right here, right now, Catalina Pardo," Stryder breathes, standing up, and kissing me chastely. "My God, your kisses weaken me."

"You're not so bad yourself, Jupiter," I quip with a devilish grin. Stryder's deep chuckles bring on another torrent of heat within me.

"I love how my childhood name spills from those sexy lips of yours." His words make my heart sputter. I rub my chest in circles trying to soothe the barrage of emotions swelling in my soul. "You feel that, don't you?" Stryder points out quietly, his eyes searching mine.

I close my eyes for a second, and smile, and then answer his question with a simple nod.

Stryder kisses me on the cheek before walking away. My body already misses his touch the moment his lips abandon my skin. Standing in the doorway with one hand in his back pocket, and the other holding the back of his neck, he smiles lopsidedly.

"Sweet dreams, Catalina," Stryder bids, waving goodbye. I return his grin and wave back. He lowers his hand into his back pocket and leaves my room.

Grabbing one of my pillows, I scream into it happily, my legs flailing against the plush bed. When I'm done with my teenage girl frenzy, I run to the bathroom for a quick shower. Dressed in fresh pajamas, all nightly routines covered, I leave my room with determined steps towards Stryder's.

With each step I take, my heart beats like a jackhammer in my chest. Is my impulsiveness getting the best of me? Perhaps, but this is what I want. Reaching the top of the stairs, I tuck a black curl behind my ear, and taking a deep breath, I walk into Stryder's room. The sounds of running water tell me he's in the shower, and like a giddy child, I jump on the bed, and hide underneath the covers.

Stryder softly sings a song about love not betraying you, but setting you free. It reminds me of Blake and his shower concertos. I hear the water shutting off, and the opening and closing of the shower glass enclosure. I'm about to have a coronary as I rethink my decision to crawl into Stryder's bed uninvited and unannounced.

Trying to control my accelerated breaths, I calculate if I still have time to run away, and go back to my room, but hearing his footsteps near the bed, I hold my breath. I hear him drying himself and gasp when something plops on top of the covers.

"I'm here," I announce, trying not to sound as stupid as I feel. I exhale when I hear Stryder's muffled chuckles through the thickness of the comforter.

"Guess I'm wearing pajamas tonight," Stryder mocks. "Stay right where you are, Cat."

Hearing the rustle of clothes in the background, I twiddle my thumbs, all to distract myself from taking a peek. The clicking of the lights being turned off makes me sigh in relief. Stryder pulls the comforter from my face playfully as he climbs into bed. I close my eyes and smile, waiting for what happens next. Stryder settles in bed next to me, his breathing sounds a little off.

"So… to what do I owe the pleasure of finding you, of all places, in my bed? I have to say this, Catalina… you are testing my resolve in behaving like a gentleman."

I open my eyes and turn to my side. The faint light of the moon outside filters in, allowing me to see him lying on his side, his elbow propped on the bed, and his gorgeous face resting on his open palm. The grin on his face is impossibly sexy, so I return his smile.

Stryder's arm uncurls, and lands on my waist. His fingertips trail tenderly upwards to my stomach, my sternum, and pausing at the base of my throat. My contented sighs draw a loud breath from his chest as I quiver under his magnificent touch. His delectable mouth trails kisses where his fingertips stopped mere seconds ago. My lips part, sucking in a sharp breath as a river of desire rampages deep within me.

"Mmm," I hum, thrilled with his closeness. His mouth and fingers dedicated solely to me, and I feel cherished beyond measure. I wouldn't change this moment for anything in the world.

"Yeah?" Stryder whispers against my skin, his tongue licking the expanse of my neck slowly.

"I'm sorry I crashed your bed like this. I just…" I stutter, trying to formulate my thoughts and failing miserably. I feel Stryder's smile against my skin. "I can't be anywhere but here, with you."

Oh God, I cannot believe I just said that out loud. I take a deep breath, trying to compose myself, but instead I go into panic mode. Am

I being too forward? I don't know what I am to Stryder. Is he going with it because I've made myself too accessible? I exhale, and finish what I have to say. "I'm sorry for being so forward." I push him away and try to get up from the bed. "I don't make it a habit to crash random strangers' beds."

Stryder's firm hand pushes me back onto the pillows. His body rests against mine; our bodies perfectly aligned to each other's, and his hands hold my head in place.

"Catalina, it's just you, the pale of the moonlight and me in this very bed. In it, there's no room for doubts or fears," Stryder affirms. "I want this too."

I squirm beneath him, the sexual tension between us building, intoxicating the very air we breathe. Squirming, I feel the twitching of his cock against the fabric of my pajama pants. *Oh, God.*

Stryder resumes his feathery kisses against my skin, his hands never leaving my face, neck, and hair. I don't know how he stays in control. My hands want to touch all of him, but my insecurities and fears stop me. Instead, I lie on my back, clutching my pillow, and restrain myself from the desires of my impulsive body.

"About crashing random strangers' beds... Tsk tsk," Stryder whispers, his throaty voice making me tremble with want. "I don't think you're being truthful. If I remember correctly, you've crashed this random stranger's shoulder more than once."

Oh, my heart. Stryder's way with words knows no bounds. It won't be long before I lose all my control and fall under his spell. I want to feel his manhood deep inside me, wreaking havoc, taking, claiming, and branding me. It's insane to feel this way. I regret not finding a release when I was in the shower... It would've made this moment easier.

Stryder's kiss awakes the wild animal trapped within me for many years. Our tongues meet again–mingling and dancing a tango. Time stops, and all that is heard in the silence of the night are our sighs, soft moans, and the movement of our humid lips.

Breaking the kiss, Stryder says in uneven breaths, "I can't be far away from you, and trust me when I say I've tried to keep my distance. Yet here you are, with me, in my bed." Sighing, he kisses my forehead, and his fingertips caress my hairline.

We are both are playing with fire, and the last thing I want is to get burned. As much as I want to lose myself in this moment, I'm not ready. My body might be, but my mind isn't, and I need to communicate that to him. My eyes search his, my hands abandoning the pillow in search for his jaw. Breathing heavily, I try to find the right words that don't sound like a rejection.

"Just lie next to me, Stryder I'm not..."

Stryder's index finger halts me mid-sentence. "Shh. I just want to hold you, and kiss you... nothing more, nothing less. As much as I want to explore that beautiful body of yours, I want to get to know you better first. Please, don't over-analyze this. Simply enjoy the moment. You're safe here with me, okay?"

I nod, sighing in relief. Placing a chaste kiss on my lips, Stryder continues his affections, keeping true to his word. With each aching minute, my body shudders and squirms, more so when his cock finds itself perfectly aligned to my swollen, hollow core. My arms instinctively wrap around his waist, pulling him closer, and he shudders in response.

"Is this too much?" I ask, halting my touch.

"No, it just feels good. So good," Stryder murmurs.

My fingertips work upwards, exploring Stryder's well defined torso. His skin is covered with goose-bumps. I'm a lucky girl, having this delectable man all to myself. I hear his contented sighs against my neck, and I know I'm in deeper than I ever thought possible.

"Stryder?" I exhale softly, happiness filling my soul. "Are you happy with all of this?"

Stryder hugs me fiercely, assuring me without words that he is. He grabs my hand and places it over his chest. His heart beats strong and lively under my palm. "Do you feel that?" Stryder asks. "This is what you've been doing to me ever since you sat next to me on that flight. My heart skips every time you're near. Every time I see you, I feel like I'm having a goddamn heart attack," he chuckles sweetly. "You consume me, Catalina."

His words embrace my heart in a way I can't describe. I'm trying to keep a level head, but he's making it so damn difficult. Pushing him onto his back, I lay against his chest, kissing the hardness of it. Allowing myself the indulgence of further exploring his torso, my trembling fingers touch his soft skin, and when my lips find his mouth we kiss hurriedly. As our intimate parts find each other through our clothing, I can feel him–all of him. Stryder groans into my mouth, his pleasure fueling mine. Using his magnificent strength, he flips us over. He breaks the kiss, breathing raggedly, and with each intake of breath, I can feel the twitching of his cock... and I'm pretty sure he can feel the tight clenching of my core.

"I'm sorry. I can control my actions, but I can't control *him*," Stryder admits, slightly embarrassed. This time, it's my index finger that stops him from speaking any further.

"Shh. Just shut up and kiss me," I plead, not masking my desire.

And kiss me Stryder does, our battered, bruised lips impossibly locked onto each other's, and as the moonlight fades away, so does our energy. We fall asleep next to each other with grins on our faces. If this wasn't bliss, then I don't know what the hell bliss is.

Stryder

Quietly slipping out of bed, I glance at the raven-haired beauty peacefully asleep on my pillow. I'm such a lucky bastard. The night we shared was intimate and perfect, and the fact that I was able to keep my passions at bay and act like a gentleman shocked me. The remembrance of our night brings on a raging hard-on, one that needs to be tamed with cold water. It may sound stupid not to stroke it, but I want to save my desire for Catalina. I'd rather deal with the pain until I can sink myself deep into her. Until then, I foresee a lot of mornings like this in my future. Dressed, I tiptoe out of the bedroom and head over to Jackson's suite. I need Kaelan's help arranging something.

"Good morning, darling boy! What brings you by so early?" Kaelan greets me happily, gesturing for me to come in.

I plant a loving kiss on her cheek, and wrap her into my arms. Kaelan lets go, but keeps me at arm's length. A knowing smile curls her lips.

"Well, I'll be damned," she declares, pulling me in for another hug. Whispering into my ear, she says, "You have the eyes of a man in love."

I nod into her shoulder, elated she can read my happiness so easily.

"How was your evening? Jackson told me about the barrage of irresponsible and unethical behavior last night. I am furious, and I'm so sorry those nitwits ruined her evening," Kaelan storms.

"Sometimes, awful moments spark the creation of new and beautiful ones. That bastard was lucky I didn't clock him on his smug, piece of shit face."

"Yes, I figured as much. Tell me Jupiter, how was your night after that?" Kaelan prompts with a wink.

I exhale looking up towards the ceiling. "Trust me, I behaved like a gentleman."

"Well that's just a motherfucking shame, Jupiter!" booms a half-dressed Jackson. He walks towards us and hugs me. "Let me take a good look at you. Uh-oh, Kaelan, I'm afraid our boy has been whipped!"

The three of us laugh at Jackson's remark. *Me, whipped? I don't think so. Okay, maybe a little.* Once the laughter fades, Jackson changes his tone; this time he's completely serious. "How'd your night go?"

Placing my hands into my pockets, and with a sheepish grin, I reply, "It was special."

Jackson whistles and claps excitedly, doing a silly routine reminiscent of our dancing days. *What is wrong with this idiot?*

"Hey, asshole," I tease, trying to get his attention. "I need flowers for Catalina. Gerberas. I want to surprise her." I look at my watch and smile because she should be waking up any minute now. "Help, please." I pout at Kaelan, ignoring Jackson's annoying ass.

Resting her palms on my shoulders, Kaelan regards me with proud eyes. "I'll take care of it. Just go back to her, okay?"

Kissing my cheek, Kaelan leaves the room. Jackson quirks his head until the door closes. When it does, he inches closer. "How did it *really* go?" Jax asks, his voice barely a whisper.

"Do you honestly think Catalina's the kind of woman that gives it away so easily?" I retort with an annoyed scoff.

Jackson quickly lowers his head in shame. "Well, did you guys at least talk?"

"We kissed. I got to say though, Jax, I'd rather snuggle with her than have meaningless sex with anyone else."

"Wow. Where is Jupiter, and what have you done with him?" Jackson quips, grabbing my shoulders and shaking them. Sniffing me, he jokes, "You smell pussy-whipped, all right." I shove him, and he declares, "I'm happy for you bro, I really am. Now go, Romeo, before your Juliet wakes up."

Saying goodbye, I return to our suite. Climbing into bed, I sigh contentedly, knowing Catalina is fast asleep. My eyes sweep her features, my mind taking it all in. My heart beats strong and full of life; it's what she does to me. I place a kiss on her shoulder, and Catalina stirs, opening her eyes slowly with a sleepy smile on her lips.

"Good morning," I whisper softly, placing another kiss on her shoulder.

"Good morning," Catalina replies in between yawns and stretches. "It's been a long time since I slept throughout the night."

I roll my body closer to hers, loving her warmth. My lips kiss hers softly. "Sorry, I just had to make sure this was real and I wasn't dreaming."

Watching her grin fills my soul with hope. Lowering my nose, I snuggle against her face. Catalina giggles and pushes me away.

"What? Tired of me so soon?" I ask, feigning injury. Catalina responds by smacking me on my shoulder.

"No, I just have needs, and using the bathroom is one of them," she answers sweetly.

I help her up and kiss her again before she leaves my room. As soon as Catalina walks out the door, I miss her. I throw myself back on the bed. My pillows hold her scent and believe me when I say there is nothing more precious or more perfect than that.

CHAPTER NINETEEN

Catalina

Stryder stands by the breakfast table, with a bouquet of colorful gerberas in his hand. Walking towards me, he kisses my cheek and gives me the flowers.

"I got these for you," he declares sheepishly.

"That's really sweet of you, Stryder," I breathe, completely blown away by his affections. Smelling the flowers, I lean in for a kiss, which he happily returns. Looking at the spread before us, I whisper softly, "You got me breakfast..."

He squeezes my hand. "Indeed I did."

The happiness I feel right now is paramount. Stryder gestures me towards the table, and we share an amazing meal all while exchanging furtive smiles and whispered affections.

"Catalina, it's tough for me to describe how I'm feeling right now, but insanely happy comes close," Stryder says with a wolfish grin. "I had a fantastic time last night."

Turning scarlet, I smile figuring out how to adequately reciprocate his confession. Before I can speak, my cell phone rings loudly on the dining table. It's Marcia. Lifting one finger, I mouth, "Sorry."

Marcia informs me there will be a teleconference call with Jackson's team and my bosses at 1 P.M. to discuss the cancelled press tour. My heart drops with the news. The time Stryder and I have left together is running out. My hand clutches my chest as the painful realization hits me. After receiving my final instructions, I end the call.

Stryder looks at me worriedly. Sighing, I place the phone on table. Once again, the damn thing goes off. It's Jackson Reese… That sneaky boy! He must've entered his number last night.

<JR: Good morning. Meeting at 1p. I'm bored. Shred it with me?">

I beam with happiness, and ask Stryder if he wants to join us. I hear his phone ringing, and look upstairs in the direction of his room.

"Hey, Reese just invited me to go 'shred it' with him. That's snowboarding, right?" I ask, giggling at my idiotic question.

"Yes," Stryder answers with a chuckle.

"Would you like to join us? I mean, I like when it's the three of us. I had so much fun last time." My phone goes off again. Jeez.

<JR: *bites nails waiting for a response*>

"Please?" I squeak. Smiling, Stryder nods–his eyes are smoldering as he rubs his palms against his thighs.

<CP: Fuck yeah.>

<JR: *high fives*. Be there in 10.>

<JR: Is Jupiter coming? *snickers* Fucker won't answer his phone.>

<CP: Yes. I'm excited!>

<JR: Woo-hoo!>

Silencing my phone, I place it on the table. Stryder looks at me seductively. The energy between us shifts and I'm right there with him, returning his desire. Words are not required as our souls are doing all the talking, and damn it, it's beautiful.

I hang onto that precious connection, my eyes following Stryder as he gets up from the chair and saunters towards me. I'm not a mind reader, but I'm fantasizing possible scenarios, all culminating in a sweet surrender. The uncertainty has me wet with anticipation, my core clenching licentiously.

Stryder takes hold of my hand, urging me to stand. Both of us breathe heavily–the air around us is suddenly thick. My arms go around his neck, and my fingers clutch the longer strands of his obsidian hair. Our eyes remain locked onto each other's, the intensity of this moment making my lips dry. As I moisten them, Stryder regards me with unrestrained hunger, his body tense. I need to remedy that.

My lips land on Stryder's as I close my eyes and lose myself in this moment. I drift to that perfect place inside my heart where it's just him and me floating in infinite space and time. One of his arms circles around my waist while the other rises to the back of his neck, finding then freeing one of my hands. His strong fingers lace with mine, and as the kiss deepens, the stronger the bond between our hands grows.

Stryder's tongue darts past my lips, teasing and suckling taking no prisoners. My free hand tugs his hair when he pulls me closer, our bodies pressed flush against each other–our riotous hearts beating fast. Stryder's hard cock twitches against my belly, the intimacy of this moment eliciting soft moans from both of us.

I unlace my hands and allow them to feel the soft, hot skin underneath his long sleeved cashmere sweater. My fingers trace his muscles, my touch making him shiver. I smile into the kiss, and my hands move towards his back, my fingernails delicately raking his hot-as-sin skin. Stryder gasps into my mouth, and his hands snake around my neck. Our passion ignites, all desire unlocked and the key thrown away.

Stryder hands find and squeeze my round buttocks, and travel down to the back of my thighs. He lifts all 180 lbs. of me effortlessly, our mouths still ravishing each other's. I wrap my legs around his waist, and whispered moans escape my throat as the hardness of his abs rub against my swollen folds. I'm so lost in his kiss I don't realize he's walking until I feel the wall press against my back.

To say I'm aroused is a complete understatement, and we're both past the point of holding back. Breaking the kiss, Stryder inhales sharply, prompting me to open my eyes.

"I want you so much, and I know you want me too. I can smell it. It's intoxicating," Stryder heaves, drunk with lust. Blushing scarlet, I look away, embarrassed that he could so easily know what's going on inside of me. Clicking his tongue, Stryder shakes his head.

"No, don't look away. Catalina, look at me," he beckons huskily, tilting my chin up to meet his smoldering gaze. "You smell amazing. I fantasize exploring your wetness with my tongue, tasting, sucking, flicking and fucking it, taking you over the edge and then some. And when I've had my fill of your sweetness, feeling your relaxed body in submission against my face, covered with your wetness... that will be my ultimate reward."

I hang onto Stryder's words, melting with each consonant and vowel that drips past his tongue. My body and mind want him, but is my heart ready? Sensing my internal battle, Stryder kisses me slowly, affectionately.

"I want your body, Catalina, but I also want your heart. I'm not asking to take something you aren't prepared to give. I'm making my intentions with you very clear, right here, right now."

His words touch every fiber of my being, reaching the deepest confines of my soul. There's nothing holding Stryder back, only me. I throw my head back against the wall thinking I need to stop thinking all together. Jackson Reese is the perfect example of this. Taking risks is what makes life an adventure, and skirting on the edge of danger and hoping for the best is a lesson I need to learn. Something inside of my head clicks. It *is* okay to enjoy this moment, and it's perfectly fine to take a calculated risk.

Snaking my arms around Stryder's neck, I trail soft kisses along his prickled skin, pausing to lick his Adam's apple. He swallows hard, and my tongue relishes the movement of it all.

"Catalina..." Stryder breathes, his voice wavering as his pleasured shudders vibrate against my shoulder.

"Please," I urge, my body quivering.

Stryder untangles my legs from his waist, allowing me to slip down his torso, feeling his sculpted lines and length. His reaction to my plea throws me off balance as my feet touch the floor. Stryder's eyes are closed, and his chest rises and falls as he tries to catch his breath. I pull him closer, and kiss his neckline. Stryder holds me tightly, his fingers gently scratching my back.

Rising on my tippy-toes, I kiss him on the lips, dismissing my fears, and give him my soul.

"I. Want. You. So Much," Stryder murmurs between kisses.

"Yes," I pant, looking into his eyes.

I fall to my knees, not once breaking eye contact. The confusion etched on Stryder's face is priceless. I glance at his bulging erection, then lick my lips, and look back into his eyes. His cock twitches, making me grin wickedly. I nuzzle my face into his crotch, using my nose to make contact with his length pressing across the front of his jeans. A guttural groan leaves Stryder's mouth, which in turn fuels my unwavering desire to my stake a claim on him. His hand grabs my hair, wrapping it gently around his fist. Through my eyelashes I see his hooded, lust-filled eyes regarding me. I open my mouth and bite softly through the thick material of his jeans, wrapping my lips around the contours of his dick.

"You don't... ahh... not unless you... ahh," Stryder mumbles, his passions getting the best of him. My fingertips gently squeeze his length as his hips roll into my mouth and hands. As I reach for the buckle of his belt, his hand takes a firm hold of mine. "You don't have to do this, Cat."

"Just shut the fuck up and enjoy it," I dare, swatting his hand away, the seductress in me coming out in full force. Once all the obstacles are out of my way, I lower his pants to his ankles. Stryder looks gorgeous as ever, his snug boxer briefs hugging his manhood. The small patch of moisture on his underwear urges me further, and hooking my fingers into the waistband I pull his boxers down.

The fine specimen of man before me takes my breath away. If perfection exists, then Stryder Martynus is perfect. His length is ideal and his girth is robust, and the swollen veins work their way through his shaft, and up to his Apollo's belt. If it's possible for a man to look beautiful, Stryder looks absolutely mesmerizing to me. Kneeling before him, I admire and adore his form.

I take hold of his hips as I allow my tongue to trace his inner thigh, working up to his balls which hang heavy and full. Stryder's body shivers under my touch and his sharp intakes of breath are a sign that I need to keep going. Placing one of Stryder's balls into my mouth, I suck on it gently, licking, and savoring his taste—allowing it to wreak havoc on my senses.

Stryder groans unashamedly at my attentions and the muscles of his legs quake with urgency.

There's something about this man that takes all of my reason and throws it out the window. I carefully extract the sac from my mouth, giving it a sweet kiss and placing its brother in its stead, showering it with the same affections. With each flick of my tongue, his engorged cock twitches, and his eyes darken as I bring him closer to that delicious edge of euphoria. His hand rests on his waist rising every once in awhile to the back of his neck, and squeezing as his groans grow deeper with want.

I lick the expanse of his Apollo's belt, relishing the feel of the thick veins against my tongue. Stryder's flesh pimples under my touch, and boosts my confidence. With my eyes closed, the tip of my nose trails his neatly groomed pubic bone. I feel both of Stryder's strong palms cup my cheeks, urging me to look at him. Our eyes meet, both of our breaths accelerated, and our hearts lock into each other's. I wish I knew what's going on inside Stryder's mind right now. There is glistening dew on the tip of his shaft that I desperately want to taste, so I crane my head, and in one swift lick, I sweep it up savoring the preamble of his essence.

"Mmm."

"Fuck," Stryder mumbles, his voice dark with desire.

My palms grip Stryder's hips, squeezing them tightly then I lick his shaft from root to tip. The quaking of Stryder's legs returns full force, and I wonder if he's holding back. After licking the moisture from his tip, I leisurely sink his cock into my mouth, and Stryder's hands land on my head, guiding, and caressing me, lost in his pleasure.

Tiny droplets of his essence seep out with each stroke of my hollowed cheeks. It's been forever and a day since I did anything like this, and it's more than sufficient to make me come. My insides quiver with excitement and dare I say I'm getting a bigger kick out this than him.

"Fuck me, Cat. Fuck me with your mouth," Stryder pants, rolling his hips.

My tongue finds the slit on the tip of his shaft and probes it tenderly, licking and lapping its wetness. My hands vacate Stryder's hips, one cupping his sac while the other clutches his root. Increasing speed, I take all of him.

My movements lack tenderness as my state of desire heightens; and primal moans escape my throat with the rawness of it all.

"Jesus. Fuck," Stryder groans, his fingernails scraping my scalp. "Slow down a little, Cat, or I'm going to come."

His enjoyment is my obsession; so I ignore his pleas. I inwardly smile when he begins pumping into my mouth furiously.

"Are. You. O-kay?" Stryder mumbles between thrusts. My hand takes a firmer hold of his balls, letting him know I am perfectly fine. Watching Stryder lose himself inside of my mouth makes me wet, my need for him seeps onto my panties.

"Cat, baby, move back," Stryder grunts, giving me fair warning. I can tell by the tightening of his balls, and the further hardening of his cock–all the more reason for me to stay latched on. Two thrusts are all it takes for the floodgates to open–his tangy seed landing on my tongue. After I devour his essence, Stryder withdraws from my mouth. Kneeling, Stryder cups my face, and his eyes search mine. Earlier there was heat, lust, and admiration even, but now, his eyes look so different: tamed, soft, and vulnerable.

Stryder's lips crash into mine, his tongue possessively licking and probing, not caring that his essence was there seconds ago. His ravenous kiss tilts me forward, his arms wrapping me into a passionate embrace. The more he kisses me, the more the walls around my heart come crumbling down. I don't know what tomorrow holds, but right here and now, there's no other place I'd rather be.

"My turn," Stryder whispers seductively, licking my earlobe.

My body shivers at his words, and under his touch both of my nipples harden, and my cheeks burn. Stryder grabs his sweater and pulls it over his head, then kicks off his shoes, and removes the boxers and jeans from his ankles. Standing fully naked before me, Stryder's body reminds me of a ballet dancer. It is trim and lean, and nowhere close to being overly muscular. His body is perfection from the top of his obsidian hair to the tips of his well groomed toes. My hands shake as I raise a fingertip to trace his sexy pelvis and abdominal muscles.

"Wow," I whisper in admiration.

"Wow? You just had my dick in your mouth and you're ogling my abs? Priorities…" Stryder quips. I giggle at his words, knowing he's embarrassed by my admiration.

"My turn," he whispers provocatively, raising me up from the floor, and kissing me as if he is thirsty for air and I own the very last bit of it.

Stryder

My fingertips trace my lower lip, savoring her kiss that tastes like me. Now it's my turn to get on my knees and adore her. It's my opportunity to explore every square inch of her body, touching, tasting, and claiming. Catalina's sweet scent mixed with her arousal is a siren calling to me, and I waste no time tracing my fingertips down her neck and her breasts which are larger than what my palm is accustomed to.

Damn. All the years I spent with thin, model-type women, completely disregarding the beauty of a voluptuous body. Catalina's elongated nipples peek through her blouse, and my fingers touch them through the fabric. With that simple touch, my motor revs again. Sneaking my fingertips underneath the cup of her bra I find the silkiest skin which prickles under my touch. As I pull on one hardened bud, Catalina moans, and her body sags against mine in ecstasy.

She trembles when my other hand feels the sides of her ribs trailing all the way down to her hip, and squeezing it gently. My fingertips inch towards the apex of her thighs, my nails raking softly against her thin leggings. As I draw closer to her pussy, Catalina's breathing becomes erratic, her kisses deliriously hungry, and her soft moans encourage me.

My hand lands on her mound, the unmistakable humidity of her arousal seeping through the fabric and onto my palm. My dick twitches, relishing the fact that my hands and mouth crave more. Breaking our kiss, I push her back against the wall and kneel before her. Hooking my fingers into the waistband of her leggings, I yank them down. She's wearing black underwear with skulls embroidered all over them. When my fingertips trace the side of her panties, Catalina quivers unequivocally.

"Forgive me if I don't take my time here with you, but I simply can't." My hands caress the sides of her hips, taking a brief moment to tame the Neanderthal inside of me. "If you want me to stop Catalina, I will. Just say the word and I will."

"Please, don't stop," she whispers.

Looking into her eyes, I smile reassuringly then look straight at her pussy. My fingertips trace the lines of her sweet spot, where her moisture is more prevalent. As I continue with my foreplay, Catalina's hands reach for my scalp, pulling my hair roughly. Tugging at her panties, I pull them down past her ankles. My tongue licks her hip bone, drawing intensified moans as I inch closer to her clit. Reaching it, I lap it, and feel it harden under my lips. Catalina's hips begin to undulate, blissfully lost in my attentions. My mouth latches onto her clit, sucking gently, bringing her closer to the brink.

"God, you taste so good, Cat. So fucking good," I breathe heavily against her swollen pussy, fighting against the compulsion to sink myself balls deep into her before I give Catalina hers. Inserting a finger into her slit, I feel her insides squeezing tightly against me. Removing my finger, I suck on it.

"Mmm," I hum, looking deeply into her scandalized eyes. Placing the finger back inside of her, I roll her moisture around and remove it, standing back to my full height. "Just taste how delicious you are to me," I whisper, tracing Catalina's lips with her wetness. Her lips part as I seize the moment and insert my finger into her mouth. Catalina sucks on it, frenzy unfolding inside those almond shaped eyes, and accepting my challenge. "That's right, baby."

I remove my finger and my mouth finds hers, our tongues tangle, and fight for power as our unique flavors mix into one amazing kiss. My hand travels down again, inserting two fingers inside of her, and the pad of my thumb rubs circles against her clit. Catalina moans harder, turned-on, and closer to coming. My hand works leisurely, but her hips undulating against my palm make my movements faster, wanting to please this gorgeous woman before me.

It doesn't take long before I feel the walls of her pussy tighten around my fingers, her moisture building. Breaking our kiss, I drop down to my knees and suck on her clit. With her hands clutching my hair, Catalina shouts my name as she comes gloriously into my mouth. Small gushes of moisture wet my lips as she rides her orgasm out. Gently removing my fingers from her sweet spot, I wipe my mouth with the back of my hand and rise to stand. Fuck me… That was hot.

Picking up my clothes, I sweep Catalina into my arms and take her into her bedroom, laying both of us on her bed. I kiss her tenderly as my mind goes wild. I pray to the heavens this wasn't a casual encounter for her, because it was the fucking world to me. Catalina lies on the bed with her eyes closed, with a sated smile on her face.

"Hey," I whisper against her lips.

She opens her eyes and two fat tears spill from them. She wipes her tears away, but more take their place. Her breath is constrained and if I didn't know better, I'd think she is holding back a sob. I expected a reaction, but not this one. I sit up on the bed, my hands squeezing the back of my neck in frustration, thinking what I could've done to upset her.

Leaning into her, I bring her closer to my chest, and grab the blanket and tuck her in. That simple gesture brings out a sob from her chest. I'm seriously freaking out. *Did I hurt her? Is she regretting this? What?*

"Cat? I can't stand to see you cry. Was it something I did?"

Catalina sits up, breathing deeply, and clutching the blanket against her chest. "You didn't. I... I just haven't felt this way in a very long time," she stutters. Moving towards the edge of the bed, she swings her legs over, swaying them anxiously. I scoot over, sitting behind her with the silky softness of her back melded tightly against my chest. Kissing her shoulder, I let her do the talking. "It's been far too long."

Realizing Catalina's tears were brought on by fear, I squeeze her tight. She feels the same way I do about her. "How long are we talking about? I know it's wrong of me to demand answers..." I ask.

Exhaling, Catalina whispers, "Four years and a few months. Not since..."

I hug Catalina fiercely, trying to comfort her, all while wrapping my head around these revelations. "Wow, four years? I wouldn't be able to go that long without sex," I confess, trying to bring some humor into the mix. It all makes sense. The way she has her guard up, her responsiveness to my affections, the tightness of her pussy as I pleasured her. I'm starting to understand. *Blake*. I need to know more about him, but I center my questions on her.

"Was it—at least good?" I ask. "For me it was. I'm struggling trying to find the right words here, Cat, but fucking amazing comes pretty close." I say, placing another kiss on her shoulder. She's not facing me, but I can tell she's smiling.

"It was incredible," Catalina replies, lowering her head shyly. "I've deprived myself of certain pleasures for a very long time. I hope you understand why I react the way I do when you kiss me. I feel like I'm going to melt into a goddamn puddle." She turns her body, and her eyes meet mine.

"I'm sorry for jumping on you the way I did. I don't know what took over me."

She's so adorable. Shaking my head, I reply, "Don't be. I just want to make sure you're okay. If this makes you feel better, that was by far the best experience I've ever had. *Ever.*" My hand reaches her cheek, cupping it affectionately. Our eyes meet and we immediately lean in for a kiss.

Catalina whispers against my lips, "I need to wash up and change."

Nodding, I look at my watch, realizing Jackson should be here any minute. After placing a chaste kiss against her lips, I dress up. Sure enough, I hear the door of our suite opening and closing.

"Ready? Snowboards and stuff are waiting," Jackson's voice echoes in the vast space of the great room.

Catalina looks at me in panic, her reaction making me laugh. "Go into the bathroom, and I'll handle him." Finger-combing my hair in the mirror, I walk out of Catalina's room.

"Ah, there you are," Jackson greets. "Where's Pardo?"

"She'll be out in a minute," I respond, trying to appear normal. Walking into the kitchen, I pour myself a glass of water, praying Catalina hurries up.

"Good morning, Jackson." Catalina greets him with a kiss on his cheek.

"Judging by the look on both your faces, I'd say it's been a good morning all around," Jackson announces with a glint of mischief in his eyes. Does anything get past him? Catalina flushes, and I'm not so far behind. I don't have a reason to hide my feelings, but at the same time, it's none of Jackson's business.

"Listen, I forgot something in my room," Catalina mumbles. "I'll be right back."

"Take your time, girl," Jax calls as she scurries down the hall.

When I hear Catalina's door close, I turn to Jackson. "Seriously, do you have to say everything that's on your goddamn mind?" I retort, annoyed.

"Whew," Jackson chides, fanning his face. "Is it just me or is it hot and tense in here? I'm getting a chubby with all of this *sexual* tension," he jokes, knowing he's getting a rise out of me.

"Just get it over with, Jax. Ask, but I'm warning you, this isn't a game to me. Choose your words wisely," I challenge, looking at him square in the eye.

"Well, it would appear you got laid, son," Jackson affirms, crossing his arms against his chest. "Am I right?"

"What in the world makes you think that?" I ask, with my poker face on.

"I don't know. You both look different. She blushed at what I said, and her eyes are relaxed, like she... well, you know?" Jackson hints, dramatically rolling his eyes, and letting out a girlish moan. *This kid has some fucking nerve. I've had enough.*

"I don't need to divulge anything, and it is best you watch your fucking mouth before I knock your teeth out, Jackson Reese," I growl.

Raising his arms in surrender, Jackson jokes, "All right, all right. Jeez! I hate when you get uptight. You start acting like an old man." Jax hunches his back, walking like an eighty year old man. Pouting his lips, he chides, "It's no fun, man. About the press tour, Kaelan is ironing out the details with *Xsports*. If they agree, we're going to Mayrofen, then Aviemore, and wrapping up at the World's in Port de Soleil. Fun times, man, so chillax."

"I think I'm in love with her," I mumble.

Jackson pats my back reassuringly. "Tell me something I don't already know, Jup," he replies flatly as he opens the refrigerator.

"Jeez, Jax. Doesn't Kaelan feed you? I'm trying to have a conversation here!"

"Hold up, asshole. Didn't you just tell me to mind my own business? This is *me* minding my own business," Jackson answers with a straight face. "Would you rather I raid the bar instead?"

Shaking my head at him, he chuckles.

"Okay. So you think you're in love. Catalina has thrown your whole axis off. I can tell by the way you look at her. You defend her like a knight, even against me, and I'm your brother from another mother!

Free this thing," Jackson exclaims, pointing to my heart.

"Give it to her. Olivia no longer matters. She's my sister, but she's a selfish cunt who never cared about you. Not every woman is Olivia. I don't know Cat well, but I do know she needs you as much as you need her."

Now I feel like a jerk. Jackson is right on all accounts. "I don't deserve her, Jax. I've never given myself a chance to heal after Olivia and I broke up. I just dived in, meeting women, fucking them and never calling them back. At first it was easy, you know? It was all about getting off, but after a while, it grew old. I hate that I gave myself away like that just because Oli wrecked my life. I want love and a partner. I want a life.

"Then I met this amazing woman, whom I don't know very much of... who is painfully honest to me and herself, who makes my balls hurt every time she's near. I don't know her past but she trusts me enough to tell me it has been four years since she's been with someone. Why?! Why is this sassy, amazing woman, whose kisses unman me, single?"

Jackson looks at me long and hard. "You want to know why she's single. It's because she's been waiting for you, dipshit. None of this was accidental, it was fate. Aren't you the one who always blabbers 'coincidences are a way of fate letting you know destiny is taking care of shit' or something like that? How about you start believing in your own bullshit for a change?"

Swallowing hard, I can't find a smart comeback to Jackson's words. He's right. He's always been right when it matters most. Grabbing Jackson's arm, I pull him in for a hug.

"Since when did you take on the role of wise old brother? Last I checked I'm older than you," I mutter, tousling his hair. Glancing towards the hallway that leads to Catalina's room, I excuse myself. "I think I better check up on her. Good talk, man."

"Yeah, yeah, yeah. Whatever," Jackson shouts as he makes a sandwich in the kitchen.

CHAPTER TWENTY

Catalina

I get ready in record time, making sure to shower and dress before Jackson gets suspicious. The door of my room opens and closes softly. Replacing the cap on my lip balm, I exit the bathroom. Stryder stands by the dresser with a pensive look on his face, but when I walk into the room, he looks up and smiles.

My heart races at the sight of him, and thinking his mouth knows parts of me a little more intimately makes my insides quiver. Stryder walks confidently towards me, and presses his lips against mine–passion, fear, hunger–all those emotions swirl between us. Cupping my jaw, he breaks our kiss, and his eyes search mine.

"I need you more than I could ever say... not only your body, but your heart. Do you think with time you could trust me with it?" he asks. Taking hold of my palm, he places it over his racing heart. "I want this to be yours, if you'll have it."

Stryder's sincere words reach my heart, but per usual, my head is second guessing everything. His eyes scream kindness and openness, traits any woman would kill for, but what will happen when this assignment is all said and done? What happens when we leave this mountain and return to our lives before we met? "Cat?" Stryder calls, as he squeezes my shoulder. "Come back to me. Please stop going wherever is it that you go when you're afraid."

"Why me?" I ask, my voice hoarse. Stryder looks at me with wide, pained eyes.

"If it conflicts you to answer that simple question, then you need to look deep inside of yourself and find it. When you do, let me know. There's a reason why I've been alone all this time. I won't drag you down a road where you can't follow," I vow, crossing my arms, and looking down at my feet–my insecurities getting the best of me.

Stryder takes a step back, combing his hair with his fingers, and breathing hard, he walks to the door with a pained expression. His eyes look sad, but his face is hard as stone. "Who did this to you? Who broke you so bad, Catalina? I mean, after what happened between us, I wasn't expecting us to ride into the sunset, but I sure as hell wasn't expecting this. I knew you were too good to be true," he says rather flatly, then storming out of the room. Seconds later, the front door of the suite slams shut.

Running towards the bathroom, I sink against the tiled floor and cry. Stryder offered me his heart and I wiped my ass with it. Holding the metaphorical grenade in my hands, I pulled the pin because I'm too chicken-shit to give us a chance at anything. The guilt I feel is immense, my idiotic move replaying in my head like a movie.

"Pardo?" I hear Jackson call. Moments later, he walks into the bathroom, and throws a sandwich into my sink. Sitting beside me, he wraps his arm around my shoulders as I cry. "Hey, you okay? Anything I can do?"

"I seriously need to stop relying on strangers for comfort."

"Um, okay, but I'm not a stranger, and I'm definitely your friend. I'm also friends with the man who walked out of here like he wanted to murder someone. Want to talk about it?"

Wiping my tears and taking a deep breath, I confess to Jackson the truth.

"I like Stryder. Like really, really like him, and I don't know how to feel about it. It scares me. Things are happening so fast and my head and heart are spinning. He's so kind and caring, and the way he's opened up to me makes me uneasy. He wants my trust when he knows nothing about me, or how hurt I am on the inside.

"He deserves better, Jackson. I mean, look at me. What can I offer to a man like Stryder Martynus? Nothing," I cry, tears streaming past my cheeks. As we sit there in silence, I notice Jackson is trying to process my words. Placing a hand on my back, he speaks.

"You know, all my life I've been the one who's hated having to face problems head on. I've resorted to alcohol to deal with my issues. For a very long time I've struggled with it. If you were to ask me my name, I'd say, 'Hi. My name is Jackson Reese, and I'm an alcoholic'. I've been to rehab twice and I'm still not sober. I'm not sure if I'll ever be… I'm a risk taker and I gamble my life day in and day out. For what? I don't know. The slopes are the perfect place for me to escape, and there are days I wish I'd never come back, but lately, I'm feeling so happy to be alive and it gives me the courage to face anything. I do know a thing or two about fear and what it's like to be afraid."

My neck almost snaps as I turn to look into Jackson's eyes. I'm the last person he should be confiding in. If the press got wind of this, it could be detrimental to his career. "Why, Jackson? You have everything in life. Success, talent, and people who love you unconditionally… Why are you telling me this?" I ask, taking hold of his free hand and squeezing it.

"When I told you you'd be the only person who would be able to tell my story, I meant it. You're not the only one who has a past. You're not the only one with a story. For the sake of your future, I'm asking you to hold my hand so that together, we can face the demons of our past, head-on," Jackson says earnestly as he squeezes my hand reassuringly. "You can fool Stryder with your wit and strength. Hell, you can fool anyone, but you can't fool me. Together, we can do this. Please understand this, Pardo. Blake is gone and he's not coming back. He'd want you to be happy. It's time to live and learn to love again. What do you say?"

"What if I'm not ready to let him go? Why were they taken from me? Everyone I ever love leaves me. Mom, Dad, Abuela, Blake, and our baby. I don't want to lose anyone again," I argue between bitter sobs.

Jackson crushes me against his solid chest, his distress mirroring mine.

"Never question God. There's a reason for everything, and while I can't answer your questions, I know I will never abandon you. You are no longer alone. You're stuck with me, Pardo. See? There are no coincidences, we met for a reason. We met because He knew we needed each other to face the storms together, that we couldn't do it on our own. I'm here for you, girl."

"Yes," my voice cracks. "I'm here for you too, Jax," I whisper as Jackson helps me up. My arms circle his waist, hugging him fiercely. I understand Jackson Reese deeply and I'm grateful we've crossed that line between duty and friendship. "Thank you."

Jackson exhales loudly then kisses my hair. "We have an hour and a half to kill before our little meeting. There's no sorrow you can't cure with snow, a board and a mountain, and we'd be so high on motherfucking life to worry about anything other than our happiness. Come. I'm not taking no for an answer."

We leave the suite in better spirits, and smiling. Picking up our equipment, we walk towards the ski lifts, where we sit next to each other, our gloved hands held together in solidarity and friendship.

"We're in this together. It's time to heal." Jackson cheers as the lift begins its journey up the mountain. "Repeat after me: Let's fucking do this!"

Laughing hysterically, I comply with his request. "Let's fucking do this!" I scream into the bitter cold blowing against my face.

Jackson cheers my act of rebellion proudly. Whipping out his phone, he tucks an ear bud under my ear guard. I instantly recognize the guitar riff: of "The Adventure" by Angels & Airwaves.

"I love this song!" I tell Jackson grinning.

"This is now *our* friendship song, Pardo. We'll listen to it as many times as we have to until we get rid of our baggage. We will be fine!" Jackson declares.

"You're awesome, you know that?"

"Of-fucking-course."

Reaching the top of the mountain, we waste no time shredding, getting on our boards and journeying down the mountain. At first I'm scared shitless, but I get the hang of it. Never in a million years did I see myself on a snow-covered mountain with an Olympic snowboarding champion beside me.

I can relate to Jackson's feelings of freedom when his board scrapes against the snow. By no means I'm a professional; and it shocks me that I can do this relatively well. He thinks I'm well-coordinated and have great balance. I believe it's all about self-confidence, something I've gained since I met Stryder and Jackson. The late morning goes by fast, both of us dismissing our anxieties and fears, and replacing them with adventure. Beyond exhausted, we return to our suites to get ready for our meeting. It's been an interesting week, full of ups and downs, and I wouldn't change a damn thing.

Stryder

With shaky hands, I return the call I've been ignoring for weeks. Jackson's right. I need to move past this if I want to have a shoot at happiness with Catalina. "Hello, Olivia," I greet as soon as she answers.

"Hello, Jupiter. How are you, baby?"

"I'm doing well. How've you been?"

"Just missing you, baby."

Laughing sardonically at her ill choice of words, I question her familiarity. "You're kidding me, right?"

"What's with the temper? Hating the Northern Territory already?" Olivia replies sarcastically.

"I'm going to make this quick and brief for my sake. Why, Olivia? Why did you do it? Do me a favor, and stop using my assignments as a shitty excuse."

Olivia pauses, her silence deafening, her sharp intake of breath tells me I've hit a nerve. "I… Why the hell are you even asking? Does it matter? This happened over two years ago!"

"I *deserve* to know. How could you say you loved me in one breath, and in the next fuck another guy?" I demand furiously.

"Because I was a stupid little girl, and didn't know what the hell I was doing! Not all of us share the same moral compass as you, Jupiter. You were away and this guy was there, and he said the right words and did the right things. What else do you expect me to say? I'm sorry? 'Cause I sure am! Jesus!" Olivia yells angrily.

"Was I not man enough for you, Oli? Was that it? I showed you with every breath in my body how much I loved you. I asked you to be my wife, for fucks sake! I shared my life with you, and I gave you everything. How could you, Olivia?! How dare you!"

"I'm sorry, Stryder. I know I messed up," Olivia pauses. "I know I did wrong, and it's weighed on me for a long time. I thought the grass would be greener on the other side of the fence, you know? I was wrong. I should've called you sooner to apologize, but I was afraid you'd reject and hate me like you do right now." Olivia halts again, her voice cracking, "It's clear to me now, more than ever, you'll never forgive me."

I try to control myself hating she's getting a rise out of me. "You fucked with my feelings, and that's a damn shame. I forgive you though, because I see things clearly now," I mutter.

"Do you think we could give it another go? Give ourselves time to heal, and try to put the pieces back together again? I still love you, and I've never stopped loving you," Olivia says, her voice above a whisper.

"I'm sorry, Oli. A wise woman told me today 'I won't drag you down a road where you can't follow.' Olivia Reese, you can't join me now, or *ever* down that road. I needed a reminder to understand why I am the way that I am. I got the answers I was looking for."

"Why, Jupiter? Why return my call if there was no hope to begin with?" Olivia cries over the line.

"My intention wasn't to upset you and for that I'm sorry, Olivia. I had to talk to you one last time. I'm moving on with my life instead of living in the past where you meant everything. In forgiving you, I'm forgiving myself."

"That's it? No hope? We're done, just like that?"

"Olivia, we've been done for a long time. I simply called to officially say goodbye." Taking a deep breath, I bid my farewell. "Goodbye, Olivia."

I hang up without waiting for her response. She was wrong about hope. I'm full of it, just not with her. Placing my phone in my pocket, I head back to the suite, realizing I'm late for the meeting. With each step I take, the easier I breathe. Closure… such a marvelous thing.

CHAPTER TWENTY ONE

Catalina

After a short yet gratifying afternoon snowboarding, I return to the suite, but Stryder is nowhere to be seen. Leaving the suite with five minutes to spare, I knock on Jackson's door. Kaelan and Jackson are exchanging looks as they direct to the dining room, and that makes me uneasy.

A steward places food on the table as Kaelan begins fussing with the screen that will connect Reese's team with my bosses. Taking a seat at the dining room table, I'm worried that Stryder isn't here.

"Kaelan, will Stryder be joining us?" I inquire, hoping her answer is yes.

"He called and said to start without him. This is a meeting between your team and ours, so his presence is not required, but don't worry dear, he'll be here," Kaelan replies, beginning the teleconference with *Xsports.*

Marcia, my editor, and Dominick Kessler, Editor in Chief of *Xsports Magazine* appear on the big screen, and we exchange friendly waves and smiles. Kaelan introduces her team and Marcia presents ours. After a few minutes of formalities, Kaelan starts the meeting.

"As we initially proposed to your magazine, we chose a handful of reporters who would be given exclusive to access to Jackson Reese's personal and professional life. Unfortunately, we encountered a snag in our initial timeline. Jackson's revised competition schedule leaves us no alternative but to cancel the tour. This decision is effective tomorrow, and all publishing houses have been duly notified.

"Jackson Reese has developed a level of professional comfort with Ms. Pardo which is crucial for success in telling his story. Having that said, Mr. Reese would like to offer *Xsports Magazine* exclusive access to his personal and professional experiences during the next three weeks. Of course, this offer is contingent on the sole condition that it be Ms. Catalina Pardo who interviews him and pens the story."

My jaw drops at the news. Jackson sits stoically, but the gleam in his eyes tells me he's pleased. It would appear Marcia is too–her excitement is evident as she nods at Kaelan's proposal. I know that landing an exclusive story is huge for our little magazine especially when sales have been slow. Marcia whispers something into Dominick's ears and he nods. Clearing her throat, Marcia speaks.

"*Xsports* will need to consult with Ms. Pardo about her availability for this revised tour, as she is owed vacation time. *Xsports* will accept the offer contingent solely on Ms. Pardo's approval. May we have a moment to confer with her?"

"Absolutely. We shall reconvene at your earliest convenience," Kaelan agrees, ending the videoconference.

My cell rings seconds later, with a very excited Marcia blabbering, "Okay, I know you hated this assignment from the get-go, and I know you have three months of accumulated vacation time…"

"I'm on board, Marcia," I interrupt, cutting her off mid-sentence.

I can hear Marcia's glee over the line, her enthusiasm is evident. "We owe you, Catalina. Thank you. You're a team player as always. Dinner on me when you get back! Now, about the story… In order to ensure authenticity with this exclusive, we want to keep all footage and sources in-house. That's not to say we aren't impressed with the footage Mr. Martynus has captured so far. If we want to succeed and sell units, I want to have *Xsports* talent at the helm. We're sending Kenny to join you," Dominick announces.

"Wh–what?" I stammer. "I don't get to work with Stry–Mr. Martynus anymore? He's an asset to my team. This is nothing against

Kenny. I believe the article will be a top seller with such a renowned photographer at the helm, and readers will appreciate the stunning photographs," I argue, trying to swallow past the lump in my throat.

"Pardo, those are *Xsports*' conditions. Kenny will be your photojournalist. It's what's right for our magazine," Marcia explains, this time leaving no room for a rebuttal. "Are you excited? How have these folks been treating you?"

"Better than I could ever deserve," I reply flatly. "Yes, I'm thrilled. Three weeks in the snow? I'm doing back flips over here," I joke sarcastically.

"I'm sorry, Cat. I really am. Dominick and I will make it up to you. Just hang in there okay? Talk to you soon, and Pardo, thanks again," Marcia says before ending the call.

I hold onto my phone with a heavy heart. If Kenny's here, that means Stryder's presence is no longer required. He could very well leave. The thought makes me sick.

"Are you okay, my dear? Kaelan asks worriedly. I shrug, clutching my phone against my chest.

"Indeed," I reply unconvincingly. Heading back to the dining table, I fight back threatening tears. Placing my head in my palms, I try to assuage the stress brought on by my bosses' unexpected requirement.

The sound of a chair being drawn beside me gets my attention. Through my eyelashes I recognize Stryder's hands, and my heart races when he squeezes my shoulder.

"Hey," he asks quietly, his brow furrowed with concern. "Are you okay? You seem stressed."

Before I'm able to answer, Kaelan and Jackson return to the table, and the video conference screen comes back to life. This time, Marcia leads the conversation.

"*Xsports* accepts the opportunity to follow Mr. Reese based on the conditions provided earlier. We have one addendum we would like to discuss. We are assigning one of our in-house photographers for this assignment. This is in no way a reflection on Mr. Martynus' quality of work. We simply prefer to use our in house talent. Mr. Martynus' work is impeccable, and he will receive credit for his work. I hope this is not an inconvenience to Mr. Reese."

Nodding, Kaelan speaks. "We accept your terms and look forward to a positive working relationship between our team and your magazine. Mr. Martynus is–after all–Mr. Reese's personal photographer, and will continue on tour, commitments permitting. I will pass along your kind thoughts."

Stryder pushes his chair back, exiting the dining room and suite, slamming the door behind him. Jackson rolls his eyes at me in sympathy as the call continues. We discuss the modified schedule, locations to be visited, and departure flight plans. I anxiously wait for the meeting to end so I can talk to Stryder. Once the call is over, I rush back to our suite.

The tension in the air is thick as I enter, and the crackling and popping of the fireplace can be heard in the background. Removing my coat, I move into the great room. Stryder stands in front of the fireplace drinking a dark amber liquid from a glass tumbler. Thinking liquid courage sounds like a good idea, I make myself a drink and approach him.

Looking straight into the flames, Stryder speaks his voice low. "Did I scare you so much that you had to find someone else to replace me?"

His words bring on shivers. *Stryder thinks I made this decision? That is preposterous!*

"No, Stryder, I promise I had nothing to do with my editor's decision. I argued against it," I plead, desperation and frustration is evident in my voice.

Stryder throws back the remaining drink in one swig, then walks to the bar and pours himself another.

"Are you going to stand there and not talk to me, Stryder?" I whisper.

As he turns to face me, I can see the pain reflected in his eyes. "Cat, I'm hurt. After all that's happened between us, my head is spinning out of control," Stryder says, stepping closer. "I want to know I'm not on a roller coaster with you, full of highs and lows, and going nowhere."

He throws back the last of his drink in one forceful swallow. His words upset me. My body quakes with resentment, his words angering every nerve in my body. My temper gets the best of me, and I throw my drink against the hardwood floor–the glass shatters into countless shards, amber liquid strewn everywhere. It takes a lot of effort not to scream. Breathing deeply, I try to control my rage.

"Do you see that all over the floor? That's me! I am broken! It takes a lot of effort and energy to smile when all I want to do is cry, scream even! This isn't about you, Stryder Martynus. *This is about me!*" I mewl, tears streaming past my cheeks. Stryder takes a step forward, his irritation gone. The closer he gets to me, the further I step back. "There's a lot you don't know about me," I whisper.

Visibly upset, Stryder bellows, "Then tell me, for fuck's sake, Catalina!" His hands squeeze the back of his neck, his frustration is visible. "What don't I know that could possibly change how I feel about you? I've been patient, trying to understand you, but the time has come for you to tell me why you're broken. Draw me a goddamn map so I can understand, because right now, *I'm fucking lost!*"

"I can't take you to that dark place, Stryder. It's better to leave things as they are. I'm working things out with myself!" I say, shaking my head.

"The hell you are, Catalina Pardo. The. Hell. You. Are. Look at me! I deserve to know. You owe me that much," Stryder demands, his voice shaking.

"The hell I owe you shit, mister! You don't know what it's like! To wake up every morning and look into the mirror only to see you survived and they didn't!" I spit angrily. "Fuck you, and your curiosity, Stryder! FUCK YOU!" I scream, walking away.

His hands reach out for mine, and I swat at them as his strong body crushes me against his chest. My fists connect to his skin, punching him repeatedly until I'm out of strength and out of breath. Out of fight, I fall limply into his arms, which hold me tightly as I cry bitterly.

"Shh, let it all out, baby. Let it go, I'm here," Stryder whispers against my hair, his palms rubbing my back in circles soothingly.

"I–I–lost e-every-thing. Bla–ke. The b-baby. My pa-pa-rents. E-every-one I–l-love leaves me!" I blubber in between sobs.

"You're coming with me right now," Stryder whispers, lifting me into his powerful hold, and carrying me up the stairs towards his room.

Kicking the door open, he lays me on his bed. He takes off my boots, yanking the covers away and tucking me in. Stryder disappears into his bathroom and comes back with a box of tissues. Climbing in bed, he cradles his body against mine, our legs instinctively tangling with each other's. Using the tissues, he dries my face like he did once before and we lay in silence–my sniffles and his breathing the only sounds in the vast space of the room. My mind replays his words and the frustration behind them. The way I reacted was uncalled for. Exhaling, saying a silent prayer for courage, I speak.

"I was seven when my parents passed away. We lived in this small apartment in South Bronx. We didn't have much. My dad worked with the Port Authority and my mom was a middle school Spanish teacher. Money was always tight, but they worked hard. Abuela pretty much raised me. I remember waking up to a bad smell in our apartment. It smelled like gas. I ran to my parents' room to wake them up.

"I tugged at my mom and she wouldn't move. She felt heavy. I figured she was really tired. I walked around their bed and my head was starting to hurt pretty badly, my vision blurry. I called out to Daddy, and when I tried waking him up, his body shifted and his eyes were open wide, but weren't blinking. I screamed and ran out of our apartment, knocking desperately on the neighbor's door. No one answered. Barefoot and in my pajamas, I ran down the emergency stairs.

"There was a police officer who was patrolling our street. I screamed to get his attention. He stopped the patrol car and asked me where my mommy and daddy were. I told him. As soon as we reached our floor, he called dispatch and asked for firefighters and response units to come by. Picking me up, he rushed us out of the building. I was upset he didn't help me wake up mommy and daddy.

"A neighbor saw us and the police officer spoke to her. She held me while he ran upstairs. Next thing I knew there were a lot of flashing lights. Then I saw two stretchers with white blankets on them. I ran towards the police officer and when he saw me, he picked me up and hugged me. He was crying. I didn't understand why. It was a breezy Sunday morning, and a draft of air flipped the white blanket that was covering daddy. That's when I understood what was going on.

"Abuela said the blessed Virgin was with me that day. I'm alive by a miracle–that's what she'd always say. Everything after that was a blur. I went to live with Abuela in Brooklyn. Even though her bodega took pretty much of all her time, she made sure I went to school, got good grades, and taught me how to play the guitar. She was there for my birthdays, graduations, and my first break up.

"Abuela was my rock you know? She got sick and eventually died of cancer during my sophomore year of college."

Stryder hugs my body fiercely. Placing his head on my shoulder, he whispers, "I'm so sorry, baby. I really am. I had no idea. No child should have to see her parents like that. I'm so sorry."

"It's okay, Stryder. Let me just continue because there's more, okay?" Stryder nods against my shoulder so I continue. "After Abuela died, I had to grow up pretty quick. My daddy was her only son and I was all that was left. I had to sell the bodega and do things normal nineteen year olds don't do. I kept Abuela's apartment in Brooklyn, and focused on school.

"I dreamed of becoming a doctor and was doing well in Pre-Med. My parents and Abuela made sure I was well taken care of after their deaths. During the last semester of my sophomore year I decided to take an elective Journalism class. My professor said my work was impeccable and suggested I consider majoring in Journalism instead.

"I did just that and never looked back. I even graduated a semester early. I was thrilled when I was chosen to do my internship at *ESPN the Magazine*. That's where I met Blake. He was my mentor and boss. With time he also became my good friend. He introduced me to his family and I instantly hit it off with his little sister who was my same age.

"Over time, I fell for him. I was twenty two and he was twenty eight. We shared the same ideals, goals and aspirations in life. I kept my feelings for him a secret, because although I was much younger than him, I acted professionally. Abuela always told me not to shit where I sleep, so when my internship came to an end, he took me out to celebrate. We went to this little bar where all the *ESPN* folks went after work."

"He asked me to dance and we did. As soon as his hands held mine, I knew I needed to tell him how I felt before I lost the courage. Just as I was about to tell him, he confessed to me that he had feelings for me since the very beginning, that he struggled with the fact that we worked together, and couldn't cross that personal/professional line while I was interning there. "I remember his eyes looking deeply into mine as he confessed his feelings for me. When we kissed, I felt happy, safe, and the fact that his family already knew me and loved me made it all perfect for once in my life. *Blake was the love of my life*.

"We dated for four years after that fateful day. We were so engrossed with our careers that we didn't talk about marriage. Who needs to rush when they've found their soul mate, right? One day, he surprised me and asked me to marry him. It was one of the happiest days of my life. Shortly after, I started feeling sick. I started losing a lot of weight, and couldn't hold anything down. It took us two months to realize I wasn't sick, but pregnant. We'd planned our wedding, but when we found out, we put off our wedding plans to focus on the baby. Once a month we spent the weekend at his parents' home on Long Island, and I was four and a half months pregnant when it happened.

"On one of our usual trips to Port Washington, the day got pretty ugly. It was grey and snowing. We checked the forecast and decided it would be okay to drive. About two miles away from Blake's home, our car got caught on a patch of black ice, and flipped several times. I remember Blake and I were laughing one minute, and the next his eyes looked back at me wide open, just like Daddy's.

"The car was upside down, and the crumpled door crushed me into place. A few minutes later I started feeling sharp pains in my womb, and as minutes passed, it just got worse. Then I saw the blood dripping from me and I knew our baby was in trouble. It took twenty minutes for another commuter to find us. By then, it was too late. When I got to the hospital I got the news I already knew–Blake and my baby were gone. Four years have passed and there isn't a single minute where I don't grieve over my losses."

My body feels beaten, a mixture of physical and mental exhaustion. Stryder combs my hair with his fingertips, his sorrow for me evidenced by the heaving of his chest.

"Is that the reason why you hate the snow, Catalina? Is that why this trip made you uneasy? Stryder asks, showering my hairline with tender kisses. I nod. "There's so much I'd like to say, and I apologize for being such an asshole earlier. I didn't know what was going on. I'm sorry, baby. My heart just breaks for you."

I turn to face Stryder. His eyes are dewy, yet a tender smile curls his gorgeous mouth up. Taking hold of his palm, I lace my fingers into his and squeeze tightly. Returning his smile, I sigh. "Now you know everything about me. Well, except for a drunken streaking incident on my twenty-first birthday," I quip, as cathartic giggles escape me bringing a much needed moment of levity between us.

Clearing his throat, Stryder asks, "Streaking? Well, Pardo, you're just full of surprises aren't you?" Stryder kisses the tip of my nose whispering softly, "You were saying?"

"When Blake held my hand or touched me, I never felt a jolt of electricity. All I felt was happiness, but with you, it's like I'm inserting a goddamn knife into a toaster. I've never felt this way before, with anyone," I confess sheepishly.

"You '*like me*' like me, Pardo," Stryder affirms with an incredulous smile.

"I believe I do, Jupiter."

Stryder sits up on the bed, pulling me into his chest. "Come here."

Acting on impulse, I straddle his lap, wrapping my arms around his neck, and resting my forehead against his.

"I'm working things out. I need some time to figure it out. I haven't turned your heart down. I simply need to free mine first, okay?" I whisper against his lips.

"Take all the time you need, Cat. I'm not going anywhere," Stryder says. "You're not the only one getting shocked around here. I feel it too." Stryder cups my jaw, his thumb rubbing softly against my skin. "I'll just have to kiss some sense into you and pray your heart follows."

My lips kiss Stryder's. His words are the most beautiful and sincere ones I've heard in a very long time. My admiration, tenderness and hope are entwined into that kiss. As our lips tangle, my heart soars because there is no better place to be than here and now. Our kisses are embers, our sighs music in the silence of the room. A single ray of sunlight works its way through the window and into our hearts.

Our stomachs grumble, reminding us we failed to eat lunch. Grabbing my hand, Stryder helps me up from the bed, and we return to Jackson's suite. Upon our arrival Kaelan beams, ushering us in, and calling out orders to the steward to serve lunch in the dining room. Jackson leans against the table, enthralled with the footage playing on the big screen television. Hearing us, he turns around, and smiles at the fact that Stryder and me are holding hands out in the open.

We all enjoy a fine lunch, talking about the great places Jackson Reese's revised tour will take us: Austria, Ireland, and France. Despite the excitement of our impending travels, a part of me dreads having someone from *Xsports* thrown into the mix. Jackson speaks, interrupting my inner worries.

"Jupiter, did you know your girl here is an awesome snowboarder? That first run we did wasn't a fluke. Look," Jackson says proudly, pressing a button on the remote.

"Oh, this I have to see," Stryder grins wickedly. I flush in embarrassment, hoping Jackson isn't mocking me.

The video plays, and my jaw nearly drops in amazement. For a newbie, I'm handling those slopes fairly well. At my side, Stryder beams, and Jackson looks at me like a proud father.

"Damn, baby, you're good!" Stryder praises, kissing me in front of Kaelan and Jackson. It's a chaste kiss, but leave it up to Jackson to make a comment.

"Is there a reason you're exchanging spit in front of me? Doesn't that go against the rules or something? Gag," Jackson quips, feigning disgust.

Not one to be meddled with, Stryder deepens our kiss, his tongue ticking my lips. I giggle and so does Jackson.

"All right, guys. Jeez. Get a room!" he exclaims. Winking, he reminds me, "I told you, Pardo. There's nothing the snow, a board and a mountain can't cure."

Smiling at his words, I break from Stryder's embrace, and hug Jackson fiercely. Before Whistler, my life lacked adventure and love. Now, I'm lucky to say I have both.

"Guys, tomorrow we leave for Austria. I hope you're ready for a fucking awesome time," Jackson exclaims, wrapping his arm around my shoulder, and wiggling his eyebrows. "Start packing it in. We leave in the morning."

"Seriously, Jax?" Stryder admonishes, shaking his head and laughing.

We return to our suite, and get our things ready for the morning. Exhausted, we enjoy a quiet dinner in front of the fireplace, wrapped in each other's arms. After freshening up, we agree to rendezvous in the great room, and camp out in front of the fireplace. With our legs tangled, kissing and caressing, we bask in each other's arms.

Stryder's strong arms cradle my body and he croons, "Sleep, my love. Happy dreams await you, and hopefully, I'm in them."

Smiling contentedly, I snuggle into his warmth, feeling safe, protected, and cherished. As the hisses and pops of the fireplace fade in the background, we fall asleep with soft smiles on our faces.

CHAPTER TWENTY TWO

Stryder

Sometimes you find things you aren't looking for in the most inexplicable of places. Sometimes those things have the power to deliver change, to make you feel the happiest you have felt in your entire life, and that is precisely what Catalina Pardo has done to me. My heart was a hollow shell, incapable of giving anything to anyone. Well, it's not empty anymore, it's filled with colors, life, and more importantly, hope.

Catalina hasn't realized it yet, but I know her well enough to know she loves me and damn if that doesn't make me happy. I can tell by the way she looks at me–her glistening eyes dark and soft, hanging onto every smile and every word, trusting, hoping, and believing in me. As long I live, I will strive for Catalina's happiness, no matter where this adventure takes us. She told me she wouldn't take me down a road I could not follow, but I love Catalina, and I'm chasing after her, just like we're chasing after Jackson Reese.

Today marks a new chapter in my life, probably the sweetest in all of my thirty four years. Placing a kiss on her lips, I slip out of bed, my entire being already missing her warmth. I run up the stairs to my room, and take a long shower, battling all urges to tame the need Catalina awakes in me. Setting my clothes aside for the day, I put on sweatpants and forego wearing a shirt.

Today we leave for Austria, making a pit stop in New York first to pick up the *Xsports* photojournalist. I don't have to make the trip, but I don't want to let Catalina out of my sight. The only motivation I have is her. The only person I want to fill my days with is her. My heart skips a beat with every step I take on my way back to her room. Standing in the threshold of Catalina's door, I look longingly at her. Catalina's long raven hair is fanned against the whiteness of the bed linens. She may not be perfect, but she's perfect to me.

Soft knocks rap against the suite door, startling me. I jog to open it, and Jackson beams.

"Good morning, Jupiter!" Jax greets as he pushes past me.

"Well come in, why don't you," I mutter sarcastically, closing the door.

"Was your night good?" Jackson asks, wiggling his eyebrows.

"I slept well. That's what I do at night, dickwad," I reply. I know he wants to know if Catalina and I did the deed.

Laughing, he quips, "Okay, no action yet. Get laid, dude. That frustration not only makes you grumpy, but it's going to make your balls explode like a cherry bomb. How do you do it, man?" Interpreting my silence, he changes the subject.

"Is Pardo up? I was wondering if you guys wanted to come with me. I'm heading downtown to visit a buddy's shop to pick up a board."

"Last I checked she was sound asleep," I reply, following Jackson towards Catalina's room. Tiptoeing like we're up to no good, we peek in, hushing each other.

"Whatever is it you're up to, I'm up," Catalina mumbles from underneath the covers. Her response makes us laugh.

Smacking my shoulder Jackson jokes, "It's your fault, asshole. Your mouth breathing gave us away. Jeez!"

This time, Catalina joins in on the laughter.

"Good morning, girl!" Jackson sings, opening the curtains next to Catalina's bed.

"Jackson Reese. Don't you know the concept of don't mess with a woman's beauty sleep? Seriously!" Catalina complains, throwing a pillow at him.

Still standing in the doorway, I chuckle at their exchange.

"Uh-oh. Someone isn't a morning person? You've got your work cut out for you, buddy. I'll be in the kitchen," Jackson announces. "Go on. I know you want to suck each other's faces off," he dramatically kisses his hand and rolls his eyes back forcing a belly laugh from Catalina. "Don't take too long. We have places to go and sights to see!"

As Jackson walks past me, I smack him in the back of the head. "Manners, asshole, manners," I mutter. It doesn't matter how old we are, Jackson Reese will always be my kid brother, and as his big brother, it's my job to keep him in line.

Catalina smiles, looking like a queen in the expanse of the bed. Tucking a long lock of hair behind her ear, she greets me. "Good morning, Stryder."

Grinning, I walk towards her, taking all of her beauty in. She must be doing the same because the heat in her eyes is unmistakable as they rake my form. My dick gets the memo, hardening quickly, and pressing against the seam of my sweatpants. Catalina is equally affected, her chest rising and falling more noticeably than a few minutes before. "Good morning, Catalina," I reply huskily. I stop by her side of the bed, smirking. Her eyes can't lie. She's definitely checking me out. "Enjoying the view, are we?"

Catalina stifles a laugh and replies nonchalantly, "Put on a goddamn shirt and I won't have to."

"To see that wicked gleam in your eye, I plan on not wearing a shirt for a long time. You're curious, Catalina. Your mind wanders off to that naughty place where you undress me and make me your little slave boy. Mmm. Am I right?"

"I'm sorry. I–I," Catalina stammers, embarrassment flushing her cheeks a deep shade of red.

"Shh," I whisper, sitting on the edge of the bed, placing my fingers against her lips. "That's okay, because I feel the same way. With just one look, you shake up my life, like a snow globe," I confess, smiling. "Sometimes it scares me, but most of the time I enjoy the thrill. You bring me to the edge and honestly, it makes me feel so young."

Catalina giggles softly. "I feel like a clumsy twenty-something when I'm around you, so I get it." Her comment makes my head quirk. *Wait. Catalina isn't in her twenties?* Seeing my shock makes her laugh harder, and she asks, "Just how old do you think I am?"

"Um, I thought late twenties, but never in your thirties," I answer sheepishly.

"Okay, let's play a game. For every incorrect guess, you have to take off an article of clothing," Catalina grins wickedly, her eyes scanning my body, "and since you aren't wearing much, they have to be good guesses."

Oh, game on, Catalina. Looking into her eyes, I say, "Twenty nine." Catalina giggles, shaking her head. I stand up and seductively remove one sock from my foot, and throw it on her lap. "Thirty." Once again, Catalina shakes her head, an amazed smile curling her lips. Leaning over, I remove the other sock tantalizingly slowly, and throw it against her chest.

All I have left to remove are my sweatpants. Catalina has this wicked gleam in her eye, like she knows I won't win. "Thirty one," I blurt with my eyes squeezed shut, with my fingers hooked into the waistband. When Catalina belly laughs, I open my eyes. When our gazes connect, she responds saucily, "No," and throws herself back onto the pillows, giggling.

"Cat, you better sit up for this then," I challenge, my voice husky. She quickly complies, dramatically sitting up, and resting her head on her elbows. I pull my sweatpants past my hips, my raging hard-on out for her viewing pleasure.

The look on her face is priceless. At first she covers her face with her palms muttering, "It was a game. I was joking!"

"Given that I've lost, and I'm standing here for your gawking pleasure, it's only fair that you tell me exactly how old you are," I demand playfully, biting the insides of my cheek as my hand squeezes my dick. For full effect, I tug myself a few times, and Catalina's eyes widen, following each stroke. "Come on, Catalina, I need an answer."

Catalina jumps from the bed and crushes her lips hungrily against mine. My lips and tongue are more than happy to comply. Pushing Catalina against the mattress, I pin her arms over her head as my mouth goes into reckless abandon, kissing whatever exposed skin I can find.

My hand lifts Catalina's t-shirt, exposing her breasts. My fingers tug at her rosy buds, and my palm squeezes her luscious beauties. My lips lap and lick her hardened nipples, and with each bit of suction, Catalina squirms beneath me, fighting for control. I lay over her, my twitching cock twitching over her pussy. The warmth and wetness emanating from her pajama pants brings out the animal in me.

"Fuck, Catalina, I want you just as bad," I murmur against her lips. Freeing her hands, Catalina works her fingernails down my back, against my ribs, and over my ass. The rawness of this moment makes me shiver as I, Stryder Martynus, cede control to this vixen. Her legs wrap around my waist, seeking that perfect friction against my cock. She tries to take off her t-shirt, but I won't allow her to break our hold.

I hold the sides of her face, kissing her deeply as I roll my dick against her softness, feral moans leaving us both. Raising my head I look down at the gorgeous woman beneath me. Goddamn, what a lucky man I am.

"Please. Please, Stryder," Catalina pants.

"There's no going back after this, Catalina. Is this what you want?" I ask, praying, begging with all my being for her to say 'yes'.

"I've had bits and pieces of you. Now, I want *all* of you," Catalina breathes.

"Fuck," I growl against her neck. "What am I going to do with you?" I remove her t-shirt, and look at her lightly tanned skin, mesmerized by its beauty. My lips kiss her silken soft skin, and she arches her back, wanting more.

"Guys? Are you ready? We gots to go, man!" Jackson calls from the hallway, his footsteps approaching.

"Shit!" Catalina mutters, pushing me off of her, grabbing her t-shirt, and covering herself.

"Dammit!" I mumble. "Jax, can you give us a minute?" I yell, hoping Jackson understands.

"Wrap it up!" Jackson calls, chuckling. I exhale in relief when his footsteps turn away.

"Fuck. I'm sorry, Cat. Dammit!" I grumble, my arm caressing her shoulder. My dick is throbbing and it's making me downright miserable. Raking my fingers through my hair in frustration, I pace in front of the bed, trying to figure out what to do. "I'm sorry, baby."

"It's okay," Catalina replies soothingly, her eyes meeting mine. "Go take a shower and think of me while you take care of it, and I'll think of you..." *Oh no, this woman. Beautiful, smart, sexy, and encouraging me? Hell no.*

"The hell I will!" I say with a sexy smile. Walking to the open door of her room, I close it, and lock it behind me.

Catalina jumps out of bed and meets me there, falling to her knees, putting my dick into her mouth. Suckling, licking, and stroking me with a passion I've never felt before. Her hand cups my balls, and her tender fingers stroke my sac bringing me to shiver. Her tongue follows suit, all while I struggle not to faint from this raw exchange between us.

Catalina's mouth does all the work, as her delicate hands clutch my hips for support. I thrust into her mouth, grabbing hold of her hair, tugging it gently. My eyes roll back, as I let myself fall under her spell. Catalina increases her tempo, making it really easy for me to come. Opening my eyes, I look down at her, and Catalina's lust-filled eyes look up to mine, showing me a side of her I've never seen before. Her confidence is mind-blowing. I'm lost between how hard she makes me, and how my love for her is growing.

"God," I croon, "your mouth is fucking amazing, Catalina. Mmm."

Letting go of my hip, she tucks her hand underneath the waistband of her pajama pants. I shake my head, thinking my mind is playing tricks, but no, her moans vibrating against my dick confirm Catalina is pleasuring herself while she pleasures me. My admiration for this woman knows no limits.

"Look at me," I implore. "I want to see you touch yourself, baby." She lowers her pajama pants, and I can see her arm jerking, her moans felt against the skin of my dick. I know she's close. Breaking our stances, I take hold of her damp hand. "Trade you."

She wraps her palm around my dick, and my fingers plunge inside of her, the pad of my thumb applying pressure against her hardened clit. Kneeling against each other, our eyes trained on one another, we draw our orgasms, restraining our sounds with a bruised kiss, my essence landing on her chest as hers drips from my fingers. Completely exhausted, Catalina leans against me as we both try to compose ourselves.

"Thirty two," she declares in ragged breaths. "Thank you, I needed that." I chuckle at her response, but when she moves an inch and winces, my laughter stops, and worry sinks in.

"Did I hurt you?" I ask, beating the mental shit out of myself for being so careless.

"No, it's just–well–lack of use," Catalina snickers, clinging to my chest. I chuckle because I never expected her to say that. I'm relieved to hear her laugh.

"You have quite the way with words, baby. You never cease to amaze me," I breathe, kissing her chastely, hoping she feels my heart only beats for her. "I promise to make up for lost time."

Her breath hitches with anticipation.

"Let's get off this floor and get ready before Jackson comes in and sees us like this."

Helping her up, I grab a washcloth from the bathroom and clean her up, then shower and get ready in her bathroom. I sing happily about dying in her arms. I hear Catalina's snickers through the glass enclosure so I sing louder. Wrapping myself in a towel, I bid her farewell with a kiss, and head upstairs, all while Jackson looks at me with the widest, grin on his face. Today, without a doubt, marks the very first day of the happiest time of my life.

CHAPTER TWENTY THREE

Catalina

My body still tingles at the memory of Stryder's hands all over my skin. Even though we weren't able to lose ourselves in each other's bodies, the moments we shared are more than sufficient to hold me over. Not to mention, I'm really enjoying the delayed gratification. Stepping out of the shower, I make sure to dress quickly. Feeling an extra oomph in my step, I decide my wardrobe should be a reflection of how I feel on the inside.

Wearing a tight black v-neck thermal shirt with grey form-fitting jeans, I step into my knee high red leather riding boots. I feel fantastic. Wrapping my hair up a fierce bun I complement it with a red silk hanky. It compliments my signature Rockabilly make-up–ruby red lips, wing-tipped eyelids with black liquid eyeliner and long eyelashes. Grabbing the handle of my large suitcase, I give the room one last sweep, and look longingly at the bed, then walk out.

I'm feeling emotional leaving this place. Everything about this press tour has changed my perception on life. Before I arrived here, I was afraid to love again, and scared of finding happiness. Now, I can't imagine my life without the people I have met on this remarkable assignment. Whistler will always be special to me, and my heart races with anticipation at what new adventures I will be a part of once we arrive to Europe. Most of all, I can't wait to see where this thing between Stryder and me leads us.

"Holy shit, Pardo! You look fuckable," Jackson says shaking his head. "Damn, Jupiter. Damn."

"Watch your mouth, asshole," Stryder warns, like a white knight.

Knowing I'll get a rise out of him, I motion Jackson over. Tapping my cheek with my index finger, I ask for a kiss Jackson Reese is all too willing to give. Smacking Stryder in the abs, Jackson walks over, pressing his chapped lips against the skin of my cheek, wrapping his arms around my shoulders, and dipping me.

His overly dramatic kiss forces a belly laugh from me, and Jackson smiles. "Now that's a proper kiss."

Stryder stands with his arms crossed against his chest, smirking. "All right, hands off the reporter. She could totally sue your ass for sexual harassment. Let me show the kid how it's done," he says, sauntering towards me. Cupping my face, Stryder rests his forehead against mine. His tongue darts out, licking my lips, nibbling my lower lip, and kisses me. My arms wrap around his neck as a sigh escapes my lips.

"All right, break it up. I don't need to be walking around downtown Whistler with a tent in my pants," Jackson chuckles. "Let's go."

Stryder and I giggle against each other's lips. When I move to grab my suitcase, Jackson halts me. "Nope, Kaelan has arranged everything. Just bring your passport, okay?"

Taking one last glance at the suite, we walk out into the glaring sunshine reflected against the beautiful mountains of Whistler. Setting foot in the SUV makes me a little teary-eyed because I'll miss this place. Stryder holds my hand, reassuring me that my thoughts are shared, a gentle smile playing against his lips.

The drive to downtown Whistler is fun, as our excitement for our impending trip to Austria grows. The SUV stops at a snowboarding shop where the owner greets us enthusiastically, thrilled Jackson Reese is there. After showing us around the backroom where snowboards are handcrafted, Jackson presents me with a gift.

"Cat, in such a short time you've weaseled your way into my heart, and being that you're in it for the long haul, what better gift than a snowboard of your own," Jackson says, placing in my hands a custom-made snowboard with skulls emblazoned all over it. The design is simplistic: red, black, grey and white, with *'Pardo: A Living Legend'* stamped across it. Tears form in my eyes at Jackson's thoughtfulness, and holding the snowboard with one hand, I hug him fiercely with the other.

"Is it too soon to say I love you, Catalina Pardo? Because I do!" Jackson says sweetly.

"No. Never! I love you too, Jackson Reese. You're the kindest, sweetest friend I've ever had," I whisper, wiping the tears from the corners of my eyes.

Stryder stands behind me, kissing my hair, his embrace reminding me that we're in this together. Nothing will ever tear apart this trifecta; deep affection, intimacy and attachment, all the things I have fought against since Blake passed away.

"Ready?" Stryder mumbles into my ear, rubbing the sides of my arms.

"As ever," I reply, looking into Jackson's blue eyes. "I have a wicked snowboard and I'm itching to break it in."

"In due time, Pardo, I can't wait to show you the big M," Jackson says, opening the door of the SUV.

"Big M?"

"Mayrhofen, that's where we're headed after stopping in New York to pick up this Kenny dude,"

The SUV pulls away from downtown Whistler en route to Vancouver, the sun slowly dims as the airport draws near. The mountaintops covered with powdery white snow I once hated, but now look forward to spending more time on them. The scenery I once dreaded is now a happy reminder of all I've gained. I've learned to be happy in such a short amount of time, and I know this day marks day one where I, Catalina Pardo, am smiling and hoping again. I was brought to Whistler chasing a story but in the end, I spun a tale of my own. Stryder's shoulder beckons me and it doesn't take long for me to fall asleep on it. I wake up startled when we arrive at the airport and board the private jet. I look out the window at the Canadian landscape passing us by as the plane takes off.

"Hey," Stryder whispers beside me. Turning my head, I smile. "You were so sound asleep I didn't want to wake you," he says, placing his hand on top of mine. Unashamed, I allow my lips to kiss his softly. Stryder makes a small noise in the back of his throat as he aims to deepen the kiss, but I pull back quickly, containing my desires.

I'm thankful to be seated on a bench in the rear of the aircraft alongside Stryder. Looking towards the front, I see Jackson watching a movie on his tablet, Kaelan working on her laptop–everyone lost in their little world.

My eyes meet Stryder's. "I know that look, Catalina Pardo. The question is, do you know you're giving it to me?" he croons.

"Whatever do you mean?" I sass, trying to mask my urge to laugh at his spot-on assessment of my thoughts.

"It's just you and me back here," Stryder whispers seductively. "How should we spend the next five hours? I have tons of ideas."

"Enlighten me."

Removing my seat belt, Stryder lays me down against the bench, his mouth eagerly finding the crook of my neck, and showering it with kisses that awaken my entire body. My fingers waste no time finding the curls at the back of his neck, and tug them gently. Small noises leave both of our mouths as our bodies align themselves.

"For starters, I would take off all of your layers and kiss every inch of your body," Stryder whispers, making me tremble. His palms trace my body hungrily, his frenzy wreaking havoc deep inside me.

Stryder's hands sneak underneath my blouse, his fingertips finding my goose-pimpled flesh and hardened nipples. Tracing lazy circles over the fabric of my bra, he teases them and the attention sends a rush of heat throughout my body. My core clenches under his touch as soft moans and deep sighs drip past my lips.

Taking a deep whiff of my skin, Stryder hums, "God, Catalina, I can sense your need all the way up here. What can we do?" Stryder's fingers land on the waistband of my jeans sneaking underneath. In no time, his fingertips find the wetness of my core. "Fuck," he mutters, gently moving his hips, his hardness pressing against my thigh. "I want you."

"I want you too," I murmur against his neck, wanting to abate the ache pooling between my legs. Stryder's hand leaves my pants and I protest at the loss of contact. Opening my eyes I see him sucking on his fingers, his tongue expertly licking all of my wetness away. I find it very hard to comprehend the need Stryder awakens in me, but I also know we're in close proximity of others and that's a buzz-kill.

"We need to stop," Stryder breathes, his statement mirroring my thoughts. "I just want you like I've never wanted anything else before. Your taste, your smell–I am having a tough time keeping my hands to myself. It's like they have a mind of their own. I'm sorry."

There are certain things in life you learn to accept and embrace. Sitting upright, my hands cradle Stryder's sheepish face. Our eyes meet in this singular and most interesting way, communicating silently our wants and needs. We both smile as we stare at each other. "This is going to be a long flight, handsome," I mumble, bringing Stryder to chuckle.

"Mmm-hmm," he replies with a grin. "How about we just get some rest? It's late and once we jump time zones it's going to get harder to play catch-up."

I nod, knowing we're moving forward in time the closer we get to New York. With Stryder's hands gently caressing my hair, I fall into a blissful sleep, feeling safer than I've ever felt before.

I wake up as soon as the wheels of the jet touch down at Republic Airport. I know this airstrip all too well, and my heart clenches when I see St. Charles cemetery to the right of the landing strip. My hand reflexively clutches my chest, remembering this is our layover before journeying on to Austria.

"Good morning, sleepyhead," Stryder purrs, hugging me.

"Morning," I mumble, feeling desperately sad, my body tense under his embrace.

Alarmed, Stryder grabs my shoulders and looks intently into my eyes. "What's the matter, Catalina?"

"Blake," I whisper, pointing to the cemetery right across the street from the small executive airport.

"Oh."

Jackson comes by with Marc, the flight attendant with three Styrofoam cups. I can't look away from the cemetery as silent tears stream down my face. There's this push and pull I feel inside of my chest. Then it dawns on me. The only way I can move forward is by saying goodbye. Wiping my tears, I look at Jackson.

"Do you think we could stop here for an hour before we leave? There's something I need to do."

Jackson's concerned gaze meets mine. "What is it?"

"I can't explain right this second. I just need a car to take me across the street," I say, hoping he doesn't overwhelm me with questions.

Nodding, he points out the small window and says, "That must be your partner over there."

Looking out of the window I see Kenneth Williams, a photojournalist and colleague of mine from *Xsports*. I try to wrap my mind around the idea that I can't be impersonal anymore once Kenny steps foot on the plane. Any misstep, and my career could be in jeopardy, something I can't allow to happen.

The jet makes a complete stop near a hangar to refuel. I put on my jacket and get ready to leave, but Stryder's hand stops me.

"Cat? Do you want me to come with you?" he asks, his worry painfully obvious.

"No, it's okay, Stryder. This is something I need to do on my own," I reply, my eyes searching his for understanding.

"Can't we just leave him there?" Jackson groans, looking out the window at Kenny. "He just screams trouble."

We all look out the window at the same time and sigh. Putting on my gloves, I give them a quick rundown. "For the most part, he's a really cool guy, but he's the one in the office that follows the rulebook to the T. We have to act professionally when he's around. He's always rubbed me the wrong way, you know? Do you guys think you can play along?"

"You don't need to worry about me, Catalina," Stryder answers, apparently unconcerned. "Worry about this knucklehead right here," he says, pointing at Jackson.

Looking away from the window, Jackson exhales, "Okay, I'll behave, but if he pisses me off, I'm shipping him back."

Stryder and I look at each other and giggle. "Quit being a five year old, Reese," I admonish, and Jackson promptly flips me the bird. I walk over to his seat, and kiss him on the cheek.

I walk towards the door of the aircraft with Stryder close behind. Looking over the threshold, I see the cemetery plots are covered in snow. As I take my first step out of the aircraft, Stryder calls out.

"I'll miss you."

I turn around quickly and kiss him. Stryder quickly wraps both arms around my waist and sighs.

"All I ever wanted is right here, in my arms. I–I–Don't take too long, okay?" Kissing my temple, he retreats back into the jet.

I march down the steps and greet Kenny. Standing tall at six feet, his bright, emerald green eyes contrast sharply with his beach blonde locks and artificially tanned skin. Kenny's always been the office jock with his super-fit bulging muscles straining against his too small clothing. Many jokes are made about how much product he uses on his pin-straight shoulder length locks. Some of the girls call him the office doll. Don't get me wrong, Kenny is a good looking guy, but his narcissism makes him unattractive. He knows he's hot and flaunts it all the time, which is a major turn off for me.

Patting him on the shoulder, I greet him with a smile. "Hey, Kenny. Welcome aboard."

Nodding, he smiles, displaying his perfectly straight and blinding white teeth. "Wow, Catalina. You look… different. Have you lost weight? Looking good, girl," Kenny replies with that saccharine tone he uses with all the girls in the office. I inwardly roll my eyes at his remark.

"Thank you, Kenny. I guess I have."

"Catalina," Kaelan calls. "The gentleman over there will be taking you. The jet is refueling so you have some time."

Waving at both Kaelan and Kenny, I walk towards the SUV with a racing heart. I need to do this. The driver opens a door for me, and I slip into the warmth of the vehicle. The driver sits and asks my destination. "St. Charles," I whisper.

"The cemetery across the street?" the driver asks, obviously shocked.

"Indeed."

Once we arrive, the driver opens the door for me. The wintry breeze blows against my face, my hair flowing freely down my back. I tread carefully against the icy sidewalk towards Blake's plot.

I've visited him many times before, but it never gets easier. Tears threaten to spill over my cheeks and my footsteps crunch against the snow as I walk over to Blake's final resting place. My hand lovingly dusts off the wet powdery snow from the headstone inscription.

BLAKE R. MACKENZIE (1976-2010)

Beloved son, amazing brother, blessed fiancé and father of an angel.

My lips find the cold stone surface, and I kiss it. The tears I had been careful to avoid spill out unbidden. Being right here and now is something I desperately need to do. Some call it closure. I really don't understand why it's called that because his memory will be forever ingrained in my thoughts, no matter how many years pass, and who I end up with. Blake and our angel will never be forgotten.

"Hi, baby," I whisper to his headstone, kneeling in front of it, not caring about the cold snow against my knees and shins. "I came by to say hi. I know it's been a while. Work has been crazy. I'm on this tour, and stopped here before I go over to Europe with the team."

Wiping my tears, I smile as I carry on, this monologue so characteristic of me for the past four years. "I don't know if you know, but Faith got engaged and I'm going to be the maid of honor. Mike finally decided to take the leap," I explain, giggling softly.

But my voice cracks with what I'm about to say next. "I–I miss you so much Blake… you and the baby. Not one day goes by where I don't miss us." Sighing deeply, I continue, "I met someone. I don't know exactly what he means to me yet. He's kind and makes me smile so much. I don't want you to think I've replaced you."

Sobs wrack my chest as I bow my head with my confession. "I feel guilty, Blake, because a part of me feels like I love him. You're gone, and you're never coming back, baby. I just wanted you to know that no matter what happens or where I find myself in this lifetime, I will always love you. Watch over me, and never leave me."

Standing up, I kiss his photograph over the headstone inscription. "See you soon." My fingers trace his gorgeous smile and deep inside of me, I feel his presence soothing me like a warm blanket, lifting away the guilt that kept me in such a dark place for all those years. Smiling, I look to the heavens and whisper, "Thank you."

Walking away from his tombstone is one of the hardest things I've ever done. There is this sense of finality in doing so, but the happiness I feel is beyond measure.

As the saying goes, "*When one door closes, look for a window*." In this case, my window is a generous and handsome man waiting for me on the tarmac; he treasures and respects who I am, and where I came from. Stryder Martynus is my future, and I hope I can be in his.

I jump out of the car and carefully walk across the slippery surface to meet him. He meets me halfway and embraces me tightly.

"Hey," Stryder whispers into my neck. "I missed you."

Nodding, I reply, "Yes."

Stryder breaks our hug and leads me back into the jet, the cold wintry breeze flapping our scarves. I stop halfway up and look up at him. We're off on a new adventure, seeking thrills, pushing boundaries, but more importantly, I'm learning to live again. Losing Blake eventually brought me love.

Looking down at me, Stryder smiles, "What?"

As soon as our lips meet, my mouth plunders his. His kisses are those of a starved man, his hand gently tugging my hair as a guttural groan escapes him. His erection is firm against my belly, sending a hot message to my insides. The contact has me whimpering.

"Stryder…"

"Yes, Cat?" Stryder breathe.

"I want to be with you," I confess, looking deeply into his eyes.

"Really?" Stryder replies incredulously, full and well understanding what I mean. I want to try having a relationship again. There are no more impediments for that to happen. "Me, too," he replies in between kisses. Stopping to catch his breath, he looks down to himself and groans. Raking his fingers through his hair, he looks at me. I take hold of his hands, not caring that they are freezing cold, and Stryder surprises me by taking my free hand, bringing it to his lips and kissing my knuckles. "This is going to be the longest fourteen hours of my life."

"Let's get on board so we can get there faster," I beckon, dragging Stryder up the steps. The smile on my face couldn't be wider or happier.

Finding our little bench, we sit down, trying to be innocuous as possible. The flight takes off shortly after. Sipping on a fresh cup of coffee; I open my laptop and try to get some work done. Stryder works on his while we exchange furtive glances and tender caresses.

Shortly after takeoff, Jackson announces a Q&A session will take place after lunch. I've already jotted down some questions to ask and this interview opportunity will allow me to present them. The only thing concerning me is Kenny's presence because while I'm here to pen a story, my questions will be based on a confession Jackson made off the record.

Stryder moves down the cabin to discuss his footage with Kenny, bringing him up to speed on the assignment. Kenny looks at me with a familiarity that makes me slightly uncomfortable. He's never looked at me that way before, and it doesn't take long before Stryder takes notice. Closing my laptop, I lay back on the bench, drained.

"Catalina?" Stryder's soft voice calls to me. Opening my eyes I realize I must have dozed off for a while because the delicious smell of lunch is wafting in the air. "Jet-lagged already, baby?" he whispers, squeezing my arm.

Nodding, I stand up and grab my toiletry bag, and march to the lavatory. Splashing my face with cold water, I instantly wake up. One glance in the mirror reflects my exhaustion. Dark circles, bloodshot eyes, and my skin is dry and pasty. I go immediately to work applying a clay mask, and twenty minutes later, I emerge from that bathroom feeling refreshed.

Lunch is served immediately afterwards and we all eat in awkward silence, Kenny watching the rest of us curiously. Jackson exhales loudly and announces the start of the Q&A session. Returning to my seat I retrieve my voice recorder and note-pad. Jackson sits beside me with Kenny and Stryder close by.

"I'm ready whenever you are, Pardo," Jackson says.

"First and foremost, thank you, Jackson, for giving *Xsports* the opportunity to accompany you on this tour. There are many questions to ask... some basic, others a little more complex, okay?" Jackson nods, so I continue. My heart beats furiously, nervous with the line of questioning I have prepared for him. Turning off the voice recorder I whisper so only Jackson can hear me.

"Jax, I'm going to be asking some tough questions. Feel free to cut me off if you don't feel comfortable answering them, okay?"

Winking at me reassuringly, Jackson replies, "You can ask me about '*that*'. Don't worry. It's time."

Sighing, I power-on the voice recorder. This will probably be the most challenging interview of my life. It's my job to ask the tough questions to get to the bottom of a story. I pray to the heavens for guidance, courage, and strength.

CHAPTER TWENTY FOUR

Catalina

"What has been one of your greatest accomplishments as a professional snowboarder?"

Jackson smiles, and scratches his chin. I return his grin, trying to make this process comfortable for him. "There have been many, but if I had to choose one? I'd say winning a gold medal in the Winter Olympics. I think a gold medal is the highest recognition in any sport. So yeah, having a gold medal is my greatest accomplishment."

"Having a gold medal certainly asserts your dominance in a world full of talented snowboarders. What has been your biggest disappointment as an athlete?"

"Well, throughout my career I've dealt with a lot of bullshit stemming from fellow competitors. Some guys out there just like to talk, and when the press gets hold of something small and trivial, like a tumble on a slope, it snowballs, no pun intended, into something big. A lot of the rivalry that exists in my sport has sprouted from inaccurate and exploitive reporting by the press. In reality, I have very few qualms with the guys I see at every single competition," Jackson replies candidly.

I can see where he's going with this. "So you're saying journalists are responsible for the bad press Team Reese has had in recent months?"

"Not entirely. In my sport, it's common to talk big about yourself to build self-confidence and inspire healthy competition. What I'm saying is the press interprets things wrong and news reports paint me out to be an arrogant asshole, when in all reality, I'm just a really cool guy."

"You're misunderstood. Is that an accurate assessment?"

"Indeed it is. Spend a week with me and you'll see I'm not the dick the press paints me out to be," Jackson replies with a smile.

I catch the double meaning behind his response and move forward, winking. "Who is a hero in your life and why?"

"That's easy! My mother has always supported me in all aspects of my life. When I wanted to play the tuba when I was a kid, she was like 'If you want to be a tuba player, be the best tuba player there is.' That was her approach to everything. I come from a family of ballroom dancers, and it was expected that I'd follow the family tradition. One Christmas I asked for a snowboard. I'd never been on a board before, and when Dad took me to the slopes near home, he saw I had potential. He told my Mom to enroll me in snowboarding lessons. The rest, as they say, is history. She never missed a practice or competition as I evolved into a professional snowboarder," replies Jackson with a grin.

Stryder walks by. "Jup, take a seat," Jackson asks, and Stryder complies, sitting beside him. I'm befuddled with his statement and try hard to withhold my laughter.

"I'm sorry. I just want to make sure I heard correctly. Ballroom dancing, as in fancy costumes, heeled shoes and sashaying hips?"

Jackson throws his head back in laughter, and Stryder joins in. "Yes. I'm a trained ballroom dancer. My Dad is a champion who now judges competitions worldwide. He still dances with his partner of over forty years when they're not judging. My sisters are professional dancers. One of them choreographs music videos for celebrities, and the other actively competes around the world. Our Dad taught us all that he knows. He's a rad dancer."

The realization hits me. This is what Stryder has been trying to tell me all along. It all makes sense! "I think you've already answered this question, but I must ask. What is your favorite hobby and why?"

"Indeed I have. I love to dance. It's all we do at family gatherings. It's how we express ourselves. It's a journey you take that helps you find yourself. Plus, it's an awesome workout. Have you ever danced, Cat?" Jackson asks with a glint of humor in his eyes.

"I don't make it a habit to dance. In fact, I avoid it at all costs. I'm Puerto Rican and I can't even dance *Salsa*, which is the dance all Puerto Ricans are supposed to have embedded in their DNA. Clearly my genes didn't get the memo," I reply, giggling but feeling slightly embarrassed. "So having that said, would you be willing to teach me if the opportunity arose?"

"Definitely, however, I know someone who's a better teacher than me," Jackson replies stifling a smile.

"Now off to some rather serious questions. Let's go back to the Olympics. It was reported after you won gold, you started exhibiting erratic behavior. You were captured on camera snowboarding naked, under the influence of alcohol, wearing nothing but a gold medal around your neck. Can you share with me what led to that?"

Stryder inhales sharply and tries to stand up, but Jackson taps him on the knee and asks him to sit. Jackson sighs deeply and replies with a steady voice, "Much has been said about that unfortunate, most embarrassing moment of my snowboarding career. It has turned into something bigger than it should've been. Every year, countless of college students in Michigan gather to run a naked marathon. It's not viewed as lewd or profane. It is simply an interesting approach to the sport of running.

"But once you become a gold medalist, representing your country, the responsibilities of being an Olympian come with a price, and image is equal to, if not more important than winning. It's no secret I was drunk when I did my own version of a victory lap. I didn't think all that much about it. It wasn't thought out in advance. I'm a guy who lives for the moment. That's what I felt like doing. It wasn't intended to upset anyone or let down my country. It was a stupid stunt that I'll never outlive," Jackson answers, looking deep into my eyes not holding back on any of his responses.

I take a deep breath in preparation for the next question, and exhale shakily because I already know the answer. "There have been numerous reports that state you're an alcoholic. What are your thoughts on those allegations?"

Jackson closes his eyes and forces a patient smile. I cringe, knowing his response could change everything. "Those aren't allegations, Pardo. My name is Jackson Reese and I'm an alcoholic, plain and simple. My team has worked tirelessly to clean up after my terrible messes, but not anymore. I've been struggling with alcohol for about two years now. I've spent time with counselors and have completed two visits to rehab. I'm not using this as an excuse by any means, but it's no secret snowboarding is a dangerous sport. The way I like to snowboard takes danger to whole new level. Alcohol is my way of dealing with the stress and demands of it."

Jackson's honesty has blown me away. I know he's proud of himself right now. Admitting you have a problem is the first step towards recovery. I couldn't be more appreciative of this, but I can't stop the momentum of this interview. "Have you made attempts to remain sober after your visits to rehab?"

"Yes. I take it one day at a time."

I'm aching to reach for Jackson's hand and squeeze it, but with Kenny close by snapping pictures, I can't run the risk of acting unprofessionally. "I only have two questions left. What was the last thing you saw someone do that really impressed you?"

Jackson turns to face Stryder, and they exchange smiles. "Actually, I saw this really awesome reporter, who'd never snowboarded a day in her life, rip a slope like a pro. Yeah. That impressed the shit out of me."

I can't help but laugh at Jackson's response, knowing he's talking about me. "This is my final question. You constantly raise the bar with the stunts in your routines by jumping out of airplanes and helicopters. What is your biggest fear?"

"The risks I take day in and day out are monumental. Sometimes I stand on the ledge of the helicopter and wonder 'Will this be my last jump? Will I make it?' And it takes a millisecond for the adventurous side of me to say 'Fuck it'... it'll be okay. I've been lucky enough to outrun avalanches here and there for the past decade, but deep down, I worry that one day I'll exhaust all of my good luck, and die in the place I love most, trapped in the snow."

I listen to his somber words with a heavy heart. Just thinking about the possibility of something like that happening to Jackson makes my chest hurt. "Whoa," I reply, my voice breaking. "That was intense. Thanks for answering every question, Jackson."

"No problem." He squeezes my hand reassuringly. "Are you okay?"

"Yeah, I'm good," I respond, lying through my teeth. "I'm just–I'm going to get a head start transcribing these so I don't fall behind." Before I move over to one of the seats on the jet, my eyes sweep over Stryder longingly.

"Jeez. You two are like kids," Jackson clucks, feigning annoyance. "I'm going to chat this Kenneth person up. Five minutes. That's all you get." Standing up, he points at Stryder and me. "Five minutes."

Stryder nods appreciatively. "No need, Jax. Anticipation is key."

My jaw drops at Stryder's smug comment. Raising my eyebrow I retort, "Oh, really? We'll see about that."

The three of us erupt in laughter, making Kaelan glance towards the back of the plane with a broad smile on her face. Shortly after, we all take our assigned seats for the remainder of the flight. I work in intervals, but my thoughts are constantly interrupted by visions of Stryder. I can't wait until we get to Mayrhofen so we can finish what we started back in Whistler.

We finally arrive in Vienna. It is eleven AM local time, but our bodies are sluggish given that we are running on Pacific Standard Time. Marc, being the ever amazing flight attendant, bids us farewell with steaming cups of coffee. I express my appreciation by giving him a warm hug.

As we set foot outside the jet, the landscape appears harsher and colder than it did in Whistler. The snow falls heavily, and the cold wintry wind is unmerciful. We tip toe towards the van carefully, as the ground is iced over.

I hear a thud followed by a whispered "Shit." When I turn around, Stryder's butt is on the ice again. It reminds me of the time he slipped and fell on our way to our rooms in Whistler. Helping him up, I dust the snow from his coat, and we both laugh so hard we spark weird looks from everyone.

It'll take us another hour or so to get to Mayrhofen, weather permitting. The van taking us there is very comfortable and in no time, I find myself napping against a very familiar shoulder. Gone are the days when the snow brought on panic. Instead, I find it comforting.

Jackson pokes my shoulder, gently announcing our arrival to the Mayrhofen Resort. "Cat," he whispers sweetly. Raising my head from Stryder's shoulder, I yawn. "We're here. I can't wait to show you the big M." My fingers rub against my eyes as my brain powers-up again. "Right now, it's perfect," he grins.

Stryder and I look at each other happily. "I can't wait," I whisper to both of them, but deep down what I'm looking forward to the most is spending quality time with Stryder. Escaping the van through the snow shower, we walk into the resort, promptly checking in. With our room keys in hand, we head towards our room. I feel beyond elated when I notice Kenny is placed on a different floor.

"Guys, get some rest. We'll aim for dinner at some point. Right now, I need a bath and a bed," Jackson announces, yawning more than once. He hugs us before walking towards his suite with Kaelan in tow.

Our rooms are next to Jackson's, and are also side-by-side. "This feels like déjà vu," I say amid laughter.

Stryder winks and calls out longingly, "See you later, neighbor."

Inserting my key, I enter the spacious room, and look around when Stryder opens a door and lands into my room. *Adjoined rooms.* We look at each other incredulously. Dropping my bags, I race towards Stryder, and his arms open wide for me. Our bodies crash against each other, our lips kissing passionately.

"Jackson," I whisper breathlessly.

"Motherfucking Jackson," Stryder repeats with a smile.

The energy around us shifts, my body humming with anticipation.

"Do you feel that?" My voice is barely a sigh.

"I certainly do. What should we do, Catalina?"

"Kiss me," I demand, and he quickly complies. His kiss is sweet, full of adoration and affection, but he breaks away unexpectedly.

"Wait right here," he calls as he runs into the bathroom. Seconds later, the sounds of running water fill the silence of the room. Curious, I walk towards the bathroom. Stryder is sitting on the edge of the large whirlpool tub, sloshing his hand in the water mixing the lavender scented oil. Lifting his head, he smiles boyishly, "Want to take a bath with me?"

His question shocks me. A part of me screams *yes* while the other feels shy. I shouldn't feel this way... Stryder and I have shared moments far more intimate than this. I hate feeling insecure in my own skin, and the thought that he'll see me fully naked overwhelms me. Stryder must sense my trepidation, because he walks over and hugs me.

"You don't have to if you don't want to. Just know that you're beautiful. Don't feel shame or embarrassment with me, baby. Don't feel afraid of baring yourself to me," Stryder whispers into my ear.

Pulling away, Stryder slowly disrobes, starting from his shoes until he stands before me fully naked in all of his gorgeous glory. His erection stands tall, his balls looking full, and stepping closer, he breathes. "Don't think. Just do."

His fingers trace my cheeks and find their way to the hem of my blouse. In a swift move, he takes it off. The sound of the material landing on the floor makes me smile. Never breaking eye contact, Stryder unbuttons my jeans and tugs them off. I stand before him in just my bra and panties. His fingers undo the clasps of my bra and my panties come off.

Stryder eyes me from top to bottom, his eyes filled with lust. I look at him long and hard too, my eyes tracing the contours of his well defined body. His body is all too perfect, probably due to many years of conditioning. Stryder eats well and his body shows it. My gaze stops to admire his Apollo's belt, which points towards unparalleled pleasure. I bite the insides of my cheek, wondering what will happen next.

"You're giving me that look again, Catalina," Stryder chuckles.

"Look at yourself and then look at me. You're impossibly handsome and I'm just–I'm just blah," I whine petulantly, all of my insecurities rising to the surface. I drop my hands to my sides in embarrassment.

"What? You are absolutely beautiful. Your tanned skin and those delightful curves that beg my hands to touch them. Perhaps your definition of beauty is different from mine, Catalina. Trust me when I tell you skin and bones are overrated. You don't have a clue how gorgeous you are to me," Stryder confesses, his eyes seeking mine. "Look at what you do to me, Cat," he says as he cups his thick cock with one of his hands. My eyes widen when I see him twitch under my gaze.

"There's no one here but you and me. You're amazing, Catalina. Turn off the brain and let your heart come out to play," Stryder beckons, walking backwards towards the vanity where his phone rests. He taps it a few times, and soft music fills the lavender-scented bathroom. "Turn around," Stryder demands, his voice husky with want. "Close your eyes."

I comply with his request, my skin prickling in awareness with his close proximity. His strong arms wrap around my waist, his tongue tracing my navel. Opening my eyes, I see Stryder kneeling before me. "God made no mistakes when he made you. You're simply exquisite," he tells me reassuringly. "I'm the lucky scoundrel who gets to love every square inch of your perfection."

Stryder trails kisses all over my abdomen, tender flicks of his tongue marking where his lips have conquered. My skin prickles, feeling the movements of his delicious mouth all over me. My breasts feel heavy, my nipples hardened by his affections. My body trembles in a mixture of fear and elation over what's about to happen. "Stryder…" I whimper.

"Too much, Cat?" he asks softly. "This won't go further than what you'll allow. I want you, and you need to know my intentions, but if you don't feel this is what you want, tell me and I will stop." The assault caused by his lips continues as his mouth nears the apex of my trembling thighs. "Just say the word and I'll stop, Catalina."

My senses are overtaken by the strong man before me, my wits scattered along with our clothes all over the floor. I want him to possess me, claim me. My body wants it desperately, but I'm afraid of the emotional consequences. Sensing my hesitation, Stryder stands and lifts me into his arms, and puts us into the tub with the comfortably hot water, with my back pressed against his chest.

"Cat. Please baby, turn off the brain," Stryder begs softly, his hands massaging the tops of my shoulders. Remembering my boldness in Whistler, I stand in the tub and turn around before him. My body is covered with bubbles and lather. His eyes darken with lust when I confidently lower myself to him.

His hand reaches out to my waist while the other cups my face. "You're so beautiful Catalina," Stryder declares before ravaging my mouth. His tongue slips inside, teasing and tantalizing mine. My palms find his shoulders, my fingernails raking his perfect skin. My actions make him groan loudly. I throw my body against his, causing a small wave of water to spill from the tub.

"Your beauty is unparalleled, but your mouth, God, it's all I crave," Stryder murmurs against my lips. "I need to stop before I lose all control. Can I just hold you?"

Smiling, I whisper, "Yes."

"You're scared. I can feel your heart beating outside your body. Can I ask why you're afraid?" Stryder murmurs. Turning around again, I lean against his chest, lacing my hands with his. I can feel his erection against my bottom, and wiggle gently for his benefit.

"It's been a long time, and I'm just worried I'll be nothing but a big disappointment."

Stryder chuckles, and holds me in place. "I find it hard to believe you'd even think disappointment could be a possibility. Cat, if only you were on the receiving end like I am, you'd know in a heartbeat just how amazing you are." Kissing my shoulders, he whispers in between kisses, "You. Will. Never. Disappoint. Me. When I take you, it won't be about fucking. Don't get me wrong. I've fucked before, but with you, it can't be about that. There's something deeper between us and I don't want to spoil whatever that is just for the sake of coming. I want it to mean something."

I nod, but feel like crying. His words resonate throughout my entire being. Stryder makes me feel safe, cherished, and loved. "I'm feeling so many things," I whisper, pausing for a moment and trying to gather my wits. "I can't name them, but you're in the center of them all, and you make me want more."

Stryder snuggles closer, our bath time confessional becoming more intimate than I ever imagined. "Cat, don't let those feelings intimidate you. There will come a time when fear will make you second guess them. I'm not asking for promises. I just want you to give yourself an opportunity to be open to them, because I feel the same way."

"Stryder?"

"Hmm?" he mumbles, his grip becoming tighter around my waist.

"I said farewell to Blake. I think in saying goodbye to him, I've kind of forgiven myself," I whisper, my hands cupping the bath water and letting it trickle through my fingers.

Stryder sits up and spins me around to face him. Raising his wet fingers to my hairline, he traces the outlines of my face. "From what you've told me, Blake was an honorable man. Kind, good, and was your soul mate. I can only hope that with time, you'll learn to love me as well. I'll make mistakes, because we're human and that's what we do, but know this. You mean everything to me, and until you realize that, I won't stop trying to convince you with my kisses, my embraces and my actions that you are worthy of loving and being loved in return. Got it?"

"Okay," I concede, closing my eyes, and enjoying this perfect of moments.

We lie there in silence until the water turns cold. Picking me up from the tub, Stryder wraps me in a fluffy towel as he takes another, and dries himself off. Holding hands, we walk back into the bedroom, both exhausted from our travels. Pulling the sheets back, I sink into the plush bed.

"Do you need pajamas or something?" Stryder asks quietly.

"No, I'm sure you'll keep me warm," I say with a smile.

"I was hoping you'd say that," Stryder chuckles as he climbs into bed with me. He pulls me close, our bodies pressed tightly against each other's. We yawn and drift off to sleep, content. We're right where we need to be, our hearts connected, counting the minutes until we can be together–united as one.

The weeks pass by in a blur. Between Jackson's hectic practice schedule and the physical demands of the terrain, I'm completely exhausted. Stryder has been patient and understanding, sneaking in cuddle time when we're not working, watching movies when we we're not too busy kissing, having quality time. I feel loved, cherished, and wanted. I'm happy knowing Stryder is the absolute gentleman, not pressing to push our desires further than where I'm prepared to go. It makes me want him even more.

I've also made good use of the board Jackson gave me back in Whistler, sneaking any moment of free time to traverse the harsh terrain on it. My body has transformed itself in the process, and all of my clothing is suddenly too large.

Jackson has remained sober throughout this trip, which makes me super proud. He has won two competitions and the world press is starting to take notice of the positive press he's creating. They've followed us since the moment we got to Mayrhofen, all throughout Aviemore, and they'll be there as soon as we arrive at Port de Soleil.

The entire team is completely exhausted between practice runs and travelling in preparation for Jackson's appearance at the World

Championships. Jackson is fast asleep on my shoulder as I lay my head against Stryder's on the bench in the back of the jet. Both of my boys are snoring away as Kenny sleeps in the front of the cabin. Shifting slightly to embrace Stryder, I accidentally wake him up, and a lazy smile spreads against his lips. Slight turbulence makes the plane rattle a little. Jackson's head lands onto my lap, and one of his calloused palms squeezes my knee. My hand instinctively brushes his hair, and a contented sigh escapes his lips.

I look up at Stryder who watches my movements with a smirk. "I can't wrap my head around it, but you seem to have connected with Jackson on a level I don't think I'll ever understand."

Smiling, I answer matter-of-factly, "Jackson is my soul brother. We just get each other. There's no other way to put it. He gets me. He can see right into my eyes and straight into my soul."

"Yeah, I can see that. He's never been upfront with anyone about his alcoholism. You managed to break through, Cat. I'll be forever grateful for that."

Sighing against Stryder's chest, I tell him exactly how I feel. "I don't feel like a reporter anymore. Not since I met you guys. I feel like I've gone on this incredible journey and discovered a part of myself I never knew existed."

Stryder looks intently into my eyes, his palm squeezing my own. "You rediscovered adventure. I don't know a whole lot about you, but when we first met, I knew there was something in you that was lacking, and that was adventure, which goes hand in hand with fun. You've changed over the past few weeks. You're definitely a different person. Everything about you is changing, including your body."

"What do you mean?" I ask genuinely intrigued.

"There's a spark in you that has you smiling all the time. It would appear snowboarding has started to trim your body. Your curves look sleeker…" Stryder says appreciatively.

His words make me giggle. "I've learned how to snowboard and I love every second I'm on the powder riding a line. I'll be forever grateful to Jackson for that. It's opened my eyes to see life from a different perspective, and as far as my curves looking sleeker, that's funny." Turning my head to look into Stryder's eyes, I say, "That spark you spoke about? Well, it happened the day I met you. I tried to ignore it for as long as I could, but in the end you won."

Stryder smiles so handsomely I almost melt into my seat. "Exhaustion has you delirious, Cat. Come here," he whispers, pulling me closer, all while my hand scratches Jackson's scalp.

My eyelids droop, content in the arms of the man I'm beginning to love, all while cradling the best friend I never knew I'd make when I left the city. Two men I love; one passionately, and the other fraternally with all of my heart.

A part of me dreads the end of this assignment. I wish I could forever stop time so I can continue to cherish these moments with these two men who brought me back to life. Only time will tell and right now, the clock is ticking.

CHAPTER TWENTY FIVE

Stryder

Upon our arrival in Port de Soleil, France, my cell phone begins chirping incessantly. As we're walking towards the van waiting for us on the tarmac, I take a quick glance at my phone and groan when I see who it is. *Olivia.*

<OR: Mom and Dad are planning a surprise birthday party for Jax. I thought you should know... xoxo, Oli>

Her familiarity makes me hesitate. Olivia must suffer from short term memory loss. She can't take a hint. We are done. Over. Finito. But this is about Jackson and when it comes to him, I have to forego my dislike for her.

<SM: Ok. Keep me posted with the details. I'll be there.>

<OR: I'll let you know as soon as I know. Miss you, Jupiter.>

Sitting beside Catalina and texting my ex brings to surface so many insecurities. With all the rush of activity and our strenuous schedule, Catalina and I haven't been able to have much one-on-one time. I know nothing has changed between us, but I'm a man who is falling in love. The need to hold Catalina in my arms and make love to her is overpowering me. Having Olivia texting me only reminds me of the hurt she's caused, which in turn makes me second guess Catalina's affections.

On our way to the ski resort where the World Snowboarding Championships are taking place, I check my email. The amount of work I'm being offered is ridiculous. There are assignments in Brisbane, Rio, Cape Town, Rincón, among many others. That's the beauty of working freelance. I can pick and choose my assignments, and thankfully there's always a steady stream of opportunities. Looking at Catalina beside me in the van makes me want to decline all of them so I can spend time with her after the press tour is over. There are only two days left, and my heart dreads what will happen. I shake my thoughts and try not to let them overwhelm me.

Arriving at the resort, Catalina jumps into the shower, and I get to work. I want to surprise her with a present. All this time I've been taking pictures of her, keeping them in a file on my laptop. I remember how much she loved my portfolio on our way to Whistler, so I figured she'd love one of her own. Picture after picture my heart whacks hard in my chest at her alluring beauty. You can see Catalina's change from the moment I snapped that first picture in Whistler to now. Her eyes reflected fear then, but now they are so full of life.

My favorite photograph is the one I took when we first arrived in Whistler. She had her guitar strapped to her back, looking at the mountains in complete awe. Even though you can't see Catalina's face, her long raven locks whip seductively in the breeze. I've never seen such a captivating sight as that. I make a mental note to develop that image and hang it on my bedroom wall. The sounds of running water ceases, so I close my laptop. I don't want her to see the pictures I'm editing for her.

She walks into the bedroom wrapped in nothing but a towel and my eyes survey her hungrily. "There she is. Feeling better?" I ask her with a grin.

"Not quite, but getting there," she replies, a little too cold for my taste.

Walking towards her I kiss her on the temple and tell her, "I'm taking a shower. See you in a bit." Opening the door I set the water on the hottest setting my body can handle, and surrender to its soothing properties. Minutes later, I hear Catalina's hair dryer. I grin mischievously because I intend on teasing her once I'm done. I exit the stall and see her eyes looking at me through the reflection in the mirror. Her desire for me is unmistakable; her lips are slightly parted as she looks at my body. Catalina is unaware I'm watching her objectify me.

Of course, my body wastes no time responding to her hunger, my dick standing tall and proud, and ready to be of service. Her gaze makes my entire body tingle with awareness, inescapably attuned to hers. Not bothering to wrap myself in a towel, I saunter towards her, and begin shaving–pretending I'm unaffected by her presence, even though my dick shows otherwise.

Done with her morning routine, a fully dressed Catalina walks past me. A swirl of electricity surges between us. I take hold of her waist, my breath quickened by her sweet scent, one I've grown to love.

"Not so fast there, Cat," I mumble, picking her up and sitting her on the space between the sinks in front of me. Leaning in, and resting my forehead against hers, I whisper huskily, "How are you?"

Catalina swallows hard. *Oh, she's affected all right.* "I feel better," she replies breathlessly.

I tut at her and challenge, "That's not what I asked, Catalina," My hand boldly cradles her left breast over her blouse. Her back arches in response, pressing it further into my palm. "How are you?" I breathe.

Catalina's breath is quickening so I tease her some more. My index finger traces circles around the fabric of her bra, gently flicking the hardened bud that is showing through. Catalina moans against my lips, lost in her pleasure, which makes me smile like the devil I am.

My other hand cups her mound, applying pressure to her clit, my thumb rubbing circles over the fabric of her leggings. "How are you?" I taunt again. With her head thrown back, Catalina moans and surprises me by bending her knees, and planting her feet flat against the counter. She's fully open to me, mine for the taking. My lips caress her neckline, my tongue lapping softly in between kisses. "If you don't answer me, I'm going to stop," I admonish, relishing in my dominance of her.

Being a man of my word, I stop touching and kissing her. Catalina's head snaps up, her eyes drunk with longing and unequivocal sensuality. I never expect her to respond the way she does next. "I feel... Like... A naughty... Little... Girl," Catalina affirms, pausing with each word.

My hands clasp her ankles and drag her closer to me. I return my palm to the apex of her thighs, cupping her pussy once again. "Mmm, and why is that?"

Catalina moans and sighs, her hips rolling unabashedly against the palm of my hand. "I was watching you," she declares in a voice that makes me want to rip her leggings off and take her hard and fast. Rewarding her for her honestly, my thumb returns to her hardened bundle of nerves, applying gentle pressure, and then releasing–a torturous move that has her near the edge. "I was looking at you in the mirror," Catalina confesses, compelling me to rub her clit faster.

Taking a deep breath, trying to control my urges I breathe, "What did you see, Catalina?" I can see she has picked up on my game because her response comes quickly.

"I saw your chest, your abs, your legs..."

I nibble her neck and stop all stimulations over her delectable body. "Is that all you saw?" I ask.

Catalina moans and looks at me irritated yet lost in pleasure. "I saw your cock. Your gorgeous and incredible cock, and damn it, I imagine it buried to the hilt in me," Catalina breathes, her unblinking eyes oozing sensuality.

I groan at her words, almost coming. My mouth crashes against hers with animalistic force, my teeth grazing against her luscious lips and slick tongue. Gone is the sweetness and patience of my earlier kisses. I'm starved for Catalina, drowning in my own lust, needing her mouth like oxygen for my lungs.

"I want you so bad, Catalina. I don't know how long we can keep this up. Please," I beg, my hands gripping her thighs.

"Then take me, Stryder. What are you waiting for?"

I look deeply into Catalina's eyes and my heart and blood simmers with what I see. Before me sits a woman who knows what she wants and I'm going to give myself to her. Here I was thinking I was the dominant one, but that would be her.

I pick Catalina up, and she wraps her legs around my waist as I take us out of the steamed bathroom, and to the bed. I practically throw her on the bed, and a surprised giggle leaves her mouth. I rip off her clothes, my lips kissing the bare skin I discover with each article of clothing that lands on the floor. Aligning my body against Catalina's bare flesh, I let my mouth go wild, nibbling, kissing, licking and marking her.

Catalina's moans are soft but constant. My hands are hurried, yet savor this moment because we always seem to be interrupted at the most of inopportune times. God knows I've been a patient man, but no more. This is our moment. I don't care if the lodge is on fire. I'm not letting this moment pass us by.

Lord knows I want to take my time, but right now, this pent-up frustration wins. "Cat," I whisper against her ear.

"Mmm?" she mumbles.

"I'm not prepared…" Catalina responds by grabbing my cock and aligning it to her entrance. "Are you sure?" I ask, feeling stupid for not thinking this through. Catalina takes hold of my hips and pulls me inside of her. Inch by inch, I slide in, her slickness luring me in. Her guttural moan sparks my own groan, our union the most perfect I've ever experienced in my entire life. "Cat," I breathe, unsure if I'm kissing or nibbling her earlobe. I feel so good right now I can't stand it.

This moment brings on a slew of curses from my mouth as she squeezes and relaxes her satin walls against my dick. "Stop doing that baby. You're killing me," I plead. I'm quickly losing control over my body; and try to command my dick not to come. I don't want Catalina to see me as Two Minute Stryder. I just can't help how my body is reacting to hers. "Forgive me, Cat, but I'm going to take you hard and fast."

With that, I take hold of her waist, my hips pumping relentlessly into her soft wetness. Her moans and my groans fill the air of the suite. One of my hands leaves her waist, and I rub the pad of my thumb in endless circles against her swollen clit. Catalina's nails rake my lower back making me push into her faster–harder.

Her walls squeeze me punishingly, and I know she's damn close. Lowering my body closer to hers, I kiss her hard and wild, and she bites my lips in response. "Stryder!" Catalina warns me breathlessly, her heart beating fast, her chest resonating against my skin.

"Let go, baby," I mumble, my hand cupping her cheek as I continue thrusting into her. She meets me thrust for thrust, her body writhing into mine. And then she comes, loudly and gloriously all over me, her wetness dripping down my dick and balls. "Fuck, baby," I groan as my own orgasm peaks. As much I want to come inside of her, I can't be an unconscionable savage.

Pulling out, I come, grunting and groaning, my essence spurting warm against her belly. Her eyes are wild as she looks at me. Catalina slides her body down, her luscious mouth wrapping around my dick, her palm gently cupping my balls. She sucks greedily whatever is left inside me, and devouring it. Beneath her long eyelashes I see her grinning in satisfaction.

Standing from the bed I run to the bathroom, quickly retrieving a warm washcloth for Catalina. I gingerly wipe my stuff from her belly, evoking from her a sweet smile that renders me stupid. Throwing the washcloth to the floor, I lay beside my love, holding her close to my chest. "Cat?" I ask softly, unsure of my words.

"Yeah?" Catalina whispers, her voice hoarse with emotion.

My fingers comb her long tresses, feeling their silky smoothness. My breath is shaky after making love to Catalina, but I think it really has more to do with the fact that my soul wants to profess its love for her. Her silence after our lovemaking session has me worried, my mind swirling with a million questions I'm too chicken to ask, so I settle for the obvious one.

"Are you okay, baby?"

Catalina climbs on top of me, her body aligned perfectly with mine. Her dark chocolate eyes well with tears as they look deeply into mine. My heart stops, thinking she's having regrets about what just happened. Dreading the worst, I caress her hairline, offering her the semblance of a smile. Catalina returns it, a lone tear rolling from the corner of her eye. My thumb catches it, spreading its moisture over my lips. I furrow my brow in concern.

"Yes, I'm okay," Catalina whispers.

"Then why the tears, Cat? Did I hurt you?" I ask my voice breaking. Catalina shakes her head, and inches towards me for a kiss which I'm all too eager to give.

"Thank you," she mumbles against my lips. My arms wrap around her shoulders, hugging her tightly, and my nose nuzzling her neck.

"You make me so happy, Catalina. I hope you know that. That was beyond words," I profess, my eyes searching hers.

There's a flicker of light in her eyes, and I know she feels the same way about the moment we shared. Catalina is quiet, but her eyes are anything but. We lie against each other, taking each other in until we blissfully fall asleep in a tangled heap on the bed.

Beep-beep.

My phone goes off, interrupting my sleep. Catalina rolls off of me onto her side with her back pressed to my chest. Lifting my phone from the bedside table, I see the cause of my disruption.

Olivia.

<OR: Kaelan is bringing Jax back home tomorrow night. His welcome home/birthday party will be on Saturday night. –Oli>

Without a moment's hesitation, I reply.

<SM: I'll be there, but I won't be alone. I'm bringing a friend. –S>

<OR: Okay… The more the merrier. Dad wants us to dance. Will you, for old time's sake?>

<SM: One dance, that's it.>

<OR: *smiley face* Splendid! TTYL, handsome. xoxo -Oli>

Placing my phone back on the nightstand, I take in the fact that tonight will be the last night of the press tour. Tomorrow Jax will be competing in the World Snowboarding Championships. Once the competition is over, so is the press tour. My chest tightens with sadness, as my time with Catalina is coming to an end. I look at her, peacefully asleep beside me. Without disrupting her slumber, I decide a shower is in order to get my mind off things.

Catalina

The sounds of running water wake me up. I sit up in bed, alone. As I look at the ceiling, my heart nearly stops thinking that tomorrow we all go our separate ways. I think back to all the special moments we've shared during this tour, how bland my life was before I met these incredible men. Stryder is dastardly handsome, but his kindness is what made me love him. *Yes. I love him.* Our time is precious and I don't want to miss a second. Tip-toeing into the bathroom, I slip into the shower with Stryder, eager to taste his lips, feel the hardness of his chest and, more importantly, enjoy the warmth that his love gives me.

Placing the last article of clothing into my suitcase, I zip it up; its sound causes tears to spill over my cheeks. *This is it.* This is the moment I've been dreading since we left Whistler. It's been a month of non-stop traveling chasing after Jackson Reese. The thought of being forever separated from Stryder and Jackson makes my head and heart hurt.

I'm thankful Stryder stepped out of the room so I can cry these tears I've been choking on for a few hours now. In two hours Jackson is slated to compete and after that, we board a flight back to New York City.

Stryder and I haven't discussed where we go from here. Deep in my heart I know our jobs will keep us far apart, assignments taking us to different places, leaving little time or space to give this relationship a chance. The thought of losing Stryder hurts more than anything. I worked hard for so long to keep my heart sheltered, preventing it from being broken again, and in the end I caved. I thought the risk was worth the reward… Now, I'm not so sure.

The door opens, startling me. I wipe my tears with the sleeve of my blouse, but it's too late. Stryder has this keen sense. He approaches me with concerned eyes, and crouching down, he sits on the floor in front of me with a furrowed brow.

"What's wrong?" he asks with a furrowed brow.

His simple question turns me into a blubbery mess. Large, fat tears stream incessantly down my cheeks. "I'm just sad, Stryder," I confess, not caring if I'm being overly emotional. "After tomorrow, I won't be with you, Jackson, or anyone on the team for that matter. You guys have grown on me, and changed my life for the better."

Sobs wrack my chest with every word. My hand rubs circles against my heart, a feeble attempt to soothe myself. Stryder tries to hug me, but I stop him.

"No, don't. I... I'll just miss you the most, Stryder. You've made me see life from a different angle. You've brought light back into my life. I'm just–I'm going to miss you terribly." Stryder inches forward using his palm to tilt my chin upwards. His hazel eyes are watery.

"Cat, you're talking like we'll never see each other again. I'm not letting you go, do you understand me? Now that I've found you, I'm not letting you out of my sight. Come here," Stryder beckons softly, pulling me forward into his chest and kissing my hair repeatedly. "Do you honestly think I'm not going to fight for you? Cat, look at me," Stryder commands, his voice cracking slightly.

"You're the light in the dark room that has been my life. You've lightened every picture within my soul with just your smile. You're my safelight," he whispers as a tear rolls down his cheek. "I can't bite back my feelings for you anymore, Catalina Pardo. I love your mouth and smile, I adore your passion and wit, your sassiness drives me wild, and your body beckons me to kneel before it. Since I met you, I see everything in colors, not just black and white. You claimed me the moment you asked me to stay with you that night back in Whistler. I'm yours Cat, all yours, if you'll have me."

His lips find mine, showering my skin with tender kisses. My hands cup his jaw, my thumbs wiping his tears away as we kiss.

"Please don't cry, Cat. I'm never letting you go, no matter how hard you fight me, I won't let your stubbornness win."

"Why, Stryder?

"Isn't it obvious, Cat? I love you," Stryder croons, his confidence unwavering.

Leaning forward, I kiss him with all my might, showing him how much he means to me.

"I enjoy your body, but your heart is what I'm after. It's what I treasure the most. I don't want to say goodbye. I want to wake up in the mornings and see you beside me. I want to go on dates with you, and kiss you while watching a movie. I want to be with you, Stryder Martynus," I confess breathlessly.

"What a lucky bastard I am," Stryder declares as he kisses me passionately. We sit in each other's embrace until it's time to walk over to the competition site.

CHAPTER TWENTY SIX

Catalina

"Looking at the standings, Jackson Reese from the USA is in first place with a score of 83.6 out of a possible 100. Let's watch him take his second run. The visibility has deteriorated over the past half hour.

Standing at the fifty degree slope top section, Reese is letting his board explore the terrain. Oh, there he goes with a Laid Out Back Flip! Impressive control and mastery of his lines, moving down the top section and... yet, another Transition! I don't know about you folks watching, but I'm waiting to see what tricks Reese has up his sleeve. And there you have it! An impressive Front Side 360 landing into a 180 Nose Butter. I think it's safe to say Reese has this championship in the bag. Making his way down the midsection, it looks like he's raising his arms to the crowd. Let's see what he does next. Approaching the ramp, oh–Will he nail it? Ladies and gentlemen, boys and girls watching that was an awesome Front Side 720! Look at him go! Finishing off with Method Air! He knows he had a perfect run. Jackson Reese has done it again!"

The incessant flashing of the cameras is blinding. Jackson Reese has won the world championship once again. Stryder and I jump excitedly and anxiously wait for his arrival at the foot of the mountain. The fact the world press is here documenting this important moment in Jackson's career speaks volumes. The goals he set for this press tour have been achieved and I couldn't be happier for him.

I see Jackson coming down the hill with his arms raised in victory. Bending over, he un-straps his boots and lifts his board, cheering, and the press goes crazy. Jackson looks at the fence where Stryder and I are standing with the other members of the press. With a wide smile, he jumps over it, lifts me into his arms and twirls me in the air.

"You did it! You really did it, Jackson! Oh my goodness! I'm at a loss here!" I squeal, overcome with joy.

Jackson smiles at me and yells over the deafening roar of the spectators. "It's all because of you! Thank you!" Jackson puts me down and wraps his arms around Stryder's and my shoulders. "This is the happiest motherfucking day of my life!" he booms, his elation visible on his face.

Jackson's team runs over and lifts him over their shoulders, cheering in celebration. The judges haven't formally announced his win, but at this point it's a formality. The fact that Jackson is here, sober at the peak of his career is a victory in itself.

Jackson walks over to his fellow competitors and shakes their hands like the good sportsman that he is. His fiercest competitor gives him a hug, and raises Jackson's arm up in victory. The announcer's voice booms over the speakers, bringing the clamoring crowd to silence. I wait nervously for Jackson Reese's name to be called, for a man to whom I'll be forever indebted, a guy I am proud to call my best friend, to be officially declared World Champion.

"Le nouveau champion du monde est JACKSON REESE!"

The crowd erupts again into a deafening roar. The members of the press bum rush towards Jackson.

"Jackson Reese, how does it feel to be on top?"

"Reese, are you sober now? Did that contribute to your win today?"

"What's next for Jackson Reese?"

Kaelan, the most eminent of assistants, steps in front of Jackson and commands the members of the world press. "Jackson Reese will not be answering any questions that are not related to the results of today's competition."

Kenny is perched on the podium snapping pictures while Jackson addresses the press. "I couldn't be more thankful to my team. They have been by my side throughout this journey. I dedicate this victory to them. I'm taking this win as validation that commitment and hard work truly pays off," he answers one reporter. "I'm going home to celebrate with my family and team. My birthday is on Friday, so what better birthday present than this! I want to congratulate all my fellow competitors. When you do this as long as I have, you become grateful to those who made you a better athlete. This win is theirs too."

After Jackson answers all their questions, we're escorted by security back to the lodge. Back inside the safety of Jackson's room, he addresses his team.

"Guys, this win isn't just mine, it's all of yours because you've put up with my shit and antics for so long. I want to say thanks to my amazing team because I wouldn't be here if not for each and every single one of you. There's no 'I' in team, you awesome motherfuckers!"

We all cheer at his words.

"There's another person who I want to thank. She's new to the family and, believe it or not, has been a huge help in my journey towards sobriety. Cat, come on up," Jackson announces, opening his arms to hug me. "You know, when this dark princess walked into my life I really didn't know what to think. Is she for real? Then I found out she was a reporter. She saw right through me, helped me realize all of my bullshit ways and in her I found a friend. A motherfucking friend for life! Have you noticed this woman has the balls to snowboard like a fucking pro?" Jackson cheers my name and everyone follows. "Seriously, Catalina Pardo, when I said welcome to the family, I wasn't joking."

Jackson picks me up and twirls me around, making me dizzy, and I laugh hysterically. "Put me down, Jackson Reese. I need my arms and legs to shred those lines, all right?" Jackson brings my feet back to the floor and gives me a one-armed hug.

"Jackson," I say, talking to him as if he and I are the only ones in the room. "I came here for a story but I'm leaving with so much more. A friendship, a family, a love for snowboarding… You know how much I loathed the snow!" My eyes meet Stryder's lovingly, "and so much more! Thank you from the bottom of my heart, Jackson Reese. You changed my life," I end, kissing Jackson on the cheek.

Jackson wipes a tear from his face with a goofy smile curving those chapped lips of his. He whispers into my ear.

"I love you more than I could ever say, Catalina Pardo. Your happiness is standing right over there."

I wrap my arms around Jackson's neck as the tenderness and finality of this moment brings on a string of quiet sobs. Kaelan quickly vacates the room so that Jackson, Stryder and me can talk privately.

"What's wrong, Pardo?" Jackson asks worried.

"I'm going to fucking miss you. This is it, isn't it?"

My voice breaks as my sobs get louder. Jackson simply hugs me reassuringly. "Hey… This is far from it. Just because we won't see each other every day doesn't mean we won't be friends. Every winter I'm going to kidnap you so we can go snowboarding. Hey, if it were up to me, I'd ask you to quit, and be on my team permanently," Jackson whispers and his words make me hiccup.

"Cat, you've helped me more than you'll ever know. I don't care what you end up writing in that article of yours because I know what's in your heart. It's the most fucking perfect, beautiful thing I've ever known... So wipe those goddamn tears. We are friends for life. You hear me?" Jackson declares.

We stand there hugging for what seems like ages. Like many things in my life, I'm afraid to let go of Jackson Reese.

Stryder

Back in our suite, Catalina and I collect our bags as we're leaving in an hour. Now is the time to bring up the subject of Jackson's birthday party in Wyoming. I know it would make his day if Catalina were there. After placing her suitcase by the door, Catalina sits on the sofa, looking exhausted.

"There's something we need to talk about, Catalina," I say, smiling. Her head snaps up. "Whoa. No need to worry. It's not bad news," I chuckle, taking a seat beside her, and intertwining our hands. "Jackson's family is planning a surprise birthday party for him this Saturday in Wyoming. I'd like it very much if you came along as my, uh, date."

Catalina beams at me. "I'd love to, Stryder. I can't wait." *Well that wasn't so bad.* Now I need to tell her about Olivia.

"As you know, Jackson's family and my family are pretty tight. My mom has been Jackson's dad's dance partner for forty plus years."

"Yes, I know that now," Catalina replies, smiling.

"Well, here's the thing. Jackson's sister Olivia and me were dance partners for almost fifteen years. With time, we started dancing into each other's lives. We got engaged and it ended badly. That part you already know," I say, shifting to look at Catalina. I can see the surprise and fear rolling into her eyes.

"What?" she asks confused.

"I've been waiting for the right moment to tell you this. I'm sorry for not telling you sooner. I just–well, I didn't know how you'd react given your friendship with Jackson. None of this changes how I feel about you. Olivia is my past. You are my present and hopefully my future."

Catalina turns away, unlacing her hand from mine.

"Look at me, Cat. The fact that Jackson's sister is my ex doesn't change one bit how I feel about you. I love you, and there's not one single doubt about that in my head or heart. If you haven't changed your mind about being my date, then you deserve to know about my history with Olivia beforehand, and not to find out once we get there," I say earnestly.

"I appreciate the heads up. I'm sorry if I can't say anything beyond that. I feel like the floor opened itself and swallowed me whole," Catalina mutters obviously upset by my words.

"It doesn't have to be that way, Cat. Does it matter if my ex was some random stranger or Jackson's sister? What matters most is that you understand my feelings are for you and that I'm not hung up on anyone else no matter who they are. I'm not going to let you dwell on this. I know your brain is going haywire processing and analyzing this. Stop. Please," I urge, worried she's putting a wall between us.

"I'll have to communicate to you the only way I know you'll listen. You leave me no choice." I stop talking and kiss her, my lips beseeching hers.

At first, Catalina's lips are firm and tense, but as I deepen the kiss, her mouth relaxes and kisses me back. Her hands wrap around my neck, her fingertips tugging the hairs on my nape, plundering my mouth eagerly. I smile, feeling content that she knows where I stand. Breathless, I break our kiss, resting my forehead against hers. "I'm sorry I didn't tell you sooner. Will you still go with me? You don't need to worry about a thing. Trust me."

Exhaling deeply, Catalina speaks. "You don't owe me any explanations. I was shocked. That's all. What should I expect at this party apart from the awkwardness of meeting your ex?"

Wiggling my eyebrows devilishly, I answer, "Dancing, lots of it."

"Well, fuck me. I don't know how to dance," Catalina complains, slumping in her seat.

I nestle closer, allowing my body to mold against hers. "With pleasure, to number one, and in regards to number two, don't stress over it," I whisper. "I don't know what is it about your pirate mouth, but it's quite the turn on."

Catalina giggles and counters, "Well, you haven't heard me just yet."

My hands lace again with hers and my breath quickens with her closeness. "When, we get back to the city, you're coming home with me. We're locking the doors, turning off phones, and I'll have my way with you."

Catalina's squeezes my hand painfully. "I look forward to that," she breathes.

Knowing we are mere seconds away from jumping into each other's laps, I stand, adjusting myself in the process. There's something I need for my portfolio.

"Come on, let's go for a walk," I say, walking towards the coat rack and grabbing her coat. Once we're dressed for the weather, I grab my bag and we leave the room.

Earlier today I saw a spot that would be perfect for what I have in mind. Walking the perimeter of the lodge, I stop at the foot of some snow-covered pine trees, and set up my tripod. Flurries are falling gently from the sky. Once the camera is set up, I instruct Catalina to stand in place. Grabbing the remote shutter trigger, I walk towards her. I draw a circle in the snow and ask her not to move out of it.

"Okay. I'm going to talk to you, ask you some questions. If you want to answer them, you can. If you don't want to, we can skip them, but the most important thing is to follow my eyes and don't look straight into the camera. In fact, try to pretend it's not even there, okay?" Catalina looks at me confused, but plays along.

"Like I have a choice?" Smiling at her sass, I extend my palm so that my fingertips trace the outline of her lips. She smiles, her eyes smoldering under my gaze. With my free hand I press the shutter button on the remote and the camera clicks away.

"Do you like this?" I ask sultrily.

Catalina blushes as she holds my gaze. "Yes," she whispers. My fingertips move to trace the contours of her jaw, and she immediately cradles her head into my touch.

"How much do you like my touch?"

Catalina's lips part, her breath quickening, steam leaving her mouth with each exhale. Catalina looks away, which surprises me, but I keep taking pictures. I get closer, and she wraps her arms around my neck, kissing me voraciously. I need to remind myself to keep pressing the shutter button.

"Are you going to ask me another goddamn question, Stryder?" Catalina clamors.

"Um, no ma'am," I mutter under my breath. "I just wanted you to kiss me so that I could immortalize this moment. I'll always carry this picture of us whenever you're not with me. Wherever my work takes me, a piece of you will always be with me. Always," I declare, clearing my throat, and grin. "I guess my plan worked."

"Oh, screw you, Stryder!" Catalina exclaims amid laughter. "If you wanted a picture, you could've asked!"

Laughing, I press the trigger, capturing her reactions. "Yes, I could've, but I wanted real reactions, like the cute sassy ones you're giving me now." Wrapping my arms around her waist and positioning Catalina in front of the lens, I whisper into her ear, "Time to look at the lens, baby." We make goofy faces at the camera. In some we kiss and in others, we simply act freely on our feelings for each other.

Turning to face her, I take hold of her cheeks. "I've loved every minute I've spent with you throughout this journey. You said you've changed. Well, so have I. I know it's too soon and I'm not asking for you to say it in return, but God, Cat, I love you. I love you so much."

Catalina kisses me softly and whispers, "Me too, Stryder." That simple utterance makes my heart soar. After a few languid kisses, the snow begins to fall at a faster pace so I rush to put my equipment away. She stands patiently beside me, waiting for me to close my bag, and be on our way. "Done with your equipment?" Catalina asks sweetly.

"Yeah," I answer, bemused. When I stand, Catalina jumps into me, her legs wrapping around my waist. Her hands waste no time clutching my hair, her lips devouring mine with a passion that surprises me. I groan into her mouth, enjoying the perfect piece of heaven that resides in there. Just as quickly as Catalina straddled me, she's back on the snow, crossing her arms, raising her chin defiantly, and smiling.

"Commit *that* to memory, Stryder Martynus," she declares, placing her hands back into her pockets, and stifling her laughter.

Trying to appear wounded and failing, I shake my head in wonder. "You play dirty, Pardo," We both throw our heads back and laugh, braving the cold back towards the lodge.

As we arrive at my building in West Village, the sun begins to rise, marking the beginning of a new day. Jerry greets me happily. "Welcome home, Mr. Martynus."

"It's nice to be home, Jerry. Meet my girlfriend, Catalina Pardo," I announce proudly, smiling at Catalina who blushes at the mere mention of her title. On our way up, a surge of electricity sparks between us and I'm counting the seconds until we make it through the door. I can't wait to show her my place. She's the first woman who has ever been to this apartment, apart from my mother and sister. My heart races furiously as I unlock the door and bring our things inside.

"It's not much, but it's my home. I'm so happy you are here," I declare, kissing her neck. Holding her hand, I show her around. She appears impressed with my gallery wall in the great room, and gasps when I show her my office and dark-room. Yawning a few times, she sits on the sofa in my office.

"Come, baby. You're tired. Let's go to bed and get some rest," I say, and bring her into my room. Her eyes take in the size of my bed, and she smiles gratefully.

"Wow, your place is amazing, Stryder," Catalina praises as she yawns once more. "Do you mind if I take a bath?" she asks sweetly. I'm only too happy to comply.

I draw a bath, adding the citrus scented oil I use whenever I feel jetlagged. I make sure to set her up with everything she needs and even light candles for relaxation. Catalina walks into the bathroom and smiles lazily. "Get comfy. Take all the time you need, okay?" I say, walking towards the bedroom.

Catalina grabs me by the waistband of my jeans. "Where do you think you're going?" she asks.

"I thought you might want some privacy," I explain sheepishly.

"Privacy is overrated. Take a bath with me, and as tired as I am, I might drown," Catalina giggles.

I strip to nothing before she's able to take off her shoes. Sitting her on the edge of the tub, I unlace her boots, reminiscent of the first time I helped her back in Whistler. Catalina's sweet smile gets my blood going. Removing her panties, I help her into the tub and we both settle into the hot water, our bodies tired from traveling.

"You know, when I bought this place I never imagined I'd see a woman in my apartment, let alone my tub."

Catalina sits up in the tub to face me. "You've never had someone over?" she asks incredulously.

"If your question is have I ever brought a woman to my place, the answer is no. This is my temple. I don't bring women here. Not until now."

"Why is that? Why haven't you brought anyone else? Is it an anal rule of yours?" Catalina prods.

"After Olivia and I broke up, I went through a phase where I wouldn't date, but would seek female companionship whenever the need arose. I was angry, disappointed with her and I thought if had meaningless sex, I'd get back at her somehow. At first it worked, but with time it became boring. I vowed to never bring someone into my home, let alone my heart. I'd do my deed at their places or hotels. It's not something I'm incredibly proud of," I exhale embarrassed.

Catalina leans into my chest, her hands squeezing mine. "It's okay. We all have our pasts. We all deal with things differently. I chose to focus on work and not live my life. I get it. No judgment zone here," she says soothingly.

Squeezing her tightly I ask, "Where have you been all my life?"

"Just down the road in SoHo..."

Kissing her cheeks, I bathe Catalina. My hands caress her warm, silken skin, my fingertips tracing her contours lovingly. She looks to me with lust-filled eyes, her lips slightly parted as I wash the most intimate parts of her.

I try to keep to the task at hand but my desire for her strays me away. My fingertips tease her nipples, which are hardened and elongated, begging to be placed in my mouth. I know Catalina is tired, but I need her and I know she wants me too. I let go of her so I can wash myself. Catalina Pardo needs to be in my bed right now. Climbing out of the tub I wrap a towel around my hips, and grabbing another, I help Catalina out and dry her. Picking her up, I lay her against my blankets having a hard time believing she's here.

"God, you look so beautiful right now," I murmur, raising my hands to my face, pretending to have a camera. My tongue clicks, emulating the sound of the shutter. "Committing this to memory," I grin, and Catalina rolls her eyes.

Beside her, underneath the blankets, my body hums with anticipation. Rolling to my side, Catalina rests her head on her elbow with a devilish grin on her face. "So…" she trails off, wiggling her eyebrows.

My lips meet hers, and the volcano that's been simmering between us begins to erupt. Our hands get busy in reckless abandon, searching, discovering, and conquering–our soft sighs echoing in the silence of my bedroom.

"Let me love you, Catalina," I whisper against the swollen flesh of her lips. Catalina nods, trembling against me. "I'm just as nervous as you are baby." I move in closer kissing her earlobe, and my palm lowers to the apex of her thighs.

I gently caress her velvety smooth lips and come in contact with her wetness. "God, you're so wet," I murmur, my dick bobbing, begging to be inside of her. I gently insert a finger into her pussy and my breath quickens when her body arches in response. Catalina's eyes are closed and her mouth is rounded as a soft moan slips past her lips.

"I need to taste you, baby. I'll be damned if I don't," I declare possessively. I get out of the bed and kneel on its edge, dragging her body close to me. I trail quick kisses starting from the instep of her foot all the way up to the insides of her thighs.

My mouth finds her swollen clit, and with a quick swipe of my tongue I tease it then suck it tenderly. Catalina's legs buckle with the contact, and cries, "Oh, fuck!"

Smiling devilishly, I reply, "Oh, fuck, is right."

Lowering my mouth to her pussy I'm greeted by her wetness. Her taste is absolutely divine–a mixture of tangy and sweet. My tongue traces circles inside her satiny skin and Catalina pulls my hair, making me groan inside of her.

"Please!" Catalina pants as the beginning of her orgasm hits her. I continue sucking on her hardened clit, hooking two fingers inside of her wetness. Her increased moans tell me I'm touching the sweet spot inside of her. Her velvet walls tighten and release with each stroke of my fingers. She's inching close, her scent drowning me in pleasure.

Catalina's nails dig into my scalp and with a loud, guttural moan she cries into the air, "Stryder!" A gush of warm wetness hits my mouth as she comes. I smile proudly, knowing that had to have been one hell of an experience for her. Catalina opens her eyes, and our eyes meet. Exhaling loudly, her body trembles fiercer than ever before. "That was intense," she whispers breathlessly.

"I know. I felt it in my mouth. You taste divine, Cat." She groans and covers her face, embarrassed. "Oh no you don't, please don't hide from me," I tease, tickling her in the ribs.

My lips find her mouth and in seconds, my dick twitches in response. Catalina pushes me on my back and straddles me. Kissing me gently, she positions my dick at her entrance and slides down on it, both of us groaning simultaneously. Catalina rolls her hips riding me seductively, and finds the perfect friction.

"Look at me," I command, hoping to show her with my eyes how much she means to me. "You've claimed me as yours, Cat. There's no going back on this. I'm yours. Absolutely yours," I grunt, bucking beneath her, the sensations so overwhelming I'm a second away from losing control.

Catalina stops at the right moment and gently squeezes my sac. As my breath evens out, she resumes her delicious torture and I feel like putty in her care. Catalina's walls tighten as she increases her tempo, knowing she's chasing her pleasure. I meet her thrust for thrust, hoping she comes because right now, I'm cutting it close. "I can't hold back anymore," she pants.

She comes loudly, her fingernails scraping across my chest, her ragged breath crying out my name. I flip Catalina over, planting her knees on the bed with that luscious bottom of hers pert in the air. Sinking balls-deep inside of her, I ride her painfully slowly, groaning at the exquisite sensation of her velvet walls against my dick. Her walls tighten again, gripping me, as another explosive orgasm builds deep within her. I quicken the pace, pumping furiously into her. This time, Catalina meets me thrust for thrust and as soon as she comes, I quickly follow, grunting her name as I unravel outside of her, my essence landing on her bottom and lower back. As we both come down from our highs, Catalina turns her body to face me, her warm, luxurious tongue licking me slowly from the base of my neck all the way up to my chin.

"How are you?" she asks, her tone of amusement reminiscent of when I asked her the same question the first time we were together.

My palms grip her shoulders, my forehead resting on hers. "You sure as fuck don't play fair do you, Catalina?" I growl, out of breath and completely overtaken by her alluring sexuality.

"Nope," Catalina replies, with a smile. "You're a stud, mister. I need to keep you on your toes."

Kissing her chastely, I go into the bathroom and notice a tinge of red on me. Alarmed, I run back to the bed and see some red on the sheets.

"Did I hurt you?" I ask, completely panicked, my eyes searching hers. Catalina smiles and looks down.

"No. Just lack of use I suppose. Nothing I can't handle, babe." Her voice is low and full of mischief. I pull her out of bed and take her with me into the shower. As the warm water hits our skin, our bodies pressed together against the tiles, we go at it again–this time slowly, because no matter how much I desire my Raven Girl, I'm not a Neanderthal. What can I say? I finally met my mate.

Once showered and ready, we quickly change the sheets and lay down. Both of our stomachs rumble making us laugh in the sunlit room. "I'm hungry. Do you want breakfast in bed?"

"Sure," Catalina replies stifling a smile. "You know what they say about giving a girl breakfast in bed, right?" My eyes bug out. "Crumbs!" she laughs.

Throwing a pillow at her, I laugh. Just when I think I know all there is to know about Catalina, her sense of humor makes me fall deeper in love with her. "You and that sass, babe… never a dull moment, huh?"

"Nope, I have to keep you guessing."

God, I love this woman.

Catalina

"Catalina, wake up!" Stryder yells frustrated with my nightmare. Opening my eyes, I sit up, completely out of breath, tears streaming past my cheeks. *It was a dream.* "Take a deep breath, please. You're scaring me."

I throw my face into my hands, crying bitterly, sobs wracking my chest. "B–b… Blake. He said goo-goo-goodbye," I cry, my chest heaving with sorrow. Stryder pulls me against his chest, rubbing his arms across my back, but I push him away, standing up from the bed and gathering my clothes. "I need to go home."

"Look at me, Catalina," Stryder asks softly. "Baby, it was just a dream. I'm here and I'm not going to allow you to go back to that place you go when you can't handle things." Exhaling a shaky breath he continues, "Listen, I don't have the answers as to why he's no longer with you. I wish I could erase all the hurt and pain life has caused you, but know this, I'm here and I'm very much alive, and I've never felt so alive in my life.

"It's all because of you. My heart beats in my chest with a force that sometimes makes me feel like it's going to beat outside of my body. You do that to me. The clock hasn't stopped ticking, the earth hasn't stopped turning, and you haven't stopped breathing. You are here with me. You are alive. Don't let your fears cower you away from this new opportunity life has given us. That's not the Catalina I know," he exclaims.

My tears are blinding and all my capacity for reasoning has left me. Grief can do that to you. Putting on my bra and panties, I try to slip my pants back on, but Stryder's hand stops me. "Why, Catalina?" he whispers into my ear, his grip on my pants unshakable. "Why do you want to leave me now? After all that's happened between us? I deserve to know why." Slumping against him, I cry.

"I don't know, Stryder! I feel a little guilty. Blake was the love of my life, and I thought he was my only shot at love. I didn't expect to feel the way I do with someone who isn't him."

Stryder loosens his grip and strokes my hair. He tilts my chin, a small smile forming at the corner of his lips. "So you feel guilty for loving me?" he asks softly, his eyes full of understanding.

"Yes," I reply, my voice cracking though my tears.

Stryder's thumbs wipe my cheeks and eyes. "Cat, I love you. I'm not going to allow you to sabotage your own happiness. Not happening. Not on my watch," Stryder declares, kissing my lips softly, conveying his adoration for me. "Turn off the brain and listen to your heart. Come back to bed with me. You're not leaving me."

I wrap my arms around his neck and kiss him deeply, and following him back to bed. Stryder returns my affections, the passion simmering between us now on full blast.

"I want to hold you close and never let go. For the longest time I thought I wanted companionship, that meaningless sex was getting old and that I wasn't getting any younger," Stryder confesses, kissing my collarbone. "I really didn't know what I was asking for, but now I know. I wanted love. I don't know what I did to deserve it, but I sure as hell am not going to turn my back on this blessing," he declares with dewy eyes. "You are my blessing." With that last word, a lone, fat tear rolls down his cheek.

"I didn't quite understand how you felt about Blake until now. Just the mere thought of losing you breaks me to pieces. I love you, Cat, and damn, I don't think I'll ever get tired of saying it."

Stryder's words of honesty shake me to my core. He loves me and I love him too. It's time for him to know.

"Stryder, I never dreamed of saying these words to another man. I love you and it makes me so damn happy to know you love me as much as you do. You say I'm your blessing. Well, you're my miracle."

Stryder picks me up and kisses me as tears wet our cheeks. What was fear and sadness turns into sheer happiness. Forget the past, they say. Turn a new leaf. Well, that's exactly what I'm going to do.

CHAPTER TWENTY SEVEN

Catalina

Spending two incredible days with Stryder Martynus has me on cloud nine. Our days consist of naps, lovemaking sessions, and meals to get us through the infinite rounds of sex that followed my small meltdown. Grinning, I quietly move about Stryder's room, collecting my clothing and getting dressed for the day. I know I'm not due in the office for a debriefing until next week, but I need to get some work done before we go to Wyoming for Jackson's birthday.

I kiss Stryder's forehead, and my heart skips a beat when he smiles deep in his sleepy state. I leave him a note on the kitchen counter, telling him I'll be back in the evening to collect my things. With an extra bounce in my step, I make my way to *Xsports*, loving hustle and bustle of the city. Yeah, I missed being home. Entering the office, I'm received with a welcome wagon of hugs, pats on the back, and an overwhelming sense that I was indeed missed. Marcia runs out of her office as soon as she hears the ruckus.

"Pardo, you're back!" she greets, and then pulls me into her office.

"Karen, hold all of my calls. Zero interruptions, no matter who they are," she calls out to her administrative assistant, then closing the door behind her. Taking a seat, I give her the slightly edited version of the Jackson Reese Press Tour. Marcia listens to my rundown with rapt attention. The more I delve into my first-hand experiences with Jackson Reese and his team, the more Marcia smiles. I end our conversation by placing a draft of my article on her desk. Smiling, Marcia eyes me with genuine interest.

"First things first, Dominick and I want to express our most sincere gratitude for taking over this story at the last minute. I know it wasn't an easy one and judging by your face, you're exhausted." Marcia says appreciatively, and smiling widely.

"No problem. It was an experience that I never, ever expected to have, but also one I'll never forget. I loved every second of it," I say, my cheeks flushing with all the happy memories.

Marcia appraises me, sitting back in her office chair with a shocked expression. "You look different, Catalina. Dare I say happy? I don't know what the cause is, but it suits you well."

Pulling her chair up to her desk, Marcia gets busy reading my draft. I stand up and walk towards the picture window that offers a view of the Hudson River. I sigh contentedly as my mind relives the past month. As I stand there, my phone chirps. It's Jackson calling.

Slipping out of Marcia's office, I take the call.

"Good morning, Jax! How are you?" I beam.

"Good morning, girl. I'm good, getting used to being home again. You know the same old. How are you? You sound... How do I put this?" Jackson pauses dramatically, then chuckles loudly, "Sated?"

"I'm happy. What else can I say?"

"Oh my fucking God. You guys did it, didn't you?!" I can't see his face, but I feel him smiling through the line.

"Now, now, you know a lady doesn't kiss and tell," I tease, bursting at the seams with happiness.

"Oh come on. Don't be so coy. I know these things. By the sounds of it, it must've been good. About fucking time he cleared the cobwebs," Jackson quips. His words make me scoff, my body shaking with laughter in the silence of the office. I get a couple of curious glances from Karen and the other folks nearby.

"Oh my God!" is all I can reply.

"So, the real reason why I'm calling is to say I miss you a bunch, woman," Jackson says wistfully.

My chest hurts a little because I feel the same way. "I miss you too. Listen, can I call you later? I'm in a meeting."

"Sure! Get to it. Have a great day. Oh, and Catalina? Tell Jupiter to ice his balls. He'll thank me later," Jackson gabs, laughing at my sharp intake of breath.

"You're fucking gross. Love you."

"Love you too. Bye," Jackson sings and hangs up.

I hold the phone close to my chest and grin.

"Who was that?" Karen asks. Before I can answer, she says, "It's none of my business, but I don't think I've ever seen you laugh like that before." My eyes widen in panic. "Oh dear. Good for you, Pardo."

"No, no. It's not like that."

Karen waves her hand at me, saying: "Get back in there," with a genuine smile.

I walk back into Marcia's office, but she's still tied up reading. Once again my phone chirps with an incoming text message.

<SM: My bed felt cold and lonely without you. I decided to do laundry to kill time. Your clothes are washed, folded, and packed. Lunch? I can pick you up... Miss you.>

<CP: You did my laundry? I'm embarrassed, but thanks. Very sweet of you. Yes. In a meeting. I'll call you when I'm ready. Miss you 2.>

Placing my phone in my pocket, I direct my attention to Marcia, who is staring at me astonished.

"So that's what it is. You're in love," she whispers.

Flushing, I reply, "In love? No. I wouldn't go that far. I just met someone and he makes me smile."

"So the rumors *are* true," Marcia says rather flatly.

"What rumors?"

"You and Jackson Reese..." Shaking my head, I rise from my seat, annoyance washing over me.

"Marcia, you couldn't be further from the truth. Jackson Reese and I are not involved, and it pisses me off that you, of all people, would fall for that kind of gossip."

"Whoa there, Pardo," Marcia exclaims, raising her palms in an attempt to diffuse the situation. "I'm sorry. You know how this business is. Everyone knows who's sleeping with whom. I'm not going to lie... I found it hard to believe when the rumor got back to me."

"So why would you assume it's Jackson Reese? He's a great guy and one hell of a host. I did meet someone during the press tour, but I can assure you, it wasn't Jackson Reese. I may be many things, but a liar is not one of them. The only thing going on between Reese and me is a really cool friendship. Kenny can vouch for that."

Marcia rubs her temples, and looks at me apologetically. "I'm sorry, Cat. I really am." Clearing her throat, Marcia taps on the printed article on her desk. "This is gold. I mean, how did you manage to get Reese to open up like this? This has Pulitzer written all over it."

Taking a deep breath, I focus on controlling the buzzing anger within me. "I did my job. I asked the right questions at the right moment and in the right setting," I reply flatly. "Jackson Reese is not the asshole we all thought he was. He's human like the rest of us." Walking towards the door I continue, "I'm taking off for the weekend. I'll be back on Tuesday to edit the article and work with Kenny on the footage."

"That's fine. When we cross this story off our list, I want you to take some R&R." Marcia nods, sighing deeply, "This is fine work, Catalina. I'm blown away. Good job." She stands from her desk and walks over to me. "I'm sorry for my mistake, Catalina."

There's a knock on the door, and I open it. Karen stands in the threshold with red cheeks and says, rather breathlessly, "Pardo, you have a visitor." Marcia and I exchange confused glances, and walk out of her office.

"There you are, Pardo," Stryder greets me with a smile, his eyes twinkling mischievously. In his hands he holds a padded envelope. "I was in the neighborhood and thought you might need the footage I took during the tour."

"What a pleasant surprise, Martynus," I say with a huge grin. I have to brush past a catatonic Marcia, who stands there with a star-struck look on her face.

"Ms. Pardo, the pleasure is mine," Stryder replies, licking his lower lip knowing he's making me blush.

"Marcia, this is Mr. Stryder Martynus. He is Jackson Reese's personal photographer."

Marcia flushes as she takes a step to shake Stryder's extended hand. "It's nice to meet you, Mr. Martynus. Welcome to our offices." She's obviously affected by Stryder's presence. I inwardly roll my eyes, but giggle because he's completely mine.

"Pleased to meet you, Marcia," he replies with a panty-dropping smile. *Great, he's enjoying this.* Turning to face me, he says, "I was wondering if you would like to join me for lunch."

"Yes. I was just leaving. Let me grab my bag."

"No problem. Take your time. I'll wait for you downstairs," Stryder winks, and begins walking towards reception. Stopping for a brief moment, he turns around, his smoldering gaze resting solely on me, "Ladies, it was a pleasure." Then he walks away.

The three of us exhale simultaneously.

"You got to work with that handsome man? I've heard of him but never imagined he was that good looking," Marcia exhales, fanning her face with her hand. "Is it just me or is it overly warm in here?"

Karen chimes in. "Nope. It's not you. That man screams sex. And that swagger? I think I need a moment."

I look at them in shock. "Ladies, what's going on with you? Get it together!"

Karen is unfazed by my words. "He can have me for lunch any day he wants, just saying. You're a lucky lady, Pardo," she winks with a knowing smile. Shaking my head, I turn on my heel, and retrieve my bag.

Walking past them I call out, "See you on Tuesday." As I'm walking away, I feel a mixture of amusement and annoyance. Whipping out my cell phone, I type a quick message.

<CP: You sure know how to make an entrance and an exit. Not cool. You left my boss and her assistant melting like ice cream. Seriously. *frown *>

<SM: I'm sorry. I couldn't help myself. *devilish face* the look on your face was priceless. Hehe. Get your ass down here. I'm hungry.>

<CP: You said ass and hungry in the same message... What do you have in mind for lunch?>

<SM: Definitely not food.>

As I wait for the elevator, I text Jackson.

<CP: I think I'm in love.>

<JR: Don't think. I know you are. Just stock up on condoms. *angel emoticon*>

<CP: *shocked face emoticon* Yes, mother. What do you want for your birthday?>

<JR: You and Jupiter here. That's good enough for me. *kissing emoticon*>

<CP: Okay, I'll have words with the travel fairy. Miss you. XOXO>

I'm giggling when the elevator doors open, and Stryder stands there with his come-fuck-me-smile and gorgeous body. Pulling on the lapels of his coat, I kiss him deeply. "I missed you, stud."

"And I missed you, Raven Girl." Lacing our hands, we walk out into the chilly New York day with grins on both faces.

After a stop at Macy's for a birthday gift for Jackson, we take a cab towards my loft in SoHo. I sit on the edge of my bed, and begin to pack for our weekend in Wyoming. Picking up my skulled emerald dress off from the floor, I add it to my dry cleaning pile, which is close to where Stryder stands. He picks it up with a huge grin on his face.

"What is it?" I ask.

"This dress… I've seen it before," Stryder replies.

"I bought it at Macy's a while back. Maybe someone else you know wore it? I wouldn't be surprised. For such a large city it sure is a small world," I answer absentmindedly.

"It sure is," he states with a confidence that brings me to attention. "Velvet Box, a little over a month ago. I was there with a date and I knocked someone over, and she fell on her ass. I helped her up. Does that ring a bell?" Stryder asks rather smugly. The cogs in my head start turning as I recall those same events.

My head snaps up. "That was you?!"

"I'm afraid so. I tried to make eye contact and you failed to look into my eyes," Stryder says, raking his fingers through his hair. "I remember how you patted my arm after I helped you up. It felt electric. Just like now." He walks over, looking deeply into my eyes, and takes me by the shoulders. "When I saw you on the flight you looked familiar, but I couldn't be sure it was you. So you see, Cat, we were destined to meet and be together. There isn't a doubt in my mind about that," Stryder declares, his voice almost a whisper.

I can't believe my lucky stars. "Faith told me 'a gorgeous man' helped me up. By the time I decided to look at you, all I saw was your back going into the lounge… I don't know what to say other than I'm so happy you found me again."

Stryder smiles and says: "Ditto." His lips connect with mine, a fiery kiss that seals once and for all our feelings for each other.

The look on Jackson's face when he opens the door of his ranch in Casper, Wyoming is priceless. Ushering us in, he makes us feel right at home. Little does he know we are more than just visiting, we're here for his big birthday bash. I waste no time pulling him over, eager for him to open his gift.

His calloused fingers break the packaging and open the velvet box. Inside is a silver bracelet with a GPS tracking dot with an inscription that reads, *"If you ever get lost, I'll know where to find you. Love, C"*

"Wow, Cat. That is so cool!" Jackson exclaims as I help him put it on.

Extending my wrist, I show him my identical bracelet. "This is an interesting take on friendship bracelets. Inside the box you'll find how to track me, so if you're ever missing me, just a few clicks on your phone or computer will show you where I am. It's powered by your pulse. Do you like it?"

Jackson nods appreciatively. Kissing my nose, he says, "I'll never take it off. You are the bomb.com. Thank you."

Stryder brings in a small cake and we sing "Happy Birthday." Judging by the look on Jackson's face, you could say his birthday wish already came true. After eating, we all settle down in front of the big

TV to watch a movie. I guess I fall asleep, because I feel Stryder picking me up from the sofa, and laying me on top of the bed in Jackson's guestroom. Exhausted, I fall asleep before the sun has even set.

The following day, Jackson kidnaps me to go sightseeing, and we even sneak in some time snowboarding in his backyard. It snowed the night before, and the conditions are perfect for yet another adventure with my best friend. Life couldn't get more wonderful than this.

Stryder

As celebrations go, when you put the Reese and Martynus families into the mix, they can be quite epic. Driving to Jackson's childhood home makes me nervous. I haven't set foot in that house since Olivia and I called it quits. I want to kick myself in the ass for agreeing to dance with her at Jackson's birthday party. The only reason I consented was because at the time it seemed like a good idea. I don't want Olivia getting the impression there's still hope for us, especially now that I've found the love of my life. I'm going to behave like a consummate professional, and I will not tolerate her bullshit mind games and manipulation tactics. Oh, she's good at those.

I press the buzzer and the door immediately opens. There stands Olivia, dressed to impress, her long golden hair slightly curled. Don't get me wrong. Olivia Reese is a slender woman who followed in the family business as soon as she learned to walk. Now thirty one with a brilliant choreography career, she has grown up to be quite the man-eater. I'm just thrilled I feel nothing when I see her.

"Hello there, Jupiter," Olivia greets me seductively.

"Hey, Oli. Ready to rehearse?" I ask, getting straight to the point.

Looking over my shoulder as if searching for someone, she says, "I thought you said you were bringing a friend. Where is he?"

Exhaling loudly, I look Olivia square in the eye, and answer her with a smug smile. "*Catalina* is out with Jackson. He's showing her around. You'll meet *her* tonight."

The shocked expression on Olivia's face is priceless. "Oh," she replies, obviously taken aback by the news. "Why didn't you tell me?" she demands, her voice breaking.

"I don't owe you *any* explanations, Olivia. I came here to rehearse, nothing more. Let's get to it. Time is running out."

Olivia's lip trembles, her eyes quickly filling with tears. *Here we go.* "But I thought, maybe, we could work things out. I apologized. How can you so easily forget our history?"

I have no patience for her games. None whatsoever. "Our history is anything but forgotten. I remember too damn well the hurt you caused me. Nothing will ever change between us. I still have my demanding career. What's going to happen? As soon as the going gets tough, you're going to seek comfort with someone else again? I don't think so. Fool me once, shame on you. Fool me twice then I'm just an idiot." Crossing my arms in front of my chest, I take a step back. "Our time is over. I'm sorry if you think I'm a cold bastard, but you killed every single ounce of love and kindness I had for you. You made your bed, now lie in it."

"I don't even know who you are anymore, Stryder! This isn't you! This woman, what has she done to you?" Olivia cries. "I've known you all my life. I know you better than anyone, and the man that stands before me is definitely not you!"

"Don't you dare bring Catalina into this," I spit furious. Pointing to her chest, I expel all the anger I've held back for years. "*You* did this to me. *You* turned me into this coldhearted asshole, and it's only *you* that brings it out. *You* bring out the worst in me. It's a little too late for you, Olivia. I've moved on. Are we going to rehearse or not? I have no time or patience for your melodrama."

Olivia turns on her heel and runs up the stairs towards her room. Shaking my head, I chastise myself for being overly harsh. *Fuck.* I think I may have crossed the line there. My bitter resentment towards Olivia brings the worst in me. I follow her to her room and see her sobbing on the bed.

"I'm sorry," I whisper, taking a seat on the edge of Olivia's bed.

"No need to apologize, Jupiter. I deserved that," she says through her tears. She hurt me, but now that I've said my peace, it hurts me to see her cry because of me. Extending my palm, I invite her to stand.

"Let's go to the hall and dance. That's the only thing I know you and I do best." Olivia nods her head and wipes her tears. A small smile appears on her face, which makes me feel slightly better. The truth is I want to get this over and done with.

Walking to the dance studio in Jax's house brings on happy memories of my childhood. What I learned here earned me two championships. I was nicknamed Jupiter after the Roman God of War because I was quite the temperamental dancer in my earlier days. Yeah, I had a reputation back then, but my love for dance helped me through some tough times. Looking at the walls with all those photos makes me smile. I was a badass on the dance floor and Olivia was my queen. Together, we made history.

As if sensing my thoughts, Olivia says, "We used to be awesome. Let's see if we still have it." Smiling, we get to work. In fifteen minutes we practice a sexy tango. I know Olivia will take advantage of this moment, but my dance will be purely for Catalina. She hasn't been shy about how "talented" I am when we're together in bed. I want to show her why I move the way that I do. It always comes back to dancing. After an hour of dancing with sweat dripping down my back, I leave Olivia and return to Jackson's to get ready for his party tonight. All he knows is that we're going clubbing in downtown Casper. I can't wait to show off Catalina to my family, especially to my folks who will be there tonight.

Arriving at Jackson's I find Catalina fast asleep on the sofa, still dressed in her snowboarding gear. That vision makes me laugh. She's gone from loathing winter to a snow junkie, and that couldn't make me happier. Seeing this transformation in her has been fascinating. Bending down, I call her name softly. "Catalina." Moaning, she rolls away, turning her back to me. "Baby?" Kicking her feet, she complains like a child being told to wake up to go to school. So I talk to her in the only way I know she'll listen. "If you don't wake up now I am going to fuck you fast and hard."

Catalina's eyes open wide, a sly grin curling her lips and making me laugh. "All right! I'm up!"

I help her stand and kiss her deeply, realizing in that moment how much I missed her absence throughout the day. Upstairs we sneak in some alone time, making love before it's time for us to get ready for the party.

Dressed in a dapper suit, I wait for Catalina downstairs. Jackson is getting ready too, so I have enough time to collect myself after today. I'm thrilled to be going out with Catalina, unafraid to show my love and affection for her in front of my family. All of this time we've had to keep our affections behind closed doors because we were working together, but now, we are free to do as we please and that independence makes me happy.

Hearing Catalina's heels click against the steps, I look up. There she stands in a red pencil dress reminiscent of a 1950s pin up girl that makes me harden in my pants. She looks heavenly wrapped in satin threads that hug every delectable curve of her body.

Racing up the steps, I meet her, my lips brushing against hers. "Wow, you look amazing."

Smiling, Catalina replies, "Why, thank you. You look handsome as well." Her dainty fingertips trace the lines of my custom tailored suit. "You clean up well, Stryder."

Her touch makes me shiver. I've been with my fair share of women, from the most delicate of flowers to man-eaters, but Catalina, she falls into a category of her own. She's sexy without flaunting her appeal. She's confident without being cocky. She's beautiful without the need of artificial enhancements to her already voluptuous figure. The one thing I've never experienced before was a dominant woman. Catalina Pardo may not realize this about herself, but she is one hell of a domme. The way she moves and craves control in the bedroom screams it.

"Stryder?" Catalina calls, her piercing gaze reaching my darkest thoughts. "Where'd you go?"

"Sorry. Yes. You look amazing," I stutter, her touch still making me wild. Her fingertips take hold of my tie and damn it if I can't feel it down inside my trousers.

"I love this tie a lot," she whispers, wrapping it around her knuckles and pulling me forward. "It has potential." Her ruby red lips kiss mine, and I eagerly kiss her back.

Whispering so only she can hear me, I tease, "If you don't behave, I will make good on my promise of fucking you, and it'll be *you* explaining to my folks why we arrived late to the birthday boy's party."

Catalina's sharp intake of breath tells me I hit a homerun. "Your folks. Thanks for the buzz kill."

Jackson's footsteps enter the room, startling us both. "Guys, come on. Let's go clubbing. You can suck face as soon as we get there. Don't get me wrong. I love porn, but I just showered and don't want to cream my pants with this indecent display of yours," Jackson jokes, feigning indignation. We all laugh at his crass joke. After all, that's who he is and he brings so much joy and laughter into our lives.

Wrapping my arm around Catalina's, we walk down the steps. Reaching the landing, I kiss her again, and tell her exactly how I feel.

"I love you, Catalina Pardo. I've never been surer of that until today."

Looking at me with dewy eyes, Catalina replies, "And I love you with all of my heart, Stryder Martynus."

CHAPTER TWENTY EIGHT

Catalina

"Surprise!" everyone greets us we enter Hellbenders. The look on Jackson's scarlet face is priceless. I'm shocked by the number of people present. I was thinking it would be a family affair, but no, there have to be at least two hundred people in attendance.

"You assholes!" Jackson turns to Stryder and me feigning injury. We all look at each other and break into laughter. Jackson moves deeper into the nightclub to greet his family, who await him at the bottom of the steps. Stryder holds my hand and walks behind Jackson.

Hellbenders is a posh nightclub in downtown Casper. The venue is three stories high with a stage and plenty of bars stocked with the best liquors you could ever dream of. The focal point is the rectangular dance floor. People are dancing so beautifully that I'm mesmerized.

Making our way down the steps to the tables surrounding the dance floor, I can't keep my eyes off the dancers. "Thrilling, isn't it?" Stryder whispers into my ear, embracing me from behind. Turning my head, I smile genuinely. "Come. I want you to meet my folks." Dragging me along, he stops beside Jackson, who is talking to a woman who looks just like him, presumably his mother.

Standing behind Stryder, I see a woman with obsidian hair just like his creep up behind him. Winking at me, she pinches both of Stryder's butt cheeks, and I can't contain my laughter. "Dammit, Mom!" Stryder exclaims, exasperated. Turning around he smiles at the incredibly elegant woman who looks more like his sister than his mother. Wearing a gold and tan dress that shows off her dancer's body and killer heels I wouldn't dare to wear myself, Stryder's mom is gorgeous.

"Jupiter," she croons, her voice elegant and cultured, "you're all skin and bones, darling." She feels Stryder's abs and arms, and then turns to greet me.

"Elizabetta Martynus, this goofball's mom. But call me Lizzie," she says, leaning to kiss my cheek sweetly.

"God! I'm sorry, Mom! This is my girlfriend, Catalina Pardo. Cat, meet my Mom," Stryder introduces us sheepishly.

"So very pleased to meet you, Lizzie," I answer with a smile.

"The pleasure is all mine," Lizzie says with a smile, assessing me curiously. "I love your dress and style." Turning to face Stryder she scolds, "Stryder, honey, you told me she was pretty, not drop dead gorgeous."

Blushing, I compliment Lizzie in return. "Thank you. I love your shoes and dress."

"Son, so nice to see you here," a man greets us with a thick Italian accent, patting Stryder on the back.

"Dad!" Stryder exclaims, obviously thrilled to see him. After embracing Stryder, his father turns to me.

"Who's the bella?" he asks, smiling handsomely.

"Dad, this is my girlfriend Catalina. Cat, this is my father, Vincenzo."

"Pleased to meet you, bella," Vincenzo greets me by kissing my knuckles like a dashing prince. It gives me the giggles.

"The pleasure is mine, Vincenzo," I reply, smiling at his affections. "I can see where Stryder gets his charm."

Jackson walks up with that devilishly cocky voice of his and says, "Everyone, please meet Cupid." He takes a bow, making all of us laugh, then Jackson pulls me in for a hug and kisses my temple.

The Cure's "Just Like Heaven" begins to play, and everyone takes off to the dance floor. I am mortified when Stryder drags me along, but with his strong arms around my waist, I follow his lead. The fluidity of his movements makes me hot and bothered, and judging by the smirk on his face, Stryder can tell.

As we're dancing, I see a gorgeous blonde eyeing us up from across the dance floor. It doesn't take much for me to put two and two together. She has to be Jackson's sister and Stryder's ex-fiancé. I look away and focus on the man before me. His dancing should be outlawed. When the song ends, Jackson drags me to meet his parents, who are sweet and kind like him. Sure enough, the blonde I encountered earlier presents herself as well.

"Olivia Reese, Jackson's sister," she sneers, extending her right hand. Standing tall and slender, Olivia Reese reminds me of Faith. Long blonde locks slightly curled, with legs that go on for days. Her beautiful green eyes sparkle like emeralds, and her is skin pale and flawless. Sighing, I extend my arm, my confidence shaken by her beauty.

"Pleased to meet you, Olivia. Catalina Pardo," I greet, feeling inadequate in her presence.

"Ah, Olivia I see you've met my girlfriend," Stryder declares confidently, kissing my temple, and wrapping his arms around my waist. I sag into his hold, relieved he came to my rescue. The night just got interesting. I swear this woman is shooting me daggers with her eyes. I fix my posture, realizing I have the upper hand here. Stryder is with me now. Eat your heart out, Olivia Reese.

Jackson

I can sniff my sister's bullshit from a mile away and there is no way I'm allowing her cuntabulous ways to put a damper on my night–or Catalina's for that matter. Oli is a self-centered, pompous brat who's always gotten her way. Yeah, she's pretty, but she's rotten on the inside. She always takes and never gives so it was no shock to me when she cheated on Stryder. That's just who Olivia is. She's my baby sister and I love her with all of my heart, but the truth is the truth.

Sensing Oli's tension after she introduced herself to Cat, I pull her to the side to have words with her. I'm her brother, after all, and this is my party. She needs to know she can't pull her shit here and get away with it, especially when Catalina is in the mix. No fucking way. Olivia looks at me with widened eyes.

"You better behave, Olivia. I mean it," I warn.

Rolling her eyes, she unleashes her venom. "Stryder couldn't be interested in that fat girl. Come on now," Olivia scoffs, her words spewing hatred.

Oh hell no. The ire I feel is enough for me to want to slap her across the mouth. Resorting to squeezing her arm instead, I seethe. "You better watch your fucking mouth, Oli. You have no right to talk that way about Catalina. She may have more curves than you, but she's not fat," I spit, nearly foaming at the mouth. "What are you, thirteen? Bullying the new kid in school... Jealous, much?" I let go of her arm, embarrassed that I share her DNA. I turn and walk away.

"Better a bully than a drunk!" Olivia yells, halting me dead in my tracks. "You're a joke, Jackson. A pathetic, alcoholic joke.

Placing my hands on my hips I allow my head to hang low. The desire to turn around and mark my five fingers across her face is tempting, but she didn't say anything that wasn't true. I look down at my shoes, noticing the multiple scuffs on the fine Italian leather, trying to distract myself from Olivia's hurtful words. Raising my head, the first thing I see is the bar with all the colorful bottles with delicious liquid inside of them. Right now I could really use a drink, or two, or maybe three. Shit. I've been good. It's been weeks since I've had a drop of alcohol. No one will notice. I deserve a break, not to mention it's my motherfucking birthday.

As I walk towards the bar, my throat feels parched, my heart racing with the anticipation of having the one thing in my system that helps me cope. Two steps away from the bar. Yes, I'm so close I can almost taste it. Then Catalina squeezes my shoulder. She worked with me to stay sober and I can't let her down.

"What exactly do you think you're doing, Jackson Reese?" Catalina questions, her voice steady. "What happened back there?" she asks, obviously referring to the exchange with my sister.

Lowering my head in shame, I reply softly, "Nothing. I just–I really need a drink."

"Jax, cut the shit. You're not getting a drink. Why? You don't need it. Don't let her words break you. You are better than that. Do you understand me?"

Catalina contends. Exhaling deeply with tears in my eyes, I whisper. "She reminded me of what I am." That last syllable breaks me the fuck apart. Catalina brings me to her shoulder and allows me to cry. I swear to God this woman is an angel.

"Shh. It's okay," Catalina croaks, making me cry harder. "You are amazing, kind, loyal, and devoted. You're remarkable just the way you are. You're my hero, Jackson Reese." She whispers, those magical words and deft fingers soothing me. Stryder is one lucky bastard. God, they are made for each other.

Raising my head from her shoulder, I meet her worried gaze. "You're the best, Cat. One of a kind. Stryder is a lucky man," I confess, giggling when she fans her face in reaction to my statement. "Do you have a sister or something?"

"Sadly no... But your special someone is out there somewhere, Jax. First, you need to focus on you. Learn to love and forgive yourself, and everything else will fall into place. Until that moment comes, you're stuck with me, bud," Catalina says sweetly, completely stealing my heart. Holding my hand, she leads me to a table where Stryder and our families are sitting.

Got to it give to my girl. Catalina Pardo is one sweet hell of a friend. I'm almost never wrong about people, and I certainly wasn't wrong about her. Smiling, I forget Olivia's bullshit and decide to enjoy this moment because after all, I am Jackson motherfucking Reese–the life of the party and I'm no longer who Olivia claims I am. *Take that, sis.*

Catalina

Kathy Reese, Jackson's mom and our gracious host, welcomes and thanks all of us for attending Jackson's party. The pride she feels for her son knows no bounds. She speaks happily about Jackson–from the moment she found out she was pregnant to his recent win in France. Stryder wasn't joking about how parties are carried out between the Reese and Martynus families.

Sitting at the family table, I see the professional dancers in their element. I dream of dancing like that one day. The one thing I'm not expecting is Kathy calling Olivia and Stryder to the dance floor. My heart sinks as I wonder what's going to happen next, but Stryder leans into my ear and whispers, "This one's for you."

I frown. A part of me wants to yank him back to his seat, but I can't act like a jealous girlfriend. Exhaling shakily, I focus my attention on Jackson, who's moved to sit next to me.

Sensing my distress, Jackson says, "The chances of those two getting back together are the same as pigs flying over the fiery pits of hell. The only thing those two are good at is what you'll see now." Kissing my hand reassuringly, he continues, "Jupiter only has eyes for you. He is it for you. I hope you realize that."

Squeezing his hand, I direct my attention to the dance floor. An interesting choice of music blares through the speakers. This is something I would dance to in a club, so imagine my surprise when Olivia and Stryder dance a sultry tango to John Newman's "Love Me Again." I swear I'm going to dissolve into a puddle of lust watching Stryder dance. His hips move, and his strong arms lift Olivia flawlessly, all while looking at me and not at her.

Stryder's mentioned how he loves to dance, but never in a million years had I imagined he was serious about being a professional. My heart quakes with each sway of his body, my mind pretending it's me who is dancing with him.

"He's totally doing this for you. You know that, right?" Jackson hints, smirking. Words escape me as I nod my head, finding it very hard to look away. As their dance number ends, I'm completely seduced, and dying to sneak Stryder into a dark corner and have my way with him.

Arriving back at the table, Stryder wipes his brow with a napkin. My eyes light up as he bends down to kiss me deeply, not caring his family is there at the table, watching us. Pulling away breathlessly, I whisper, "You're incredible."

"I had to keep my eyes focused on you to get through that dance. She means nothing to me," Stryder reassures, looking deeply into my eyes.

The remainder of the night goes by pleasantly. I take turns dancing with Jackson and Vincenzo. Every time Stryder tries to dance with me, someone else interjects, so my anticipation only grows. Stryder has just excused himself from the table, presumably to get us drinks, when Jackson's voice booms through the speakers, thanking everyone for attending.

Stryder walks onto the dance floor and signals me to join him. I shake my head in panic, while Vincenzo takes my hand and walks me to his son. The lights dim, and Chris De Burgh's "The Lady in Red" starts playing. I remember this song all too well. My Mom and Dad used to dance to it when I was a little girl.

Stryder takes hold of my waist, and we begin dancing to the romantic ballad. He sings into my ear as we sway. "I swear this song was written about you, Catalina," Stryder whispers, his fingertips tracing my lips. "I love you."

Looking into this man's eyes, I forget where I am and who is watching. Hell, I can't even remember my name. I wonder if this is how Cinderella felt when she danced with Prince Charming at the royal ball. Taking hold of his cheeks, I pull him in for a kiss, and as soon as our lips meet, I feel complete. We kiss, unhurried, savoring each other's mouths and letting our love speak for itself.

A couple of whistles and cat-calls bring me back to the present. Stryder chuckles and turns my torso for a dip which sparks a round of applause from everyone at the club. "I love you, Stryder Martynus," I declare breathlessly.

Smiling, he returns my affections. "Your touch blows me away, Cat. Your lips leave me speechless, but this?" he pauses to place his hand over my racing heart, "This is the most perfect, beautiful instrument of your body." Resting his forehead against mine, he exhales. "I want in. You already stole my heart. It's only fair you take me as well. We're sort of a package deal."

Wrapping my arms around his neck, I kiss him passionately. The love I feel for Stryder is beyond anything I've ever experienced before, and when you love like this, it changes your life completely.

The song ends and I flush, realizing everyone witnessed our very public display of affection, but that feeling lasts a second. When you're in love and with the man you love, sometimes you just have to stop caring what other people think and follow your heart.

After a remarkable weekend in Wyoming, Stryder and I return to the city refreshed and ready to return to work. I have a few days in the office and then I'm on vacation for three months, which sounds wonderful. For the first time in years I'm looking forward to spending time away from my job.

Stryder and I haven't discussed our plans. He mentioned being offered work overseas, but didn't say if he was going to take the assignments. We've been enjoying each other's company, and we've been inseparable since the day we met. Tuesday rolls around quickly, and I reluctantly make my way back to work. Jackson texts me on my way there, saying he's in Vancouver again, this time snowboarding with some friends for fun. A part of me is insanely jealous, wishing I was there with him, and not here about to enter my office building.

Settling into the office takes some getting used to. After being away for so long I have so much work piled up, hundreds of emails to go through, and final adjustments to the article I penned about the press tour. It's nice to share a coffee with Collins again, and banter around like we used to, but the Jackson Reese Press Tour has changed me. Suddenly the walls of this office I've always loved seem too small. My body misses the snow and the outdoors, and I feel nostalgic and borderline sad with the change of scenery.

An incoming text from Jackson cheers me up.

<JR: How's my girl doing? Miss you. *kissing emoticon*>

<CP: Up to my elbows talking shit about you in my article. You won't miss me much when I'm done. *tongue sticking out emoticon* Jkjk. Miss you bunches.>

<JR: About to go up the Purcell Mountains. Dodgy slopes but you know me, I live for the thrill. So... How's things? Can you walk? *angel emoticon*>

<CP: Be safe. P.S. You're a jerk. Of course I can walk. The same thing can't be said about our mutual friend. *devil emoticon*>

<JR: Woo-hoo! That a girl! But seriously, are you happy? Is he all you ever wanted?>

<CP: Yes and yes.>

<JR: I'm glad. Gotta jet. TTYL. Love you, Pardo!>

<CP: Love you too!>

As I'm placing my phone into my messenger bag, I feel an envelope in the way. Intrigued, I open it. Inside is a picture of Stryder and me from that impromptu photo shoot in Port De Soleil encased in a black and silver frame with a skull on it. Engraved on the frame is the quote: *"Life is Love"*. My heart flutters at the beauty and sensuality of the image. Kissing it, I place it on my desk next to my monitor so I can look at it all day. Picking up my phone, I text Stryder.

<CP: I found your present. All I can say is I love you.>

Almost immediately, I receive a response.

<SM: Life is love and you fill me with both. Ti amo, mia bella.>

Grabbing a granola bar from my desk drawer, I make my way to the conference room where everyone is gathered watching the news. Not paying attention to them, I take my seat at the conference table and doodle on my notepad. It's not until I feel Marcia's hand touch my shoulder that I look up. I see her, Collins and Kenny looking at me with worried faces.

"Kenny?" I ask, feeling scared, but not knowing why. "Kenny? What's the matter?" My voice rises. He just stands there with a horrified expression.

"Pardo, come with me," Marcia says, picking up my notepad and guiding me into her office.

"What the fuck?" I mutter under my breath. Walking into Marcia's office, I see her big TV is on with the volume turned up rather loud. It's displaying a snow-covered mountain. "What the hell is going on, Marcia?" When she doesn't respond, I approach the television to get a closer look at the news ticker.

Then the bar of red overtakes the screen with the breaking news.

For those of you just tuning in, today at approximately 1:00 P.M. local time, a group of men were snowboarding down Purcell Mountain when an avalanche struck. We can confirm that Olympic gold medalist and world champion snowboarder Jackson Reese is among those who are missing. The images we are about to show you is raw footage of the incident taken by Reese's personal videographer.

As the boys are going down Purcell, a large slab of snow cracks underneath them like a mirror. My hand flies to my mouth as a terrified cry leaves my throat. The jagged piece of ice rolls down the front of the mountain as a cloud of ice and snow swallows my best friend and two others whole.

I blink twice, trying to process the image. I feel lightheaded, my stomach turning as sickness comes up my throat. Overwhelmed with the news, I frantically search for the closest trash can, and empty the contents of my stomach. Collins, Kenny and Marcia are by my side.

"No, no, no!" I mumble. "He could survive that right?" I look at Kenny, but he looks back at me grief-stricken. "He's not dead! Why are you all crying?" But it's me who's sobbing. Running out of Marcia's office I stumble to my knees. "No, no, no! He's not dead. He's not dead! Goddamn it, Jackson! You're not dead!"

Collins wraps me in his arms as grief takes over my body. I'm screaming at the top of my lungs, wailing, my hands clutching my heart. "We just texted each other. No, Jackson! You can't do this to me! Goddamn it!" My skin-curdling cries bring everyone out from their cubicles. "No, not Jackson! God, not Jackson!"

Kenny holds my hands, his eyes full of tears. If anyone at *Xsports* knows how special Jackson is to me, it's him. "Kenny, please tell me Jax is okay. Please!" Kenny only shakes his head, making the nightmare of this moment very real. I push him and Collins off me. "This isn't funny. This is a lousy prank, people." I say, laughing maniacally because this couldn't possibly be real. Looking to my sides, I see everyone crying. Clasping my hands to my face, I scream as loud as I possibly can, my throat burning. *"God, why do you take people away from me? Why? What have I ever done to you? Why did you take him too?"*

I scream almost incoherently into the silence of the office. I try to stand on my own, but my legs give out as darkness consumes me.

"Catalina?" I hear a voice in the distance. Shaking my head, I keep my eyes closed enjoying the silence. "Catalina?" I hear the voice calling my name again. Opening my eyes, I see Faith beside me, squeezing my hand. Blinking twice, I make sure I'm not imagining her there.

"Faith? Why are you here?" I ask, my speech completely slurred. My head feels numb. I look down and see an IV hooked up to my arm. "Where am I?"

Faith, dressed in her doctor's coat, looks at me worried. "Babe, you're in the hospital. You fainted at work. Your blood pressure is low. How are you feeling? What do you remember last?"

It takes me a moment to remember, but then the realization hits me like a freight train. *Jackson.* My grief returns instantaneously as tears stream down my face. I feel drugged so I begin to choke in between sobs. "Stryder!" I cry, looking in the room for him. "Stryder!"

Faith sits on the bed beside me and hugs me fiercely. "He stepped out. He's been here since you were brought in, and *that's* a conversation we'll have as soon as you're better," she winks.

Seconds later, Stryder walks into the room, his handsome face marred with sadness, and that's when reality finally sinks in. Jackson is gone. Taking hold of me, Stryder hugs me fiercely to his chest, both of us crying, not understanding how cruel life can truly be.

"Baby, they found two bodies but not his. We can't lose hope, okay? If we do, then what's the purpose of this all? He isn't gone. I feel it in my heart. Our best friend can't be gone. He just can't," Stryder croaks in a low voice.

I just lay here on this hospital bed and cry. A nurse comes in and puts some medicine in my IV line, and shortly afterwards I fall into a deep sleep.

It's been a day since my darling friend Jackson Reese went missing. All news outlets are saying all efforts of a rescue mission have been exhausted. They are now using all of their resources to find Jackson's remains. The doctors let me go home this morning and prescribed anti-depressants, claiming I had a psychological breakdown brought on by the news of Jackson's terrible accident. I took that bottle of pills and threw them in the nearest trashcan. I know I will miss Jackson Reese for as long as I live.

I would rather cry myself into a grave than live my life numb. Jackson Reese was the brother I never had, the best guy friend any girl could have, and the champion who won my heart. He gave me the greatest gift, Stryder Martynus, a man I love with all my being who turned my dull life into glorious Technicolor the day he walked into it.

Grief does weird things to you. For some, it breaks you down, for others, life simply moves on. Jackson Reese was a force of life to be reckoned with. He showed me how to live again by reminding me of what's important: friendship, hope and love.

Life isn't about giving up or cowering to our human weaknesses. It's about living, like jumping out of a helicopter with a smile on your face, not worrying about what might happen, or if you make it down alive. Life is about living, and loss brought me love. That's what I learned while chasing after Jackson Reese.

EPILOGUE

Catalina

It's been two days since Jackson went missing. Everyone has pretty much declared him dead, but Stryder and I keep hoping for good news. Jackson's parents have been in touch, and they believe it's time to set plans in motion for a memorial service. As I lay in my bed with Stryder fast asleep beside me, my fingertips absentmindedly play with the silver bracelet around my wrist.

I sit up in bed, looking at my bracelet with wide eyes. I remember the GPS Tracking Dot feature… *powered by your pulse… if you ever get lost, I'll know where to find you. Love, C.*

Jumping out of my bed, I search frantically through my closet for the jewelry bag that had both of our bracelets. I remember jotting down Jackson's ID number on the instruction manual. Frustrated, I yell when I can't find it. Stryder jumps out of bed, alarmed. This is the first time he's rested since the nightmare of Jackson's disappearance began. With worry etched on his features, he takes hold of my hands. Through my tears, I try to explain to him about the bracelet. His eyes light up and he joins in my search efforts, finally finding the jeweler's bag inside my suitcase.

I power up my laptop, my hands shaking uncontrollably. As my fingertips enter the bracelet ID, the "Locating now..." hourglass takes forever. My heart races with every second that passes. I gasp when the GPS narrows in on a location a few meters away from the search site at the Purcell Mountains.

Repeated pings blink on the screen of my laptop. I look at Stryder with excited eyes as both of us realize that our dear friend, the champion of our hearts, is not dead, but very much *alive.*

To be continued...

SPECIAL EXCERPT

Please enjoy this excerpt from:

finding Reese.

a SAFELIGHT novel vol.2

IMY SANTIAGO

PROLOGUE

Jackson

The deafening sounds of the helicopter's rotors come to a stop once it lands on top of the Purcell Mountains. Kicking Horse to be exact. Grabbing my board and backpack from the cargo bins, I trek away from the helicopter. Chris and Rem are riding with me today. These guys are not only my buddies, they're also members of my snowboarding team. In the cockpit, the pilot lifts his thumb and I follow suit, letting him know we are good to go. The rotors roar back to life and the three of us crouch, shielding our faces from the snow that spirals as the chopper takes off.

God, I love the Canadian terrain. While Wyoming has some cool spots to snowboard, it's got nothing on British Columbia. The harsh weather conditions and roughness of the terrain, not to mention the threat of danger, beg me to shred the lines of this gorgeous mountain.

As the helicopter flies away, I survey the wintry landscape. Adjusting my polarized goggles, I look at the horizon, admiring the perfect azure sky. The sun glares blindingly against the icy mountaintops, and the howling wind lifts the powdery snow and blows it in all directions. Resting my gloved hands on my waist, I take in the incredible view. Kicking Horse has an elevation of 8,033 feet, and little old me is standing right on top of it. That's fucking awesome if you ask me.

The boys arranged this little expedition as a birthday present, and after spending a great weekend with my family in Casper, an outing like this is the icing on my cake. Fresh back from the press tour and winning first place at the world snowboarding championships in Port de Soleil, France my life is pretty darn good.

The walkie-talkie strapped to my chest chirps as home base makes contact. "How's it looking up there, Jax?" Robert asks, his voice cracking over the radio.

Robert Karlsson, the *Swedish Son* as he's known by folks in the industry, is a former Olympic champion and my coach. He was my childhood instructor when Dad enrolled me in snowboarding lessons when I was seven years old. I can thank Rob for my career in snowboarding. He saw something different in me, and from day one he believed in my potential. While we've struggled with my alcoholism, he's never turned his back on me. It saddens me that Rob is inching towards retirement. He won't be able to follow me around the world like he used to. I'm treasuring whatever time we have left together as athlete and coach.

"Oh, if you could see the view right now, Rob! It can't get any better than this."

"The weather conditions are passable, Jax, but I'm warning you, the snow is dry, and this mountain hasn't seen major ice movement for quite some time. There's an avalanche watch nearby, but the target team thinks if you stay away from the east side, it should be a decent ride. Just be careful with crevasses. We need you back in one piece, okay?" Rob cautions.

"Roger that," I reply nodding, eager to start our run. "I want to point out the visibility is low, and the wind is blowing something fierce. Base, let's get this party started. See you on the other side."

Strapping the radio back on my chest, I gather the guys for a safety brief.

"Did you guys hear the radio call?" I ask Chris and Rem. They nod, and await instructions. "Okay. Here's the plan. We need to go down in intervals just in case the ice patch is as loose as Base thinks it is. Rem, you go first and I'll go mid. Chris, stay close behind me and be careful. Got it, guys?"

Chris and Rem nod, then strap their boots onto their boards, and I follow. As I lock the last strap over the point of my boot, the winds shift direction, and then come to a complete stop. I feel a chill rising from the base of my spine, and working its way up to my scalp. There's an eerie feeling unfolding in my gut as I hear the howling wind in the distance.

The confidence I had this morning dissipates. A part of me wants to call Base and abort this run. I can't quite pinpoint what it is, but the bad feeling in my gut increases tenfold. It took a lot of convincing on my part to get the team to sign off on this run, especially Rob, so I can't pussy out. Let's just hope my lucky streak continues, and I'll be shaking off this bad feeling once we reach the bottom of Kicking Horse.

In the distance, I hear the rotors of the helicopter and I know that's Gabe, my videographer, ready to document the journey down. Looking to the guys, I call, "All right, guys, it's now or never. Let's have fun, and remember to stay away from the east side of the slope if possible. Let's do this."

Rem nods, and jumps down the steep ledge of the mountain. Watching him trek down unharmed builds my self-confidence. Seconds later, I hear Chris' characteristic whooping as he follows close behind.

It's such a peaceful feeling, trekking down the mountain hearing the sounds of your board scraping against the snow, the light spray of powder landing all over your goggles and going up your nose. These are the little things that mean so much to me when I'm riding. I enjoy the silence as I become one with nature. It fills my soul with feelings I can't even begin to describe.

But there's something off about this line in particular. There's an eerie feeling I simply can't shake off. Maybe I'm just over-thinking things, or Rob's resistance this morning somehow shook all of my confidence away, but a part of me feels this could be it.

A loud crack on the side of the mountain straightens my spine, followed by a shrill scream from Chris. Looking behind him, I see a cloud of snow and ice barreling down the mountain. The ground shakes as nature reclaims its territory. I let out a guttural roar to warn Rem, and he looks back at the monster behind us. I can't see his eyes, but I can tell he's scared by the way he's flailing his arms trying to figure out how to outrun it.

I journey over, trying to find a safe spot to land, and hopefully escape the avalanche. A garbled cry for help comes from behind me, and I turn my neck just in time to see Chris sucked into the claws of the avalanche. "NO!" I scream, horrified.

I've lost all sense of place and time, but my body seems to be taking me to safety as my board zigzags down to the west side of the mountain. I've been able to avoid avalanches in the past, but this time around, I'm not so lucky. It takes another second before the avalanche sucks me under.

My body is tossed around like a rag doll until I'm buried beneath the snow. It's packed in around me tightly; I can't move my legs or arms, and as the snow settles, it feels like I'm encased in a pool of hardened cement. It's becoming harder to breathe with each passing second, and I'm resigned to the fact that I will most likely die.

My mind replays memories of my life before me like a movie, and bitter, frustrated tears stream down my face, crystallizing quickly as the freezing cold sweeps over me. I've always feared dying like this, trapped in the place I love the most, in the snow. My thoughts are of my family, especially Mom and Jupiter. My tears quickly become painful sobs as the contractions of my cries tighten the snow pack around me. Catalina... My best friend and confidante. The news of my death will crush her.

I wrestle against the hardened blanket of snow and ice to move my arms, and after a few seconds of unwavering persistence, my arms come free. My hands desperately push the snow away from my chest, trying to get hold of the radio. With shaky fingers I press the call button.

"Base, this is Jax. Do you copy? I'm trapped, but I'm okay. Can anyone hear me?" Taking small, measured breaths, I wait for a reply, but all I get is static. "Base, this is Jax. I'm on the western quadrant of the mountain. I'm alive. Can anyone hear me?" Once again, static feedback rings in the small pocket of snow surrounding me.

No, no. This can't be happening. My body shakes violently as the freezing cold goes through all of my layers. I'm finding it hard to breathe, and if no one comes soon, I'll be dead from hypothermia.

I'm so cold I can't feel my limbs, and the more breaths I take, the more exhausted I become. My life as I know it hangs by a thread. Exhausted, I close my eyes and say a prayer. I ask God to have mercy on my soul. While I'm not the most spiritual of men, I think He's always had my back. All the stupid shit I've done, all the risks I've taken, I've always risen from them all.

The clock is ticking. I need to dig myself out somehow and go home. I refuse to let this be my end. *Catalina–the bracelet–look for me, please!*

"Base, please. This is Jackson Reese. I'm alive. Someone come and get me. Please," I cry into the radio, praying someone answers.

I'll keep trying until my dying breath. This is not how I was destined to die. Not here and not like this. Closing my eyes, I rest.

What happens next is all in God's hands.

LOST LOVE BOUND FOREVER

A poem by Ashley Heather

I look into the chocolate pools that make up your eyes
You're here, I begin to shake, and my heart rate starts to rise

As your hand brushes my cheek
A finger silences me as I'm about to speak

Shaking your head you pull me in close
I welcome the embrace; along your jaw I stroke my nose

I inhale you in, your smell, your scent
You here holding me, this is what was meant

A sexy smile appears, on your lips so lush
Slowly they meet mine, two pairs in a crush

Gently at first and then much more deep
I feel you taking me over, into my bones you seep

Hold on to me, don't let go, grasp me tight
I need to be here, safe in your arms all through the night

Feeling you, smelling you, it makes me whole
This love, this connection, the joining of two souls

With soft fingertips, I reach up to your face
The outline of your lips I gently trace

A vice grips my heart, in anxiety and fear
My world begins to crumble as you suddenly disappear

Shaking hands reach for you, grasping and frantic
I'm caught in a moment of dread, distress elevates to panic

Tears fall and my eyes begin to stream
This can't be happening, it has to be a dream

You left, I'm lost, and I'm all on my own
You were my center, my life, the place I called home

I'd give anything for you to be able to stay
Please let him come back to me, I beg, hope and pray

Then right on cue, I wake, cold and alone in our bed
Hugging your pillow, with a silent sob, I lay down my head

Gone forever, from me you were taken, it was your time
My beautiful Angel, I love you, now let your light shine

ACKNOWLEDGEMENTS

As my debut novel, chasing Reese. will always have a special place in my heart.

To say it was a labor of love is an understatement. There are so many people I have to thank, and the truth is, I would need to write a separate volume to enumerate the amount of people who have supported this book and my dreams.

The first thanks I must extend goes to my fiancé, Jc, who endured countless nights going to bed alone, managing my bitchy mood after nights with little or no sleep, and made sure my workstation was stocked with chocolate and coffee to get this project done. It has been a long year and a few months getting this project off the ground. Thank you, baby. Remind me to get you something amazing, and no, I can't deliver Helen Mirren. I love you.

To my daughter Izzabella Grazia, who remarkably understood, as best as a toddler can, that mommy needed time to write. One day she will learn I wrote the SAFELIGHT series for her. Izzy, Mommy isn't perfect, but the one and only perfect thing she helped make was you. One day, I will make good on my promise to give you a home with your own bedroom and lots of happiness. Mommy's trying. I love you with every fiber of my being.

I also want to thank Kimberly Ito, my editor at Sakura Editing, who made me strive for greatness while working with me on chasing Reese. If anything, I can say my writing evolved during the editing process, and I owe the final product to Kimberly.

My gratitude goes out to Marisa Shor, my cover designer at Cover Me, Darling, for this awesome book cover. She saw my vision and delivered such a remarkable piece of art that is the cover of chasing Reese. She also managed my neurotic emails and made me laugh with her replies. Thank you!

There are authors who have been instrumental in my development as a writer. Some have answered emails, and others have simply inspired me by their works alone: E.L. James, Jodi Ellen Malpas, Raine Miller, Katy Evans, K. Bromberg, Lily White, Colleen Hoover, and many others. If you read closely, you'll find small tributes to these authors throughout the book.

There are two authors who I want to make mention of, who played a major role during this journey. First and foremost, I extend my most sincere gratitude to Sylvain Reynard for inspiring me to sit in front of the computer and write again. My love for his writing knows no bounds. In fact, my heart flutters thinking he may, at some point, read this. Know that my love for your characters, especially *The Professor*, is going on three years strong. Thank you.

K.L. Shandwick, thank you for taking a chance on stupid, silly me. You showed me the ropes, listened to my disappointments, showered me with compliments, sent me on interesting writing challenges using – ahem – videos, and even scolded me when I tried to write dingle berries instead of balls in a sex scene… Your friendship and vote of confidence means *everything* to me. Thank you. I love you.

To Alannah Carbonneau, Ashley Heather, and Marian Girling: Ladies, you have been my rock, and the way you champion my work makes me giddy. You were there for me when the going got tough. I could never repay you for your kindness, and I feel immensely blessed with your friendship.

Being an Independent Author means you need to foster positive relationships with blogs. There are over one hundred blogs I want to extend my deepest appreciation. You know who you are. Thank you. A special shout out goes to Chantel Sharp with *Smutty Book Friends*, the first blog to ever take notice, and Isa Jones & Joanne Swinney with *Isalovesbooks*, who promoted and supported my dreams relentlessly. From the bottom of my heart thank you.

A notable mention goes out to Jimmy, Isa, Nicola, Autumn, and Shanna. In the beginning you guys worked so hard, and you believed in me when I had a hard time believing in myself. Thank you.

Last but not least, I want to thank the readers and reviewers who fell in love with my story without ever reading the finished product, and talked about it on Social Media and Blogs. The way you have supported my writing journey takes my breath away. Thank you, for without you, *I am nothing*.

Love you madly,

-i

ABOUT THE WRITER

IMY SANTIAGO

I love to read stories about loss, heartache and redemption, so it didn't shock me that I would end up writing stories revolving around those central themes. I write with my heart, using my life experiences and emotions to dictate the tone and path in which my fictional characters embark in my long list of stories. I believe in the power of friendship and to always remain hopeful because life is always full of pleasant surprises. If you were to ask me if I consider myself an author, I would tell you no–I am not. I'm just a girl who loves a good story that makes you ponder life choices and the darkness that envelopes a broken heart. My stories are about loss, friendship, hope, and love. When I'm not writing, I'm enjoying a quiet life with my family on Long Island New York (yes, on–that's how Long Islanders roll).

Connect with me:

www.imysantiago.com
@SAFELIGHTauthor
@legalimy
ImySantiagolegalimy
@legalimy
@legalimy
@legalimy
tsu @legalimy

SAFELIGHT Playlist:
http:open.spotify.com/user/legalimy/playlist/26L8Q9AUYh36Zmxqgby2m
Goodreads
http://www.goodreads.com/author/show/8425449.Imy_Santiago
Amazon
amazon.com/author/imysantiago

www.ingramcontent.com/pod-product-compliance
Lightning Source LLC
Chambersburg PA
CBHW032150190626
46814CB00005BA/1922

* 9 7 8 0 9 8 6 3 5 8 0 4 3 *